REDEMPTION

LAUREL
DEWEY

THE
STORY PLANT

The Story Plant
The Aronica-Miller Publishing Project, LLC
P.O. Box 4331
Stamford, CT 06907

Jacket design by Barbara Aronica-Buck
Jacket illustration by Karen Chandler
Author photo by Carol Craven

ISBN-13: 978-0-9819568-7-9
Visit our website at www.thestoryplant.com

First Story Plant Hardcover Printing: June 2009
First Story Plant Paperback Printing: March 2011
Printed in the United States of America

To David.
Your clear, editorial eye is only overshadowed by your devoted,
adoring heart.
I love you.

My gratitude goes out to Sergeant Wayne Weyler of the Mesa County Sheriff's Department in Grand Junction, Colorado, who helped with research and story accuracy.

Thanks to the many experts on geology, religion, crime patterns, and esoteric philosophy who contributed minor and sometimes major information for this book and who wished to remain anonymous.

Kudos to Peter Miller for saying, "Yes" and giving this book another chance.

As always, many thanks to Lou Aronica for his invaluable assistance and excellent editorial recommendations.

"No bitterness, no hate, and no regret
disturbs my mind.
In great exalted thoughts, in mighty dreams and aims,
in sudden gleams of light and spheres unknown,
there lies the greatest wealth.
Through sorrow, grief and darkness breaks the light
which leads us in the end back to the ocean
of all souls wherein we find
redemption
from the world of man."

Oscar Brunler

"There has to be evil so that
good can prove its purity above it."

Buddha

CHAPTER 1
DECEMBER 27

"Barmaid!" Jane Perry yelled above the din of the smoke-laced barroom. "Two more whiskeys for me and two tequilas for my friend!" Jane came to an unsteady halt in front of the waitress, her back to Carlos. "You got that?" Jane said, her eyes asking another question.

The waitress cautiously looked at Carlos before quickly locking back on to Jane's iron gaze. "Yeah. I got it." The waitress headed back to the bar.

Jane nervously lit her fifth cigarette of the hour and surveyed the sparse crowd mingling in the center of the bar. The dim lighting painted heavy pockets of darkness across the tables and chairs, making it difficult to discern faces. A dozen beer-splattered Christmas garlands hung carelessly against the nicotine-soaked walls. It was the bar's inept attempt to define the holiday season, but the cheesy decor reminded Jane of topping a dead tree with a broken angel. The Red Tail Hawk Bar was located on East Colfax in Denver, Colorado—a location that supported seedy establishments and attracted drug deals, bloody brawls, and twenty-dollar hookers. The clock with the beer keg image read 4:45. Within thirty minutes, Jane knew the grimy hole would be packed with hardcore drinkers and enthusiastic partiers, all looking to find a warm refuge from Denver's December chill and to extend their stoned post-Christmas revelry. Her jaw tightened, a sign that the stress was taking its toll. The deal had to go down tonight, and it had to go down exactly as Jane planned it. Wearing a mask of bravado, she turned around. "You said 4:30. We're fifteen minutes past that. I'm not used to waiting!"

8 REDEMPTION

"Chill out, Tracy," Carlos replied in a lazy tone, his oily, black hair obscuring his pockmarked, swarthy visage. "I told you I'd hook you up. This is a busy time of year. Santa may have stopped sliding down chimneys two days ago, but Camerón and Nico are still in business."

Jane drunkenly moved around the pool table. "Shit, man, I'm jonesin'."

"Have another shot," Carlos suggested, motioning over to the approaching barmaid and her tray of shot glasses.

"Two tequilas," the barmaid said, setting the shot glasses in front of Carlos, "and two whiskeys," she managed to stammer as she slid two shots in front of Jane and surreptitiously tilted her head toward two men who had just entered the bar.

"Is that them?" Jane asked Carlos, dismissing the waitress and angling her pool cue in the direction of the front door.

Carlos squinted against the poor lighting. "See? I wasn't fuckin' with you!" Carlos raised his hand, catching the eye of Camerón and Nico, who made their way through the syrupy darkness.

Jane felt her heart race as the two Columbians moved toward the pool table. They were as imposing as she expected. Both were in their late thirties, but their road-ravaged faces made them appear fifteen years older. They seemed to drag the darkness of the bar behind them as they loomed closer. Camerón was the lead guy, but Nico was clearly an equal partner.

"Hey," Carlos said, proud to be part of this nefarious deal. "How's it goin'?"

"It's goin'," Camerón said, sizing up Jane.

"This is Tracy," Carlos said. "She's *real* happy to see you guys!"

"Are you?" Camerón replied, his black eyes boring holes into Jane's face.

"You got the stuff?" Jane asked, crushing her cigarette into a nearby ashtray.

"You think I'm stupid enough to bring a quarter kilo inside a fuckin' bar?" Camerón quietly replied with a sharp timbre to his voice.

"Where is it?" Jane said, undaunted.

"First things first," Camerón announced. "You check her out, Carlos?"

"Yeah, she's got the fifteen Gs."

"No gun?" Camerón asked Carlos, never taking his eyes off Jane.

"You think *I'm* stupid enough to bring a gun inside a fuckin' bar?" Jane retorted, echoing Camerón's prior statement. She noted a stream of patrons entering the bar and realized if she didn't move things along, the set-up was going to get complicated. "I got your cash." Jane opened her leather jacket to reveal a fat envelope secured in an inside pocket. "Where's my coke?"

"You gotta love these trust-fund snow junkies!" Nico said with a cocky grin.

Camerón stared at Jane for what seemed like an eternity. Jane matched his steely glare, hoping he couldn't hear the deafening beat of her heart. Finally, Camerón nodded. "Take a shot to kill that edge and then we'll go out to the car," he suggested.

Jane grabbed one of her two shots and quickly knocked it back. "Let's do it," she declared, taking a drunken step away from the pool table.

Camerón eyed the remaining shot of whiskey, shrugged and drank it. Jane turned toward him as the last drops of liquid slid down his throat.

"What the fuck—" Camerón said, checking the aftertaste. He grabbed Jane by the arm. "How do you get drunk on tea?"

Jane started to react, but Camerón moved too quickly. He jerked Jane's body toward him, opened her leather jacket, and pressed his palm against her side. "She's wired! *She's a cop!*" Camerón pulled out his nine-millimeter handgun and aimed it at Carlos. "You dumb motherfucker!"

Jane caught Camerón's hand, moving it just enough off target for Carlos to escape the deafening gunshot. The shockwave sent the bar into a frenzy. Patrons ducked for cover as Jane skillfully punched the butt of her pool cue into Camerón's groin, causing him to drop the gun. She kicked the pistol under the pool table with her boot as Nico drew his gun, aiming it squarely at Jane's head. Jane rapidly swung the cue at Nico's forearm, deflecting the gun before it discharged. A split second later, Carlos leaped onto the pool table and took a forceful dive onto her body. The loosely hung fluorescent light fixture above the pool table crashed down as Jane hit the wooden floor with a hard thud. As the fluorescent tubing exploded around them, Carlos landed a brutal punch to Jane's right cheek.

"Fuckin' bitch!" Carlos screamed, nailing Jane with another savage smack.

Jane managed to roll onto her back and slam the side of the pool cue against Carlos's forehead. The momentary dazing afforded her the opportunity to struggle to her knees, just as a burly male bar patron jumped into the mêlée. Chaos broke loose as the muscle-bound guy pounded Carlos's head against the pool table until he passed out. Jane, slightly woozy from the two punishing blows that Carlos had delivered, ducked under the pool table and swept Nico's handgun under a nearby chair. But as she turned her body, the thick envelope of cash slid out of her jacket and onto the floor, spreading several hundred dollar bills under the pool table. Jane reached for the envelope, but Nico quickly snagged it and disappeared with Camerón into the dark recesses of the bar.

Jane achingly emerged from underneath the pool table just as the beer keg clock came loose and smashed to the floor. A stream of blood spilled from Jane's lip and she stood, disheveled, amidst the chaotic aftermath.

All eyes in the bar focused on her.

But one set of probing eyes was more intensely interested in her than the rest.

CHAPTER 2

"We need everybody to please exit the bar now!" A gray-suited, Denver Police official in his mid-thirties made the strident request. His cocksure swagger caught the attention of Jane, who sat on a stool with her back against the bar.

"You need a couple stitches, Detective," the paramedic suggested to Jane.

"I'm not a detective. I'm a P.I. And I don't need stitches!" Jane insisted, pushing the paramedic's hand away and lighting a fresh cigarette off the dying ember of the one still in her mouth.

"You got punched in the face pretty hard—"

"I'll take an aspirin!"

"Bennie!" The cocky officer called out to one of the investigators. "You put a call in to Weyler?"

Jane heard Sergeant Weyler's name and her stomach tightened. Until five months ago, Weyler had been her boss at Denver Headquarters. But more than that, Weyler was someone Jane considered a friend, as much as anyone could be Jane Perry's friend. The dapper, well-dressed black sergeant had supported and defended Jane throughout her ten-year tenure working homicide at DH, even though that often meant looking the other way when Jane showed up at work hungover. She hadn't seen the fifty-seven-year-old sergeant since late July, when she met him for coffee to tell him she was turning down his offer to promote her to sergeant. Jane had thought long and hard about taking the job. But after solving two of Denver's high-profile multiple homicide cases that summer, the subsequent barrage of media attention given to both cases, the death of her father, and her decision to quit drinking, Jane needed to take a break.

At first, Jane had felt a sense of freedom. It was as if a door was opening into a new reality. But capturing that reality and breathing it in was not always easy. There were days when she sensed she was on the verge of finally figuring out her life, but most days, her enlightenment was dim at best. It was easier to focus on the grittier, more tactile side of her existence. By early August, she had felt the itch to prove her investigative might. Jane made a quick sale of her father's property, netted $100,000 after taxes, split the profits with her younger brother, Mike, and opened up a one-person, 200-square-foot downtown office on August 9 called "J.P.I." for Jane Perry Investigations.

Her proverbial "fifteen minutes of fame" that summer provided Jane with a couple good cases that included nailing a group of counterfeiters for a prominent Denver bank. But she wanted to capture bigger fish. It wasn't that she wanted more media attention. Being in the spotlight was the last thing Jane craved. She had granted only one interview after putting the Stover and Lawrence homicide cases to bed—a one-on-one exclusive with Larry King on CNN. As far as Jane was concerned, everybody and their brother had watched that interview. She received phone calls from people she hadn't talked to in years. Suddenly she was being courted by dozens of news organizations to be the "talking head" on every headlining criminal case. Against others' advice to cash in on her name, Jane turned down all offers, including a lucrative book deal, preferring to pour her mental acuity into what she did best: solving crimes.

And then there was that little detail of dealing with her addiction to booze. She hadn't touched a drop of liquor for nearly six months, earning three sobriety chips from her AA group. She kept the chips in her left pants pocket, nervously rubbing them against one another whenever her nerves spiked. Hearing Weyler's name yelled across the bar caused Jane to start rubbing the hell out of those chips. Jane knew that Denver PD was concurrently pursuing the same powerful cocaine ring. She had taken on the intimidating sting independently—partly to prove herself as a legitimate investigator away from Denver PD and partly to show up Headquarters for what she perceived as inept management. But in the past two weeks, Jane had been approached by the FBI in relationship to the drug ring. After nearly three months of working the case, she was making good headway and was so close to nailing the top players, she could taste it. The FBI, in turn, was working its own angle, but it became clear to the Bureau that Jane was better positioned within the inner circle. She was promised a large financial payout from the Bureau once she delivered concrete evidence to them. She agreed to turn her wires and all documented one-on-one proof over to the Bureau as long as she could continue to have complete anonymity. The Bureau agreed to all of her demands but stipulated that Jane quickly wrap up the case.

Jane surmised that the Bureau's desire to move forward had to do with DH's simultaneous investigation of the drug ring and *their* desire to be the first to nail the group. DH was still smarting from the fallout of the Stover family murder and subsequent Lawrence double homicide that had left nine-year-old Emily Lawrence as the sole witness. The further complication of a DH cop's sinister involvement in both cases had not exactly been a shining moment for Headquarters. The apparent race between the Bureau and DH to successfully apprehend the movers and shakers of the ring had far more long-range implications than just scoring an important case. Jane knew that if she aided the Bureau, she could help herself to a lucrative future of independent law enforcement that would be on *her* terms. However, if she screwed it up, her connections with the FBI would be cut, and with it, any real chance of establishing autonomy.

And Jane *knew* that Sergeant Weyler was fully aware of it all.

Weyler's ability to know everything that was going down was uncanny. He had friends everywhere—in every jurisdiction and in almost every state. Underneath his quiet, reserved demeanor, was a man who could move mountains with a single phone call. He didn't accumulate friends and acquaintances, nor did he respect every cop he supervised. However, his respect for Jane was evident and that respect had never once waned after she chose to leave DH. In fact, Weyler had called Jane at her home on many occasions, but she never returned his phone calls. Her reluctance to talk to him was partly due to her desire to create distance between herself and Headquarters. At least that's what Jane told herself. The bigger reason was that she knew her desire to show up DH by infiltrating the drug ring and handing the group over to the FBI was a blatant slap in Weyler's face. While Jane's intention was never to disrespect Weyler or make him look bad, reconnecting with him would be professionally awkward.

"Weyler's on his way over!" the investigative cop yelled back to the cocky detective.

"I gotta put a topical antibiotic on your lip," the paramedic informed Jane.

"Whatever. Just make it quick," Jane said, feeling the need to get out of the bar.

The barmaid crossed to Jane, hovering nearby with a piece of paper in hand.

"Hey, Rose," Jane said, slightly uncomfortable. "I want you to know that you did everything I asked you to do and you did it well. Tell Jerry I'm sorry everything got fucked up, okay?"

"Jerry left. He asked me to give this to you," Rose said, handing Jane the piece of paper.

The paramedic was just about to apply the topical antibiotic to Jane's lip when she read the note. It was a bill made out to "J.P.I." for damages totaling $3,000.

"What the hell?" Jane yelled, drawing the attention of several crime scene investigators. "What's Jerry smoking?"

"The pool table's got a rip in it, we gotta get a new light fixture, hire a crew to clean up the blood, *and* we gotta plaster the wall 'cause of the gunshot hole."

"Like you've plastered all the *other* gunshot holes? And blood? This is *The Red Tail*! The *same* dive that's known as 'Slaughterhouse Central!' You know as well as I do there's more blood pounded into the cracks of this floor than any other bar on Colfax!"

"I'm lucky to still have a job after what I agreed to do for you," Rose nervously whispered. "Jerry says it's $3,000 and that's what it is. And he wants the money in three days or he's pressing charges against you *and* contacting the media, which, as Jerry said, is not gonna do much for your 'Larry King reputation.'"

Jane turned to the paramedic. "Give us a second?" The paramedic tossed the antibiotic ointment tube into his portable medicine kit and walked away. Jane turned to Rose and spoke confidentially. "I thought we made a deal! I don't give a shit about some 'Larry King' reputation! But I *do* give a *serious* shit about protecting my future ability to work undercover. If Jerry talks and exposes what went down here to the media and uses my name, he's putting both my business and my safety in jeopardy!"

"I don't know what to tell you," Rose offered with the slightest hint of compassion. "He said three grand in three days or he talks. And he means it."

Rose started to walk away, but Jane stood in front of her. "I don't have $3,000. Every penny I have went into building my business and working this case. We're talking thousands of dollars. I had to think up a lot of creative angles to make things happen. And I mean *creative*." Jane realized she was sounding too desperate. She dialed her tone back a notch in intensity. "Look, a lot of the pieces of this case fell apart tonight. But I'll figure out how to make them come back together. And when I deliver those assholes to the people who want them and see some cash, Jerry will get his money. But it won't be in three days!"

"You know Jerry as well as I do. It's his way or...his way. Maybe you can sell some stuff..."

Jane stared into the distance. "Yeah, well, the thing is, Rose, the only thing I've got that I'm willing to sell is my ability."

Rose shrugged her shoulders. "I'm sorry, Jane." Jane reluctantly stepped aside, allowing Rose to walk away. She turned to face the bar and caught her shadowed reflection in a large whiskey bottle. It was moments like this when the desire to numb her senses hit hard. Her head started to pound in a syncopated beat. She wasn't sure if the pain in her head was due to the beating Carlos had given her, the stress of the case, the anxiety over a $3,000 bill she couldn't pay, or the prospect of being revealed by a two-bit bar owner. Her vision began to blur as a distorted face warped into the whiskey bottle, awash in a purple glow. Jane's heart raced and she quickly clamped her eyes closed.

"Hey, are you okay?"

Jane spun around, startled to see the paramedic. "Leave me alone, would you?"

"How many fingers do you see?" the paramedic asked, holding up his thumb, first finger, and middle finger.

"Two," Jane said, collecting herself. "Your thumb's not a finger!"

"Well done!" a male voice chimed in. Jane turned to find the cocky PD official standing next to her. "Looks like you got your ass kicked," he said to Jane.

Jane regarded the paramedic. "Give me the ointment and leave us alone."

The paramedic obliged and walked away.

"You sure you don't need stitches...Jane?"

"Excuse me?" Jane asked, surprised this guy knew her name.

"I recognized you under the wig. Nice try."

Jane touched the blond wig to make sure it was still securely on her head.

"This is awkward for you, isn't it?" he said, a self-satisfied smile pasted across his face.

"Why?" Jane said, trying her best to remain stoic.

"Come on, Jane. I've heard enough about you through the grapevine at DH to know this whole scene is hard on your ego. By the way," he said, extending his right hand, "my name's Kenny Stephens."

Jane let Kenny's hand dangle. "What do you want, Kenny Stephens?" she replied with a mean edge to her voice.

Kenny broke into a wide grin that exposed his whiter-than-white teeth. "Well, for starters, *Jane*, I'd like to know where you scored that big envelope of cash."

"Yeah, I bet you *would* be interested," Jane replied, turning away.

"Seeing as one of the perps got away with the envelope, minus the three hundies that fell out," Kenny said, revealing three crisp one hundred dollar bills, "I'd think you'd be alarmed. Or maybe, those who *fed* you the cash would be alarmed?"

"Nobody fed me the cash."

"Really? Shit, we're talking, what? Thousands?"

"Fifteen thousand, Kenny," Jane replied matter-of-factly, wishing Kenny would let her leave.

"Fifteen grand of your *own* money? I'd be slitting my wrists if that happened to me!"

"Easy come, easy go," Jane said, attempting to get past him.

"You act like it was Monopoly money." Kenny eyed Jane with heightened precision. His brow furrowed. "Oh, wait, don't tell me." He abruptly turned. "Hey, Bobby!" Kenny yelled over to one of the crime scene investigators, "you got that pen on you?"

Jane's gut clamped down. She knew what was coming but maintained her poker face.

Bobby tossed the pen across the bar to Kenny, who slapped one of the hundred dollar bills onto the bar. He drew a mark across the bill and turned to Jane. "You gave those guys counterfeit?"

Jane was aware of the tenuous predicament she was in, but kept up the front. "Guess so."

"I don't get it. Are you trafficking on the side with a counterfeit operation?"

"No, Kenny, I'm not making extra cash by *making* extra cash. Where I got the money is none of your goddamn business!" She wasn't about to tell Kenny that she'd secretly stashed a box of "cash" from the counterfeit operation she successfully bagged for the Denver bank. Jane knew it was legally wrong, but she figured that Denver PD used confiscated counterfeit cash in undercover operations in order to trace its subsequent destinations, so why couldn't she? The phony money had turned out to be her saving grace when she started her undercover drug investigation.

"I'm curious, Jane," Kenny continued with a perverted sense of professional muscle, "what's a lady like yourself doing hanging in a Colfax bar with a bunch of lowlifes during the holiday season? Have you sunk that low since you made that decision to turn down the sergeant's job at DH?" Kenny moved closer to Jane, whispering. "I'd think with your little alcohol problem, you'd want to stay away from dives like this."

His words cut through Jane's heart. She didn't know anything about him, but *he* knew of her achingly private battle. That was a deep, unforgivable violation. A raw vulnerability enveloped Jane, but she was damned if she was going to show it. "Where in the hell did DH find you? Was it online at assholecops.com?"

"Funny," Kenny responded dryly.

Jane snatched her coat. "Excuse me," Jane said, moving away from him.

"If you're worried that Carlos, your date, is talking, he's not. But that's okay. We know he's just a lackey."

Jane turned to Kenny. "He's not my date."

"Did I say 'date?' I meant stooge. Right? Only a fucking idiot wouldn't check to see if you're wired before setting you up with some of the top guys." Jane stopped. "Wasn't that what Camerón was grabbing for right before he turned and aimed his gun at Carlos? By the way, nice little *Matrix* move you did in deflecting the gunshot. *Classic!*"

Jane couldn't understand how Kenny knew how everything had gone down. She was tired of his arrogant manner and decided it was time to play hardball. "I'm not giving DH my wire."

"We don't need your little wire. We've got tons of audio of these guys. We just needed two things to wrap it up: fingerprints and a good, clear video of them in action. You wouldn't think that a dump like this would install video cameras, would you? And once we get the prints off the two guns they dropped and you kicked out of sight, it's a slam dunk! Give us a few a more hours, and DH will go on the books with this collar!"

"This is *my* collar, you son of a bitch!" Jane said with venom. She stood within inches of Kenny's face. "I've been inside, working alone for three months."

"And DH has been working it for eight months. But you knew that, right? Did you actually believe you were gonna show us up? I don't think so. Guess you wasted three months for nothing. God, that must totally suck for you."

Jane stared at Kenny, feeling her entire world crumble beneath her feet.

"Oh, and by the way, Jane. DH didn't find me on the Internet. I applied for the job...after *you* turned it down. So when you see the name *Sergeant* Kenny Stephens under my mug when the media shows me announcing the collar, you can appreciate the irony." Kenny capped his statement with an arrogant smirk. "Ain't life a bitch?"

Jane felt a feverish rush. Even though Kenny was built like a weight lifter, she knew she had the power at that moment to pummel his head into mush. But since she was looking at losing everything she had worked for, certain bankruptcy, and the possibility of being revealed by name to a drug mob...well, she figured that an additional charge of murder wouldn't help. She turned and walked to the exit.

"I'll give Weyler your best, Jane!" Kenny yelled out to Jane.

Jane kept walking toward the exit without a word, except for thrusting her middle finger backward in the air before slamming the bar door shut and walking into the bleak December chill.

CHAPTER 3

The late December night air stung Jane's cheeks as she walked to her '66 ice blue Mustang. She'd parked the car within fifty feet of The Red Tail Hawk's front door with the idea that she could quickly rip out of the establishment if necessary. One thing about Jane, she was always thinking ahead and factoring in what may or may not happen in any given situation. It was this highly calculated approach to life that defined her investigative method and had paid off in the past with numerous high-profile collars. That's why the chaotic battle inside the bar completely caught her off guard. She had worked and reworked every possible angle before ever embarking on the set-up with Carlos—everything from planning the ice tea for whiskey substitution with Rose to maneuvering the meeting at the joint's only semiprivate pool table, one situated on a raised platform with three walls surrounding it. Jane had strongly debated whether to take her Glock into the bar as a safety backup, but she had concluded that to hide a wire and a gun would be pushing her luck.

Jane ducked into her Mustang and slammed the door just as a flurry of snow whirled against the front window. The crimson glow from the bar's neon sign reflected an eerie blood wash effect against the car's interior. Drawing a squashed pack of Marlboros out of her jacket pocket, she pulled out a cigarette and lit up. For Jane, the first hit off a fresh cigarette was always like a flood of anesthesia that softened the edges. She pulled the smoke in, allowing the burn to penetrate her lungs. Looking off to the side, Jane noticed a lone prostitute on the corner. It was typical fare for this part of Denver. She noted how the hooker's blond wig was askew and exposing a tendril of dark hair. Jane thought how trashy it looked and then caught a glance of herself in her rearview mirror. Her short-cropped blond wig had been pulling double-duty hours over the last three months and was starting to show the wear. Jane yanked the wig off her head, exposing her pinned up brown hair. Removing the barrettes, Jane shook out the tangles and took another drag on her cigarette. She returned her attention to the prostitute. A cheap, white, cropped faux fur jacket fit snugly around her narrow frame. The hooker tugged self-consciously at her tight-fitting, pink miniskirt. That single action caused Jane to regard the girl with greater interest.

On closer examination, she looked no older than sixteen. Probably a runaway, Jane thought. She was trying to give off a tough vibe, but Jane could see the fear and vulnerability bleeding through her eyes. Jane knew that look all too well. She'd seen the same face staring back at her in the mirror when she was a teenager. Under the smeared black eyeliner, cheap rouge, and fire-engine red lipstick, there was an odd innocence to the girl. She still retained enough baby fat to send up a red flag to anyone with a perceptive eye. The more Jane watched her, the more she reeked of inexperience. It was the way the kid bit her lower lip as she glanced from side to side. It was the apprehension in her step. Give her another year on the street and all that would be walled up inside a crusty exterior.

A tall, lean guy crossed Colfax Avenue and approached the kid. Jane noted how the girl's entire body seized up as she caught sight of him. That single movement convinced Jane that this girl had never turned a trick in her life. The kid exchanged a few words with the guy, but then things turned ugly. The guy slammed the girl's body against the wall, just a few feet from an alley that skimmed the bar. He had one strong hand on the girl's right shoulder and the other was working its way up her short pink skirt. Jane peered more closely at the guy and got out of her car.

"Hey!" Jane yelled with a punctuated clip.

The john turned his head toward Jane but still kept a tight grip on the girl's shoulder. "Mind your own business, bitch!" He turned his attention back to the girl. "A deal's a deal!" he said in an intimidating tone.

Jane moved closer. The girl's eyes darted to Jane. They were brimming with tears. As Jane moved within a few feet of the kid, it became clear she was all of fourteen.

"You like 'em young?" Jane said to the guy as the snow spit against her face.

The guy turned back to Jane, pissed. "Unless you want to do a three-way, get the fuck outta here!" With that, he jerked the girl by her wrist toward the darkened alley. "Come on!"

"So, Rick," Jane yelled out, "how old is Chelsea now?" The guy stopped dead in his tracks. "She'd be, what?" Jane continued. "Thirteen. No, fourteen. As old as this kid right here. Fourteen. You know how I remember Chelsea's age, Rick? I nabbed your sick ass twelve years ago when I worked assault at DH." Rick turned around, squinting at Jane through the falling snow. "I also personally wrote up the restraining order that barred you from having any contact with your then two-year-old daughter."

Rick glared at Jane. "Perry?"

"Yep. Take your hand off the girl, Rick!"

"I never touched Chelsea in that way," Rick said his hand still firming gripping the kid.

"Ten years in prison and your old lady moving out of state with Chelsea never gave you a chance. Are you gonna let this girl go?"

"I gave her a twenty for a blow job and she ran off with the money before services were rendered! What are we gonna do about that?"

"She's gonna put the twenty toward a bus ticket back home so she can finish ninth grade and start high school with a clean slate. And if that doesn't sit well with you, Rick, I've got a Glock under this jacket," Jane said, lying through her teeth, "and I'll use it to blow off your dick so you won't have to worry about blow jobs in the future. What's it gonna be?" Jane unbuttoned her jacket as if she were reaching for her pistol.

Rick quickly let go of the girl. "Fuck, Perry! You're crazy!"

"And you'll be dickless if you don't get the hell outta here!"

Rick backed up several steps, then spun on his heels and took off down Colfax.

Jane turned to the girl. "So, tell me. Is the reason you ran away from home worse than living out here and dealing with scum like him?"

The girl shook her head, still trembling from what had just transpired. "No.... No, ma'am." There was a soft, southern drawl to the girl's frightened voice.

Jane's perceptive ear tuned in. "Tennessee or Alabama?"

The girl's eyes widened in surprise. "Tennessee. Just outside Nashville."

"Denver to Nashville. That's gonna be about $150 plus whatever food you need." Jane dug into her jacket pocket and withdrew her wallet. She pulled out every last bill. "All I have left is $160. Here," she said, handing the cash to the kid. "We'll have Rick's twenty pick up dinner, okay?" The girl took the money in stunned silence. "There's a runaway shelter one block down on this side of the street. It's next to the gas station. You can't miss it. Ask for Hilary and tell her you need a ride to the bus station. If you leave tonight, you can be home around this time tomorrow. But do me and your family a favor. Wash off the face paint and ask the shelter to give you a pair of jeans and a sweater. You don't want to get off the bus dressed like this and give your mother a stroke! And call your folks before you leave so they know you're coming home. Okay?"

"Yes, ma'am," the girl stuttered.

"And by the way, if I ever catch you working the street again, I'll kick your ass into next week. Understood?"

The girl smiled. "Thank you," she whispered through a well of tears. She started down Colfax and then turned back to Jane. "Hey, how'd you know I was fourteen?"

Jane shrugged her shoulders in an offhand manner. "I just did."

The girl turned and continued toward the shelter. Jane felt a sharp stab of pain around her jaw where Carlos had punched her.

24 REDEMPTION

For the first time that night, she realized how much the beating truly hurt. She took a final drag on her dying cigarette, crushed it into the wet pavement, and headed back to her car. Once inside, she angled the rearview mirror toward the light of the bar's neon sign and examined her battle scars from the bar brawl. Her right cheek was starting to swell. Likewise, her cut lip was beginning to show signs of bruising. For a second, Jane flashed back to a bloody night nearly twenty-two years before, when she was fourteen years old and her cop father, Dale, nearly kicked her to death in a drunken rage. It was an incident that had haunted and defined Jane for many years, and one which fueled so much primal anger. It was also a memory that, up until nearly six months ago, had triggered her need for a fifth of Jack Daniels in one sitting.

Jane was just about to fall back into the violent flashback when she thought she saw a face looking at her in the reflection of the rearview mirror. She shifted the mirror to the old sedan parked directly behind her Mustang. However, between the shadows that cut through the curtains of falling snow, Jane couldn't see a figure in the car. The only thing she could identify was a crystal hanging from the sedan's rearview mirror.

Paranoia kicked in as Jane sat back in the seat. She slipped her left elbow toward the driver's door lock and pressed it down. Reaching under her seat, she pulled out her Glock, placed it in her lap, and stared straight ahead. Jane's mind raced with various scenarios of who she may have seen—a mob lackey hired to stay outside and wait for her exit, a Denver detective planning to trail her moves, or...nobody. It was the psychological price Jane paid for getting involved in dicey clandestine work, and it was taking its toll on her psyche. She snuck another look in the rearview mirror and was shocked to see that the sedan was gone. Jane looked around. She couldn't believe she had missed the stealthy exit of the mysterious car. She tuned in to the moment, surrounded by the fast falling snow, and listened to her gut. When all else failed, Jane Perry could always rely on her sixth sense. And right now, her gut was surprisingly free of turmoil.

Checking her watch, she noted it was just after seven thirty. She deduced she could head home and order a pizza and ruminate on how her life was going to hell or she could attend the regular 8:00 AA meeting in the basement of the Methodist Church a few blocks from where she lived. Being a Friday night and a couple days after Christmas, Jane figured the meeting would be filled with people who were equally engaged in gnashing their teeth over their individual dramas. "What the hell," Jane muttered to herself as she clenched a fresh cigarette between her teeth, slid her Glock under the front seat, and peeled away from the curb.

She pulled into the parking lot of the Methodist Church at 8:10 with the butts of two cigarettes still smoking in the ashtray. Traffic had been heavy due to the snow, and the parking lot was crammed full of cars. Several other vehicles stacked up behind her Mustang in search of parking spots. Jane was about to give up when she eyed a sliver of cement next to a far curb. Banking her wheels so that half of her car was on the curb and the other half on the cement, Jane managed to squeeze her Mustang into the space. As she crossed to the back door of the church, she sensed prying eyes focused upon her. She quickly turned around. The only action she noted was three AA members sucking on the dying embers of their cigarettes before heading down the back steps of the church. But as she followed the others down the steps, Jane could still sense the intense gaze of someone out in the snowy darkness.

As Jane expected, the church basement was packed with well over sixty people. The 1,000-square-foot room felt hot and dank as she maneuvered around the crowd, all tightly stuffed onto the couches and chairs with only the cushion of their down jackets between them. She located a metal folding chair and wedged it between two couches in the back, just behind the table that held the coffee and a bowl of packaged crackers and cheap candy. The meeting had started on time, and the customary recital of the Twelve Traditions was completed. Another female member read the Twelve Steps.

"One: We admitted we were powerless over alcohol—that our lives had become unmanageable," the woman said with a shaky voice. "Two: Came to believe that a Power greater than ourselves could restore us to sanity...."

Jane peered around the crush of bodies, noting a lot of new faces. Their hollow eyes gave them away. It was the look of every alcoholic new to the program—a lifeless, blank stare that gradually filled with hope as the weeks progressed. In Jane's peripheral vision, she caught an old man staring at her. When she looked over at the gentleman, she realized he was drawn to her beaten face. He gently patted his own cheek as if to say, "What happened to you?" Jane shrugged her shoulders and mouthed, "It's okay" in an offhand manner, trying to minimize her awkward appearance.

"Three," the woman continued reading, "Made a decision to turn our will and our lives over to the care of God *as we understood Him*. Four: Made a searching and fearless moral inventory of ourselves...."

That's where Jane tuned out the woman's voice. It was appropriate. For whatever reason, Jane was stuck on Step Four. She wasn't sure if she just didn't want to work the program or if the words simply weren't connecting with her. Somewhere deep down, Jane could appreciate the significance of the Twelve Steps, but the words weren't integrating into her psyche. At times, she likened it to crossing a rickety bridge over a roaring river and wondering how in the hell that compromised bridge was going to safely lead her to the other side. The straightforward declarations within each of the Twelve Steps resonated with millions and made the difference between pursuing a chaotic life or a serene existence. Yet for Jane, the words felt flat and meaningless. She had no idea how to begin a "searching and fearless moral inventory." Jane could fearlessly defend herself or someone she loved against any number of oppressors. But to boldly delve into the deep, dark regions where the demons play...well, she didn't know how to begin such a daunting task.

"Would anyone like a twenty-four-hour chip?" the evening's appointed leader asked the group. A petite, red-haired woman in her thirties raised her hand. "Great! Come on up and get it! How about thirty days?" An angular, crusty old cowboy in his seventies got up from the couch and collected the chip. "Ninety days?" Three people dislodged themselves from their seats and pocketed their three-month chip. "Six months?" Jane was two days shy of snagging that chip, but figured it would be bad luck to add it to her collection before the actual date. The distribution of sobriety chips continued with nine months and finally one year. Finally, it was time to cruise around the room and make introductions.

"I'm Joanie and I'm an alcoholic."

"Hi, Joanie," the group responded in unison.

"I'm Alex and I'm an alcoholic drug addict."

"Hi, Alex."

Once again, Jane's mind wandered. Perhaps it was because of the serious discomfort caused by the throbbing pain around her eye and lip. But whatever the reason, when it became Jane's turn to introduce herself, she missed her cue. The older woman to her left gently touched her arm, bringing Jane back into the room.

"I'm Jane. And I'm an alcoholic." The words fell tiredly, sounding more as if she were ordering a bag of fries than declaring a life-affirming revelation.

"Hi, Jane," the group responded.

Introductions continued for another five minutes. Then it was time to open up the meeting to whatever topic crept into the minds of the group. Jane shifted her aching body in the hard chair and waited for what she expected would be a sad drone of post-Christmas despair. She was about to zone out again when a wiry, dirty blond woman in her late forties spoke up.

"I'm Michelle and I'm an alcoholic addict."

"Hi, Michelle," the group dutifully responded.

"I've been sober and drug free for three years, Christmas Day. I think that day is appropriate because that's when I had my big spiritual awakening. But there were lots of moments that served as spiritual awakenings. I just didn't recognize them at the time. When they're happening, you're usually so wrapped up in whatever shit's goin' on that you don't realize that the hand of God just touched you and transformed your existence. Like three and a half years ago, I'd been drinking pretty much for four days straight and decided it would be a great idea to get in my truck and go for a drive. But I was so fucked-up that I forgot I had forty-two empty beer cans and two empty bottles of Jose Cuervo rollin' around the backseat." The group chuckled in a knowing manner. The woman continued. "So I'm driving and getting more pissed at everything in my life. And I don't realize I'm going over ninety in a forty mile an hour zone. I also don't see that there's a turn just up ahead. I come up on that turn and try to make it, but it's hard to carve a turn going ninety miles an hour when you're sober, let alone drunk. So my truck banks on the divider and then flips twice, landing on its hood. For some unknown reason, I don't fly out of the truck window. I'm just hangin' upside down and all around me are those forty-two crushed beer cans. The two empty glass bottles of Cuervo had smashed and the chards were embedded in my face. But I didn't feel anything. I was like, 'Fuck! This sucks.' Then a state trooper drives up. It didn't take him more than a second to put two and two together. He says, 'Well, lady, you sure did it to yourself.' I say, 'Get me the fuck outta here.' At least, I tried to say it. I didn't know that I'd almost bitten my tongue half off. The ambulance shows up and they use the Jaws of Life to pry me out. Next thing, I'm in the emergency room and there's the nurse shoving this paper in my face, saying I have to sign it. They'd sewn my tongue back together, but it was swelling up and they said that in less an hour it would be so swollen that I wouldn't be able to swallow and I'd die. So I had to sign the piece of paper to let them operate again and save my life. And I thought, 'Wow. I have a clear choice right now to sign my name on a piece of paper and, in doing so, choose to live. Or I could just lay here and die in less than an hour.' That was profound, you know? So I signed the paper.

And you'd think that that would have been the great moment of change for me, right? Wrong.

"Chasing death was my newest addiction. The closer I got to death, the more fun life was. When I got out of the hospital, I started mixing booze and drugs. I lost my job. I lost my house. And the whole time, I cursed God for abandoning me. I ended up in a homeless shelter in the worst part of town. Every possession I had fit into a duffel bag and I got that stolen the second night there. A week later, I got the shit kicked out of me in the alley over a bad drug deal. A week later, right before Christmas, I got raped by three guys. I figured that was it. God had forsaken me and there was no reason to go on. So, on Christmas Eve, I locked myself in the shelter's bathroom and downed a bottle of Valium and a fifth of Jack. I lay on that tile floor and waited for God or the Devil to come get me.

"That's when it happened. I stepped out of my body and looked down at myself lying there. For the first time in my life, I looked at myself as I really was. I saw how much I hated myself and how fucking angry I was at everybody and everything. And in the same moment, I realized that all the shit in my life, all the stuff that I thought was so awful and had led me to that cold, tile floor, had served a greater purpose. All the things I thought were terrible were actually spiritual awakenings that were trying to lead me toward my higher Self. Yet, each time they happened, I wasn't ready to grab on to the towline and pull myself to shore. That didn't mean God wasn't there the whole time. He was beside me, but He was also within me. Those are the only words I have to explain it. I looked down at myself and for the first time in my life, I felt love and compassion for that person lying there. I never loved myself until I was on the edge of death. I spoke to God. I thanked Him for the car accident. I thanked Him for getting beat up. I thanked Him for getting raped. And I thanked Him for the grace of a quick death or a better life. And this time I meant it.

"The doctors said I should have died that night. None of them could understand how anyone could survive what I did to myself.

But I've never questioned it. I just know that the synchronicities of my life are neither good nor bad. They are all opportunities to move closer to the God within." The woman peered down at the worn, blue carpeting and wiped away a tear with the back of her hand. "Someone told me that temptation precedes growth," she whispered. "Now I know what that means."

The group was silent. Jane sat stone-faced. She'd heard plenty of stories over the last few months from group members, but this one drove deep into her core. A swell of emotion inexplicably crept up on her as her thoughts shifted to that winter night almost twenty-two years ago. She remembered stepping out of herself and looking at the battered and blood-soaked body that lay unconscious on the dirt floor of her father's workshop. But for Jane, there was no compassion or love for that girl on the floor. There was only the desire to die so the pain would cease. The taste of salt brought Jane back into herself, and she furtively wiped a tear off her face. The cut on her lip throbbed. She knew the only way to temporarily short-circuit her pain was via a strong dose of nicotine. Jane quietly stood up and made her way to the stairs that led outside.

Thankfully, the snow had ceased, leaving a dry layer of caked, white powder on the black asphalt parking lot. The orange streetlamps cast a distorted glow against the world. She lit a cigarette and inhaled deeply. Jane looked around the parking lot as the stillness enveloped her. She figured a gentle walk might help, so she drifted toward the front of the brick church. Once away from the glare of the streetlamps, she stopped, gazing into the black velvet December sky.

"Hey," said a soft voice from the darkness. Jane turned quickly to her right. A round-faced woman in her mid-sixties sat on the cement steps that led to the church's front door. "Sorry," the woman said. "I thought I should say something so you knew I was here and didn't freak when you saw me."

Jane's first thought was that she'd never heard a woman in her mid-sixties use the word "freak" unless she was using it to describe someone who she considered weird. "Okay," Jane said. There was an awkward silence between them as Jane drew two drags off her dying cigarette, blowing the smoke away from the woman. The woman shifted her backside on the cold steps and wrapped her long, wool coat around her chest. "You know, it's warm downstairs. And there's hot coffee if you want it."

"Oh, I'm sure. Thank you," the woman replied, not moving a muscle.

Jane regarded the woman out of the corner of her eye. She appeared slightly plump under her heavy purple coat. Her lilac suede boots rose above her calf, under what appeared to be a violet wool dress. On her head, she wore a jaunty, multicolored bouclé hat. What really caught Jane's observant eye was a thick, single braid of salt-and-pepper hair that reached to the middle of the woman's back. The words "well dressed Bohemian" rang in Jane's head. This woman was no road-ravaged drunk, she thought. This was a woman who lived well, albeit alone, and swigged a bottle of good red wine every night as she watched the *Arts & Entertainment* cable channel. For some unknown reason, Jane decided to do what she hardly ever did: strike up a conversation with a total stranger.

"I remember my first time coming to a meeting," Jane offered, flicking her cigarette onto the curb. "I hung right around these same steps, sucking down a half pack of Marlboros before going down in the basement and meeting the folks." The woman turned to Jane with a nervous smile. "My name's Jane."

The woman looked into Jane's eyes. "I'm Katherine Clark."

"Oh, no, no," Jane admonished Katherine in a joking manner. "*No last names.* It's like the hotel marquees on the Vegas Strip. "Liza." "Elton." "Siegfried and Roy." I'm Jane P. and you're Katherine C."

"Kit," the woman said, an undercurrent of nerves still below the surface. "Everyone calls me Kit."

"Kit? Okay."

Kit peered at Jane's beaten face. "Looks like you got smacked pretty hard."

Jane shrugged it off. "I just had a little run-in with a pool table."

"And the pool table won?" Kit quickly replied.

"Fuck, no! It's a goner!"

"Okay," Kit said with a smile.

Jane eyed Kit. "If you don't mind me asking, what are you, mid-sixties?"

"I'll be sixty-eight next year."

"One thing I've noticed talking with the Basement People here—"

"The Basement People?"

"That's what I call them. I'd rather say I'm going to see the Basement People than say I'm going to a meeting. Personal preference. Anyway, I've noticed a definite distinction between your generation of drunks and what's out there today. There was a certain dignity to your group that you just don't see anymore. Your liver could be the texture of pâté, you might be perambulating around on two legs that look like thick dowels, you could fall asleep on the kitchen floor clutching a drained bottle of scotch, but you *still* managed to get up every morning and make it work. Goddammit, I respect that!" Jane slid another cigarette out of her pack and lit up. She handed Kit the pack of cigarettes.

"No, thank you."

"Oh, come on. You can't give up one addiction without starting a new one."

"No, thank you."

"Suit yourself." Jane slid the pack into her coat pocket. "But understand that meetings are sponsored by R.J. Reynolds. We gotta numb the pain, right?" Jane said with a nervous edge to her voice.

"I need to feel my pain," Kit said, her eyes trailing across the ground.

"Running is always a popular one. That's what I do now. I run in circles around my block like a fucking nut. And *coffee*. I'm a coffee expert. *Gourmet* coffee, not the cheap shit. I bet I've got close to twenty pounds of coffee in my freezer. If one's good, twenty's better. That's the alcoholic creed."

"I haven't heard that one."

"We Basement Folk have a pithy saying for everything. 'Fake it 'til you make it.' 'One day at a time'. And of course, 'Let go and let God.'"

"That's a good one."

"It's one thing to say it, Kit C. It's another thing to actually *do* it."

"You don't sound as if you enjoy being here."

"Who in their right mind would enjoy this? Regurgitating your past in front of people with initials for last names. 'Naming it and claiming it.'" Jane peered off into the distance. "I used to hang out with drunks in bars three or four times a week. Now I get to hang out with these drunks, drink bad coffee, eat crappy candy, and listen to stories of redemption. You know, Kit C., there's nothing more tedious than listening to drunks prattle on about redemption! It's like paying a whore to read you the Book of Revelations. What's the fucking point?"

"You don't think a drunk is worthy of redemption?" Kit asked, really studying Jane's face.

"Sure, why not? Let's hand redemption out to everybody!"

"You always use sarcasm to skirt an issue?" Kit asked with a penetrating stare.

Jane turned to Kit. There was something different about this woman—a quiet intensity. At once, it attracted and repelled Jane. "Well, yeah. It usually works."

"But those who know you don't let you get away with it," Kit declared.

The conversation had turned far too personal for Jane. She felt the need to either buffer her well-built wall and change the subject or return to the dank basement. Jane chose the former. "So, have you started your personal inventory?"

"My personal inventory?"

"Oh, right, this is your first time. Step Four: 'Make a searching and fearless moral inventory of ourselves.' According to the Big Book, "We search out the flaws in our makeup which caused our failure. Being convinced that self, manifested in various ways, was what had defeated us, we considered its common manifestations.'"

"You memorized that well," Kit responded.

"I could memorize a phone book. It doesn't mean I know the people in it."

"I think I have," Kit said, looking off to the side.

"Have what?"

"Made a moral inventory. I had to. I had to understand why I did things that, in retrospect, were careless and responsible for destroying others."

"I think 'destroying' is a bit over the top."

"Not in my case. I've spent years in 'moral inventory.'"

"Well, good for you," Jane said, taking another drag on her cigarette. "They're just words to me these days. A million questions but no answers."

"What if the answer is that there is no answer? Just faith?"

"Faith? There's a fucking dark pit if there ever was one!"

"Don't you believe in God?"

"In that power greater than me? Sure. Why not? Better to believe than not believe and be caught with your pants down when your time's up, right?"

"But you still can't let go and let God?"

"Well, Kit C., therein lies my daily struggle." Jane stared aimlessly into the night sky. "I'd let go and let God if I thought He knew what the hell He was doing."

Kit stared at Jane in a probing manner. "Do you *really* mean that?"

Jane thought about it. "Yeah. I do," she said as the realization hit hard. "I guess that makes me the ultimate control addict. I want finite answers to infinite questions. I want black-and-white solutions to gray problems. Today is something I just gotta get through. And tomorrow is full of apprehension." She felt herself slipping into the void. Jane Perry would never usually allow herself to be so vulnerable in front of a stranger, but there she was, standing in the shadows and saying things she had only thought about in these last few months. "You know, Kit C., we think we've got it all figured out and that the dark night of the soul is behind us. We become aware that we have a problem and we think that's the beginning of the light shining into our lives. But it's just the beginning of the rocky ride. It's the first layer of the onion after you dig it out of the ground. It's full of dirt, and you peel that layer away and the layer underneath is still a little dirty, but as you continue peeling, the onion gets cleaner. But you know what happens when you get to the center of the onion, Kit? There's another fresh, dirty onion waiting for you. It never ends."

Kit pulled herself up with the help of the metal rail. "Enlightenment is a lifelong process, Jane P. Just a whole lot of fresh onions waiting to be peeled."

Jane came out of her daze and looked at Kit. "Well, that's fucked."

Kit smiled broadly. She picked up her purse, which looked more like a tapestry carpetbag than the typical purse a sixty-eight-year-old carried. "I've got something in here that'll help take the pain away and make your face heal faster."

"You got a bottle of Jack in there?"

"No, but I have this," Kit said, handing Jane a small, amber glass bottle.

Jane hesitated as she took the bottle. Using the reflected glare of the orange streetlamps, she made out the word on the label. "Arnica?"

"It's a homeopathic remedy for bruising. Take four pellets under your tongue every fifteen minutes for the next couple hours and then take four every hour tomorrow. You should see marked improvement if you get on it right away."

Jane regarded Kit with a puzzled look. "You a doctor?"

"Oh, God, no. A doctor wouldn't know what the hell those were!" Kit zipped up her purse and carefully moved off the steps and onto the snowy pavement. "See you soon." Kit started off into the darkness, away from the church.

"You're not going to the meeting?" Jane called after her.

Kit turned. "Not tonight, Jane P." With that, she turned the corner and disappeared from Jane's sight.

Jane stood in the semidarkness, debating her next move. There were fifteen minutes left in the meeting. But the thought of dragging herself into the basement was becoming less appealing. She looked at the bottle of Arnica and thought, "What the hell." Jane popped four of the tiny white pellets under her tongue and headed to her Mustang.

She pulled up in front of her brick house on Milwaukee Street ten minutes later, just as the snow began to fall in a blinding diagonal arch. Jane grabbed her Glock from under the driver's seat and tucked it halfway down the front of her jeans. Stashing the blond wig in her coat pocket, she dashed for the front door. She'd left the television set in the living room on "mute" before going to The Red Tail. The erratic glow served as the only light in the room as she tossed her Glock on the kitchen table. Turning to the television, she was greeted with the words BREAKING NEWS across the bottom of the television screen. Jane knocked back another four pellets of Arnica as she watched a sheriff's deputy from California hold up a flyer with the photo of an angelic-looking young blond-haired girl. Jane almost hit the volume button on her remote control, but was overcome by the extreme weariness of the day's events. She clicked off the television and turned to head down the hall to her bedroom when she noted the blinking red light on her answering machine.

Punching the button, she was shocked to hear Sergeant Weyler's voice.

"Jane. It's me. We just missed each other at the bar tonight. I need you to call me ASAP on my cell or at home. I don't care how late it is. We have to talk."

The machine beeped, signaling the end of the message. Jane hit the ERASE button and walked into her bedroom, slamming the door behind her with a violent swing.

CHAPTER 4
DECEMBER 28

Jane's morning routine had dramatically changed since she got sober. Instead of stumbling over Corona bottles and trying to ignore a hangover, her new ritual began with a trip to the freezer to unearth a bag of gourmet coffee. There were over twenty one-pound bags of pricey coffee waiting for her, with names like Madagascar Vanilla and Swiss Almond Roast. On this morning, Jane selected a dark oily bag of Italian espresso beans. The aroma alone was enough to jolt her body into adrenal ecstasy.

Jane flicked the "percolate" switch on her high-tech chrome coffeemaker and then threw on a pair of sweatpants, a light sweatshirt, and a hooded jacket. Thankfully, the weather outside was sunny and dry. It was typical for Colorado: snow and bone-chilling cold one day, sun and T-shirts the next. This served the Denver mantra, "If you don't like the weather, wait ten minutes."

Jane tied her running shoes and headed out the front door for the next leg of her morning ritual. Jane kept a pack of Marlboros and a lighter tucked under her front doormat. Before her feet hit the sidewalk, she took her requisite three drags off a cigarette before softly dipping the glowing ember into a can of sand that stood next to the doormat. She held the potent plume of smoke in her lungs and felt the power of the nicotine take hold as she unraveled the Friday edition of the *Denver Post*. She peeled off the front section and set off on her run. Not many people can easily read while they're running, but Jane had perfected this unusual talent.

Jane flipped the paper over and continued scanning the front-page stories. The headline, MISSING CALIFORNIA GIRL, 12, WORRIES HOMETOWN caught Jane's attention. Wrapping a dangling strand of hair around her ear, Jane quickly read the first few paragraphs. According to the story, a twelve-year-old girl named Charlotte

Walker from Oakhurst, California—a small tourist town known as the unofficial "Gateway to Yosemite National Park"—was missing and presumed kidnapped. The last known sighting of Charlotte, an only child, was outside a drive-through barbeque restaurant on the main drag on Christmas day. One of the employees of the fast-food joint, a teenage girl, described how she saw Charlotte getting into a beat-up four-door Chevrolet that was heading out of town.

Jane jogged to a halt and stared at the cheerful school photo of the child. It appeared to be a photo of pure innocence. Charlotte's soft blond hair curled around her ears as her round, hazel eyes stared sweetly into the camera. She noted the kid's lips. They were exceptionally pink, slathered with a shiny gloss, and what Jane would describe as "plump and pouty." There was the expected quote from the grieving mother: "It's not like Charlotte to get into a stranger's car. She's a good, sweet girl." Jane looked back at Charlotte's school photo. Throughout her career, Jane had always had the ability to look into the eyes of a victim or a perpetrator and instinctively *feel* the truth or lie beneath their surface. Staring into the eyes of Charlotte Walker, something felt off.

Jane jogged back to her front steps. Removing the partially spent cigarette from the can of sand, Jane lit up and drew four deep drags into her lungs. The sound of the telephone caught her attention as she unlocked the front door.

"Jane, are you there?" Jane stood motionless as she listened to Sergeant Weyler's determined voice on the machine. "Pick up for God's sake!" Jane started to reach for the telephone but pulled back. "Goddammit, you're standing right there, aren't you?" Jane peered at the machine with a puzzled look. "I know you got my message because the phone rang four times instead of two!" Jane muttered a frustrated "Shit," remembering that she was dealing with a man who was as good as she was at deciphering little things such as how many times a phone rings before and after a message is heard and then erased. "Stop avoiding me for Christ's sake and call me right away!"

40 REDEMPTION

Weyler slammed down the phone with a hard *click*. She knew he wanted to talk about what had gone down at the bar the night before and her involvement in the case both she and DH were chasing. But her stubborn pride wasn't going to give in.

Jane moved with gusto toward the heady aroma of coffee that awaited her in the kitchen. She took a long sip and caught a glance of her reflection in the chrome coffeemaker. She couldn't quite believe what she saw, so she walked down the hallway to the bathroom. Yes, her face showed the signs of a beating, but the bruising and swelling was much less severe than she ever expected. "Humph!" was all Jane could mutter as she made her way into her bedroom. Finding the bottle of Arnica on her bedside table, she was reminded of Kit Clark and the somewhat pointed conversation they had shared the previous night. For good measure, Jane popped another four pellets of the homeopathic remedy into her mouth and prepared for her day.

The focus of the day would be straightforward: figure out a way to pick up the pieces from the debacle at the bar, gather together what she had for the FBI, and convince Jerry to give her extra time on the $3,000 bill for bar damages while persuading him to not put her life and career in jeopardy by alerting the media. In Jane's mind, it all seemed perfectly plausible and possible to achieve.

But that was before she checked her cell messages en route to her downtown Denver office. There were three messages, all from her contacts at the FBI. The first two were short and to the point. "Call us." The third message was equally succinct: "The deal's off." Jane felt as though she'd been kicked in the teeth. She redialed her contact's number while driving erratically through the maze of Friday morning traffic, only to hear the taped voice mail recording. As her mind whirled with the various scenarios, none of which were appealing, Jane left the only message she could think of: "No one tells me the fucking deal's off until *I* say so!"

Jane's mind was elsewhere as she pulled into the parking lot that framed her two-story walk-up office building. She tore out of her Mustang and raced up the stairs that led to suite twenty-two and J.P.I. Her cramped, one-room, 200-square-foot workplace was in great need of a decorator's touch. The walls were bare, except for a trio of glass sconces across from her desk. Stacks of large boxes crowded Jane's cluttered desk, which had just enough empty space to fit the circumference of a coffee mug. That spot was soon filled with said coffee mug as Jane ripped through the phone book in search of the bar's number. Finding the number, Jane dialed and waited more than ten rings before Jerry picked up.

"This is Jerry," a gruff voice answered.

"Jerry. It's Jane. We gotta talk."

"You got my money?"

"That's what we've got to talk about—"

"Nothin' to talk about, Jane. Three grand or I call Channel 7 News."

Jane was tired of being dictated to by a low-class slob. "How about this? I caught you serving shots the other night to three kids who were underage. It'll take me less than two hours to get the paperwork served to shut you down."

"Well, it'll take me less than two minutes to dial Channel 7 News and expose you for who you are! I want my money tomorrow or I talk!"

"Rose told me you'd give me three days!"

"I changed my mind. I want my story about you on the Saturday night news. Better ratings. And if you fuckin' shut me down, I'll just use that action against you in my story!" With that, Jerry hung up.

Jane threw her handheld phone against the closed door, narrowly missing the vertical opaque glass pane. Jane peered outside, staring into the crush of cars parked beneath her in the lot. Three months of grueling investigative work was over and she was broke, both physically and financially. The walls started to cave in on Jane. She stared blankly into the parking lot, not focusing on anything in particular, until the sudden glint of a reflection caught her attention. She looked to where the sparkle of light emanated from and clearly saw a dangling crystal hanging from a rearview mirror. Peering more closely at the car, she realized it was an old sedan. She remembered the mysterious sedan with the identifying crystal that had been parked behind her the night before outside The Red Tail.

In her peripheral vision, Jane quickly noted a figure obscured against the vertical opaque glass in the hallway outside her office. Instinctively, she reached for the Glock in her shoulder holster, and then realized she'd left it underneath her car seat.

"Who's out there?" Jane yelled, a nervous edge creeping into her voice.

The figure moved toward the door. Jane looked around for an object she might use as a defensive weapon. But before she could grab anything, the door opened.

It was Kit Clark.

"Hello, Jane P."

CHAPTER 5

It took Jane several seconds to get her bearings as she stared incredulously at Kit.

"I figured you'd be surprised to see me," Kit said, closing the door. Jane attempted to sort out the scene in silence. Kit looked down and saw the handheld phone Jane had thrown in anger. She picked it up and placed it on Jane's desk. "That must have been what I heard hit the door." Kit dropped her tapestry satchel against the lone chair reserved for clients. "Your face looks much better. I told you that Arnica works."

"What in the hell is going on here?" Jane said, regaining control of her domain.

"Are you going to offer me a seat?"

Jane searched valiantly for words to match her confused thinking. "We talk outside the meeting and...what? What is this?"

"I guess I'll offer myself a seat," Kit replied, pulling the chair away from the desk and plopping her round frame into the cushion.

"Wait just a goddamned minute!" Jane said, coming to her senses.

"Sit down and I'll explain everything to you," Kit replied succinctly as she removed a series of envelopes and folders from her satchel.

A bolt of anger erupted inside of Jane. "No! *I* will explain it to *you*! You don't follow me from a bar to my private turf outside an AA meeting and talk to me as if you're one of us and then just waltz in here! That was sacred territory last night!"

"I understand and respect that," Kit said in earnest.

"The fuck you do!" Jane yelled, feeling terribly exposed and vulnerable.

"Hell, I don't care if you're a recovering alcoholic! That doesn't make you less of a person in my eyes. Frankly, it makes you more human. If you were all bravado and no vulnerability, then you couldn't work from your heart, and I *know* you work from your heart. Last night, it was imperative for me to look into your eyes and really see *you*."

"What are you talking about?"

"You do the same thing with others before you agree to form a relationship."

"Excuse me?" Jane said, in a semimocking tone.

"You did it with me last night! You looked into my center. You felt who I was."

"Jesus...."

"Let's not play games, Jane P. Time is of the essence, and I don't have any desire to fill that time with bullshit."

"Get out!" Jane ordered Kit, pointing toward the door.

Kit dug her backside into the chair and flipped her long, salt-and-pepper braid over her shoulder in a defiant thrust. "No! I'm not leaving until you hear my petition."

"If you don't move your ass out of that chair—"

"What are you going to do, Jane P.? Take a pool cue and knock me across the forehead?" Kit let that statement sink into Jane's ears.

Jane was dumbstruck. Kit had somehow witnessed the fiasco at The Red Tail the previous night. Grabbing a small digital clock, Jane slammed it on the desk. "Five minutes and then you're out of here!" Jane sat down.

"Do you believe in fate?"

"Do I believe in fate?" Jane repeated with a wicked edge.

"Yes or no, Jane P."

"You just chewed up twenty seconds of your time with a dumb question."

"Oh, you're going to play tough with me?"

Jane tapped the back of the digital clock. "Four and a half minutes, Kit."

Kit angrily slapped the clock off Jane's desk, sending it against the wall. "Scratch the badass cop act! That's not who you really are!"

"You don't know who the fuck I am!"

Kit sat forward. "Yes, I do! I followed the Emily Lawrence story very closely this past summer," she said, referring to the high-profile homicide case that had propelled Jane's name into the public eye. "I was fascinated by the case and the way you so deftly solved it. When I found out you were going to be on *Larry King Live*, I taped the show."

"What are you, a detective groupie?"

"Far from it. I'm deeply interested in *any* story that deals with a child and a murder. I saw you on Larry King's show. I looked into your eyes and I saw a kindred spirit. You can stiffen your back and say 'fuck you' until the cows come home. I know it's all a comfortable front to hide your pain and disarm stupid people so they don't see how sensitive you really are." Jane cringed at Kit's backhanded compliment. Having her vulnerability exposed skewed her normal leveraging capabilities. "I don't want you to think I'm sucking up to you, because I don't suck up to anyone. Now, I do need to get to the point of my visit. It's a matter of life and death and time is running out."

Jane didn't know what to make of Kit's disturbing appeal. "Life and death?"

"I assume you're aware of the breaking national news story of the moment?"

"What?"

Kit removed the *Denver Post* from her satchel and slid it toward Jane. "Charlotte Walker, age twelve, kidnapped from her hometown in Oakhurst, California."

Jane stared at the photo of the hazel-eyed child. "What about it?"

"I think I know who has her," Kit replied in a shaky voice.

Jane furrowed her brow like a judge debating the sanity of a defendant. "Yeah?"

"I'm not 100 percent sure, but my intuition is a helluva lot sharper these days. And it *does* add up if you look at his pattern."

"Whose pattern?"

Kit leaned forward and spoke with defining authority. "*Lou Peters*. He'd be thirty-three years old now. He's slim, has sandy brown hair, resembles a Greek god or Brad Pitt, take your pick. He's utterly charming and smart. That's who Lou Peters is. What he *did* was kidnap, rape, and kill my granddaughter, Ashlee, fourteen years ago in Northern California. Big Sur, to be specific. That's where I used to live until I couldn't live there anymore. Too many memories. Too much pain. I live in Boulder now."

Boulder. To Jane, this pronouncement was akin to saying, "I'm a Leftist and proud of it!" When Jane was a member of the Denver PD—traditionally, a conservative band of folks—they delighted in a running jag of derisive comments about the 100 percent organic, free-range-thinking town that sat twenty miles northwest of Denver. Comments such as "He's from the People's Republic of Boulder," "Welcome to Boulder, where the streets run red from all the bleeding hearts," or "There's only one age in Boulder: New Age" offered an example of what cops thought of the town.

"Here," Kit handed Jane a photo. "That was taken of Ashlee and I just a week before Lou kidnapped her."

Attached to the photo with a paper clip was a business card made on a home computer. Kit had found a yin-yang symbol in her clipart and positioned the small circular design above her name, address, phone number, and e-mail. Jane sat back and looked at the photo. A younger, more vibrant Kit was seated cross-legged on the grass, her back against a giant redwood tree. Ashlee lay across her grandmother's lap, comfortably leaning into Kit's body and tilting her head lovingly toward her shoulder. Her slim, agile body wrapped around Kit's rounder frame, showing off her tanned legs and bright red toenail polish. The child's shoulder-length brunette hair was parted into two braids with crimson ribbons tied on the ends. Her form-fitting yellow T-shirt showed off her well-developed breasts and the subtle outline of bra straps. Ashlee's frayed shorts were also tight fitting, but cut modestly several inches above her knee. Jane looked into the child's hazel eyes and saw a kid with a beautiful inner light. There was a sweet joyfulness about her—an incredible effervescent quality that literally vibrated off her body. It seemed almost incongruous that the girl was no longer on this earth. She handed the photo back to Kit.

"You keep it. That's a copy," Kit instructed. Jane reluctantly slid the photo under the flap of a nearby file. "Lou Peters went on trial for Ashlee's murder. There were the usual attempts to create as much reasonable doubt as possible, thanks to devious defense attorneys who bully elderly witnesses until they doubt what they *know* they saw, and then put so-called 'experts' on the stand who have no business being there...." Kit took a breath, her emotions getting the better of her. "Lou was rightfully convicted of Ashlee's murder and sentenced to life imprisonment. However, there was always a cloud of doubt that his attorney kept encouraging throughout the appeals process, focusing mostly on the semen left on a condom that was found near Ashlee's body." Kit handed a stack of manila folders to Jane, each bursting at the seams with newspaper clippings, handwritten notes, and police reports. "Every last detail you need to know about Lou Peters's trial is in here. I was there in that courtroom every day. When I wasn't in the courtroom, I was making myself at home with the detectives on the case, getting them to make copies of any relevant material they could release to me."

Jane gave the bulging files a cursory exam and surmised that Kit must have been a veritable treat to deal with during the trial. In scanning the files, Jane found a mug shot of Lou, dated June 26, 1990. Here was the photo of a nineteen-year-old guy who allegedly raped and murdered a fourteen-year-old girl, and yet he looked more like a Calvin Klein model in a T-shirt ad. Between his tousled light brown hair and piercing blue eyes, Jane knew that Lou could easily beguile and infatuate any number of girls. In her years at DH, Jane had viewed a lot of mug shots. But this one was different. Jane detected a profound heartache behind Lou's eyes.

That brief but nagging perception disarmed Jane. Criminals were criminals. There were no shades of gray allowed in her book.

"I couldn't let go of it," Kit interjected, taking Jane's attention away from Lou's photo. "I had to know what Lou did to my beautiful girl. Every ghastly detail. I know that sounds sick, but I was responsible for what happened."

"How were you responsible?"

"Ignorance. Stupidity. Confusing discernment with judgment." A deep gulf of emotion caught in Kit's throat. "My daughter, Barbara, has never forgiven me for what happened to her only child. But no one will ever know how I've punished myself over the years. When the prosecutor showed the photographs of Ashlee's battered body, her face bashed in with a rock to the point where you couldn't identify it as a face any longer, I made myself look at the photos and carve those images into my mind. I listened to the testimony of the medical examiner when he described how she had been raped repeatedly with the handle of a hammer over the fourteen days that Lou held her captive, and finally how Lou had raped her before he killed her. They always threw in the word, 'allegedly' because the goddamned condom they found wasn't a solid match to Lou's semen. Tried to make my Ashlee out to be a whore at fourteen years—"

Jane tried to get a gut feeling for Ashlee's case. Drawing a cigarette out of a nearby pack, she was just about to light up when Kit raised her voice. "Please don't smoke. I can't be around the toxins. Besides, there are No Smoking signs posted all over this building."

Jane lowered her lighter and plucked the cigarette out of her mouth. Yes, there were signs all over the place, but Jane never let a pesky sign stop her from doing anything. "Fourteen years ago," Jane said, thinking out loud, "the DNA technology—"

"Wasn't what it is today," Kit said, finishing Jane's sentence. "That was one of the big problems. All they could surmise was that there was a one in a hundred chance that Ashlee and Lou had been in close contact. They determined that from a drop of blood found on her hip. But because Ashlee and Lou knew each other, the defense shrugged it off as opportunistic contact."

Jane's ears perked up. "They were friends?"

Kit let out a long, tired breath. "Friends...I don't know. Lou rented a guesthouse that sat behind my house off Highway 1. He liked the place because it was quiet. It was tucked in a stand of trees and skirted the creek down below. It was the one and only summer he lived there. Ashlee always came to visit me from San Diego for the month of June. She loved Big Sur. She loved the ocean, the people, and the freedom. My daughter and son-in-law were really strict with her. Barbara tends to be repressed, just the opposite of her ol' mom. But Ashlee was a free spirit who couldn't be contained." Kit's eyes moistened with bittersweet tears. "She was an old soul. It sounds arrogant, but Ashlee flourished with me. She was my twin flame. I bought her clothes that her parents would never buy her. Other things, too, like bright blue eye shadow and red nail polish. Every fourteen-year-old girl needs those! I taught her how to meditate and do yoga and to understand the significance of Native American animal totems. We'd knock back shots of wheatgrass juice and burn Nag Champa incense. I gave her books on the Dalai Lama and love poems by Rumi. Ashlee lived a bread-and-butter existence at home. She yearned to break out and taste life! Thankfully, I could give that gift to her. *I* took Ashlee to her first R-rated movie." There was pride in Kit's statement. "There wasn't violence in the film, just nudity. I think violence is abhorrent, but nudity is beautiful. All the things we shared together were our little secrets. It made me feel very special, and I wanted to continue that relationship with her. So I didn't create a lot of boundaries for her."

Boundaries. God help us, Jane thought. Yet another buzzword of the New Age community.

"When she first laid eyes on Lou, she was smitten. She was fourteen and coming into her sexuality. And like I said, Lou was nineteen, built like a Greek god, and walked around half the time with faded jeans and no shirt so everyone could see his tanned physique. She'd talk to him and he would talk to her. It was always innocent, at least on Ashlee's part. *Lots* of girls were taken with Lou Peters. That's how he lured them into his web."

"There were other girls?"

"Oh, yes! Ashlee wasn't the first. She was the first he killed. But he raped at least two other fourteen-year-old girls before Ashlee!"

Jane observed Kit's presumptuous attitude. "Was that proven?"

"It was never used at his trial because the assaults took place when he was under eighteen. And since the two girls in question never pressed charges, it became a moot point."

"You knew these two girls?"

"No, I just know it happened. I had a very reliable source."

"Hold on. Two fourteen-year-old girls get raped and there are no charges? What about the girls' parents? Weren't they at all interested in justice?"

"Justice? Please. There's no such thing as justice in our court system!"

"Yeah, I hear you. But you're telling me it's common knowledge that two fourteen-year-olds are raped in your community by the same guy and nothing is done about it?"

"That's exactly what I'm telling you."

"Why would you rent your guesthouse to a guy who raped two fourteen-year-old girls and then allow your own granddaughter to fraternize with him?"

Kit lowered her head. "First off, I didn't know he raped those girls until *after* Ashlee's murder. However, we spent a great deal of time together talking. I'd have him to the house for dinner or coffee and we got to know each other. He had issues—"

"Issues?"

"He had problems...*severe* problems rooted in his childhood, which he openly shared with me in great detail."

"Like what?"

"He suffered horrific physical, mental, and sexual abuse at the hands of his mother—"

"Sexual abuse by his *birth* mother?"

"Yes. The woman was insane. She should have been locked up."

"Why would a nineteen-year-old guy tell you, his *landlord*, something that personal?"

"Look at me, Jane P. I give off that 'Earth Mother' vibe. I was always the 'cool gal' who lived in Big Sur. I made a good living as an artist. I did my share of Big Sur seascapes, but I was famous for my nudes. Both men and women. Sometimes together in the same painting. I was cutting edge."

"Yeah. Right. Cutting edge," Jane said, not impressed.

"I was an outspoken militant against anything that stifled human development. I still am! I marched in Salinas for migrant farm worker reform and boycotted any number of items to draw attention to injustice. Most important, I was respected as one who would not condemn you, no matter your sexual preference, religion, lack of religion...you get the point. People could tell me anything. *Anything.* They knew I could be trusted to keep their secrets and I wouldn't turn them in—"

Jane's ears perked up. "Turn them in?"

"For drugs," Kit said, being more specific. "You know, pot, coke, whatever."

"Yeah, right. *Whatever*," Jane said, a stinging tenor of judgment in her voice. Jane hated drugs. They had become the defining core of most crimes she investigated. "It's always wise to keep your personal supply line running smoothly, isn't it?"

Kit regarded Jane with a sideways glance. "I smoked pot. No hard drugs."

"In front of your granddaughter?"

"No, of course not!"

"And she never smelled it on your clothes or your furniture or in your house?" Jane was quickly turning the conversation into an interrogation.

Kit's back stiffened. "I always smoked it outside, and what in the hell has that got to do with the reason I'm here?"

"Just trying to get an accurate visual, Kit," Jane said in a cool tone. "So, back to you being the 'Earth Mother' and Lou confessing his deep, dark sexual secrets to you."

Kit took a moment to organize her thoughts. "I was aware that his childhood trauma created some twisted ideas in his head, much of them circling around fanatical Christian fundamentalist religion, sex, violence, the Devil, and on and on."

"Sex, violence, God, and the Devil? This shit didn't send up a red flag to you?"

"Back then, I bought into the New Age sermons about not judging others. Like I said before, I sadly confused proper discernment with judgment. So while my left brain was concerned about Lou's disturbing comments, my right brain kept admonishing me to not judge him!"

Jane had to force herself not to roll her eyes when she heard right brain/left brain. She understood the difference between the logical mind and the creative mind, but she hated the New Agers and their patent terminologies. "Okay, after Ashlee's murder, you hear stories about two fourteen-year-old girls supposedly raped by Lou—"

"Not *supposedly*! He raped those girls, Jane!" Kit stressed, jabbing her index finger several times onto Jane's desk. "Those rapes proved that Lou Peters had a criminal mind as well as a criminal pattern. That's the most important part of all of this! *Lou has a definite pattern.* The two girls he raped were both fourteen years old. Ashlee was fourteen years old. The girls were brunettes. Ashlee was a brunette. The girls had hazel eyes. Ashlee had hazel eyes. The pattern is a complicated, psychological mesh of Lou's tweaked perspective. Lou's mother was a brunette with hazel eyes. I know it sounds like bad, cookie-cutter psychology, but there it is. Choosing a fourteen-year-old also had meaning. Lou was fourteen years old when his mother raped him."

"His mother actually physically raped him?"

"I already told you that!" Kit replied, sounding a bit irritated.

"You said she sexually abused him. That's a broad umbrella term these days. It can run the gamut from fondling and masturbation to exposing him to porn or making him watch her have sex with another guy."

"Well, Lou's mother did all that *and* she raped him with her own goddamned body. Get the picture?"

"So, what's the meaning around the number fourteen?"

"I was getting to that. During our conversations, Lou mentioned a saying to me many times: 'The Power of Fourteen.' It was a strong belief he had. He said that when a boy or girl reached fourteen years old, it signified a pivotal moment in his or her development. It was at that age, he said, that a child was highly impressionable and could easily be altered spiritually, mentally, physically, and emotionally. His feeling was that whatever occurred in your fourteenth year framed and defined who you would become as you grew into an adult. As much as I hate to admit it, 'The Power of Fourteen' theory has merit. I've paid more attention over the years, and I have noticed that it *is* a defining age. Look at that little girl in Utah who was kidnapped and held captive for all those months. What was her name? Elizabeth.... Elizabeth Smart. She was fourteen years old when that occurred. I know that tragedy and trauma can strike at any age, but there *does* seem to be something to the whole 'Power of Fourteen' idea."

Jane nervously rubbed the old scar on the right side of her forehead. She had been fourteen when that defining moment in her young life occurred. And that runaway kid on the street in front of The Red Tail...she was fourteen. Coincidence? Jane wasn't about to entertain a warped theory from the mind of Lou Peters. "You believe that shit when a Devil incarnate like Lou says it?"

"Even the Devil speaks the truth sometimes, Jane P. He just doesn't couch that truth in love. But that doesn't take away from the fact that truth or insight can pour from his lips."

"I'm afraid I see the world as a bit more black-and-white than that, Kit."

"This is not a black-and-white world. If you see it that way, you create polarity. And when you do that, you're not open to the wonderful, frustrating, enlightening gray middle part."

"Cops don't see gray. We can't. It would eliminate that 'polarity' we call 'guilt.'"

"Lou's own experience proved his theory. He was actually speaking about himself. His mother raped him when he was fourteen, and that event altered and twisted him and turned him into what he became. It's the classic cycle of victimization."

Jane had listened to the "abuse excuse" too many times during her career. If she applied that reasoning to her own violent childhood, she would be working the other side of the law instead of enforcing it. "Do me a favor, Kit. Don't use Lou's childhood trauma to sell your appeal. A lot of us got the shit kicked out of us and we're not out there raping and killing people."

Kit eyed Jane carefully. "I was right," she said, more as an acknowledgment to herself than a statement to Jane. "I saw it in your eyes during that Larry King interview. I saw your pain. I just wasn't aware where it came from."

Jane was not used to anyone so readily peeling away her well-built, protective armor. Sergeant Weyler was the only other person who saw through Jane's tough shell, and that pissed off Jane no end. She leaned forward, digging her elbows into the desk. "Cut to the chase, Kit. You said that Lou has a pattern?"

"Yes. First, I have to tell you what happened last year. Lou's lawyers fought hard and were able to convince the court to reexamine the semen from the condom. The DNA proved beyond a shadow of a doubt that it was *not* Lou Peters's semen. That opened up the door. There were four weeks of emotional court appearances, all of which I went to and witnessed in California. Barbara and Paul, her husband, didn't attend. They live in Henderson, Nevada, now and can't go through the pain all over again. There were the same attorneys and the same asinine 'expert witness/ doctor' who testified that Lou Peters was a good Christian who had been wrongly accused. I wanted to offer my two cents, but the prosecutor felt I was too much of a loose cannon. The judge ruled that reasonable doubt existed, and Lou was ordered out of prison on bond. He's set to have a new trial in twelve months, and will probably get off, knowing his luck."

Jane looked down at the newspaper and Charlotte Walker's school photo. "So he's out on bond and suddenly he's responsible for Charlotte Walker's kidnapping?"

"I took a good look at Lou Peters in that courtroom last year. I listened carefully to the personal testimony he gave to the judge. I was completely open to the idea that he was reformed and not a danger to society anymore. But every time I looked into his eyes, I saw darkness and a willfulness to repeat his past behavior. I knew he was going to do it again. I didn't know when or where, but it was only a matter of time. That's why I've kept my eyes wide open this past year. When I saw the bulletin about Charlotte Walker yesterday afternoon, my gut told me to act on what my heart felt. And believe me, my intuition is a lot sharper these days."

"Well I'm not getting the hard and fast connections between Lou and Charlotte."

"After his release from Chino Prison, he moved to Mariposa and then over to Oakhurst, California."

"How the hell do you know that?"

"His bondsman told me."

"*You know his—*"

"I made a point to get to know the guy, and he liked me as much as he hated Lou. He was more than happy to share Lou's relocation destination with me, off the record."

Jane leaned back in her chair and observed Kit. Up to this point, Kit's kooky, pot-smoking, New Age spouting attitude had lowered her credibility in Jane's eyes. But now the word *chutzpah* was warranted as a description, and Jane respected people with *chutzpah*. She attempted to picture Kit, with her long hair in a braid and 'Earth Mother' aura, walking into the coarse environment of a bail bondsman and winning him over. That took guts and the kind of unflagging determination that Jane rarely saw anymore.

But still, she had questions. Serious questions related to supposed patterns. "Charlotte Walker is twelve years old. And she's blond. That kind of blows your 'Power of Fourteen' theory. Not to mention the pattern of choosing brunettes—"

"I'm aware of that. But I've also done a great deal of study on the criminal mind and those who choose patterns versus random hits. A criminal doesn't start off with the same pattern he ends up using. The pattern builds upon itself as the criminal feels more confident in getting away with his crime." Jane was well aware of this fact, but was interested to see exactly how much research Kit had done. "Lou started out raping two girls who were both fourteen. Unfortunately, I don't know if there were differences in his approach between victim one and victim two. What I was able to gather from reliable sources years ago was that victim one was raped and let go immediately. Victim two was held for a period of several hours before he let her go. He realized he could get away with it, and so he decided to add to his pattern with Ashlee. This time, he held his victim in a remote location and for a longer period of time. He didn't stay with Ashlee twenty-four hours a day during the two weeks he had her. He'd ride his motorcycle to the cabin where he had her tied up, spend a few hours there, and then motor back to town. He worked his maintenance job, went to the market, and ate at the coffee shop—all with the premeditated intention of creating alibis during those fourteen days. Finally, after fourteen days, for whatever reason, it was time to add to his criminal pattern. He raped her with his penis, not the hammer handle, and then he killed my Ashlee." Kit eagerly dug into her satchel. "I've got reams of information on this kind of offender—"

"That's okay. I know the beast," Jane assured Kit. "So why would Lou now go for a twelve-year–old blonde?"

"I've given that great thought. Once criminals get away with a certain crime, they don't so much change their patterns, they *add* to them. I have a very strong feeling that Lou is adding something different to this one. Something twisted. I can't explain it. As I said, my intuition is stronger these days. Maybe Lou's prison time convinced him to alter his 'Power of Fourteen' theory."

"What does his bail bondsman say about his behavior since he got out?"

"The gentleman told me that Lou called him to let him know he moved from Mariposa to Oakhurst. Then he called him again a couple months later to let him know he was having phone problems but it would be resolved soon."

"Why would Lou call his bail bondsman about a phone problem?"

"That's what makes Lou's mind so criminal. He understands what is expected of him and he goes out of his way to do things that he doesn't have to do in order to earn points with those in authority. But it's all done with a highly manipulative motive. He is an A-One class charmer, believe me! Lou once alerted one of the guards at Chino Prison that his cell door wasn't locking correctly, knowing full well that alert would get back to the warden and make him look like an up-front fellow! It's all about external impressions with Lou. He professes to be a strict, fundamentalist Christian who believes in the importance of family because he knows that sort of posturing will work in his favor." Kit was obviously tiring quickly. "Look, we'll have plenty of time to talk about Lou when you and I travel to California."

"Whoa! Hold on! I didn't agree to take this case!"

"I looked up on the Internet what private investigators get per day. Since you're relatively well known, I factored that into the equation. I came up with five hundred dollars a day as a fair fee. Meals, hotels, fuel, and anything else you require is on me—"

"Kit—"

"I'm hoping you can figure this out in ten days or less for the sake of that child. Either way, I'm prepared to give you five thousand dollars up front for the job—*in cash.*" With that, Kit withdrew a thick envelope from her satchel and slapped it on Jane's desk. "It's in hundreds. I hope that's all right." Jane looked dumbstruck at the envelope. "Feel free to count the money. It won't insult me."

"Where did you get five thousand dollars?"

"From my savings account, of course. If that's not enough, I can withdraw more. But you'll have to let me know right away since I want us to get going tomorrow."

Jane's head was spinning. "I have another case—"

"You mean that debacle you were involved in last night at The Red Tail?"

Jane bristled at Kit's "debacle" description. "Yes, that one—"

"Do you truly like dealing with those lowlife scumbags? That swarthy fellow last night would have put your lights out if that big bruiser hadn't intervened! From what I witnessed, you'd do well to hightail it out of town for a bit!"

"It's a little more complicated than that!"

"Jane P.! A twelve-year-old girl's life hangs in the balance! *What is there to discuss?*"

Jane quickly realized that Kit's fervent tone was probably the same one she used when she debated any number of pet political causes. "Kit, there is not enough hardcore evidence for me to link Lou with Charlotte Walker's disappearance. Your gut intuition isn't enough to convince me to travel all over hell and back with you—"

"I'd do this alone. But I don't have the energy, nor do I possess the credibility and knowledge that you have. And tell me, Jane P., how many times did *your* gut intuition lead *you* to a killer?"

"It's not my gut talking here! It's *yours!*"

"And you don't trust my intuition. I see. Well, get to know me and you'll see that my intuition is right!"

"That's not good enough for me!"

"When I sat down in this chair, I asked you a simple question: Do you believe in fate? The reason I asked that has everything to do with my intuitive abilities. Call it fate or coincidence, but isn't a coincidence simply a *co-incident?*"

"You're losing me, Kit—"

"Call it coincidence or synchronicity, it's the same beautiful magic. Life serves them up to everyone; the trick is understanding the messages they seek to deliver." Kit leaned toward Jane. "Forget about logically explaining them. They *defy* explanation! When you begin to recognize how these 'coincidences' weave in and out and of your life, only *then* will you understand the governing power of a higher plan."

The conversation was becoming too spiritually deep for Jane. "Yeah, okay, I—"

"You want concrete examples of what I'm saying? *Fine.* How about this: Because of my interest in children, I collected every-thing I could find on the Lawrence murder case you were involved in this past summer. Then I see you on Larry King's show and I'm drawn to you. I can feel that you're a kindred spirit. And then yesterday afternoon, I'm watching CNN and they break the story of Charlotte Walker's disappearance in *Oakhurst, California*! Within two hours of seeing that story, for no reason at all, I feel a *calling* to go for a drive. I get in my car and what do I see immediately? A red-tailed hawk circling above me! The Native Americans will tell you the red-tailed hawk is a messenger. It is telling one to pay at-tention to all signals and coincidences! And so I drive for miles, let-ting my intuition lead me the entire way, until I end up in Denver on Colfax Avenue. That's not exactly the neighborhood I choose to frequent. But there I am. And I'll be damned if I don't look up and see The Red Tail Hawk Bar. Well, it couldn't get any clearer than that now, could it? *Coincidence?* Not to the untrained eye! I walk into the establishment and who do I see at the pool table but Jane Perry. At that moment, it all came full circle: my odd kinship with you, Charlotte's disappearance in Oakhurst where Lou re-sides, the circling hawk, the bar, and you. Now, I know to a skeptic, that line of reasoning wouldn't hold water. But to the intuitive person, those connections are solid!" Kit sat back, seeming a bit worse for wear after her passionate plea. "Open your mind, Jane P. There are greater things in heaven and earth than we'll ever know. *Pay attention*! The synchronicities in life boggle the mind!"

Jane recalled the subject of synchronicity at the AA meeting the night before. And yet, she still wasn't convinced. No matter how much money Kit threw at her, she wasn't about to embark on a wild-goose chase that would make her look more foolish than she did getting the crap beat out of her in a Colfax bar. And there was still that little issue of saving her current case and making things good with the FBI. Jane let out a deep sigh and rubbed the scar on her temple as she tried to engender a softer, less strident voice. "Kit, I'm sorry. I need more."

"Money?"

"Proof."

"We'll find proof when we get there. Isn't that how it works? Learn as you go?"

Jane looked at Kit with an empty stare. "I'm sorry."

Kit's face fell. In stunned silence, she gathered the files and envelope of money together and carefully tucked them into her satchel. Jane recognized a sudden frailty as Kit rose to her feet and walked to the door. After a good, well-thought minute, she turned to Jane. Her voice was choked with emotion. "When I said this was a matter of life and death, I was referring to Charlotte Walker's life...and *my* death." Jane stared at Kit in questioning silence. "I have inoperable, terminal lung cancer. Just hit stage four. I've got maybe another three months left. I don't want your pity. I want your help. I couldn't save my Ashlee from Lou. But I believe I *can* save that little girl in California with your assistance. I *have* to go there. My life *must* come full circle. I can't die knowing I've lived an unfinished life, Jane." Kit got control of herself. She reached into her satchel and brought out an eight-inch square, purple suede drawstring bag. "I know you're cautious of anything that is 'woo-woo'," Kit said, gently moving toward Jane's desk, "but humor me. This is a bag of animal stone totems I use for divination. Would you draw one out of the bag for me?"

If it had been anyone else, Jane would have replied with a string of obscenities. Kit opened the bag and Jane reached in, drawing out a flat stone the size of a silver dollar. Carved onto one side was a slithering snake.

Kit's eyes widened, as if she were witnessing a pivotal moment in history. "The snake. My God! You're on the verge of radical transformation. Your soul is ready to shed the skin of the past and move on to a more enlightened path."

Jane did her best to hide a sarcastic smile and not utter an equally cynical retort. Instead, she handed the stone back to Kit. "I'm still not taking your case."

Kit dropped the bag into her satchel, sans the snakestone. "You keep it. It'll remind you of where your soul wants you to go." She headed toward the door. "Oh, keep an eye out for proof that the animal you chose is legitimate. Very often, the universe delivers the animal to you in some form, as cosmic proof of its validity. Just another synchronistic event." Kit exited the office and disappeared down the hall.

CHAPTER 6

The sooner Jane could suck nicotine into her lungs, the sooner she could think clearly and possibly save face with the FBI. Nervously pacing outside her office building, Jane dug one hand into the pocket of her jeans and anxiously rubbed the three sobriety chips. Drawing her hand out of her pocket, Jane dropped the flat snakestone totem she'd pulled out of Kit's purple drawstring bag. Jane knelt down to retrieve the stone. Boojey-Woojey. That's what it was, Jane insisted. Just another crackpot, New Age gimmick. And yet...she was beginning to experience too many strange things that couldn't be easily forgotten. Like the past summer. Jane had experienced strange dreams—mystical, precognitive dreams that eerily alerted her to key signs to look out for. At first she had chalked them up to a bender or the result of quitting booze cold turkey. She tried to detach from the dreams, believing that by not acknowledging them, she could pretend them away. But she could never deny the disturbing realization that the images in those ambiguous dreams definitively led her to a cold-blooded killer. It was in these quiet moments alone that the memory of those staccato images haunted her. Jane looked down at the snakestone. "Radical transformation." Those were the words Kit had used to describe the auspicious totem. "Ridiculous," Jane muttered under her breath. She had half a mind to fling the stone into a nearby mound of fast-melting snow. But for some reason, she slid it back into her pocket to keep her sobriety chips company.

Four more attempts to reach her FBI contacts were unsuccessful. The feeling of being out of the loop allowed Jane's thoughts to turn paranoid. Was Jerry calling Channel 7 News and spilling her story to the investigative journalist at the station? She mused how fragile one's moment in the spotlight could be. Six months ago, the media had called her an "adroit heroine" after solving a chain of brutal slayings while working for Denver Homicide. She was fending off phone calls from *Larry King Live*, *60 Minutes*, *20/20*, *Dateline*, and Diane Sawyer, all begging to nab the exclusive interview with the hottest commodity in town. She wouldn't have agreed to any interview if it hadn't been for Sergeant Weyler and his suggestion that granting one solid tête-à-tête would concurrently satisfy the masses and help out Denver PD. While Weyler personally favored the more intellectual offerings on PBS, it was he who encouraged Jane to grant Larry King the exclusive. "He's smart," Jane remembered Weyler telling her. "He doesn't go for the jugular. He won't piss you off like Diane Sawyer will. You'd deck Diane Sawyer inside of five minutes." Jane smiled at the recollection. And that's how she'd ended up on Larry King's program five months ago. And now? Now she was twenty-four hours away from falling off that precarious ladder and having her name and reputation dragged through the muck. "Radical transformation, indeed!" Jane mused.

After three more hours of shuffling papers on her desk and not a single phone call, Jane scooped a disorganized mass of files into her arms and headed home. Halfway there, her cell phone beeped, alerting Jane that she had a voice mail message. Jane grabbed the phone and eagerly retrieved the lone message.

"Hey, Janie, it's me!" The voice was Jane's younger brother, Mike. The perpetual adolescent cadence to his voice suggested that he was fifteen years old rather than thirty-one. "I just turned on the TV and saw all the hotshots making their big announcement. I looked for you, but the only guy I recognized was that Weyler dude. You're probably out celebrating. Hey, I'm confuzzled. Didn't you say you were working this alone?"

Jane sped home. Tearing into her house, she quickly grabbed the remote and angrily turned on the TV. Scanning quickly, she landed on a Denver news station.

"...Weather should be warmer than usual over the next few days, Kent."

"Thanks, Brock. Recapping the headlines this afternoon in Denver. An hour ago, Denver Police announced a successful close to an eight-month cocaine drug sting...."

The TV flashed video from the press conference. Ten Denver cops and detectives stood behind a long table stacked with kilos of cocaine. Standing to the far right was Sergeant Weyler, impeccably dressed in one of his tailored suits and crimson ties. The room was filled with a claque of photographers and rabid reporters.

"This is by far the *biggest* takedown of cocaine in Denver's history." The jacked-up, cocksure voice belonged to none other than Kenny Stephens. *Sergeant* Kenny Stephens. That's exactly what it said under his pumped up frame. DH had done exactly what they intended to do: use Jane's print and video evidence at the bar to seal their investigation. And there was Weyler—Jane's mentor, confidant, and friend—standing in front of the cache. While many of the other cops gloated, Weyler's expression remained pensive with a decipherable irritation under his seemingly calm surface. Looking more closely, that tension appeared to be most evident when Kenny opened his mouth. "As a bonus for the Denver PD," Kenny continued, "nearly fifteen thousand dollars in counterfeit bills was found when we raided their location." The TV cameras focused on the fake money. "So that makes this catch a double win for Denver!"

Jane stared helplessly at the screen as she sunk into the couch. She lit a cigarette and took a long drag. "Fucking assholes," she muttered to herself. The more Jane mused on the fallout from this event, the madder she got. She sunk her left hand into her jean pocket and nervously started rubbing the metal off the sobriety chips. "Fucking assholes!" Jane screamed in a flinty rage as she threw the remote control with gusto against the living room wall. Unexpectedly, one of the channel buttons depressed when the remote hit the wall, causing the TV to switch to CNN.

"We want to run the video that was just released this hour to the media by the Walker family in Oakhurst, California," the female news anchor reported. "Apparently, this video—which we're going to loop—shows twelve-year-old missing child Charlotte Walker at her birthday party this past year. The family wanted the public to get a better idea of what Charlotte looks like...."

Jane was still stinging from the PD's announcement and didn't immediately look at the television screen. But the playful, somewhat flirtatious giggle caught her attention. Turning to the screen, Jane observed Charlotte Walker in her backyard, opening birthday presents and surrounded by her mother and friends. A smattering of teenage boys who looked to be a few years older could be seen sitting on chairs around the yard. Charlotte's mother, a heavyset woman who appeared to be in her mid-thirties, beamed and fawned over her exuberant daughter.

But what really caught Jane's eye was that Charlotte Walker looked nothing like the photo released to the media. She wore a cropped denim jacket that was buttoned just enough to reveal a white tank top beneath it. Her low-rise, tight-fitting blue jeans exposed a two-inch gap of tummy and a well-formed backside. From Jane's point of view, Charlotte gave off a much older vibe than twelve. There was the thick black eyeliner, rouge, and red lipstick. And there was the odd, long, rainbow-colored wig Charlotte wore loosely on her head that skimmed the middle of her back. It looked similar to the wigs that rabid sports fans don in football stadiums. *Attention getters.* That was the first thought that crossed Jane's mind as she watched Charlotte in her birthday video.

A quick glimpse of a reflection in a window showed the camera operator to be a plump woman in her mid to late-thirties. Charlotte tore the wrapping off a large box and pulled out a red leather jacket.

"Hold it up so Aunt Donna can film it, Charlotte!" her mother said.

Charlotte dutifully flattened the red jacket against her chest and happily posed for the camera. There was no shyness with this girl. The camera zoomed closer, slightly going out of focus. As Aunt Donna adjusted the focus ring, the TV screen filled up with Charlotte's face. Her hazel eyes stared at the camera in a provocative manner. "I *love* my new coat! It's *beautiful*! *Thank you!*" she squealed at the camera.

"Try it on!" Aunt Donna instructed as she zoomed the camera back to reveal Charlotte from the waist up.

Charlotte unbuttoned her jean jacket and removed it, revealing a tight white tank top underneath. That's when Jane's heart started to pound. She stared at the TV screen in disbelief. As Charlotte slipped on the red leather birthday jacket, the vertical emblem emblazoned on her tank top was easy to identify. It was a slithering vertical snake.

Jane withdrew the snakestone from her pocket. She held the stone up to the TV screen; it was a perfect match to the image on Charlotte's tank top. Jane's incredulity quickly turned into a growing indignation. Her mind raced as she plunged the chips and the stone back into her pocket and headed down the hall to retrieve her Glock.

She furiously sorted through the files she'd brought home. Jane found what she was looking for: the photo of Kit and Ashlee and the accompanying address card. Jane knew exactly where Kit's apartment complex was located.

It was approaching four thirty in the afternoon as the sun sunk beneath the Rocky Mountains. Jane gunned the Mustang toward Boulder, cigarette tightly clenched in her teeth. With each passing mile, her righteous ire became more acute. Nobody was going to screw with her. *Nobody*.

Just shy of five fifteen, Jane skidded to a halt in front of Kit's apartment building. She stormed out of her Mustang, noting Kit's road-weary Buick with the identifying crystal hanging from the rearview mirror. Securing her Glock inside the waistband of her jeans, Jane entered the apartment complex. Upon finding Kit's apartment, she banged on the door. "Kit! Open up!" Jane yelled with edgy cop supremacy.

Kit opened her door. "Jane P.! This is a surprise. Why all the pounding?"

Jane forced her way into Kit's apartment, which wasn't easy, as the door had a soft obstruction behind it. A pervasive aroma of patchouli incense wafted through the air. Once inside, Jane was all business. She slammed the door and stormed into the tiny living room that held a couch, lounge chair, several floor lamps, and a television that was tuned to CNN. On the screen, Jane noted the same continual loop of Charlotte Walker's birthday video. Jane eyed the narrow kitchen, then plowed down a short hallway, canvassing Kit's bedroom and tiny bathroom. Satisfied that Kit was alone, Jane returned to the living room.

"What the fuck is going on, Kit?" Jane yelled with authority.

Kit stood calmly perplexed by Jane's behavior, her unbraided salt-and-pepper hair covering the front of her violet caftan "In relation to what?" Kit replied innocently.

"What kind of a con are you pulling?" Jane said with pointed determination.

"Con?"

Jane dug the snakestone out of her pocket and held it up to Kit's face. *"This!"*

"What about it?"

Jane eyed the television. The video loop was repeating the moment when Charlotte removed the jean jacket to reveal her tank top. Jane moved to the TV and slammed the snakestone against the screen, clearly showing a side-by-side, nearly perfect copy of the snake motif on Charlotte's top. "Explain that!" Jane demanded.

Kit walked to the television, smiling. "Look at that! I told you the universe would provide confirmation of the radical transformation you're about to experience!"

"Cut the New Age shit, lady! You don't come into my office and play some fucking game with me and then—"

"I'm not playing a game!" Kit said, taking offense at Jane's statement.

"The hell you aren't!"

"Take it down a notch! The neighbors are going to think I'm being assaulted!"

"Do you have information on the Charlotte Walker kidnapping? Are you protecting somebody?"

"*What?* I told you my instinctive feelings about Lou Pet—"

Jane quickly pulled aside her jacket to reveal the Glock. "*What do you know about Charlotte Walker?*" Jane said pointedly.

"Nothing more than what I've heard and seen on television!" Kit eyed the Glock. "Is that meant to intimidate me?"

Jane stood firm. "Where's your little bag?"

"What bag?"

"The purple bag this thing came out of!" Jane said, waving the snakestone.

"It's in my satchel where I left it," Kit calmly replied.

"Get it!"

Kit let out an exasperated breath and turned to retrieve her satchel. She pulled out the purple drawstring bag and handed it to Jane.

Jane backed up a step. "Open the bag and drop the contents on the floor."

Kit looked at Jane incredulously. "Why?"

"Because every single stone in that bag has a snake on it! That's what makes your con so effective! Dump the bag, Kit!"

Kit let out a sarcastic snort and did as she was told. The stones fell onto the carpet, mostly landing face up. There were stones with carvings of ravens, hummingbirds, eagles, crows, and more. But not a single snake. Jane scanned the stones, her mind working overtime on her next move.

"Anything else you'd like me to do while you've got your gun out?" Kit asked, each word dripping with disdain.

Jane turned her attention from the stones to Kit's face. Studying it carefully, she saw a steely willfulness and no fear. What Jane *didn't* see was the slightest aura of duplicity that graced the visage of so many con artists she'd dealt with in the past. She draped her jacket over the Glock. "Explain it," Jane demanded.

"The snake? I can't. *You* pulled the damned stone—*I* didn't!"

"So, it's just a *coincidence* that the *same* goddamned image appears on the shirt of a missing child *you* are so interested in finding?"

"What did I tell you about coincidences in your office? Are you paying attention? This is beautiful! This is confirmation!"

"Stop talking in riddles! I'm not Alice and this ain't Wonderland!"

Kit casually turned and sunk her body into the lounge chair opposite the TV. "Maybe it is. Maybe this is all a grand illusion. You know, the Buddhists believe—"

"Don't change the subject, Kit!"

"Was I changing the subject?"

Jane looked around the room and saw two large suitcases and one extra large duffel bag near the front door—the "soft protrusion" that prevented Jane from easily gaining entrance when she arrived. "You're skipping town?"

"You make it sound like I'm running away. I'm going *toward* something!"

"You're gonna go track down Lou in California?"

"Someone has to do it!"

"You driving that shit-pot car parked outside? What is it? Nine, ten years old?"

"Nearly fifteen, actually."

"You wouldn't make it to Grand Junction before something started to clatter under the hood!" Jane observed to Kit. "You're *seriously* planning on dragging your sick ass in a relic of a car over a thousand miles so you can prove your point?"

"So I can save a child, not prove a point."

"What are you gonna do when you get there? Look up Lou in the phonebook and say, 'Hey, Lou. Kit Clark, here. Did you take that sweet little Charlotte, and if you did, could you please bring her back?" Jane's voice was thick with a snide, syrupy rebuke.

Kit eyed Jane like a schoolmarm would an unruly student. "I'm not sure what exactly I'll do when I get there. But whatever I do, I *will* find Lou."

Jane thrust her hands onto her hips with great drama. "You're *nuts!*"

Kit smiled. "You look like Wonder Woman when you stand like that."

Jane regarded Kit with as much cop bravado as she could muster. "I'm only gonna ask you once: did you have advance knowledge of Charlotte's birthday video?"

"Of course not!" Another thought crossed Kit's mind. "*Oh!* Did you hear that Charlotte's mother believes her daughter was wearing that *exact red leather jacket* shown in the video when she disappeared on Christmas? The girl from the barbeque shack—the one who says she saw Charlotte getting into a car with a man—wasn't sure whether Charlotte was wearing the jacket. Let me tell you, I have been *glued* to the TV!"

Jane turned her back to Kit, attempting to sort out everything. "This is insane."

"By the way," Kit's voice took on a sound of compassion, "I caught the local news and the big story about the cocaine bust." Jane soured at Kit's statement. "That should have been *your* collar, right?" Jane turned, looking at Kit with a nasty glare. "Well, wasn't it?" Kit asked, unmoved.

"Yes," was all Jane could utter.

"So I assume that case is no longer number one on your priority list?"

Jane knew where this was going. "That's a fair assumption."

"There's nothing else pressing that requires you to don that blond wig and get the shit kicked out of you?" Kit's eyes danced with sweetness and respect for Jane.

Jane recognized Kit's gentle jab and the crafty humor behind it. She tucked the snakestone in her pocket. "I want it understood up front that I'm not completely convinced Lou Peters kidnapped Charlotte."

"Understood. Prove me wrong and you get some time away from Denver. Prove me right, and you can save a little girl's life. I'd call that a win-win situation."

Jane marveled at how Kit made the whole agreement sound so ridiculously simple. "Can I have three grand by tomorrow morning?"

"You can have *five* thousand, and you can have it right now," Kit said offhandedly, removing the envelope of cash from her satchel and handing it to Jane.

Jane opened the envelope and ran her thumb over the stack of hundred dollar bills. "We do this my way, or we don't do it at all."

"Of course. You're the expert. That's why I hired you for the job."

"I'll pick you up at nine o' clock on the nose tomorrow morning."

"Make it six. We can't waste a second."

Jane grimaced inside at the thought of a six o'clock pick up, but she nodded in agreement.

Kit stood up, extending her hand to Jane. "Thank you for accepting my offer. Your decision will alter the course of many lives."

Jane shook Kit's hand with an anxious heart. That last statement would keep Jane up the rest of the night.

CHAPTER 7

Jane had a long list of things to do before her appointed six A.M. pickup. First on that list was the trip to The Red Tail to deliver the three grand to Jerry. Jane noticed how disappointed Jerry looked when she plunked the wad of cash on the bar. He would have happily foregone reimbursement just to get his two minutes of fame trashing Jane's reputation on the Denver news.

Jane's next stop was equally important to her. In the past, ten days or more away from home didn't require much preparation. But ever since Jane had replaced her alcohol addiction with a gourmet coffee addiction, it was important to have appropriate provisions on hand. By the time she left The Gourmet Grind, she'd purchased fifteen assorted four-ounce bags.

Back home, Jane cleaned out the trunk of the Mustang to accommodate luggage. Checking the weather for Oakhurst on her laptop computer, Jane noted that rain was in the forecast for the next two weeks. Out of curiosity, she researched the weather data for December 25—the day the girl at the barbeque restaurant saw Charlotte Walker get into the mysterious car. Oakhurst had sunny skies that morning, but clouds formed midday, turning into hard rain. That certainly erased any footprints left by the kidnapper as well as any scent at the scene of the crime.

This was all based on the assumption that Charlotte was *indeed* kidnapped. Jane wasn't ruling out anything. It was December 25. Perhaps the kid took her Christmas cash and left town to party forty-five miles southwest in the "big city" of Fresno?

Or maybe Charlotte was a runaway and she skipped town to ditch her parents. The birthday video was full of giggles and grins, but that was just "surface crap" to Jane. Jane never accepted at face value the images or behaviors that anyone presented to the public. She knew all too well from her own violent childhood that appearances can and do deceive. Even when Jane and her brother, Mike, showed up at school with bruises or swollen lips, there was the carefully rehearsed explanation that had nothing to do with the truth. Maybe, Jane thought, Charlotte Walker was getting the shit punched out of her and ran away. That'd make it easy. No bad guy and no dealing with Lou Peters.

Perhaps Charlotte's mother was fighting a custody battle. Where was Charlotte's father? Only her mother was quoted in the *Denver Post* story and there was no sign of her dad on the birthday video. The skipped town possibility, runaway theory, and custody battle idea would all be explored by everyone on the case, since the kidnapping was fast becoming a major news story with possible out-of-state transport of the alleged victim.

Jane clicked on the television to have some noise in the background while she packed. It quickly became evident that Charlotte Walker's case had become the number one story in America. Fox News led their report with a banner headline in stark block letters that read, THE SEARCH FOR CHARLOTTE WALKER. Rival cable news network MSNBC plastered, MISSING INNOCENCE ON CHRISTMAS DAY with a treacly graphic of a yellow rose leaning against the word "innocence." Typical. Charlotte's disappearance had become the same kind of hardcore small-screen tragedy that fires up every newscaster's loins. It was the brash, unrehearsed, flying-without-a-safety-net reporting that fueled news stations from all across the country. It was women and men with microphones pounding the pavement, climbing over ten-foot hedges and endearing themselves to unsuspecting friends and family of the victim so their network could catch the exclusive interview with someone—*anyone*—who could shed light on the missing kid's disappearance.

And then there were the pundits. They came out in droves. They had no other job but to offer their "expert commentary" on every blip of new information. None of them had any more knowledge than anyone else, but because of their credentials—psychology, medicine, law, FBI, behavioral science, body language—they became instant media stars. And they were all riding the edge of a family's worst nightmare. Jane knew the drill: Nothing sells a breaking news story like a missing girl from a small, wholesome town. Nothing except the trial of the SOB who *murdered* that girl.

Murder. That was something Jane couldn't deal with again. She'd had her fill that past summer of slaughtered bodies and the dying eyes of a ten-year-old she couldn't save. The memory had incited grisly nightmares and whiskey binges until her life came crashing down around her. Perched on the fragile slope of new-found sobriety, Jane wasn't sure she could mentally handle another case where the child ended up dead.

Jane glanced at the TV. A bevy of ubiquitous yellow ribbons dotted the rain-soaked trees and fences around Oakhurst. These symbols of remembrance and town unity were standard fare for any missing child case. The poster with Charlotte's cherubic photo was displayed across the screen, and Jane scrutinized informal circles of children and women holding candles in prayer vigils as they softly sang "Amazing Grace," while a misty rain fell around them. Bergman himself couldn't have filmed the scene with more grim lighting. It was a well-orchestrated, all-American, yellow-ribbon spectacle, perfected and packaged by the media over the years, thanks to the numerous headlining child abductions. Instead of the *Junior Miss Pageant*, Jane pondered, it was the *Junior Gone Missing Pageant*. Through it all, Jane couldn't help but wonder if somewhere out there Charlotte Walker was wearing her red leather jacket while watching this national television exhibition and laughing her ass off.

After packing, Jane settled under the glare of the kitchen lamp with a fresh pot of Columbia Supremo steaming beside her and read through the thick files Kit had given her before leaving the apartment that afternoon. Kit kept copious notes during the initial trial, along with a neat, chronological stack of newspaper clippings. There were also copies of short reports made by detectives and given to Kit. While the reports didn't offer any earth-shattering information that couldn't be gleaned by court documents and Kit's detailed trial notes, it did show that at least one detective brought in to work the case from Carmel, California, seemed friendly and willing to offer more than the stock "I'm sorry for your loss" statement. There was a loose note with a header that said, FROM THE DESK OF CHARLES SAWYER, dated, August 10, 1990. The typewritten note read:

Dear Ms. Clark,

After our phone conversation last week, I researched your two requests.

In regard to Stacey Peters, state records indicate that this past February, Ms. Peters was found hanging from a closet rod in a San Francisco hotel room. At the time of her death, there was no permanent residence listed for Ms. Peters, nor did she own a vehicle. It appears she was homeless and possibly engaging in prostitution. Her death was listed as autoerotic asphyxiation, complicated by a significant amount of heroin in her system. From what I can gather, Ms. Peters had not been in contact with her son for nearly four years. This corroborates the information given to you by Lou Peters.

As for your second request, I have been unable to locate any documented material that can prove the two alleged rapes of underage girls by Mr. Peters. I appreciate that you trust your sources. However, without legal documentation or the voluntary verbal revelation by the victim or victims, I'm afraid there is no way the alleged rapes can be brought forth in the current indictment of Lou Peters. I realize this may put Mr. Peters's case more firmly in the defense's court.

I regret that I could not report back to you with more positive news. I was brought into this case as an adjunct investigator and will soon be transferred onto another homicide investigation. However, I will continue to take a private interest in the outcome of Lou Peters's case.

Sincerely,
Chuck Sawyer

"Lovely choice of death, Ms. Peters," Jane murmured after rereading the words "...death was listed as autoerotic asphyxiation." This sexual ritual is defined as asphyxia caused by intentionally strangling oneself—typically hanging—while masturbating in order to intensify the orgasm through reduced oxygen flow to the brain. Jane likened the insane act to masturbating in the bath water and dropping in an electric toaster at the point of climax. The entire act and those who practiced it—including the few who lived to tell about it—was the ultimate hedonistic, sexual power trip. Jane surmised that it said a lot about Stacey Peters and her insatiable obsession with satisfying purely carnal needs without recognizing that the likely tradeoff for five seconds of temporary pleasure was permanent death. But what did that prove? She was a sick woman who caused her son irreparable psychological harm, but it didn't necessarily provide a viable reason for his possible actions later in life. If that theory could float, Jane argued, *she* should be able to have carte blanche in *her* expression of rage toward others with no repercussions. Deep-seated anger had been her fulcrum for years. When she drank, the red-hot ire burned like acid. With nearly six months of sobriety, the vitriolic outbursts had subsided. But the undercurrent of rage bubbled like a volcano just before it erupts.

Jane wondered why Kit had asked Detective Sawyer to locate Lou's mother. Was she expected to give testimony against Lou? What was she supposed to say? "I raped my son and that's why he's fucked up now." Mothers weren't known for tipping evidence against their own flesh and blood. That fact was even more applicable when *said mother* would be admitting a grotesque felony against *said son*. So what was Kit's reasoning for asking an obviously busy detective to track down Stacey Peters? It seemed incongruent to Kit's second request: verifying the alleged rapes of the two fourteen-year-old girls when Lou was underage. One request could curry sympathy from a compassionate jury; the second could convict him by showing prior criminal acts.

Jane shuffled pages and found a roster of case detectives and their accompanying office numbers. She found Sawyer's name and number and looked at the clock. It was 6:30 Colorado time. Sawyer easily could have changed numbers in the last fourteen years. Still, Jane felt a need to talk to him. If anything, she wanted to get another cop's bead on Kit Clark. She also wouldn't mind his take on Lou Peters and what, if anything, went wrong in respect to the case. After all, he didn't have to say that he would take a "private interest" in Lou's case. Knowing fellow cops as Jane did, she was positive that after fourteen years, Chuck Sawyer had formed clear opinions about the case. Maybe, Jane speculated, that opinion was that the evidence against Lou Peters was weak and that, perhaps, he was the wrong guy? If Jane could immediately find enough evidence that Lou was not guilty of Ashlee's murder, she could easily deduce that he had nothing to do with Charlotte's abduction and save herself a wild-goose chase across the country.

The whole case was eliciting far too much conjecture and doubt for Jane. She lit a cigarette and reasoned that she took the case out of desperation—not a shrewd motivating factor. If she'd had the three grand to give Jerry on her own, she would have done it and pressed on with obtaining local cases—cases that didn't revolve around fourteen-year-old mysteries that were supposedly tied to the number one missing child story at the moment. Jane realized that she could be walking from one humiliating fiasco in Denver into an even greater chaotic chasm in California. To her knowledge, nobody else was making the nefarious connection between Lou Peters and Charlotte Walker. Investigators would automatically look at family members first and rule out their involvement. After that, all felony child sex offenders living in the area where Charlotte went missing would be interviewed and crossed off the list as their alibis proved true. This would certainly include Lou Peters. Then the search would depend upon any tactile evidence, eyewitness accounts, knowledge of any rifts with friends or boyfriends, or simply the possibility that Charlotte had just left town. Jane reflected on the very good possibility that her high-profile connection with this wild hare of a case could be the final nail in her professional coffin. "Fuck," was all she could muster.

Jane dialed Detective Charles Sawyer's number. As expected, she got a neutral recording that didn't offer much insight into who the number belonged to. A male voice said, "I'm either away from my desk or out of the office. Please leave your name and number and I'll return your call as soon as possible." After the beep, Jane left a rocky-worded message for Detective Sawyer, stating her name and then realizing that anyone but Detective Sawyer who received this message might recognize her name and make immediate connections if Jane alluded to the Lou Peters case. She wanted to do everything possible to keep her name and Lou Peters's name as far apart as possible. Jane recovered her full throttle cop voice and finished off the message with, "I need to connect with Detective Sawyer regarding a cold case." She gave her cell phone number and hung up. With the New Year's holiday less than a week away, Jane figured she wouldn't be hearing back from anyone anytime soon.

She poured another cup of coal black java and returned her attention to the files. The summary of details regarding the location of Ashlee's body and the cause of death was written in typical offhand fashion. "On June 23, 1990, the fourteen-year-old victim was found approximately 7.2 miles off Palo Colorado Road within the Pico Blanco wilderness area...." Jane located Lou Peters's mug shot in the file and noted the date: June 26, 1990. They find the body and three days later they nab a suspect. Fast work, Jane figured. They either felt 100 percent sure that they had their perp or they moved too quickly out of desperation to nail the killer and got the wrong guy.

"Victim's nude body was discovered lying on her back on a southeast limestone outcropping by hikers.... Victim's head suffered fatal blows from a heavy, jagged object. Indications at the scene show that a limestone-included rock [see photo] was used to deliver the fatal blows." Jane looked through the files for the photos and then realized that Kit obviously was not given any.

She continued reading. "Due to significant heat generated by the exposed limestone, victim's body was partially 'cooked,' thus attracting condors to the site. This accounts for the partial removal of flesh in victim's upper right thigh, torso region, and eyes. Accounting for heat, exposure to wind and rain, and postmortem effects of scavengers, estimated time of death is between June 20 and June 21, 1990." Jane skimmed the page. "Latex condom found next to victim's body. Particulate matter ranging from grains to several, one-centimeter chips found pressed into latex. Ejaculate present. Extreme lacerations on labia indicate repeated rape using the handle of a narrow, wooden object prior to death...." Turning the page, Jane saw a cop's crude drawing of a cabin and its location in relation to where Ashlee's body was found. The detailed description explained the drawing. "Cabin is located approximately 350 feet over a ridge from where victim's body was found. It appears to be an old abandoned structure once used by the Boy Scouts.... Victim was held in a closet [see photo]. Perpetrator affixed several four-foot-long mirrors inside closet. Remnants of rope and a gag were found inside closet. Also, five battery-powered camp lanterns were found. A single hammer [see photo] was located at the rear of closet. Streaks of blood on wooden handle indicate this object was used to rape victim...."

Jane had a fairly gruesome visual of the scene. She downed the last of her coffee, poured another cup, and skimmed several more pages until locating Ashlee's toxicology report, dated July 7, 1990. "Toxicology shows sustained levels of Valium in victim's bloodstream." Valium? Jane mused on the finding and then quickly deduced that the perp kept Ashlee drugged throughout most of the kidnapping. She checked back in the notes and confirmed that no ropes or restraints were found on Ashlee's body when it was found on the limestone. While she couldn't be sure, Jane figured that the murderer made sure Ashlee was unconscious—possibly from the Valium—when he removed her from the cabin and carried her nude body to the place where he finally killed her. But why drag her body out of the cabin to kill her? It seemed a bit dramatic to Jane. Then again, she had dealt with a few homicides over the years where the murderer seemed obsessed with sending a message either by the way he arranged the body after death or by staging the corpse in a location that was meaningful to only him.

Sorting through additional pages, Jane ran across a page titled, WITNESS STATEMENT. It seemed that there was a lone witness—a Mr. Bruce Zatkin—who reported in great detail to investigators what he saw. The sixty-three-year-old retired civil engineer was camping in Pico Blanco with his wife for the week of June 16 to June 23, 1990. Their campsite happened to be less than half a mile from where Ashlee was held in the abandoned cabin. Under oath, Zatkin swore he observed Lou Peters on six separate occasions during that eight day period walking alone on an unused trail, carrying what appeared to be small bags of food. Zatkin later testified that each time he saw Lou, his gait was "deliberate" and always in the direction of the cabin's location or away from it. "I didn't think much of it the first couple times I saw the guy," Zatkin wrote in his declaration, "but then it just seemed strange. It looked like suspicious behavior...." As Jane read the detailed transcript, she wondered why Zatkin didn't follow Lou if he thought there was reason to be concerned. Apparently, the investigator wondered the same thing and inquired about it. "Hey, I don't want people bothering me," Zatkin said, "and I don't bother them. If I'd known what was going on with that little girl, I'd have contacted the authorities immediately...." Jane read between the lines of Zatkin's statements. Here was a fellow who was obviously devastated that he could have possibly prevented Ashlee's grisly murder. The transcript made it clear that Zatkin thoughtfully made many mental notes on Lou's comings and goings and was more than happy to share his information and impressions with investigators. So what happened at the trial with Zatkin? Jane dug through the files in search of anything that would answer that question. She came up empty-handed. Did he fold? Did he refuse to testify? Did he change his story? The prosecutors had a mature, respectable, highly observant lone witness who was obviously not a flake. That's gold to a prosecuting attorney. What happened?

The more she read, the more questions she had and the more she wished she could talk one-on-one with Detective Sawyer. Jane leaned back in her chair to stretch her back. In doing so, she knocked her hand against another file. A white, legal-sized envelope fell out of the file and caught Jane's eye. The word BARTOSH was written across the outside in an enraged cursive twist. Clearly, Kit was either irritated at something else when she labeled the envelope or she was taking out her ire on whoever Bartosh was. Jane opened the envelope and removed all the contents. After several minutes, it became clear that Bartosh was Dr. John Bartosh, the appointed defense expert that Kit had angrily alluded to during her initial office visit. The now sixty-five-year-old had, until recently, lived in the Big Sur area. He had been there since the early 1970's with his wife, Ingrid. From what Jane could gather, this psychologist and doctor of theology had experienced a hardcore spiritual awakening in 1973 that lead him to practice a strict form of Christian Fundamentalism. At age thirty-three, he started a fundamentalist church in Big Sur called "The Lamb of God Congregation" which was determined to counter and destroy what Bartosh labeled the "free love and drug culture" of Big Sur during that time. He quickly emerged as an outspoken leader in what he referred to as his "personal crusade against secular society and the destructive power that society has on young people."

Jane had to wince at some of Bartosh's narrow beliefs: a woman's place was in the home, a wife must do what her husband tells her as if "God himself was speaking through him," sexuality between a husband and wife was for procreation only, God was a vengeful God bent on judgment and destruction of sinners, pubescent boys and girls were easily tempted and had to be sheltered from anything "worldly," girls and women needed to be modest in *all* forms of their behavior and dress.... Jane's head was spinning as she read one archaic, narrow-minded idea after another. It was hard to fathom that this kind of man was described as "charismatic" by his followers and was happily accepted into the Northern California community as someone who could "kick the Devil out of town."

There was one reference after another to the way Bartosh decoded the Bible's teachings and most of them were, in Jane's opinion, too literal. Much of that literal translation had to do with raising children in a loving, yet strict, fear-centered existence that taught them to trust the church and detest the secular world. Jane read an example of Bartosh's extremely literal teaching: "In Proverbs 22:15 we are told: 'Foolishness is bound in the heart of a child; but the *rod* of correction shall drive it far from him.' When punishing your child, you must *only* use a rod. A rod is the Biblical form of chastisement that our Lord speaks of and freely encourages. Explain the use of the rod to your child and he/she will come to accept that God is speaking through the rod. Always pray with your child after chastisement and compel him/her to tell God that he/she is sorry for sinning against Him. Seeking God's mercy will bring him/her closer to our Lord." Jane took a long drag on her cigarette to digest that little gem. After being on the receiving end of a lot of rods, belts, and sundry implements as a child and teenager, Jane knew that if someone told her God was speaking through them, she would have quickly become an atheist. "Always pray with your child after chastisement and compel him/her to tell God that he/she is sorry for sinning against Him. Seeking God's mercy will bring him/her closer to our Lord," Jane reread. Was that mercy for the child or the parent, she wondered?

Jane resumed reading and discovered that, amazingly, one family after another joined Bartosh's church, determined to protect their children from the evils of the Cultural Revolution. He became a trusted counselor whose advice was followed without question. Jane gleaned from the pages of information that Bartosh's main conviction was that the Devil had a tight grasp on every individual, and that led to Sin with a capital "S." She had to smile at some of Bartosh's ideas. One idea, in particular, professed that a young girl in her early teens must guard her thoughts every hour of the day. If she allowed herself to entertain the notion of what a boy's lips would feel like on her cheek, there was no telling where that illicit thought could lead. As Jane continued to read, she noted a recurring theme: *Fear.* The Devil was to be feared. One's thoughts were to be feared. The possible *results* of one's thoughts should definitely be feared. Youths didn't feel *enough* fear and needed to actively generate more fear to save their souls. And, of course, sex was dirty.

It was truly mind-boggling, Jane decided, that this self-appointed moral authority was respected enough to be repeatedly called upon to offer opinions in child development. At some point, Jane deduced that Bartosh's polished Christian celebrity attracted the eye of law enforcement. In turn, they began utilizing his supposed knowledge and effectively marketed him as an expert witness in cases where the clinical judgment of a psychologist was needed. For all Jane knew, some of the officials may have been good Christians of other less rigid churches who assumed Bartosh was a trustworthy man whose unblemished reputation could provide valuable insight into the behavior of the criminal mind. "Sure. Why not?" Jane surmised. It was identical to the way the media sucked on to someone with a high-profile name or pertinent occupation during a child abduction case and allowed that individual to hold court on TV, even though that person was only offering general hypotheses that often generate no new ideas on how to find the missing kid. It was smoke and mirrors, but it worked every time. It looked as if Bartosh had perfected that magic act all the way to the Lou Peters trial.

Jane discovered that Dr. Bartosh had met Lou in the late 1980's. Lou joined The Lamb of God Congregation after his mother abandoned him and he spent nearly all of his fifteenth year on the street. Lou was welcomed with open arms by the church members, who Bartosh commented in court testimony, "adopted Lou as their own." For over two years, Lou lived in the various homes of "Council" members on a rotating basis. Even Bartosh and Ingrid invited Lou to stay with them. From reading Bartosh's account, Lou was "a strapping young man with a deep devotion to God and a keen sense of high morality." Bartosh was clearly taken by Lou's enigmatic quality and happily encouraged him to spread the word of the Lord to the church and beyond. Curiously, by Bartosh's own admission, Lou's engaging personality and handsome face proved to be a winning combination when it came to drawing young people to the church. In one document, a detective had underlined the following sentence, attributed to Dr. John Bartosh: "Lou Peters helped the church recruit more teenage girls than in all the years previous to his affiliation with the institution. He's been sent from God."

There was a minor notation buried in the sheets of court papers that made reference to Bartosh being aware of Lou's abusive childhood. One line stood out to Jane: "Lou's morally-destructive childhood is a clear example of how wantonness and sexuality destroys the fabric of one's soul and how God can lead one back to His arms." It became clearer to Jane that Dr. Bartosh believed he had found the ultimate Christian poster boy for his church in the form of Lou Peters. Here was a young, enthusiastic, pied piper for God who was a walking, breathing model of someone who had been exposed to the most corrupt sin imaginable but was saved by his faith in God.

Fast forward to one year ago, when Lou's attorneys brought his case back in front of a judge to appeal his conviction and request a new trial. When the DNA on the condom found next to Ashlee's body—the one piece of evidence that swayed the jury to convict—was clearly proven to *not* belong to Lou Peters, the thirty-three-year-old's luck changed. Dr. Bartosh's stanch belief in Lou became a defining factor in a case weak on other concrete scientific connections and blood evidence. The last few papers in the pile illustrated Bartosh's unwavering belief of Lou's innocence, which may have given the judge the crucial validation he needed to release Lou on bond while he awaited a new trial. Kit's handwritten notes on yellow legal pads alluded to the fact that Bartosh—now living in Grand Junction, Colorado, where he was building an extension of The Lamb of God Congregation—had monthly visits with Lou in prison, where he acted as an "advisor, pastor, and motivator for Jesus." Motivator for Jesus? Jane thought that was an odd choice of words for Bartosh to use in court.

By the time Jane finished reading and gathered together everything she needed for the trip, it was nearly four in the morning. She was just about to light her tenth cigarette of the night when Jane heard the familiar *thump* of the *Denver Post* knocking against the front door. Clenching the cigarette in the corner of her mouth, she opened the front door to retrieve the paper. Staring back at her from the top of the fold was none other than *Sergeant* Kenny Stephens. There he was with his cocky grin and his muscular build standing in front of the cocaine-laden table at the press conference. Jane felt an angry edge creep up on her. Her eye then caught the name of one of her FBI contacts who was quoted in the second above-the-fold headlining story. "We've been asked to be part of the Charlotte Walker team and we will use every tool at our disposal to bring this little girl back to her family," Jane read.

She looked back at Kenny Stephens's self-important moniker and slammed the paper onto the nearest chair. Suddenly, all those fears about being part of the Walker case and how it might ruin her reputation dissolved into the background. Within minutes, that familiar fire began to burn in Jane Perry's belly.

CHAPTER 8

DECEMBER 29

It was only a fifteen-minute morning run, but Jane was at least able to get her heart racing and knock the cobwebs out of her head before picking up Kit. After a quick shower, she slipped into a form-fitting pair of black jeans and a long-sleeved crimson shirt. A scuffed pair of black western boots and her black leather jacket completed the look. Patting her left jeans pocket and finding it empty, Jane picked up her pants from the night before and withdrew her three sobriety chips and the snakestone. Rolling her eyes sarcastically at the stone, she buried it along with the chips in her pocket. Catching her reflection in the bedroom mirror, Jane stopped to examine her injured face. She found it amazing that only two days ago she had sported visible signs of getting smacked in The Red Tail Hawk Bar. And now, save for the slight line of a cut lip and some insignificant surface bruising around her eye, the effects of the fight had almost vanished.

Jane eyed her bedroom for the bottle of Arnica, locating it on the nightstand. She collected it and stuffed it into her jacket pocket, brushing her hand against the short-cropped blond wig she had shoved into the same pocket when she returned from the bar. Jane flung the wig on her unmade bed and started to walk away when she reconsidered. One never knew when a wig could come in handy during an investigation.

As was customary when she left on a trip, Jane phoned her brother, Mike, to let him know she'd be gone for ten days and to ask him to bring in her mail and newspapers. His tired, obviously half-asleep voice assured her that he'd follow through. Jane noticed the blinking red light on her answering machine. Hitting the PLAY button, she heard Sergeant Weyler's voice. This time, however, it wasn't punctuated with urgency or irritation. If anything, Weyler sounded fed up.

"Hello, Jane. Sergeant Weyler calling. *Again.* I can appreciate that you don't want to talk to me based upon the headlining story in today's *Post* and on last night's evening news. Fine. Understood. I know perfectly well that your inside work played a major role in the drug bust. If anyone should have been paraded in front of those cameras, it should have been you and not that damned snake." Jane's ears perked up at the word, "snake." She'd never heard Weyler use that terminology before now. "Be that as it may, here's my question: Would you please reconsider my offer and return with the upgrade of *sergeant* to DH? You'd be doing me——" With that, the machine cut off Weyler with a piercing beep.

Snake. She touched the stone in her pocket. For a moment, she considered the idea that Weyler's use of the word "snake" was some kind of sign. Then, catching herself, Jane couldn't believe she had entertained such a ludicrous notion. It was just a coincidence. Very odd, but a coincidence, she decided as she erased Weyler's message.

Jane downed her third cup of coffee and finally felt awake. She slipped her laptop into its case, wedging it securely into the duffel bag filled with pounds of coffee and sundry items, including the stack of files Kit had given her. The morning light was just starting to crest over the rooftops on Milwaukee Street when Jane slammed her Mustang into gear and headed for Boulder.

Two trips to Boulder in two consecutive days. That was some kind of record for Jane Perry. As she curved around the exit off Highway 36, Jane amused herself with what it would be like if Boulder ruled the world. Instead of Law and Order enforcement, there would be the Peace and Harmony Patrol. Cars would certainly be outlawed, and everyone would be riding bikes. Recycling would be mandatory. Tofu would be a major food group. And Ralph Nader would be president of the United States.

Just a few minutes past six, Jane slipped into a parking space in front of Kit's apartment. She no sooner knocked on Kit's door than the door quickly opened.

"You're late!" Kit said, securing her knit scarf under her multicolored winter coat. A billowing pair of purple, wide-legged trousers that poked out from beneath the coat were securely tucked into a well-worn pair of Sorrel boots.

"It's 6:05—"

"That's five minutes we've lost on the road!" Kit replied, sliding three heavy suitcases and one bulging duffel bag out the door.

"You're taking all this?" Jane asked

"We're going to be gone for ten days. It's winter. Winter clothes are heavier. Plus, I have my books and herbs.... I have *a lot* of herbs." Kit struggled with the zipper on the duffel as she reopened it to squeeze another bottle of herbal pills into the pocket.

Jane caught a glimpse of what looked like pounds of herbs in bags, bottles, and teabags. There was also an equally enormous amount of books shoved tightly into the bag. "You're reading all those books?" Jane asked, clearly overwhelmed by the sight.

"No, Jane P., I just carry them for ballast!" Kit said in a mocking tone. "Could you please take these two out to your car?"

Jane lifted the duffel and cringed at the extreme weight. "You got rocks in here?"

"Actually, yes, I do. Be careful. They do chip easily."

"Can't you take out a few herbs and leave them here?"

"Those herbs are what's keeping me alive. I won't do chemo or radiation because I won't be able to function. And I *have* to be able to function! Come on, let's go!"

"Wait a second. You got any grass in this duffel?"

"I have *barley* grass powder that I put in my morning 'green' drink—"

"You know what I'm talking about, Kit. You got marijuana in this bag?"

Kit let out a long, tired sigh. "What if I do?"

"Take it out and leave it here! This is a police investigation. I can't have a private citizen traveling with me who's carrying drugs! And I *don't* want to hear that you're smoking it for medicinal purposes!"

Kit pursed her lips and unzipped the duffel bag, exposing a mind-boggling assortment of herbs, books, empty mason jars, and rocks. She removed a plastic sandwich bag filled with pot. "This isn't some sort of trick so you can arrest me, is it?"

"Just hide the grass!"

Kit stuffed the bag into a drawer. "And you're bringing along your cigarettes?"

"Yes, I am. And don't try to lay some left-wing bullshit argument on me that they're just like pot!"

"I would *never* say that! Those packs of 'cancer sticks' are *far* worse than my little bag of weed. Do you have any idea how many chemicals they add to those cigarettes? You'll be smoking those *outside* our hotel room! I can't afford to inhale toxic fumes!"

"Right." Jane surmised it was going to be one helluva road trip.

As Jane packed Kit's baggage into the trunk of the Mustang, Kit took a hard look at Jane's car. "You said *my* car was too *old?*" Kit queried Jane.

"This is a '66 Mustang with a brand-new engine that purrs and goes so damn fast, we'll be in California before you're halfway through your kilo of herbs."

Kit sat in the passenger seat. "I see I'm going to have to put up with your sarcasm for the duration of this trip." She removed a sausagelike pillow from her satchel that made an unusual hissing sound and placed it behind her neck.

"Your pillow hissed."

"It's filled with buckwheat. It conforms to the neck."

"Buckwheat? Like the grain?" Jane said, getting into the car and closing the door.

"Go on. Get it out of your system. Say your sardonic response and let's go."

"What?" Jane replied, jamming the key in the ignition. "I'm glad you've got that pillow. If we get hungry, we can always take a knife to it and cook up some pancakes."

Kit sniffed the air inside the car. "Do I smell *ground coffee?*"

Jane opted to remain taciturn as she peeled away from the curb and headed west. "There's a lot of good information in those files you gave me," Jane told Kit as she banked the Mustang onto Interstate 70.

"Keeping those notes and records occupied a great deal of my life over the last fourteen years," Kit said, staring out the window at the lifeless winter landscape.

"There's a few people who intrigue me. Detective Sawyer is one of them."

"Chuck! He was a compassionate ally. Lovely aura, too. It was yellow with beautiful violet striations. Magnificent!"

"You've lost me."

"He's *evolved*, Jane. He's very much in touch with his Higher Self."

"What do you mean?"

"We all have a Higher Self and a Lower Self. The God Force wants us to always work within the realms of the Higher Self—the Self that is pure and motivated solely by love."

"And the Lower Self?"

"The Lower Self is where the devils play. It's the dark essence that dwells within each of us. It's the unenlightened, vulgar place that pulls us down and prevents us from seeking our greater Truth. Everyone has a Higher Self and Lower Self. We have to choose which one we want to activate for our greatest good."

Jane gave the idea serious thought. "So, these Higher Selves and Lower Selves can operate at the same time?"

"Of course!" Kit replied. "For example, when you drank, you dwelt in your Lower Self. You were sucked in and succumbed to its persuasive tongue—"

"*Persuasive tongue?* Sounds like you've been reading cheap porn."

"Porn! That's an *excellent* example of indulging in the Lower Self. But when you choose to allow compassion and love to chart your course in solving a crime...like with that little girl, Emily Lawrence, this past summer, well, you evolve to a greater plane of awareness."

"Getting back to Detective Sawyer, what else do you know about him?"

"I just had a few interactions with him and they were fourteen years ago. He was in his mid-fifties back then, so he's probably retired by now."

"Oh," Jane said, crossing Detective Sawyer off her mental list of people who could lend a hand.

"Why the interest in him?"

Jane felt the need to keep certain things to herself. She wasn't going to debate or discuss matters that she felt weren't of any consequence to Kit. And besides, one of her reasons for speaking to Detective Sawyer was to get his bead on Kit. "Just curious," Jane said offhandedly. "By the way, why did you ask Sawyer about Lou's mother and to look into the possible rapes Lou committed when he was underage? Weren't those two requests at cross purposes?"

"No, not at all. Lou spent hours telling me about his mother and what she did to him when he was a child. Some of it was so disturbing, I...well, I wondered if it was truly possible. But it did indeed happen."

"Well, say Stacey hadn't killed herself. Say Detective Sawyer was able to contact her and she agreed to testify in court. Who was that supposed to help? Lou?"

"The truth is the truth, Jane. P."

"*What?*"

"The truth is Lou was raped by his mother. It happened many times and it played a critical role in his development and his subsequent psychosis."

"But, Kit, don't you see? Bringing that kind of information to a jury could have easily turned *Lou* into the victim, instead of Ashlee."

"They were *both* victims. And I'm sure Stacey Peters was a victim of some sort of psychological torture or she wouldn't have perpetuated the evil! Don't you see? It's the *perpetuation* of the darkness that has to be stopped! If we just keep attacking these people with hatred instead of love, the cycle will continue! I've learned the hard way, Jane P., that the only way to stop that cycle is through *forgiveness*. And there is *no* room for forgiveness in your heart if it is filled with anger and retribution!"

"Oh, God!" Jane's ire forced her to shift in her seat and push down on the accelerator momentarily. "You honestly believe that left-wing drivel?"

"That forgiveness and love are the keys to moving forward? You're damn right I do! And there's no left or right wing to it! There's nothing *political* about forgiveness!"

"If we're gonna start talking about sympathy for the violator—"

"Not sympathy. *Forgiveness!*"

"Why do I hear a sympathetic tone to your voice?"

"It's *compassion*. The *same* compassion one can only hope the criminal will attain in his or her lifetime. That's one reason I don't believe in the death penalty."

"Oh, God," Jane said, shaking her head. "Some people need to die, Kit."

"Have you ever taken a life?" Kit studied Jane's face.

Jane didn't want to answer the question. The memory was still too raw. "Yes," she replied quietly. "I didn't like it. But I would do it again if I had to."

"I sense a hint of compassion for the poor soul you killed."

"I *don't* have compassion."

"Yes, you do. If you didn't, you'd talk about it with no emotion."

"You have compassion for Lou Peters?"

"Yes," Kit responded without missing a beat.

"After what he did to Ashlee? You sat in the courtroom and heard what he did to her in graphic detail. How do you walk away from that with compassion?"

"Back then I didn't have compassion for him. I had hatred. The kind of hatred that boils inside and eats away at your spirit and perspective until it eats away at your body. And then there was the inevitable deep depression. But isn't depression really just anger without enthusiasm? All the hatred I held inside didn't affect Lou one bit. But it sure as hell affected me! I gave myself cancer. I take full responsibility. I gave myself cancer because I couldn't let go of the hate or the anger. You can't live like that and expect it not to affect you in some way." Kit stared out the window. "When you're dying like I am, if you're smart, you look at life differently. Pettiness and retribution take too much energy. You want answers. You allow yourself to look beyond the polarized righteous indignation that prevents you from seeing other possibilities. There's a reason why Lou turned out the way he did. I had to understand it and that's why I asked Detective Sawyer to locate his mother."

"If you're gonna tell me that Lou's past absolves him from punishment—"

"I wouldn't be going to California to save another young girl if I believed that! I strongly sense that Lou's past is dictating his present actions and he must be stopped!"

"I hear something else in your voice. You want to save that girl but...there's more." Jane turned to Kit to see if she could gauge any reaction to her statement.

Kit sat expressionless. "You know what I hear in *your* voice?"

"What?" Jane replied, realizing that Kit wasn't taking the bait.

"I hear someone who is still living in her past. A past filled with violations and deceit that you can't let go of. You identity with the victim too well, Jane P."

Jane kept her eyes on the road. "My past is my past."

"No, it isn't. It's alive and well and written all over you. It's the jerk in your hand when you pull a cigarette out of your pack and light it. It's the way your eyes drift off to the side when a memory slips through and reminds you of the reason you rage. I don't know what happened. But I know it still owns you. If you could forgive whoever—"

"You ever had the shit kicked out of you, Kit?" Jane's voice was icy. "I mean it literally! *Kicked* out of you!"

"No."

"Well, I did! And it didn't just leave scars like this one," Jane said, pointing to the old scar on her right temple, "it left permanent scars inside that prevent me from being like other women."

"You can't have children?"

"Correct," Jane replied in a curt tone.

"I'm sorry."

"Don't be. Just know that there are a lot of us walking around who don't have any compassion for the violator because we can still feel their footprints on our flesh."

"When you hold on to that anger, Jane, you think you're punishing the violator. But you're killing yourself. You have this backward notion that forgiveness is a favor you offer to the violator. But in reality, forgiveness is a gift you give to yourself."

"Sounds like a bumper sticker."

"Think about it, Jane P. Just think about it."

They drove in silence for almost ten miles before Kit started to shift uncomfortably in the passenger seat.

"What's wrong?" Jane asked.

"I have these pains occasionally. It'll pass."

Jane's protective instinct kicked in. "You want to lie down in the backseat?"

"No. We have to keep driving. Every second is precious. Let's just talk."

"Okay." Jane thought for a moment. "What about Bruce Zatkin? The witness who says he saw Lou at Pico Blanco—"

Kit let out a hard sigh and shook her head. "Bruce. Yes. He was a good man."

"*Was?*"

"He's dead. As far as I'm concerned, the defense team and the whole bloody bond hearing last year bears responsibility for his death. He was a good, intelligent man; a man whose story never changed and who *never* wavered in his memory of what he saw, no matter how the defense lawyers attempted to use his own words against him. I know that Bruce did not want to get involved in the case again. Being the sole witness fourteen years ago, there was a lot of pressure on his shoulders to confirm what he saw. I could see the stress had taken a hard toll on him. He held a lot inside and it finally got the better of him. He died of a heart attack last fall."

Cross another off the list, Jane thought. "It's important for us to unearth Lou's criminal patterns; patterns of prior acts that create the motive for him to strike again."

"You're speaking about the two rapes prior to Ashlee?"

"Yes. Who were your sources for that information?"

"Genevieve Paulson. She was one of my regular nude models. Very zaftig."

"A fat, nude model is the sole source you trusted?" Jane asked skeptically.

"I sense judgment! Just because Gen's job didn't have a dress code doesn't mean her information wasn't reliable. Cops use informants who are strippers and addicts!"

Jane couldn't argue that point. "What kind of woman was Gen? A gossip?"

"Absolutely not! She got the information however she got it. Gen wouldn't lie to me. Her only weakness was a high-strung personality and nervous disposition."

"How does a nervous woman get the guts to pose nude on a regular basis?"

"It was part of her therapy. And it worked! *Much* better than the drugs!"

"*Drugs?* She was a junkie?"

"*No!* A little pot to calm her down...occasionally a downer to get her relaxed...."

"You supplied these drugs to her?"

"No! She brought her own bag of stuff to our sessions!"

"Exactly how fucked up was she during the sessions?"

"She was calm...very calm...sometimes she'd nap."

"She was unconscious?"

"*Resting*, is a better word."

"Tell me, are her eyes *open* in any of the portraits you painted of her?"

"I painted them as open," Kit begrudgingly conceded.

Jane shook her head in disgust. "Well, bump zaftig Gen off the 'talk to' list!"

"Because of the drugs!"

"Yes! You are *so* lucky you didn't push to get her on that stand fourteen years ago or you'd have ended up with more guilt than you already have! All it would take was a savvy defense attorney to find out that she smoked dope and dropped downers—"

"You make Gen sound like the poster child for Woodstock! Anyway, it wouldn't have worked for her to testify. She hated Lou. Didn't trust him."

"Why?"

"He judged her, of course, for her choice of work. She also didn't care for his constant spiritual condemnation. On more than one occasion, he apparently took her aside when she was leaving my house and preached the gospel to her. Isaiah, Genesis, the book of John, Revelations. He'd go on chapter and verse. When she told him to shove it up his ass, *she says* he set his mind to disrupting her life."

"How?"

"Little things. He left handwritten notes in her bag saying: 'Jesus is watching you,' 'God loves the sinner but hates the sin.' She also accused him of rooting through her bag and taking a photographic magazine that was full of black-and-white nudes. I guess he was doing what he thought he should do to take the Devil out of her life."

"Was she able to prove Lou stole the magazine out of her bag? Or was Genevieve *asleep* when he did it?"

Kit rolled her eyes in silent contempt. "You can think whatever you wish about Gen. She was good people."

"Okay, let's say Lou did rape two other girls," Jane deliberated out loud. "How did he meet them? What was their connection? Were the girls friends? Was it random?"

"Where are you going with this?"

"Patterns, Kit. Remember? We're looking for *patterns*. If Lou is the psycho you say he is, he's developed patterns that he repeats or builds upon with each subsequent criminal act. Determining that pattern could possibly help us figure out if he nabbed Charlotte Walker."

"Do you think it's possible that the pattern could change drastically from someone he knows to someone he just happens upon?"

"Anything is *possible*. The question is whether it's *probable*. And my experience has proven that if a pattern works for a criminal, he doesn't change it."

"You said a few people intrigued you. Who else?"

"Dr. John Bartosh," Jane declared as she wound the Mustang around the rock-faced highway and passed Idaho Springs.

Kit's mien appeared to shift into a dark space, rimmed with resentment. "Yes. He *was* quite the intriguing little man in this whole nightmare, wasn't he?" There was a sudden, mean twist to Kit's voice that didn't escape Jane's perceptive ear. "I assume you read all about his religious beliefs? Every single backward, preschool perception of God and how things work in this black-and-white world!" Kit's ire was growing; her eyes narrowed and her mouth tightened with each bitter memory of Bartosh.

"He's definitely a fan of the gospel," Jane said in an offhand manner.

"You mean, *fanatic*, don't you?" Kit asked in a truculent tone, as if Jane wasn't up to speed in regard to Dr. John Bartosh's archaic world perspective.

"There was a tedium to his moral diatribe."

"*That's* putting it mildly! Jane, it went beyond his juvenile religious point of view! That asshole basically single-handedly orchestrated Lou's release last year! Putting him on the stand as if he were a goddamned expert! That man is pure evil. He's going to have a shitload of karma to deal with when he leaves this world!"

Jane couldn't help but smile at Kit's rancorous turnaround. "Evil, huh? Weren't you the one who was just telling me that anger solves nothing and compassion is the key to understanding our fellow man? Hmm. What would *Buddha* do in a case like this?" Jane was purposely pushing Kit's buttons.

Kit reeled in her emotions and let out a sigh. "What *would* Buddha do?"

Jane didn't get the desired vitriolic retort she expected, but she wasn't giving up. "Is it because Bartosh is a fundamentalist? If so, I thought you were all about loving everyone, no matter their sexual deviations, drug use, or warped psychological issues. Weren't you the cool gal in Big Sur who didn't judge anyone's religion? Why doesn't that apply to Dr. Bartosh? Maybe what you *really* mean to say is that you don't judge more mystical religions like Buddhism—"

"Buddhism is not a *religion*. It's a *philosophy*," Kit quickly interjected.

"Don't change the subject! If you say you don't judge religion, then you damn well better embrace even the most fundamental of the fundamental Christians!"

Kit stared straight ahead. After a long minute, she spoke. "You're right." Jane looked closely at Kit to see if she was being sarcastic. She wasn't. "If somebody wants to become a narrow-minded Christian Fundamentalist, so be it. I guess my main concern is Bartosh himself. I take umbrage with the way he created this image of being 'the expert' and selling that brand to law enforcement. He may well be a Biblical authority who can quote the Good Book verbatim. But that doesn't mean he also has the insight to provide a clear, unbiased viewpoint of a psychologically damaged person like Lou in a court of law! He's blind to Lou's psychosis, Jane! *Blind!* He trusts in Lou's innocence so deeply that he used Congregation money to put up his bond!"

Jane was stunned. "*Bartosh* paid Lou's bond? You didn't mention that!"

"I'm sorry. There's just so much to this story...." Kit shifted in her seat. "But I think the fact that he did that shows you how committed he is to Lou being innocent! I guess what really pushes my buttons is that Bartosh consistently uses hardcore fear to perpetuate his dogma. There's nothing more negatively motivating than fear!"

Motivating. The word triggered a recall for Jane. "Bartosh had monthly visits with Lou in prison. There was something about how he was Lou's advisor, pastor, and 'motivator for Jesus.' What does that mean?"

"That's one of the many pithy terms he uses. He urges his flock to become 'motivators for Jesus'...to promote, provoke, do whatever they have to do in order to push their doctrine onto others. They all have this fervent need to convert as many people as they can as part of the 'Great Commission from Christ.'"

"I thought The Lamb of God Congregation was just in Big Sur."

"Oh, no. He's apparently got a congregation going in Grand Junction. But that's not all. Bartosh has devotees all over, thanks to his monthly newsletter and audiotapes. You should read one of those newsletters! The flagrant ranting! Anyone who doesn't believe the doctrine is considered unclean and risks the hammer of God upon them."

"The hammer of God?"

"Another one of his pithy sayings. It's one of his favorites. He actually wrote an article years ago titled, 'The Hammer of God Will Fall on All Sinners.' Lou gave me a copy of it when I lived in Big Sur."

"Why'd he give you a copy?"

"I don't know. Why'd he take the nude photo magazine out of Genevieve's bag? Lou liked to make his religious statements in a covert manner. I think he enjoyed a certain amount of subtle drama. His mind is complex and twisted."

"What did Bartosh mean by the 'hammer of God'?"

"Vengeance. 'The hammer of God will befall you if you don't follow His way.'"

"Is that 'His' with a capital 'H' or 'his' as in Bartosh?"

"Good question. I think Bartosh truly believes he speaks for God. So, perhaps 'his way,' is one in the same! He's religiously arrogant and has managed to convince a helluva lot of people that his literal way is the only way to redemption. And I mean a *very literal* doctrine of the Bible. The Lamb of God Congregation leaves no room for interpretation. Their whole structure is built on a single level of toothpicks. There's no texture. No tangents. And there's certainly no questioning of anything once Bartosh has defined it! What a suffocating existence! It's what Bartosh leaves out or simply *refuses to see or acknowledge* that makes him worthy of scrutiny, Jane." Kit balled her fist and punctuated the air. "*His religion is his identity.* Do you truly understand what that means?" Jane glanced toward Kit, not appreciating the significance of her statement. "When your religion is your identity, questioning it is akin to questioning your existence." Kit turned, staring out the window. "Threaten someone's soul who believes the way he does and you threaten their life." Kit pinched her lower lip as if she were trying to make sense of an elusive idea. "I can't put my finger exactly on what it is about Bartosh that deeply bothers me. Maybe it's his utter blindness. When I said Bartosh was pure evil, perhaps I misspoke. I don't know if he's evil by nature. But I do think he does evil things because he chooses not to see."

Jane sensed that the whole discussion was causing Kit physical discomfort. "What do you say we take a break in a bit? I could use a smoke—"

"Yes. A break. Good idea."

They agreed to stop at one of Kit's favorite health food stores on the I-70 route. Getting off the highway at the Frisco exit, Jane's desire for nicotine was only outdone by Kit's craving for a cup of freshly juiced carrots. Kit ducked into Alpine Natural Foods as Jane took a deep drag on her cigarette. Mounds of recently plowed snow framed the area, creating a cocoon-like shelter. The high altitude mountain air was a startling change from the more moderately temperate Denver climate. A gust of icy wind swept across the parking lot, stinging Jane's cheeks and causing her to wrap her leather jacket tightly around her chest. Her thoughts wandered and came to rest on the phone message that morning from Weyler and his offer to bring Jane back to DH with a promotion to sergeant. Had the ball-buster Kenny Stephens been given the ol' heave-ho? As much as Jane's innate curiosity was piqued, she couldn't bring herself to return Weyler's call. There was too much water under the bridge. Too much pride. Jane sunk her left hand into her trouser pocket and made contact with the trio of sobriety chips. It suddenly occurred to her that by tomorrow at this time she would officially be six months sober. Six months. She took a long, hard drag on her cigarette. There'd be four chips rattling around in her pocket fairly soon. And yet, somewhere deep down, Jane didn't feel a sense of accomplishment or pride. There was just a stone-cold emptiness that was hungry and needed to be filled.

The sudden buzz of her cell phone jerked Jane out of the self-imposed daze. Checking the incoming number, she noted a "541" area code that she didn't recognize.

"This is Jane Perry," she said with her usual cop edge.

"Jane? Hello! I'm glad I caught you!" The voice was unknown to Jane, but extremely cheerful and casual.

"Who's this?" Jane asked.

"Oh, excuse me. It's Chuck. Chuck Sawyer. I guess you and I need to talk."

CHAPTER 9

"You there?"

Jane quickly got her thoughts together. "Yeah. I'm here." She turned around to check if Kit was still in the health food store. "I didn't expect to hear from you. I got the idea you retired."

"Yeah, you figured right. I moved to a little town in Oregon with the wife. Real quiet. Farm people. Honest, good-hearted folk, you know?"

"Uh-huh," Jane replied, not quite knowing what to say. She remembered Kit's description of Chuck's "lovely aura" that propelled him toward his Higher Self. Jane couldn't believe that image actually crossed her mind as she lit a cigarette.

"The boys at the department still keep in touch with me," Sawyer continued in an unaffected manner. "I got a call this morning and they told me about your message. They said it sounded sort of urgent."

"Yeah." Jane quickly attempted to figure out what angle she should take with Sawyer and how much she should divulge. "They're reopening the Lou Peters case. I'm working solo, doing preliminary investigative work right now."

"You working the angles to what? Keep Lou in or out of prison?"

"You know he's out on bond?" Jane asked, taking a deep draw on her cigarette.

"Yeah. I caught wind of that last year. I still keep my ear to the ground."

Jane couldn't determine whether Sawyer was happy, angry, or indifferent about the news. She wanted to work the conversation carefully, but she also needed to get information before Kit emerged from the store. "I realize the Peters case was a while back and everybody's memory gets foggy—"

"Yeah, but I kept good notes. You want to hear something weird?"

Jane hesitated. "Okay."

"I was in the garage a few weeks ago and I ran across a box of files that I took after I left the job. Half the files in that box had to do with Lou Peters. Quite a coincidence, wouldn't you say?"

Jane was hearing the word "coincidence" too much lately. "I guess so."

"I'm standing in the garage looking at the files as we speak. I ruminated about that boy for years after it was over. He's the kind of kid who sticks in your craw."

"You doubt his guilt?" Jane offered, figuring it was time to cut to the chase.

"Hell, I've asked myself that question over and over. I doubt the evidence, but back then we didn't have the solid DNA we have now." Sawyer reiterated much of the data Jane already knew about how Ashlee was found. "A lot of minutia was lost or simply not discovered. Plus, it'd been raining hard for half a day with a summer wind that howled like a banshee. Between the rain, the limestone, the sand from the creek bed, and the lack of scientific technology, the circumstances gave some leeway to the perp."

"Anything stand out to you?"

"Sure. Plenty. There was the condom that was recovered. The crime scene guys reported finding a particle of something shiny on it. I'm reading here...'Particle is dark green, akin to mica.'"

"Mica? Okay. What's the significance of that?"

"She was lying on limestone. While there may be mica residue in limestone or cross-contamination from the sandy creek bed, mica isn't dark green. It's typically black or white in color, sometimes cloudy clear."

"The report said, 'akin to mica.' Not that it was mica."

"Yeah. Shiny. Dark green."

"Limestone particulate?"

"Limestone is gray with very light green flecks. Not dark green."

"So why your intense scrutiny of the particle?"

"It was found on the condom. How did a particle with no inherent connection to that immediate area get transported onto a condom? There was nothing rocklike in the closet where Ashlee was held. I don't know...." Sawyer's voice trailed off.

"What is it?" Jane sensed Sawyer wanted to offer more.

"You know that gut feeling you get when some supposedly insignificant discovery is more than what it appears to be?"

Jane knew that familiar feeling all too well. "Yes."

"That's what this dark green particle was to me."

"So what happened when you went further with the information?"

"I didn't. I was brought in as part of the 'B' team. I didn't have the stature to go further with things."

"You think this green particle could have exonerated Lou?"

"Exonerated or maybe been the solid proof of guilt they were looking for. Maybe I'm putting too much emphasis on the thing. My wife's always after me for not letting things go from the past that pull on my mind and keep me awake at night."

"Does the Lou Peters case still keep you awake at night?"

There was a significant pause on the other end of the line. "Sometimes," Sawyer responded in a quiet, somewhat troubled manner.

"What else pulls on your mind about Lou Peters?" Jane asked, blowing out a stream of smoke into the icy morning air.

Sawyer let out a hard sigh, as if dredging up the past was too painful. "Well, frankly, *Lou Peters*. Have you met him?"

"No."

"I wonder what the kid looks like now? He'd be what? Thirty?"

"Thirty-three."

"There was always something about that kid. Something... hinky."

"Hinky. Yeah, got you." *Hinky* was a popular word cops liked to use when describing a person or situation that didn't seem quite right but they didn't have enough evidence to prove anything more nefarious. *Hinky* was like a cop saying, "My gut says something ain't right here."

"Brass remarked how intelligent he was," Sawyer continued, "and I'm not saying he wasn't. It's just that he seemed to be intelligent by proxy."

"By proxy?"

"That's the best way I can describe it. You'd look at the guy and some of the words he used just didn't seem like the vocabulary of a nineteen-year-old kid with his background. And his theories, or whatever you'd call them...they seemed to have a ring of something else."

"Something else?" Jane was trying to get Sawyer to be more specific while keeping one eye on the door to the health food store.

"He went on about 'The Power of Fourteen.' How fourteen-year-olds are vulnerable to the secular world's temptations and must be strongly persuaded to follow God in order to be saved. That certainly raised a few eyebrows with the boys at Headquarters. The prosecution ended up using Lou's words against him in court by pointing out that Ashlee was fourteen and she was held exactly fourteen days before she was murdered."

"Is that concrete? The data I read put the time of death between June 20 and 21."

"No, it was determined to be fourteen days from her disappearance to her death."

There were so many questions Jane had for Sawyer and so little time to squeeze them in before Kit returned. "From what I read, you guys nabbed Lou very quickly. What led everybody to Lou?"

"Right off the bat, he seemed too cool in his shoes. The guy was a good-looking young man and I have a feeling that he's used it in the past to his advantage."

"In what way?"

"There were rumors, completely unsubstantiated, that Peters raped two fourteen-year-old girls prior to Ashlee's death."

"You believe that?"

"There was no proof. Just small-town talk. You can't connect the dots on gossip. I looked into it, but I could never definitively find the missing link. God, I'm gonna sound like one of those whacked-out conspiracy theorists, but I wonder if there was some major cover-up on Peters's behalf."

"For what purpose?"

"I'm not sure. The female individual I talked to was 100 percent clear that the rapes happened but refused to testify."

Jane's mind immediately focused on Genevieve Paulson, Kit's "zaftig," drugged out, nude model. "Was your source Genevieve Paulson?"

"I don't know what her name was. She called Headquarters and I picked up the phone. We talked for less than three minutes. She wouldn't give her name and she sounded scared to death. She had a high-strung quality in her voice. When I asked her to come down to give a written statement, she told me to go 'F' myself, but she didn't say 'F.' Then she hung up. It was the first and last call I got from her."

Sawyer's description of "high-strung" mirrored the exact words Kit used to describe Genevieve. "Was the voice young or old?"

"Hell, I can't remember. I just recall that the woman sounded terrified."

"Terrified of what?"

"Death."

"Death?"

"Yeah. But there was that dichotomy of her salty tongue. She was scared but she was tough. It was like, 'Nobody's gonna tell me what to do.'"

"What else about Lou Peters raised suspicion?"

"His syrupy charm, for one. That wasn't working on the investigative team. His story would change. He kept getting his times wrong regarding his whereabouts. First he said he vaguely knew Ashlee, and then when we pressed harder, he admitted that she was a passing friend."

"So, I don't get it. He kidnaps Ashlee and—"

"Personally, I don't think he kidnapped her. I think she went willingly. There was no sign of a struggle at Ms. Clark's residence near Jade Cove, so we all agreed she wanted to go with him. He had a motorcycle. What fourteen-year-old girl isn't gonna feel special if some good-looking nineteen-year-old guy pays attention to her and offers a ride on his motorcycle?"

"So he took her for a ride without a struggle. Then what?"

"Maybe he told her he was going to take her for a romantic drive on Highway 1. Maybe he told her he wanted to show her a special place. Whatever happened, he ended up driving about an hour north until he turned into Pico Blanco. He obviously knew about the abandoned cabin. The church conducted Christian Youth outings at Pico Blanco. The cabin was a favorite place for the kids to congregate and share their love of God. Certainly, nobody was staying there overnight. The cabin was falling apart and filthy. It was more a place or point of reference for the kids when they were at Pico Blanco or a shelter to go to in case of storms."

"Lou conducted these Christian youth outings?"

"Yes, most of them. He was a huge draw for kids. Let me rephrase that: *girls*."

"Right. Was there any paper trail tying Lou to the crime?"

"Yeah. Receipts. Peters bought five battery-operated camp lanterns that were found in the closet at the cabin. Paid cash for them and kept the receipts for some reason. We found the receipts in his house and traced them back to a camping store in Monterey. The gal who sold him the lanterns testified in court that Lou Peters bought those lanterns from her, along with the rope and padlock they found at the scene. The date on the receipts was exactly a week before Ashlee's disappearance. So we figured he was buying this stuff and shuttling it to the cabin in preparation for what he planned to do."

"And the Valium?"

"We never sourced it. He could have purchased it on the black-market, stolen it from a friend, or just had someone give it to him."

"The lanterns and rope with receipts in his possession are considered circumstantial evidence?" Jane offered in an attempt to elicit a telling response.

"Every time we'd get a good indication that he was doing what we thought he was doing, there'd always be a viable reason for the evidence. That's one of the reasons why his attorneys had such a slew of ammo for the appeal."

"Give me an example," Jane said, squashing her cigarette butt into a pile of fallen snow with the heel of her boot.

"Peters's attorneys claimed that Lou purchased the rope and padlock to secure the cabin and the lanterns as backup light if the kids got stuck there during a storm. And, of course, Lou's prints were all over the cabin. But there were also close to twenty or twenty-two other prints from teenagers and others who all belonged to The Lamb of God Congregation. Lou's tire tracks from his motorcycle were also there. But so what? He was up there all the time conducting these Christian Youth outings."

"Wait a second, there were mirrors mentioned in the crime report. Several four-foot-long mirrors that were affixed in the closet where Ashlee was kept. And the hammer she was raped with."

"No receipts in his possession on those items, unfortunately."

"Fingerprints on the hammer?"

"Not conclusive. A lot of the blood was wiped off the handle."

"What was your take on those mirrors?"

"Humiliation. Ashlee was naked and tied up in that closet. We assumed she was in a fog because of the Valium. But when she woke up, she'd see her nude body and the blood and, I imagine, feel total degradation and terror. It was an in-your-face attempt to jolt the child."

"Jolt her into what?"

"Submission, maybe. Or...." Sawyer considered the idea. "If Lou *was* tied to this, then maybe the mirrors were a twisted attempt to convince her to convert to his form of Christianity out of shame for what she was."

"She was fourteen and a virgin."

"Maybe he assumed she wasn't a virgin because she looked mature for her age. People with sick minds make assumptions about young girls who develop early. She was also a free spirit. To a hardcore fundamentalist like Peters, Ashlee was a dangerous girl."

A thought suddenly came to Jane's mind. "Were Lou and these kids from The Lamb of God Congregation up there constantly, or were there breaks? And if there were breaks, were Lou's tire tracks found during those breaks when he could have been setting something up or holding Ashlee?"

"There were plenty of breaks and there was abstract evidence of Lou's presence during those breaks. That was the main drive of the prosecution's case against Lou. The tire tracks were fresh enough when we found them to make good imprints of them. But then we found out that there were at least 185 other people in the general area who had the same tires on their motorcycle. The defense really got a leg up when they found a camper who had been in Pico Blanco during Ashlee's disappearance. He had a motorcycle with the same tires on it. Now, there *was* a reliable witness who claims he saw Peters coming and going during Ashlee's disappearance—"

Jane informed Sawyer of Bruce Zatkin's death.

"Oh, Christ," Sawyer said with a heavy sigh. "He was the only credible link that put Lou at the cabin during that time. God, Peters seems to have such luck. He was always good at explaining away a lot of things. He could explain his prints by saying he was there many times with the kids. But on the other hand, it also gave us a reason to believe that he chose the cabin for its obscure location and because he knew how to get in and out without being seen."

It was Jane's turn to let out a hard, frustrated sigh.

"Hey, I hear you," Sawyer softly responded. "This case will make you sigh a lot."

Jane looked through the double glass doors of the health food store and saw Kit standing in the checkout line. She knew her time with Sawyer was limited. "Anything else about the case stand out to you as significant?"

Sawyer gave a thoughtful pause. "When I saw the photos of Ashlee's body and the crime location, the first word that came into my head was 'sacrifice.'"

"Sacrifice?"

"It looked like some perverted offering to the gods. Do you know the story of Pico Blanco?"

"No." Jane was feeling edgier as she watched Kit move up one place in line.

"It's known as The Sacred Peak. There's a story about Pico Blanco that involves the destruction of the world in a great flood. Very Biblical in nature, although it's told from the Native American point of view. The story goes that when the waters rose, the summit of Pico Blanco was the only land that remained exposed. At that place, the sacred birds met." Jane's attention was suddenly focused on Sawyer's words. "The Eagle, Crow, Raven, Hummingbird, and...."

"Hawk...." The words spilled out of Jane's mouth before she could contain them.

"Yeah. You know this story?" Sawyer sounded duly impressed.

"No. I just—" Jane felt a strange shift around her. "So the Hawk?"

"Well, Hawk is the main character in the story. Hawk plucked a magical feather from the head of Eagle, and carrying it, dove to the bottom of the sea. He then planted the feather in the earth. This caused the waters to recede and recreated the world. Hey, I'm no scholar in Native American beliefs, but I do remember reading something about how Hawk is the messenger and signifies paying attention to signs...."

Jane was silent. It was too bizarre. Certainly there was a viable explanation for this odd callback to that damn story Kit told her. And The Red Tail Hawk Bar.... No, the whole thing was a convoluted coincidence, Jane thought to herself as an electrical pulse ran up her spine.

"Anyway, like I said, it looked like an ancient sacrifice to the gods of Pico Blanco, the way Ashlee was laid out on the rock."

There was a thick silence between Sawyer and Jane. Jane caught a glance of Kit paying the cashier. "So," Jane said in a last ditch effort to drag information out of Sawyer, "you think Lou killed Ashlee?"

"I wouldn't put money on it. But I also wouldn't want to be alone in the same room with him."

"So, say he killed Ashlee. Given what you know about him... what does your gut tell you? Could he do it again?"

"Again? What do you mean?" Sawyer's voice was suddenly agitated.

Jane was afraid that her driving desire to learn more had forced her hand. She retreated. "It's just a hypothesis. I have to look at all possibilities given the retrial that's coming up for Lou."

"Oh, I see. Okay." Sawyer seemed satisfied with that answer. "I don't know. Given the right circumstance...the right prodding... maybe he could kill again.... That's saying if he indeed killed the first time." Sawyer let out a soft chuckle. "God, I envy you," he said in a confidential tone. "I hear the fire in your voice and I get that gurgle in my belly again. Jesus, I hope my wife didn't hear me say that. She'd have a fit if she knew I was shaking loose old ghosts from the past."

"Hey, I always say that I'm the job. But only another cop understands that."

"I hear you!" Sawyer chimed in with a familiar camaraderie. "You know what I say? I tell people I worked the job until the job worked me."

Jane related well to that statement. "Nightmares?"

"Sure. But then you figure out how many shots it takes to make them stop."

Jane felt the unintentional sting of Sawyer's words. "How many does it take now that you're off the job?" Jane asked in an uncharacteristic familial tone.

"Zero," Sawyer replied in a proud tone. "I have thirteen years."

Thirteen years? Jane couldn't imagine being sober for thirteen years. She was a day shy of six months and still felt that she was struggling to crest a very steep hill. Jane sensed her professional guard slipping. The only other time she let herself do this was during conversations with Sergeant Weyler. There was something comfortable about Sawyer's voice, like a soft place to fall. "Thirteen years," Jane said, her words stumbling out of her mouth. "That's a goddamn lifetime."

"Yeah. But it's a life worth living, Jane." Sawyer hesitated, sensing a greater need from the person on the other end of the phone.

Jane saw Kit heading for the glass double doors. "I gotta go. Thanks for returning my call."

"My pleasure. You got me thinking again. It feels good."

"All right, well—" Jane started to hang up when Sawyer spoke up.

"Hey, you know who you should talk to? Dr. John Bartosh. He headed The Lamb of God Congregation. There's something about him."

"In what way?"

"I don't know. When you talk to him, you'll see what I mean. You gotta do it."

"Okay." Jane turned around as Kit exited the health store. "Thanks again." Jane hung up and stealthily slid the cell phone into her coat pocket, unbeknownst to Kit.

"Ready to go?" Kit yelled across the parking lot.

Jane turned around and nodded. As she walked to her car, she realized she hadn't asked Sawyer for his impressions on Kit. Still, she mused, if Sawyer had any misgivings about Kit, he certainly would have offered them. Climbing into the car, Kit took a sip of her carrot juice and gingerly placed a bag of groceries behind her seat.

"I got us some healthy treats for the road," Kit said with a joyful ring. "Carob covered almonds, yogurt sticks, sesame crunches, spirulina energy balls—"

"Spirulina energy balls? What the—"

"They're better than coffee and they'll do wonders for your colon! Your shit will be green and glorious!"

"Lovely," Jane muttered as she retrieved a phone book from under her seat.

"Who are you looking for?"

"Dr. John Bartosh. He's in Grand Junction now, right?"

"What in the hell are you doing?" Kit's demeanor turned suspicious.

Jane continued to flip through the phone book. "We'll be in Grand Junction in less than three hours. I want to talk to him face-to-face."

"Why would you want to bother with Bartosh?" Kit's tone was becoming increasingly indignant. "You'd be matching wits with an unarmed man! Jane, trust me, spending time with Bartosh is like being awake during your own surgery."

"I've got a high pain threshold."

"He's as much fun as root canal without the positive outcome!"

"Positive outcome?"

"At least with root canal, the agony eventually stops."

"Kit, in order to work this case, I have to get to know all the people who are involved. Bartosh fits into that category."

"He won't talk to you when he finds out you know me."

"So I won't tell him." Jane slid her finger down the page of names and found Bartosh's phone listing and address.

She had to look twice at the name of the street: Eagle Road.

·· **CHAPTER 10**

"Jane, Bartosh will not agree to talk to you! He doesn't trust anyone in the secular world!"

Jane's attention was still drawn to Bartosh's street name: Eagle Road. Was this another one of those coincidences that had been occurring rather frequently lately? Ten minutes before, Detective Charles Sawyer had described the legend of Pico Blanco where Ashlee's body was found. There were the sacred birds: the Eagle, Crow, Raven, Hummingbird, and Hawk who helped the waters recede after the great flood. Bartosh could have lived on any street. Why did he happen to live on Eagle Road?

"Jane?" Kit said, sounding like a schoolmarm. *"Did you hear me?"*

"Yes," Jane said, coming back to her senses. "He doesn't trust the secular world. Fine. I'll pretend to be someone else. I'll play a role. I'm good at that."

"What types of roles have you played in the past?"

"A hooker, a junkie, a drug dealer. I played dead in a morgue once so I could hear a conversation between two perps who came to view their dead brother."

"Dear, I don't think any of those roles will be helpful in dealing with Bartosh. We could possibly use the playing dead one, but it would be a stretch."

"For Christ's sake! I can figure out a workable angle so he'll agree to see me!"

"Not with your sailor's mouth, you won't! All it'll take is one slip-up of 'fuck' or 'shit' and you'll blow your cover! And *then* what?"

Jane sat back and looked at Kit intently. "I thought you had faith in me."

"I do," Kit replied without reservation. "But you don't know the born-again Christian lingo. They have their own way of speaking so as to properly identify one another. Just like African Americans and Texans."

"You're shittin' me!"

"Do you know the difference between a Fundamentalist, an Evangelical, and a Protestant?"

"We're doing Christian riddles?"

"You don't know, and yet you're willing to go into Bartosh's lair unprepared! Fundamentalists are Christians who believe the Bible is the *literal*, incrrant word of God, and is correct not only in its religious or moral teachings, but also in its scientific and historical claims. God *literally* created the world in six days. God *literally* created Eve from Adam's rib. Jesus *is* God. Evangelicals are Christians who say they have a more personal relationship with Jesus. Bartosh is a Fundamentalist and he's as *literal* as they come! His Fundamentalist dogma allows him to be unburdened by introspection."

Jane smiled at Kit's clever observation. "And Protestants?"

"Protestants are middle of the road, wishy-washers who aren't committed to Jesus with the proper fervor that's needed to spread God's Word. Fundamentalists and Evangelicals believe that it's not enough to say you believe in Jesus. It's every *true* Christians' mandate to talk about Him by 'The Great Commission of Christ.' Protestants are known as the 'sidelines.' To Fundamentalists and Evangelicals, Protestants are a dying sect of Christianity; a group with no firm mission statement. Protestants keep their faith private, whereas the New Christian constantly witnesses for Jesus. Then there are the secular elitists."

"And they are?"

"Also doomed because they have no real religion at all. Secular elitists are usually East Coasters. The gin and tonic crowd. Daddy's old money. You'll hear the words 'secular elitist' coming out of Bartosh's mouth a lot *if* you get in the door!"

"What else?"

"Oh, there are too many to list. 'Wonder-working power.' It's from the Bible. It's also a line in an old gospel hymn that sings of changing the world through divine, not human, intervention. The New Christian carefully drops it into conversations. Some believe that by saying 'wonder-working power,' it's a sort of wink-wink code to let others know you are part of 'the chosen.'"

Jane was impressed by Kit's grasp of the subject. "How does a pseudo Buddhist like you know all this stuff?"

"Well, when I'm not chanting, burning incense, or designing intricate sand mandalas, I actually read outside my scope of spiritual interest. In order to know the beast, you must study them."

"You mean, in order to *hate* them?"

"I don't hate them!" Kit's said. "I don't *trust* them. There's a single-minded, arrogant attitude that many of them possess. I wouldn't accept that behavior from anyone—a Jew, an Arab, *or* a Buddhist! It just so happens that Jesus got tagged as the sacrificial lamb two thousand years after they sacrificed him the first time!" Kit continued to clue in Jane with additional lingo: "Witness for the faith," "Divine mission," and "Having the heartbeat." "Isn't the true purpose of talking to Bartosh so you can find out about Lou? Well, how can the subject of Lou Peters logically happen without it looking suspicious? Bartosh is desperately paranoid. Bring up Lou and you'll see what I mean."

"Why is he so paranoid?"

"Bartosh truly believes that secular society is out to get Lou. He's firmly *committed* to Lou's innocence. If you make one wrong move, we're screwed!"

"How are we screwed?"

"By Bartosh delaying us! We need to get to California as quickly as possible!"

Jane turned and stared out the car window, quickly thinking of angles. She would need to create a win-win situation where she appealed to Bartosh's sensitivities. "What trips his trigger?" Jane asked out loud. "God, right?"

"Yes," Kit answered uneasily.

"What else?"

"Youth. The destruction of the moral fiber that is tearing apart families—"

"So, engaging him in a thoughtful exchange about society and the plight of our young people might spark his interest?" Jane said as she started to melt into the character she needed to become to nail a one-on-one tête-à-tête with Bartosh. "Our young people are at risk, Kit. It is only through our Lord and Savior, Jesus Christ, that we can salvage their future."

Kit shifted in her seat. "Okay, you're scaring me. Stop it!"

Jane dropped character. "You believe I can do this now?"

"I believe you can parody a religious role. But I'm not sure you can get your foot in the door and maintain that role for longer than a few minutes."

"Kit, I went undercover and played a child's mother for over one month. I had an entire town hoodwinked by the con." Jane said with a proud grin as she pulled out her cell phone. "If I can play a kid's mother, I can sure as shit play a goddamned, God-fearing, Christian woman for a fucking hour!"

"We're screwed." She let out a weary sigh. "I can't talk you out of this?"

"Why should you? You afraid I might learn something pertinent to your case?"

Kit turned away with an uneasy shift in her seat. "I've told you everything. There's nothing to hide." Jane's ear noted a slight upturn in Kit's voice with the words: *There's nothing to hide.* It was the same cadence that Jane always defined as a false statement. With Kit, the underlying tone was not malicious...just untrue. "Go ahead!" Kit continued with a flick of her wrist. "Have your little chat with Bartosh."

"I need to see people and get a flavor for who they really are. Hell, if I could talk to the *dead*, I'd do it!"

"You *can* talk to the dead. I talk to Ashlee every day."

Jane realized she stepped over the line. "I'm sorry. I didn't mean to cause you pain with that statement."

"Oh, Jane. You can only cause me pain if I give you the power to do so," Kit replied with a decisive tone as she reached into the backseat and pulled a book from her bulging traveling bag. "If you're going to do this, let's get it done! *But think this whole charade through before you call him!* How are you getting your foot in the door?"

Jane noticed a customer leaving the health food store, deeply involved in a magazine article. The light bulb went on in Jane's head. "I'm a journalist...for a Christian magazine. And I'm writing a story on how to save today's youth from the temptations that will certainly bring down our great nation." Jane turned to Kit with a look of "What do you think?"

A serious, somewhat frightened look enveloped Kit's face. "Okay. That may work. Just don't get cavalier. Bartosh may grant you your interview, but he's not stupid. If he senses an ounce of deceit on your part and then chooses to investigate you on the spot and *then* finds *me* attached to you—Kit Clark, one of his most potent critics, well, *do the math!* We could easily get put into a *very* embarrassing predicament that could stick us in Grand Junction for days sorting it all out when we should be driving at lightning speed to California!" Jane nodded in agreement. "You better wear a skirt and blouse to see Bartosh. He doesn't think much of women who wear pants. I saw a secondhand store on the way into town. You can find a conservative outfit in there. Now, what magazine do you work for?"

Jane grabbed her laptop and did a quick search for leading Christian Magazines. "I'm a freelance writer for *Christian Parenting Today*." Jane declared as she snapped the top of the laptop shut.

"Are you using your real name?"

"No, of course, not. My name is...." Jane looked around the parking lot and saw a posted sign that read: THIS SPOT RESERVED FOR JACKIE. Jane turned to Kit. "My name's Jackie. And my last name is...." She casually turned over Kit's book, a New Age tome titled *Finding Your Inner Light & Joy*. Pointing to the words "Light & Joy," Jane revealed, "Lightjoy! Jackie Lightjoy!"

"That's a name you'd give a cartoon character who lives on a spaceship and drives a phallic-shaped car!"

"Hey!" Jane said with a straight face as she dialed the number. "The Lightjoy family has dealt with that kind of derision for generations. And we *don't* appreciate it!"

"Hello?" The voice on the other end of the line was soft, gentle, and female.

In an instant, Jane went into character. "Hello!" Jane replied in a quasi-reverential manner. "My name is Jackie Lightjoy and I'm a writer with *Christian Parenting Today.* Is this where I can reach Dr. John Bartosh?"

"Yes. I'm his wife, Ingrid. What can I do for you?"

Jane felt a hot rush of excitement. It always happened when she was knee-deep in a fresh ruse. "Mrs. Bartosh," Jane continued in a respectful tone, "I've heard so many wonderful things about you from my colleagues at the magazine."

Ingrid Bartosh was taken aback. "Well...thank you. My husband is usually the one attracting the accolades...."

Jane thought quickly. "That's understandable. But you make it possible for him to shine and carry The Word of God."

"Oh, my," Ingrid was touched by Jane's words, "How can I help you, dear?"

Jane flashed Kit a pious smile of victory and launched her pitch. "I'm writing a story...a *cover* story, for *Christian Parenting Today* on the many secular obstacles that are negatively affecting today's preteen children. *Especially* young girls." Jane caught a peripheral glimpse of Kit's reaction. It was a contemptuous roll of the eyes and then back to reading her New Age book.

"Well, that's certainly an appropriate subject," Ingrid replied in an ultra-contained tone. "What was your name again?"

"Jackie. Jackie Lightjoy."

Kit couldn't resist. "Beam me up, Jackie Lightjoy," she whispered.

Jane responded with a swift finger to her mouth to mime, "Shh!"

"Jackie, yes," Ingrid continued, "My husband isn't here at the moment. This is the morning he heads The Brotherhood Council. He has some time available two weeks from Wednesday to speak on the phone—"

"I was actually hoping to do something sooner and in person if at all possible—"

"In person?"

"I'm traveling through Colorado on family business. When my editor called to give me the assignment, it was just pure luck that one of the best contacts for our story lived in this wonderful state. And frankly, I do enjoy meeting people face-to-face."

"Yes, of course," Ingrid said in a halting manner. "It's just that my husband doesn't usually speak to the media without fully researching the organization—"

Jane was quickly reminded of Bartosh's paranoia. A dead end was imminent. Jane was forced to do the unthinkable. She began to cry crocodile tears. "I understand," Jane said with an audible catch in her throat. Kit looked up from her book and stared at Jane in bewilderment. "I'm sorry. I usually don't get emotional like this. It's been a tough week for me. Well, for our whole family. I said I was in Colorado on family business and, well, that business was the death of my seventeen-year-old niece...Janie."

"I'm so sorry. May God bless and keep her in his Divine home," Ingrid said with sincere affection. "How did she pass into His arms?"

"Well," Jane poured on the intense emotion, "I hate to say it, but the darkness got hold of her. She turned from Jesus and chose the Devil's temptations. First it was drugs and then it was alcohol and then it was...." Jane drew in her breath. "Sexual deviancy."

"Oh, dear," Ingrid said with great empathy. "I am *so* sorry."

"Thank you," Jane said in a choked whisper. Kit continued to watch this dramatic performance with a questionable gawk. "Apparently, Janie went to some horrible...." Jane made sure she confidentially whispered the next two words, "*sex party*. Things got out of hand and she was strangled to death by one of the boys at the party."

Jane could easily determine that Ingrid was sympathetic to the alarming story. "Have mercy on her poor soul," she said in a faraway voice. "You say she was...seventeen?"

"Yes. Seventeen."

Jane heard Ingrid's voice catch. Somehow, the false story had struck a nerve with her. "It's difficult at times to understand God's plan for us and those we love so dearly."

"This wound to our family is still so fresh in our hearts." Jane took a breath and went for the clincher. "To have your own flesh and blood die during an orgy forces one to step back and take comfort that the *wonder-working power of God* will heal our souls." Kit's mouth dropped open as she regarded Jane with a bemused gape.

There was a thick pause on the phone.

"Where did you say you are right now?"

"About three hours from Grand Junction," Jane said, her heart pounding as she felt the tug of the fish on her deceptive line.

"I'll make this interview happen for you, Jackie," Ingrid said. "Perhaps this is Jesus' way of getting the message out to other young girls at risk so that we can save a soul who is on the edge."

"God bless you, Ingrid. *God bless you!*"

Jane hung up, dissolved out of character, and looked out into the distance with a self-satisfied grin.

"And the Academy Award for the most deceptive and absurd performance that used the words 'wonder-working power' and 'orgy' within the same breath goes to...."

"Kit," Jane said, turning on the ignition, "you ain't seen nothin' yet!"

CHAPTER 11

With one hand on the steering wheel, Jane quickly checked her cell phone for messages and retrieved one from her brother.

"Hey, Janie!" Mike said in a singsong manner. "Just checkin' in. Picked up your mail and watched some TV while I was here. Hey, that Sergeant of yours...ah, *Weyler?* He stopped by while I was there. Looked like he was goin' to church the way he was dressed. Anyway, he *really* wants to talk to you. I told him you were drivin' to California. Oakhurst, right? He seemed kinda pissed about that... I told him to give you a call on your cell. I went ahead and gave him your new number. That's okay, right? See ya."

Jane clicked her phone shut and let out a long sigh. Mike could never keep a secret. For Sergeant Weyler to show up at her house meant he was not going to accept her silence. Now he had her cell number. Great.

Kit read her New Age book until she nodded off. Jane took advantage of the respite from conversation to push her concerns about Weyler far back in her mind and go over the information she'd discovered in the last hour about Ashlee's murder.

Jane pulled a pad of paper from the leather satchel that was tucked behind her seat. She placed it on her lap and withdrew a pen from the visor. Detective Charles Sawyer had turned out to be a gold mine of information. However, with each question, Sawyer had brought up even more questions and possibilities that were equally perplexing. Jane put the pedal to the metal and started jotting down some of the more puzzling points that Sawyer had revealed.

Foremost on her mind was the mysterious dark, green, shiny particle found in the condom. The fact that Sawyer had obsessed so much on that particle meant something to Jane. Cops have an odd gift—a built-in radar that lights up when they're given incongruous information. It could be a word, a piece of evidence, a person, or a situation that trips the radar. Once the radar is tripped, the gut starts to clench, acknowledging that something is askew. It had happened to Jane hundreds of times, and each time that radar had proven to be right on the money. However, determining the incongruity often required weeks or even months of hard investigation.

The two alleged rapes Lou Peters was accused of committing were a good example of nagging incongruity. After talking to Sawyer, the possible rapes took on a more sinister aspect, especially with the introduction of the anonymous caller who had spoken to Sawyer fourteen years ago. "High-strung." That was the term he had used to describe the female caller. "Terrified." That was another description of the woman. Terrified of death, Sawyer theorized. Jane mused that could be presumptuous. Then again, that old radar could have kicked in when Sawyer was talking to the female caller. So the next logical jump, if death was indeed a fear, was the usual conspiracy link: a cover-up. Jane wrote that word in capital letters on the yellow pad with a question mark. A cover for Lou, she wondered, or a cover for the real killer?

Thinking back on the conversation with Sawyer, Jane noted the suspicious purchases by Lou of lanterns and rope. Certainly noteworthy, Jane figured, and just a bit too coincidental, given the seemingly premeditated nature of the items. Then there was the Valium used to drug Ashlee. That seemed to be available out of nowhere. Jane figured the perp would need a significant number of pills to last fourteen days.

Fourteen days. Ashlee was fourteen. Was the time between the kidnapping and the murder significant or just coincidental on the killer's part? If Lou was the killer, and if he was responsible for kidnapping twelve-year-old Charlotte Walker, did that mean Charlotte was destined to die on day twelve? She counted twelve days past Christmas Day, counting Christmas as the first day, and came up with January 5.

Jane's mind bounced to the discussion of Pico Blanco and the limestone outcropping where Ashlee's cooked body was found. Sawyer recalled the "sacrificial" pose of the body. "Like an offering to the Gods," he told Jane. Strange terminology, she thought, and yet it gave Jane a crisp image of how Ashlee had been posed by her killer. An unexpected shudder jolted Jane as she flashed on the grisly impression. A feeling of raw vulnerability washed over her, and for a split second, the comforting contemplation that a shot of Jack Daniels would feel good at that moment. Even though the consideration lasted less than a heartbeat, Jane was somewhat stunned and enticed at the same time by the notion. "How many shots does it take now?" she recalled asking Sawyer, only to discover that he was a full-fledged member of the first-name-only club. Jane still felt daunted by Sawyer's thirteen years of sobriety. "But it's a life worth living...." Sawyer advised. To Jane, that statement was analogous to *faith*. At that critical moment, trusting in anything was proving to be difficult. She yearned to encounter the black-and-white answers that led to black-and-white conclusions. But amidst the odd occurrences that had taken place in her life over the last few days, Jane was left with a sense that she was freefalling into a gray abyss filled with strange coincidences and even stranger wraith-driven connections.

As if on cue, she felt the edge of the snakestone totem rubbing against her sobriety chips. Radical transformation, Jane thought. *Insane logic*, she assured herself. That snakestone was as insignificant as the odd connections to the sacred birds of Pico Blanco and their legend. The Eagle. The Crow. The Raven. The Hummingbird. The Hawk. It was all just a disjointed linking of coincidences, Jane told herself as she took the Horizon Drive exit off the highway into Grand Junction and headed toward Bartosh's house on Eagle Road.

Bartosh's house was located in the center of Grand Junction, just off Main Street in what looked like an old, established part of town. Passing a 7-Eleven on the corner, Jane pulled into the parking lot and grabbed the conservative skirt and blouse she had purchased from the secondhand store. She emerged from the 7-Eleven's bathroom looking prim and proper. Checking her reflection in the window, Jane decided that by pulling her layered, long brown hair back into a discreet ponytail, she could project an even more virtuous appearance. She grabbed a pack of black barrettes and, seeing a small notepad and pen combo nearby, Jane collected it as well, figuring it would work as a good prop.

Back in the car, Jane brushed her hair back into a neat ponytail and asked Kit to borrow her tape recorder and a blank tape to use during the interview.

Kit handed Jane a blank ninety-minute tape. "Where are you going to stash me? Neither Bartosh or his wife can see me with you."

"I can drop you off at a health food store and pick you up when I'm done."

"I'd normally say fine, but I'm feeling rather unsteady at the moment."

"Unsteady?" Jane asked, concerned. She realized that her worry for Kit was more deeply rooted than she expected.

"It happens a lot lately. The only thing that helps is if I lie down and rest."

"That's easy," Jane said concisely. "We'll move the bags from the backseat up front and you can lie down back there. I'll park the car halfway down the block from where they live. Problem solved."

Kit nodded as Jane backed out of the parking lot and headed into Bartosh's neighborhood. The weather in Grand Junction was light-years away from typical Colorado winter offerings. The temperature was a mild fifty-five degrees; warm enough to make jackets optional. Turning on to Eagle Road, Jane noted that the street was positively idyllic and pristine. The homes were solidly built, many made of brick, and looked as if they could withstand a hundred-mile-per-hour sustained windstorm without losing a shingle. But to Jane, it looked like a Disney movie set with false front homes that appeared too clean to be true.

Jane located Bartosh's modest one-story brick house and continued down the street half a block before parking. She cleared the backseat and Kit maneuvered her large frame into it. Jane collected her props and started to head off when a thought crossed her mind. "Do you know what the Brotherhood Council is?" Jane asked Kit.

Kit thought for a second, adjusting her buckwheat pillow. "It's an elite, fraternal group of men Bartosh gathers together to discuss Church matters. They're handpicked by Bartosh. It was quite the honor back in Big Sur to be part of the chosen few."

"Why just men?"

"Well, for one, Bartosh doesn't acknowledge the Goddess. And two, he lives in an old paradigm where men make the rules and women make the meals and babies!"

Jane rolled her eyes. "Okay," she retorted sarcastically.

"Don't you get uppity," Kit warned.

"*Uppity?*"

"Uppity! Bartosh and his misguided members *hate* uppity women. Women are bred to look congenial, have no personal opinions, stay in the background, and suffer. Not necessarily in that order...so don't try to push the envelope and show how bloody smart you are or he'll know you're not one of the tribe!" With that significant statement, Kit punched her buckwheat pillow into a ball and closed her eyes.

Jane smoothed a few stray hairs and walked up the block, transforming herself into the antithesis of Jane Perry. Arriving at Bartosh's door, Jackie Lightjoy rang the bell.

CHAPTER 12

"Mrs. Lightjoy?"

Jane tilted her head and flashed a demure smile as she extended her hand. "Mrs. Bartosh. It's a pleasure to meet you."

Ingrid shook Jane's hand with one hand and cupped her other hand around Jane's knuckles. The gesture was a universal body language sign that told Jane a lot about Ingrid. This was a woman who thought with her heart and was motivated by a strong need to feel the pain of others.

"Please, call me Ingrid," she said as stood aside to let Jane inside the door.

"And you must call me Jackie," Jane insisted as she moved inside the house. She was immediately taken by two things: a dense, almost claustrophobic, overheated environment, and the soft, nearly trance-inducing taped music of a choir singing "Jesus is the way and the light." Ingrid was wearing a beige skirt that flowed well past mid-calf down her narrow hips and a pressed, white, button-front shirt that was generously cut to obscure whatever upper body the woman possessed. Her wavy gray hair with occasional streaks of brown underneath fell softly against her narrow shoulders. On her feet, she wore a pair of beige loafers that Jane surmised were purchased in the sensible shoe department. Ingrid appeared to be in her early sixties, although her moist, peachy-rose face was devoid of both makeup and excessive lines. Jane did note a certain downturn in her mouth and what looked to be a quiet sadness in her hazel eyes.

"I have coffee set up in the family room," Ingrid said as she led Jane past the dimly lit living room, through the antiquated 1950's-style kitchen and into a large room with mustard shag carpeting. To call this a "family room" seemed odd to Jane. The furniture, which consisted of a well-worn plaid couch, a single leather recliner, a large coffee table, assorted straight-back chairs, and a floor-to-ceiling bookcase with a large cross cut out of the top center portion, did not seem conducive to family gatherings. The initial dense feeling Jane felt when she walked into the house seemed stronger in this stuffy room. There was no television, nor anything that reeked of jovial entertainment. The walls were blank except for three two-by-three-foot pictures of Jesus. One was an extreme close-up of His face and blood dripping from the crown of thorns atop his head, the second a traditional Christ on the cross crucifixion pose, and the third, a standing image of Jesus dressed in a flowing robe and knocking on a wooden door. Between the hot, confining environment, the drone of choir music, the feeling that Jesus was watching her from all angles, and the nauseating mustard shag carpeting, Jane felt the need to gird her loins for the job ahead.

"My husband is finishing up ministering to a Congregation member on the telephone." Jane glanced toward a well-lit, adjacent room less than five feet from where she stood. She could see the edge of a large desk, a small lamp, and a male hand balled up in a fist. While she couldn't hear the private conversation, Jane noted how the fist bounced quietly yet purposefully off the desk as the muted voice made a point. For some odd reason, the idea of Oz behind the curtain popped into Jane's mind.

"Please have a seat." Ingrid motioned to the plaid sofa. Jane sat down. Ingrid took a seat next to her, placing her hand on Jane's arm. "I briefly explained the story you're writing for *Christian Parenting* to my husband, as well as your personal family tragedy involving the nature of your niece's death. I'm sorry. Her name again?"

Jane immediately noted Ingrid's forward behavior mixed with an added edge of righteous justification. Even though the story Jane had told about her "niece" was fabricated, she felt a sense of indignity as a tenor of judgment rang clearly in Ingrid's genteel voice. "Janie," Jane replied.

"Yes, Janie," Ingrid said. Jane wasn't sure if this was some sort of test, but she figured she successfully passed the first hurdle of remembering her fictitious niece. Ingrid's eyes drifted to the side, as if recollecting a bittersweet memory. "Seventeen years old, you said? Life hasn't even begun at seventeen, has it?" Ingrid looked back into Jane's eyes, seemingly in search of a deeper answer.

"No, it hasn't," Jane softly replied.

"I have a plate of sugar cookies!" Ingrid said in an abrupt, incongruous change of subject. "They were left over from my husband's Brotherhood Council meeting. Do you like sugar cookies?"

Jane couldn't care less. "They're my favorite!" Jane took a bite of a cookie while Ingrid eagerly awaited her review. "Homemade?"

"Of course! Store bought won't do! The Brotherhood loves them. I'm *known* for these cookies," Ingrid said with an almost childlike candor.

Jane figured the only woman who needed to brag about her cookies was *Mrs. Fields*. But then again, she'd entered an odd, new world, and she had to blend into it. Ingrid poured Jane's coffee and stood up. "Aren't you going to join us?" Jane asked.

"No. You came here to talk to my husband, not me. And he only drinks coffee when he has to stay up late writing an article for the newsletter."

Jane recalled Kit mentioning Bartosh's newsletter. "Newsletter?" Jane asked, taking a sip of the boiling brew. Jane noticed a somewhat burned quality to the coffee, a decidedly bitter taste that cheap pre-ground beans often produced.

"Yes. It comes out every other month. We've been publishing it for over a decade. It's the way Congregation members keep in touch with what's going on."

"How many members do you have?"

"I don't know the exact number. We print close to seven thousand newsletters each go-around. But, the Congregation numbers far exceed that. And we have new members joining constantly, what with our members traveling overseas and ministering to the thousands of lost souls in the Middle East, China, India.... I'd be happy to gather together some back issues for you if you'd like."

"I'd love it. Thank you!"

Ingrid's attention focused behind Jane. "*This* is the man you came to see!"

Jane turned around to find Dr. John Bartosh standing five feet from her. His entrance had been so stealthlike, it caught her off-guard. Jane stood, extending her hand. "Dr. Bartosh! My name is Jackie Lightjoy. Thank you so very much for taking the time to speak with me today."

Bartosh shook Jane's hand with a firm grasp. "You're with *Christian Parenting Today?*"

"Yes. I freelance for them. It gives me more freedom to spend time with my husband and children, while still doing God's work."

Bartosh silently took in the scene, quietly judging and ana-lyzing every word. Jane's plastic smile belied the rapidly rotating wheels of observation that whirled inside her head. After the grave warnings and descriptions from Kit regarding Bartosh, she half expected to meet a repulsive ogre. Instead, the man who stood before her was mid-sixties, barely six foot tall, wore a crisp white business shirt, a dark suit with outdated lapels, polished black oxfords, and a plain wedding band. His complexion was ruddy, which tended to amplify the various strands of strawberry red hair that mingled in his mostly gray, wavy conservative coiffure. Jane was immediately taken by Bartosh's steel blue eyes and their pen-etrating glare. She could easily understand how anyone lacking self-confidence might feel trepidation under such an intense gaze.

Bartosh's fixed stare upon Jane lasted longer than normal. "You look familiar."

Jane realized Bartosh must have seen her photo or her appear-ance on *Larry King Live*. She needed to quickly work a believable angle. "I get that a *lot*."

Bartosh's eyes continued to analyze Jane's face with a third-degree gaze. "*Very* familiar," he said with emphasis. Ingrid joined the facial scrutiny.

"Julia Roberts," Jane said with a singsong tone.

"Excuse me?"

"The actress? People say I look just like her," Jane lied. She waited for the celebrity name to register with Bartosh. It did not. "*Pretty Woman?* The movie?"

"The one about the harlot?" Bartosh stated with severity.

Jane was unmoved. "Yes, that one. But—"

"I wouldn't want to look like anyone who promotes prostitution to the masses."

If Bartosh was trying to use intimidation to wear down Jane, he was in for a long battle. While Jane Perry would have responded with a dizzy slur of four letter words, Jackie Lightjoy simply smiled. "Perhaps I should cut my hair to avoid the comparison."

"Perhaps...." Bartosh thought for a second. "Lightjoy," he mused, crossing to the only lounge chair in the room, across from the couch. "I've never heard that name before." He sat down, never taking his eyes off Jane.

Jane sat on the couch. "It's my married name." Silence. Jane took up the challenge. "My husband's family hails from England." Stream of consciousness kicked in. "A tiny village near Southampton. When his ancestors came to the States, they took on the name of their village, which happened to be Lightjoy. It could have been worse, my husband jokes. His second cousins hail from Duck Bottom." Silence. Jane took a sip of Ingrid's burned offering and continued. Pulling out the tape recorder, she placed it on the coffee table. "Do you mind?" Jane asked, pointing to the recorder. "I have a pad for notes, but I find that a recorder helps me get quotes exactly right."

"Fine," Bartosh said concisely, and Jane pushed the RECORD button.

"I'll leave you two alone and get those newsletters, Jackie," Ingrid said before quietly vanishing into Bartosh's office.

Jane took a breath and started to speak when Bartosh interrupted her.

"I smell smoke," he said, his tenacious eyes focused on Jane. "*Cigarette* smoke."

"I was afraid of that," Jane replied, never wavering from character. "As your wife may have told you, I've been in Colorado on family business and, unfortunately, surrounded by individuals who are smokers."

"It's a filthy habit."

"I couldn't agree with you more," Jane said, briefly flashing on the soothing image of inhaling a deep drag of nicotine-laced smoke. "It's such an addiction. Some say it's worse than addiction to heroin."

"Addiction is addiction," Bartosh said tersely. "It's simply a lack of self-discipline. And where there is no self-discipline there can be no self-rule."

Jane seriously considered the statement and found it oddly provocative. "May I use that in the article?"

"If you wish," Bartosh brusquely replied, sitting back in his chair but maintaining a strong, cautionary posture. "What happened to your niece is unforgivable." The statement appeared to come out of nowhere and rang with resounding judgment. "It's a perfect example of what occurs when one falls prey to the Secular Humanist manifesto and the Culture of Darkness."

Jane had no idea what the Secular Humanist manifesto espoused, but she played along, with a callback to her conversation with Kit. "I agree. It's *secular elitism* at his worst." Jane waited for the catchphrase to take effect before continuing. "We're all sick about what happened to Janie. It's what makes the story I'm writing for the magazine so much more meaningful to me. Did your wife tell you about the theme of our story?"

"Yes. I'm sure she related to you that I usually don't agree to do any interviews without prior written correspondence."

Jane nodded and took another painful sip of the bitter java. "May I ask what changed your mind?"

"It's not *what*, Mrs. Lightjoy, it's *who*. *Our Lord and Savior Jesus Christ.* Based upon situations that have come to my attention over the past three weeks, it's become apparent to me that His fervent message is being ignored by our young people, and because of this, *great* suffering will befall the children very soon." Bartosh's visage took on a grave appearance. "I wrote about this *exact subject* in our last newsletter. My words, it seems, have become prophetic. But that doesn't surprise me. God has always used me as a vessel to spread his message."

"May I ask what situation occurred that allowed us to have this interview?"

A dark pall befell Bartosh. He spoke with a contained fury, edged with anguish. "Three weeks ago, one of the Brotherhood Council members informed me of a perverted group of men and women known as 'A.C.U.S.': Adult Child Union Society. The group encourages girls as young as twelve to have sexual intercourse with adults, as well as take part in sadistic ritual abuse." Bartosh hesitated, obviously sickened by what he was about to divulge. "Once-a-month, they organize a 'Night of the Virgin' where adult members sacrifice their preteen, virginal daughters or female family members to the highest bidder in a silent auction."

Jane felt a peak of ire. Years ago, she had cut her teeth at the Department working some of Denver's most disturbing child sexual abuse cases. The lucky child victims, Jane always said, were those who died during their torment. The survivors lived their lives in tortured shells.

"When I returned home and my wife informed me of the manner in which your niece was murdered and then your story theme for *Christian Parenting,* I realized that it wasn't a coincidence."

Coincidence. There was that damn word again, Jane thought.

"As always, our Lord was speaking loud and clearly to me. He was telling me to use the Christian media to expose this repulsive, secular splinter group." Bartosh appeared trapped in a moment of personal darkness, and his eyes drifted off to the side. "When young girls are led astray from The Way, their transgressions impact so many for decades. One sinful action can produce thousands of hours of anguish...." Bartosh fell silent for another long moment before regaining his focus and turning back to Jane. "I put full blame on the secular elitist society for creating this soil in our culture that allows a group such as A.C.U.S. to conceive their madness. *They don't have the heartbeat!* The power of the secular media to impose a Godless message on our youth is truly unforgivable. They wrap their message in a seductive package that most young girls cannot resist! Exactly what message are the perpetrators of smut and carnal lust sending to young girls when they represent youngsters as harlots or glorify drug addicts? You can't walk into a store these days without being bombarded with a visual reminder that young, innocent girls are sold as a public commodity for the prurient enjoyment of those who lack discernment and self-discipline. There was a time when there would be an outcry if a girl of eighteen were sexualized in public. Now, a child as young as twelve can be exploited in the media and no one thinks twice about that kind of sickness. When a nation turns a blind eye to rampant exploitation of innocence and then encourages it by purchasing the smut, is it any wonder why a group like A.C.U.S. formed and appears to be flourishing with unrepentant abandon?"

"Have you alerted the authorities about A.C.U.S.?"

"*Secular* authorities?" Bartosh asked with disgust. "Yes! You know what I was told? 'We'll check into it.' Well, good for them! That means we can look forward to at least another ten years of bureaucracy before someone saves those innocent young girls! *I* go to the people who I *know* can spread the word and make a *real* difference! Members of our Congregation have invested nothing less than their *souls* in this Divine Mission. I've told them that it is a mandate from God and will be a Crusade like none they have ever seen! *We are in the fight for our final redemption.*" Bartosh took a deep breath. "If we lose this fight, the hammer of God will fall, Lucifer will rule, and darkness will engulf this earth, erasing the beloved blood sacrifice of our Lord, Jesus Christ." Bartosh sat back, seemingly spent from the enormity of what he had just shared with Jane.

Jane dutifully jotted down his words on her notepad, nodding her head.

Bartosh leaned forward, his hands tightly clasped. "Hear, O heavens, and give ear, O earth: for the LORD hath spoken, I have nourished and brought up children, and they have rebelled against me." Bartosh recited the words with an unflagging flair, as if he penned them himself. "Ah sinful nation, a people laden with iniquity, a seed of evildoers, *children that are corrupters*: they have forsaken the *Lord*, they have provoked the Holy One of Israel unto anger, *they are gone away backward*." Bartosh took another meaningful, deep breath. "Isaiah, Chapter one. Verses two and four, respectively."

Jane let the moment reverberate before speaking. "This is why I bring a recorder. These moments need to be captured on tape in order to appreciate their magnitude."

Bartosh settled back, grasping the arms of the chair with white-knuckled tension. "Do you believe in signs, Mrs. Lightjoy?"

What a question, Jane thought. Her mind drifted for a split second to the snakestone and the hawk. "Of course."

Bartosh proceeded to blame the secular elitists for everything from teaching evolution theory in grade school to premarital sex and bestiality. "What is the result of this secular sadism? Christians have become the most persecuted people on this earth. The wonder-working power of Jesus is defiled. His sacrifice is spit upon. We cannot depend upon the sideliners to bring the children back to Him." Bartosh was clearly on a roll. For the next ten minutes he gave Jane one example after another of secular sadism. There was the demonstration by the American Atheists in New Canaan, Connecticut, against the crèche, claiming that the image stirred violence because it encouraged disturbed people to enter the neighborhood and destroy it. "So, the answer is to have no crèche at all so we don't attract destructive perpetrators! If I were to apply that kind of logic to life in general, I would stop eating so I don't incur the wrath of those who have no food!" Jane had to smile at the wry comment. The examples continued. In one Texas school, no one was allowed to exchange Christmas cards. In Northern California, no Christmas hymns were allowed to be sung at a holiday pageant. "They cry from the rooftops, 'It's a violation of the separation of Church and State!' And I respond that it is a violation to separate God from His people in the name of secular propriety!" Bartosh pounded his fist on the coffee table to emphasize his point. *"The change must take place with our children.* If they are not taught to fear God and worship His name, we are destined to live in the abyss and subsist on the pustules of Lucifer for eternity." Bartosh once again leaned forward, his piercing blue eyes boring holes in Jane. "Are *you* raising your children to fear Him?"

"Absolutely," Jane said with unflinching commitment.

"Do you have any daughters?"

Jane figured it was best to stay out of that dubious loop. "No. Two sons."

"God has blessed you."

"Were you and your wife so blessed?"

A dour look befell Bartosh. "Yes. A daughter." His ruddy cheeks flushed suddenly with an angry crimson cast. "But she's no longer with us."

"No longer—"

"She's in Lucifer's hands now," he said with a terse upturn of his voice.

"I'm...so sorry," Jane said as she watched Bartosh's eyes drift to the floor in a solemn yet odd, unsettling manner.

In a faraway stare, he looked up at the picture of Jesus, knocking on the wooden door. "The Lord will knock on the door of your heart and all you need to do is answer and obey His Law. Those who refuse will experience the hammer of God and live forever in the pit of darkness." For a moment, tears welled up in his eyes. It was a startling human moment Jane did not expect. Bartosh swallowed hard and pressed the memory deep into his gut. He regained control and sat up with newfound conviction. "Christians kept quiet for so long and played the passive role. Turning the other cheek! That just allowed the secular Humanists to view us as doormats. But they don't anymore! We are a powerful, unified group of people with a common cause! I was telling the Brother-hood Council this morning that *we have to ratchet up our ministry to a new level!* We will no longer seek *tolerance* toward us. *Tolerance* is requested by those who are too weak to stand up and grab what already belongs to them by a Divine declaration! And that Divine declaration is the literal teachings from God in the Holy Bible! Congregation members have taken their rightful ownership of Jesus!"

Jane bristled at Bartosh's sanctimonious conviction. "Ownership?"

Bartosh explained that "ownership" entitled church members to proselytize with greater conviction. He sat back, satiated in his piety. "Do you know what I call our Congregation members?" Jane shook her head. "Motivators for Jesus!"

Jane recalled the term from the court files. "Motivators for Jesus. What an unusual terminology. Could you explain how one motivates for Jesus?"

Bartosh scowled at the question. "It's very simple. One's heart tells him."

"What if one man's heart says one thing, while another man's heart—"

"When Jesus' love fills your heart, the answer is always the same: spread His word and save the world from destruction! That's simple to do when you own Jesus!"

Jane shifted the conversation to Bartosh's psychology doctor-ate, only to learn that he did not acknowledge it. Psychology was part and parcel of the secular humanist decree; his theology doc-torate more closely affirmed his beliefs.

"I was ignorant of The Way at that time in my life. I came to know Jesus as my devout Savior and Lord when I was thirty-three—the same age that our Lord was crucified. Divine Irony, I always tell my Congregation. He died for me at thirty-three and I was reborn at that same age. Part of being reborn is starting fresh. Some people change their name; I decided to disassociate myself from my psychology degree, as I felt it was part of my past and lacking relevance for my life as a leader of a Church."

Jane was taken by Bartosh's statement, since it seemed he used the psychology doctorate to validate his services when asked to testify in court cases. "Isn't psychology useful for uncovering personality traits that can become destructive later in life?"

"Not the way the secular world practices it. They spend too much time making obscure associations that almost always have to do with sexual perversion or sexual abuse at a young age."

"You don't believe that sexual abuse can lead to sexual perversion later in life?" Jane asked, her mind using Lou Peters as a prime example.

"That's a secular argument. Expose two brothers to the same sexual abuse at a young age. One will come out unscathed and the other, a twisted killer."

Jane couldn't disagree. Then there were those who were exposed to abuse as she and her brother were and neither ended up on the wrong side of the law. As far as coming out "unscathed," well, that was a dicey determination. Jane felt comfortable enough to make a leap. "Have you ever had personal contact with anyone fitting that description?"

"What description?"

"A killer," Jane said in an offhand manner.

"No."

"With all your years of ministering, I assumed you'd meet a killer."

"No," Bartosh said with a definite shake of his head.

Jane couldn't let it go. "That's amazing."

"I assure you I have never been in the presence of a murderer. Now, our newsletter is sent to the incarcerated. Some of *them* may be of that ilk, but I have no personal relationship with them. We also have our Ministry Forum on the Internet. It connects brothers and sisters who are shut-ins, or in hospice, or in prison, as well as anyone in the Congregation who wishes to discuss timely matters of our faith."

"How do you justify the secular quality of using the Internet?"

"I gave that question soulful prayer. After much thought, I realized God wanted the Forum. When I received that word, I had no choice but to follow His wishes."

Jane wasn't sure how God expressed interest in the Congregation going online, but she figured she'd let that question ride. She recognized an emerging pattern with Dr. John Bartosh: his tenacious, fundamental belief centered upon his direct line to Jesus. That heavenly connection allowed for any number of services, publications, and the like to come into fruition. In Bartosh's eyes, "The Great Commission of Christ" demanded that he be the middleman for Jesus, a translator of His wishes for those whose ears weren't as finely tuned to the bigger heavenly plan.

Ingrid quietly padded into the room, carrying a handful of newsletters. "I don't want to interrupt you two," she said, gently crossing to Jane and handing her the reading material. "I've included issues of timely importance from the most recent to when we first started our newsletter almost sixteen years ago in California."

Jane glanced at the newsletter's bold name: **THE CONGREGATION CHRONICLE**. Underneath, the subtitle read, WE ARE WARRIORS FOR JESUS!

"I'm still learning my way around the Forum," Bartosh interjected. "That's why I put Ingrid in charge of monitoring the daily traffic. We call her the 'Matron of the Forum.'"

"Monitoring?" Jane speculated that the Ministry Forum was about as exciting as dry toast. Still, she maintained her plastic smile of appreciation. "Sounds wonderful."

"It's another way The Lamb of God can spread The Word," Bartosh said in a self-satisfied tone. "Often, we see members who print on the Forum—"

"You mean *post*, dear," Ingrid tenderly corrected her husband.

"Right, *post* on the Forum. I often see names of those who have moved away, are in hospice, and so forth, and am more than happy to respond to their questions and faith-related concerns. We have a Congregation brother in Chicago named Thomas, another brother, Matthew, in South Dakota, I believe. Ah, Manuel, Simon, Phillip...."

Jane noticed that, aside from Manuel, all the names belonged to the Disciples. She wanted to ask if Judas was on the Forum, but decided against it. "How ironic," she said instead, "most share their names with the Apostles."

"No irony. As I said earlier, when one is reborn into the true faith of God, you cast off the old world. For some, that means changing their names to align with the heartbeat of true Christianity."

"Who chooses the name?" Jane asked.

"They do, of course. They choose a Biblical surname that resonates with their new identity."

"Did you change *your* name?"

"No. I was blessed with the name John. Of all the names, it's the one I would happily choose. I have always had an affinity for John the Baptist."

"Why is that?"

"His faith was as strong as mine. He was willing to sacrifice it all—his body...his life...to serve Jesus." Bartosh soulfully spoke from the depths of his heart. "I resonate with his unyielding conviction. My devotion to Jesus, Mrs. Lightjoy, is unwavering. One is only as strong as his faith. It defines you. It motivates you. It narrows your perception to what is ultimately required for your own salvation. Some might say I have tunnel vision when it comes to my beliefs. I say, so be it when our Lord Jesus is standing at the end of that tunnel."

There were a few thoughtful moments of silence before Ingrid's soft voice broke the solemnity. "It looks like you need a refill on your coffee, Jackie."

Ingrid reached for the cup just as Jane put her hand on the saucer. The joint encounter forced the remaining coffee to spill over Jane's skirt. Jane quickly stifled a crude exclamation as she recovered the cup.

"Oh, my goodness, Jackie!" Ingrid said with genuine concern. "I'm so sorry! It's my fault! Let me help you!"

"It's fine. Don't worry," Jane said, more interested in continuing the interview.

"Perhaps Mrs. Lightjoy can attend to the spill in our lavatory," Bartosh advised.

"Really, it's not a problem," Jane assured them. "We have so much more——"

"We can't have you walking around with a nasty stain on your skirt!" Ingrid said. "The bathroom's just down the hall."

Jane realized these people weren't used to hearing the word "No." With reluctance, she followed Ingrid across the family room and down a narrow, dark hallway lined with more portraits of Jesus and a dense grouping of photos. The bathroom was equally suffocating. With only one small window over the bathtub, the room felt like a tomb—a musty, pink-walled, Christian-themed catacomb with plaques of Biblical verses and guest towels embroidered with blue crosses and the words JESUS SAVES. Jane tried to imagine what it was like to live in this house. She'd been there for less than forty-five minutes and she could feel the stranglehold of religious judgment cutting off her natural spontaneity. To grow up in such an environment would be akin to a slow, deliberate ache administered directly to one's heart. As the thought crossed her mind, Jane recalled Bartosh's comment of his daughter, a girl "no longer with us" and "in Lucifer's hands." There was something unsettling about the way he talked about his nameless child and the distant look that came over him and then angrily vanished.

Jane heard the muffled ring of a telephone and felt an urgent need to get back to continue the interview. She quickly tossed tap water on her skirt to dilute the coffee stain, sopped up the moisture with one of the "Jesus Saves" guest towels, and returned to the darkened hallway.

Midway down the hall on the left wall, Jane noted a three-foot square collage of photos attached with plastic pins to a large cork-board. She moved closer to the photos, straining to make out the faces in the faded light. Many of the photos were taken in Big Sur, California, and the roaring surf could be seen in the background. There were numerous five-by-seven photos, formal group shots of Congregation members with dates below each photograph. Jane stole a quick look down the hallway. She could hear Bartosh talking to someone on the telephone. His tone suggested that he was counseling the individual. Turning her attention back to the photos, she searched the crush of smiling faces and landed on the one face she was most interested in: Lou Peters.

There was Lou standing with a group of twenty girls and a few boys in front of an old cabin. The bottom of the photo read LAMB OF GOD YOUTH GROUP—PICO BLANCO, EASTER HOLIDAY, 1990. This was the youth group Charles Sawyer mentioned and the cabin was most likely the same cabin where Ashlee was murdered only a few months after this photo was taken. Jane moved closer, getting a better look at Lou. He wore a plain white T-shirt and faded jeans. His tanned, muscular arms wrapped covetously around two smiling, young teenage girls who stood on either side of him. Lou did indeed remind Jane of a model with his engaging grin and penetrating blue eyes. As an avid student of body language, Jane couldn't help but analyze the photo for anything unusual. Lou's posture was confident, with the enticing tilt of his body toward the camera. The girls on either side of him looked about thirteen years old and the epitome of virginal innocence. Jane snuck another look down the hallway to make sure she was still alone. She could still hear Bartosh's muted voice on the telephone. Looking back at the photo, Jane noticed that everyone looked genuinely happy except for two girls standing in the front row. They were around thirteen or fourteen years old. Both had brown hair and were neatly dressed in jeans and long-sleeved shirts. But in Jane's eyes, their posture gave them away. Jane read it as reticence textured with anger. Or was it fear? Whatever it was, their body language clearly demonstrated that they didn't feel comfortable.

Jane detected that one side of the photo showed a skirting image of a girl's left arm. Running her fingers along the edge of the photo, she could see that part of the photo had been purposely tucked underneath an adjoining photo on the corkboard. A quick overview of the other photos showed that none of them overlapped. Jane pulled the pins from the photo and held it under the best light available. Jane was instantly drawn to the girl. She was seventeen or eighteen, by Jane's guess, with a slim build and penetrating eyes. Her long brown hair fell past her shoulders, framing a narrow face that seemed both tired and agitated. Whoever she was, she did not look like she belonged in the photo. She had a cocksure stance that, coupled with that enigmatic stare, made her a force to be reckoned with. It was as if she was imparting a secret message with her steely glare. She reminded Jane of herself at that age—chock-full of attitude and brimming with rage. Jane instantly felt that familiar tightening in her belly that signaled a significant moment. It was the same feeling Charles Sawyer talked about when he noted the shiny, green, micalike particle inside the condom.

Jane weighed the consequences of her next action. The hallway was dimly lit. The question of how detailed-oriented the Bartoshs were came into play. Jane made the split-second decision and quickly rearranged the photos to fill in the missing gap. Just as she was pushing the last pin into the final photo, she heard footsteps padding toward the hallway. Jane turned and stealthily slid the stolen photograph down her shirt.

"Is everything all right?"

Jane turned around to find Ingrid staring back at her with a questioning look. "I think I got most of the stain out," Jane said. Ingrid was silent as she regarded Jane with an uneasy look. Jane's heart began to pound. "We should probably wrap up the interview so you two can get back to work," Jane said, walking toward Ingrid with the plastic smile firmly pasted across her face.

"My husband is occupied with an important call. He told me to wish you the best with your article and he looks forward to reading it when it's published."

That was that. Jane realized she was being summarily dismissed. There was no point in arguing. Bartosh had spoken and his will would be obeyed.

Jane collected her notebook, Congregation newsletters, and tape recorder and headed for the front door. "Thank you again for arranging this interview."

"It was my pleasure," Ingrid said, grabbing a tan jacket and slipping it on. "I'll walk you to your car."

A moment of tension gripped Jane. "Oh, you don't have to do that—"

"I always walk my guests to their car." Ingrid crossed to the front door.

Jane followed, feeling a mix of anger and frustration building inside her. Ingrid may have come off as sweet and gentle, she may acquiesce to her husband's wishes, but this was a woman who was also used to getting *her* way. What a formidable team the Bartoshs made, Jane thought. "I parked up the block more than halfway," Jane offered.

"Exercise is good for the soul," Ingrid piously replied as she started up the block.

They walked in silence. Jane peered into the distance toward her Mustang. She was fairly certain that Kit was still prone on the backseat. A million diversionary tactics swarmed in Jane's head, most of which included chokeholds and takedowns. Sadly, those would not work in this situation.

Jane's mind was still spinning when Ingrid spoke up. "May I ask you something?"

Jane's gut seized up. "Yes, of course."

"Did you notice a profound change in your niece's personality?"

Jane felt a momentary release of tension. "I don't know for sure. I only get to visit my sister once or twice a year, so—"

"People don't go from good to bad overnight, Jackie" Ingrid interrupted, staring straight ahead. She appeared to be searching desperately for personal answers.

"Well, let's see," Jane said, using the opportunity to stop walking. "We visited with the family this past summer and...yes...yes, I did notice changes in Janie."

"Was she more introverted? Did she stay in her room most of the time? Was she agitated at the slightest things?" Ingrid's tenor was plaintive.

Jane looked at Ingrid and the pieces clicked. The reason Ingrid granted her the interview was because she felt she had found a kindred spirit in suffering. "Is that how your daughter acted before she died?" Ingrid's eyes welled with tears as she sadly nodded. "She was seventeen?"

"Yes," Ingrid whispered, the pain of that memory still raw. "Children are God's greatest gift. He only honored us with one child and we did everything to raise her so she would know His love and follow The Way. But she was a defiant one from the moment she took her first breath. She questioned us *all the time*. As you can imagine, that didn't go over well with my husband." Jane vicariously liked this girl. "She had sort of calmed down and we thought she was on a better road, and then she became a teenager and everything fell apart. By the time she turned fourteen, it was all we could do to deal with her willfulness. We prayed, but she just got angrier and more out of control. I kept encouraging her to let God into her heart, but she'd have none of it." Ingrid's voice became agitated. "I couldn't understand why she wouldn't let Him in! She was just too obstinate for her own good!" Ingrid's mind drifted faraway.

"How did she die?" Jane carefully inquired. Ingrid remained in a daze. "Ingrid?"

Ingrid turned back to Jane with a foggy countenance. "She just left. One day she was here and then she wasn't."

For Jane, talking to Ingrid was like interrogating an uncooperative witness. "I'm sorry. I don't understand. She left?"

Ingrid looked off to the side, pulling up the memory. "She was gone less than a day when I emptied the trash basket in her bedroom. That's when I found it. I didn't know what it was. And I certainly never thought my seventeen-year-old daughter would!"

"What did you find?" Jane asked, more like herself than Jackie Lightjoy.

"A pregnancy test," Ingrid stated, loathing each word. "And it was positive."

Jane finally understood all the circumventing. The Bartoshs' daughter was "dead" as in "dead to her faith."

Ingrid stared into the distance. "She turned from God and chose to follow the path of sin. For my husband...for us...she was doomed. She had allowed herself to be taken in by the dark forces."

Jane had heard a lot of appalling family sagas during her tenure as a detective. But getting pregnant out of wedlock at seventeen didn't rank high on her "tragic" scale. However, for the Bartoshs, it was obvious that a pregnant daughter was a stab in the back and a slap in the face for all they stood for. To them, their daughter might as well have robbed a bank and killed a cop. "You haven't talked to her since then?"

"No. The phone has rung a few times over the years and I've answered it to find air on the other end. One time, I said, 'Mary? Is that you?' But there was no response."

"Mary. Pretty name."

"We named her after Mary, the mother of God. *The virgin.* But it seems her namesake turned out to be Mary Magdalene!" Jane waited for Ingrid to add "*the whore,*" but she opted to silently infer that with the raise of an eyebrow. A chilled gust of wind kicked around them, signaling an approaching storm. "We need to get you to your car!"

"Why don't you go back to the house? I'm fine," Jane urged.

Ingrid started up the block. "I always walk my guests to their car."

Jane countered with a quick diversion. "Looks like we're in for a storm!" She yelled the comment louder than necessary. Ingrid regarded Jane with an odd look.

"Appears so," Ingrid said quietly.

Jane spoke again, this time even louder, hoping that Kit would wake up and hide. "Are we supposed to get snow?" They were within ten feet of the Mustang.

Ingrid was puzzled by Jane's loud voice. "I don't know. Maybe."

Jane decided to take aggressive action. She moved toward the driver's side and stood in front of the backseat window, doing her best to casually block Ingrid's view. "Well, once again, thank you for arranging all of this!"

Ingrid's eyes fell past Jane and into the backseat. "Well, my, my." Jane remained unmoved, even though her heart pounded out of control. "Looks like you've got an extra load."

Jane turned around. Now her heart raced faster. Kit was gone.

"That's quite a heap of luggage you're carrying," Ingrid offered.

Jane's eyes drifted to the pavement. Next to the left front tire she saw a small pool of vomit that trailed around the hood of the Mustang. Surreptitiously, Jane skirted the immediate area for any sign of Kit. But there was nothing.

"Yes," Jane said halfheartedly. "I really should be going. Thank you again." Jane unlocked the car door, eyes eagerly scanning the neighborhood. Once inside the Mustang, she started the ignition and looked out the window to where Ingrid was still standing. "Bye!" Jane said, wondering why in the hell Ingrid was still standing there. Ingrid took a few steps back and gave a little wave but stayed in place. Pulling onto the tree-lined street, Jane trolled up the block. Checking in her rearview mirror, there was Ingrid, *still* standing and waving. "Goddammit!" Jane said under her breath, her mind racing with awful scenarios that involved Kit. She crawled up the street another two hundred feet.

That's when she saw it.

CHAPTER 13

It was just a quick flash of purple, but Jane quickly identified it. That type of billowing clothing only belonged to one person.

The dark plum fabric from Kit's left trouser leg stuck out from an oak on the right-hand side of the street. Jane tapped the accelerator, cruising toward the tree. There was Kit, her back flattened against the front of the tree, doing her best to hide from Ingrid. Her long braid had bits of bark and leaves stuck to it and her face was ghostly pale. For an instant, Jane noted a faint sense of disorientation coming from Kit. Checking the rearview mirror, Jane saw Ingrid inexplicably still standing in the street. But Jane's concern for Kit superseded the need for secrecy. She hit the brakes and motioned for Kit to get in the car. Kit shook her head and waved Jane onward with a flick of her wrist. Jane checked the rearview mirror again. Ingrid was in the same spot.

"Shit!" Jane exclaimed. Leaning over to the passenger side, she rolled down the window. "Kit! Get in the car!"

"Is she still back there?" Kit asked, coming back to her senses.

"We're far enough away! She can't tell it's you! Get in!"

"No," Kit quietly replied, her voice weak, "We can't risk it! Drive 'round the block and pick me up here in ten minutes." Kit choked on a rattled cough. "Go on!"

"You're sick! She can't tell who the hell you are from this distance! Now get your ass in the car or I'm coming out to get you!" Jane unlocked the passenger door and pushed it wide open.

"Goddammit, Jane!" She hesitated briefly and then made a beeline for the Mustang, keeping her back to Ingrid. Once inside, she slammed the door. "Drive!"

Jane accelerated, checking her rearview mirror. Ingrid was still there.

"I saw vomit around the side of the car! What happened?"

"It's nothing."

"The hell it's nothing! *What happened?*"

"I woke up and felt nauseous. It happens occasionally. I've learned that if I can get up and walk in the fresh air, it subsides. So that's what I did. I had every intention of getting back in the car before you showed up, but...." Kit turned away, trying to gather her thoughts. "I thought I saw someone...."

"Who?" Jane asked, concerned.

Kit looked out the window, sadness briefly engulfing her. "I was mistaken."

Jane finally reached the end of the block and turned. "Well, it's good you didn't get back in the car. Ingrid would have seen you for sure. She walked me all the way to the car. Some kind of odd Christian courtesy."

Kit smiled. "My special Guides were obviously watching out for me."

"Huh?"

"They knew I couldn't be seen by Ingrid and so they designed an opportunity for me to get out of that car. It's just fascinating...." Kit's eyes twinkled at a private memory.

Jane tried to think of any way to help Kit. "Maybe if you'd do some cancer drugs, you wouldn't get sick like this."

"I won't poison my body."

"But you could lengthen your life."

"You mean like buy myself another six months? I don't need six months."

Jane found the comment odd. "You don't need—? What?"

"I don't need six months," Kit repeated, more to herself.

"What *do* you need?" Jane asked, feeling more than a little confused.

"I need...my balls." Jane regarded Kit with a questioning look. "*My spirulina energy balls!* Where are they?" Jane directed her to the backseat. Kit eagerly grabbed the bag and brought out two dark green balls the size of kumquats. "Here, try one!"

"No, thanks."

"You've got a long drive. They'll give you tremendous energy! *Here!*" Jane reluctantly took the spirulina ball and popped it into her mouth. "Not bad, huh?" Kit questioned as she happily took a bite from the remaining health treat.

"Yeah, tasteless algae has always been a personal favorite," Jane replied, swallowing hard to get the gooey mess past her throat.

Jane's cell phone rang. She retrieved it from her bag and snuck a look at the caller ID. It was Sergeant Weyler. Jane snapped the phone shut and tossed it into her bag.

"Who is it?" Kit asked.

"Nobody."

"Who is it?"

Jane let out a tired sigh. "Sergeant Weyler. He's my old boss at DH."

"Did you tell him about my case?"

"Of course not!"

"Is he a good man?"

"*Weyler?* Yeah, of course he's a good man."

"Trustworthy?"

"Top-of-the-line trustworthy. Why?"

"Maybe he can help us. You know, documents, information—"

"Whoa! *I* am working this case for you! I don't need Weyler!"

"Why so defensive? Do you respect this man?"

"Absolutely!"

"Then we shouldn't discard him out of hand in case he could be of assistance!"

"I am *not* talking to Weyler! Period! End of sentence. Case closed."

Kit observed Jane like a suspect. "Why are you so afraid to talk to him?"

Jane told Kit about Weyler's offer to return to DH as a sergeant.

"'Sergeant Perry calling from Denver Headquarters,'" Kit enthusiastically mimicked. "I think it's got a helluva nice ring to it! Call him back and say yes."

"You don't think I can make it on my own?" Jane was seriously insulted.

"Stop acting like a child! You can make it on your own, but maybe you can make it *better* in a larger organization and with the support of this Sergeant Weyler. And I bet they give you one helluva good dental plan!"

"Kit, enough!"

Kit finished her spirulina ball and changed the subject, wanting to know what happened with Bartosh and if he was still practicing paint-by-numbers piety.

"It went fine. He felt my article was a sign from God."

"What happens when your article never appears in the magazine?"

"*C'est la vie*, as they say in France," Jane replied in a cavalier tone.

"Well, 'Cover your ass,' as they say in the U.S. You should call him back to follow-up with more questions. Makes the whole thing look aboveboard. Then maybe a call down the road to say the article's not going to happen. Blame it on your editor."

"Shit happens. Stories get shelved all the time." Jane gunned the Mustang onto I-70, heading westbound. "Did you know the Bartoshs had a daughter named Mary?"

"No. Why?"

"She left home at seventeen quite suddenly. She was pregnant."

Kit turned to Jane, stunned. "Bartosh told you this?"

"No. Ingrid."

"Where'd she go?"

"Who knows. They haven't heard a word from her since she left."

Kit tried to piece together a timeline. "She must have left before Lou's trial, because I never saw any teenage girl that belonged to the Bartoshs in the courtroom."

Jane weighed the pros and cons of her next move and decided it was worth the risk. She dug the five-by-seven photo out of her shirt and handed it to Kit. "Take a look at the girl on the far left-hand side."

Kit's eyes bugged out. "Where did you get this?"

"It was one of many photos in a collage in their hallway—"

"You *stole* this photo?!"

"That hallway was so dark, you couldn't see your future. They'll never miss it!"

"Jane P., they *will* miss this!"

"You don't understand the feeling when your gut twists and you just know you're on to something but you can't put your finger right on it—"

"You mean it felt *hinky*?"

Jane was seriously taken aback. It was the last word she ever thought Kit would bandy around, let alone use correctly in a sentence. "Yeah...*exactly*...that's exactly it."

Kit seemed satisfied by Jane's response and studied the photo. "Okay. So, what about the girl on the far left side?"

"How old is she?"

"Sixteen.... Maybe seventeen."

"I'm saying seventeen. What do you bet that's Mary?"

Kit looked closer at the photo, this time with more interest. "It could be anyone."

"Look closely. She's got Ingrid's features. And just that part of the photo where she appears was covered up." Jane started factoring the timeline in her head. If Mary was seventeen in that photo, then she left home in 1990. Since Kit didn't see her at Lou's trial, Jane figured Mary left home sometime between Easter and that summer.

Kit saw the written reference to Pico Blanco on the photo. "That's the cabin."

Jane inwardly grimaced. She kicked herself mentally for forgetting the significance of the cabin and handing it to Kit. "Here," she said, reaching for the photo.

"No," Kit said, holding on tightly to the photo. Her eyes fixated on Lou. "You see how handsome he is? Is it any wonder he enticed girls?" Kit fell into a trancelike state. "I wonder what he looks like now. He was clean-shaven with an army haircut at the bond hearing last year. Prison took away some of his youthfulness. But he still had that blue-eyed come hither look that traps and tricks the unsuspecting child...."

Jane gently took the photo out of Kit's hand, securing it in her satchel. "I'm sorry."

"So many memories...." Kit contained her emotions and asked what Jane thought of Bartosh. When Jane said she agreed with much of what he said in relation to the sexualizing of young girls, Jane noted how Kit took it as a blatant defense of a man she could never respect.

"I don't buy the religious end," Jane argued, "but I agree with him when he talks about how young girls are enticed to act older and sexier than they should. It sets the stage for chaos and sexual predators. Sexual predators are always looking for the perfect victim."

Kit bristled. *"Perfect victim?"*

Jane took it down a notch. "A cop sees three types of people in this world: victims, predators, and none of the above. Victims put off an energy—" Jane knew she was treading on dangerous ground. She didn't want to dredge up more painful memories for Kit. But she wished she could explain clearly what her years as a cop had proven to her: some people put off either a conscious or unconscious vibe to predators. Her experience showed that there was always an inherent weakness in the victim. The predator hones in on that weakness and takes full advantage of it. Sometimes, that weakness was sheer ignorance; ignorance that provocative clothing, actions, or behavior tripped a predator's senses. It didn't mean the crime was justified. But from Jane's perspective, there were many cases where the victim was either drunk, stoned, in known dangerous locations, or fraternizing with people who had, in Jane's estimation, obvious criminal intent. But to try and explain this to Kit was pointless. And the last thing Jane wanted to do was give Kit the impression that Ashlee asked for what she got.

"Are you talking about free spirits?" Kit asked.

Jane couched her response carefully. "To a sexual predator, a 'free spirit' is asking for it, *especially* if the predator is coming from some warped religious point of view. Bartosh made a comment that I agree with: 'Where there's no self-discipline there's no self-rule.' Self-rule and self-discipline work both ways. Free spirits usually don't have either."

"What do you suggest we do? Shove everyone into a box and crush their vitality, only letting them out to breathe and stretch before slamming them back in the box? Isn't that what *Bartosh* tells parents to do with their children? Create little robotic drones who can't think for themselves, let alone act without first consulting with the Great Master in Grand Junction? That technique obviously didn't work on his own kid!"

"There's a place between the box and infinity, Kit."

Kit considered Jane's words. "Children should be allowed to make mistakes and not pay with their lives as punishment."

"That reasoning works in a perfect world. Charlotte Walker made a conscious decision to look a certain way when she left her house on December 25—"

"That's an unfair statement, Jane!"

"You watched that goddamned birthday video, what? A hundred times? Did you really *look* at it with an eye of perception? I bet Charlotte knows how to get exactly what she wants. She learned how to use a wink, a smile, a turn of her head to get attention from boys. I imagine there are a lot of teenage boys in Oakhurst, California, who could tell me how hard it is to keep their dicks soft around her."

"You're walking a fine line right now, Jane P. When you insult Charlotte like that, you insult my Ashlee and her memory!"

This was exactly the reaction Jane wanted to avoid. "I am not disrespecting Ashlee's memory." Jane reworked her approach.

"Look, what I'm saying is that Mrs. Walker doesn't get it. I've seen a million Charlottes. No dad in her life—"

"You don't know that for sure—"

"Trust me, she's an only child with a single working mom. Close ties to *female* family members. Remember Aunt Donna who ran the video? Where were the men in that video?"

"It was a five minute clip. You can't delineate Charlotte's life based on that!

"I'd bet you a million bucks that when I probe into this kid's world, there will be an *insignificant* number of men in her life compared to women. No men. No positive male role models. No balance." Jane could feel herself melting into Charlotte's private world. "Mrs. Walker lets her kid dress and act older than her years because, bless her ignorant soul, she would rather be Charlotte's best friend than her parent. The irony is, deep down, Charlotte doesn't want her mother to be her best friend. *She* wants her to be her *mother.* And what Charlotte doesn't realize is that Mom is vicariously living through her daughter. She thinks it's cool when Charlotte dresses up in her red jacket and tight jeans and the boys stare at her. Because before Charlotte's mom packed on the extra hundred pounds, she was quite the looker and the boys loved her. But her looks faded. She got hard, and after the boys and men left her, Charlotte's mom decided to hate men because, in her mind, men are just fucked up, useless trash. Sperm donors. Heavy lifters. But to little Charlotte, men are a mystery. They're a color she's never seen. So she goes out looking. But she goes out with only half the information in her hip pocket. She doesn't know who she is because we are only as strong as where we come from and who rocked our cradle. She's missing half the puzzle—*a father.* She unconsciously searches for that missing puzzle piece. But because she's so needy and desperate for that male energy, she thinks that all guys want to help her and be her friend. *That's* the vibe that attracts the predator. But she doesn't recognize the monster when he pulls up and says, 'Need a ride?'"

Kit took it all in before speaking. "Well, your theory doesn't wash completely. My Ashlee had a father!"

"Was he present in her life?"

"Paul was a good provider—"

"You didn't answer my question. Was there any emotional involvement?"

"Paul is complicated. He prefers to take the path of least resistance. I'd say he is emotionally challenged. Now more than ever."

"So Paul wasn't a strong presence in Ashlee's life. Doesn't that fit what I said? Physical or emotional absence, it makes no difference. Mom was the strong one."

"I wouldn't call Barbara strong. I'd call her reliable. Structured. Unbending. Unforgiving. Hateful...." Kit's voice trailed off. "Nobody tells Barbara what to do. I think Paul decided it was easier to just go along rather than argue with her." Kit looked at Jane. "What about you? Did you have a strong father figure?"

Jane moved into the fast lane and accelerated to eighty-five miles per hour as she neared the Colorado/Utah border. "Strong in what sense? Physical strength? Yeah, in spades. Strong in the emotional sense...no."

"Yes, we touched on this briefly in your office. Your childhood wasn't comforting."

Jane shook her head at Kit's careful adjective. "My brother and I shared a childhood that was as comforting as fingernails scraping across a chalkboard."

"You mentioned there was physical abuse. What happened?"

"This is not about me."

"You were a victim, Jane. And your father was a predator. So, based on what you've told me, what weakness did your father see in *you* that sparked his rage?"

"I am *not* a victim! I'm a survivor—"

"Who began as a victim! What did you represent to your father?" Kit wasn't going to let it go. "You *had* to represent something to him for him to go off on you!"

"I won't be psychologically analyzed with bumper sticker philosophies!"

"*I* think it's a question worth investigating! You talk about patterns. You're right. We all have patterns we repeat. You spend *so* much time analyzing and observing others, but you've never taken the time to observe yourself! Isn't that part of the AA platform? 'Make a searching and fearless moral inventory.' Step Three, is it?"

"Step Four," Jane said, pulling in her emotional wall.

"But that's where you get stuck, right?" There was a sting in Kit's voice.

Jane accelerated to ninety miles per hour. There was stony silence until, "I'm going to say it once and then we're never gonna talk about it again. I got beatings all the time protecting my little brother because that's what my mother asked me to do on her deathbed. I would have died for my brother and I nearly did one night when I was fourteen. My dad dragged me out to his workshop behind the house and beat me with his belt and punched me until I fell against his worktable and cracked my head open." Jane pointed to a visible scar on her right temple. "So I figured one of us needed to die. I grabbed a gun that was on the table and pointed it at him. I should have shot the son of a bitch, but I froze. And that cost me." Jane revved the Mustang past ninety-five miles per hour. "He beat me to the ground and then kicked me in my groin until I passed out. I woke up alone, still on that same floor and soaked in my own blood. I didn't get help because my dad was a cop and I knew if I told anybody, he'd kill me the next time. And as much as I wanted to die, I couldn't risk it because I'd promised my mother I'd take care of my brother. And you see, Kit, I keep my promises, no matter the cost. So there it is. My dad was a fucking, twisted nutcase. But he's a fucking *dead* nutcase now thanks to a stroke and a boozed up liver." Jane's voice was taut with bile. She moved uncomfortably. "I want to get out of this outfit and get a smoke. There's a gas station and convenience store up ahead. We're stopping."

Kit remained silent as Jane exited the off-ramp and cruised to a stop in front of the store. After filling the tank with gas, Jane grabbed her jeans and shirt and headed into the store. Ducking into the bathroom, she quickly changed clothes and then returned to the cashier's station. For a brief moment, her eyes scanned the magazine rack. She was suddenly aware of one cover shot after another of young girls in alluring poses and pouty close-ups.

"Can I help you?" the clerk asked.

Jane looked up in a slight daze. "Yeah, thirty bucks for the gas and a pack of Marlboros."

The clerk took Jane's money, handed her the cigarettes, and then clicked the MUTE button on the TV remote to turn on the volume.

"We're here in Oakhurst, California with Clinton Fredericks...."

Jane immediately focused on the television when she heard the name.

"For those of you who are unaware, Fredericks is a self-proclaimed 'Gonzo' crime profiler," the reporter continued. "A guy who likes to put himself firmly into the center of the action in many of the most disturbing cases. He's the author of three bestselling books, including *Profile of a Killer*, which is based on the infamous—and some say tragic—capture of Rudy Weiss. Thanks for joining us, Mr. Fredericks!"

As Jane stared at the TV screen, a foreboding suspicion came over her. The camera cut to the forty-something Clinton Fredericks, seated outside of what looked like a fast-food restaurant on the main drag in Oakhurst. He was dressed in drab olive slacks, a well-worn crewneck sweater, and a battered navy rain slicker. Fredericks looked as if he were reporting from the front line of a war-torn, Third World country. His intense blue eyes sparked to life the minute the camera hit him. "Media whore." That's what went through Jane's mind when Fredericks addressed the reporter.

"Good to be here!" Fredericks responded, dragging his thick fingers through his already tousled dirty blond hair. "I want everyone to know that I'm working exclusively with Charlotte's mother and all those who love this child and want her safely returned to her happy home and the bosom of her dear mother. I made a personal promise to Mrs. Walker today. And that promise was that I would do whatever it took to analyze this horrific kidnapping, profile the individual who took her child, and bring her beloved daughter back into her loving arms."

Jane tuned out Fredericks's brash voice. The Walker case was quickly turning into an uncontainable circus and Clinton Fredericks was the unofficial ringmaster. Based on what Jane knew about Fredericks's method of operation, Mrs. Walker had made a dangerous choice in allowing this egocentric, self-serving ass into her private world. As with all headline-making crime cases, the vultures were descending. But based on Clinton's dicey track record, *this* particular vulture could hasten Charlotte Walker's death.

If Jane was going to successfully work the Walker case, she would need to know how to stay four steps ahead of Clinton Fredericks. There was only one person who intimately knew how Fredericks operated. And he was less than eight hours away.

CHAPTER 14

Jane quickly inhaled sufficient nicotine into her lungs before getting back into the Mustang. "We've got a problem," she stated, peeling out of the gas station and heading back onto westbound I-70. "Clinton Fredericks is now part of the Walker team."

"Why is that name familiar?" Kit asked with a troubled look.

"Rudy Weiss? Eighteen months ago?"

"Right. The psycho who kidnapped that bank teller in rural Arkansas."

Jane nodded. "Fredericks profiled him, tracked Weiss to his backwoods trailer, and then negotiated one-on-one for three days on live TV with Weiss to let the woman go and give himself up."

Kit's eyes suddenly bugged out as she recalled the tragic ending. "That woman got killed!"

"Yeah. A lot of people blamed Fredericks's devil-may-care attitude for her death. He supposedly convinced the sheriff to storm the trailer. Weiss killed the woman when they blew down the door and nearly took his own life before they grabbed him."

"How did Fredericks get involved so quickly with Charlotte's kidnapping?"

"He's an opportunist asshole. He sees a headline story involving a missing girl, a bevy of cameras, and the chance to take center stage and redeem himself. Fredericks didn't waste a second getting in good with the mother. The idiot woman agreed to give him carte blanche on the case. She's so fucked and she doesn't even know it!"

"You think Fredericks could get Charlotte killed, don't you?"

"He's had eighteen months to think about what happened. Of course, he spent most of that time promoting his book on Rudy Weiss, doing guest spots on TV, and playing the cable news pundit.

I strongly doubt that Fredericks has spent much time evaluating his ego-driven need to become the story instead of report it."

"How does he work?"

"I have no idea." Jane hesitated slightly. "But I know somebody who does."

"Who?"

"My cousin, Carl. Carl Perry. His dad and my dad were brothers. We lost touch over fifteen years ago. The last time I saw him, he was a pothead, loved his tequila, and was hammering out stories for whatever underground rag he could get to print his shit."

"He's a writer?"

"Yeah. I guess he's pretty successful now. He writes for *Rolling Stone*. He's traveled around with tons of well-known people, usually rock stars. Probably has access to all the free dope he can smoke."

"How does Carl know Clinton Fredericks?"

"*Rolling Stone* hired Carl to do a story on him after the Rudy Weiss debacle. It was called 'Profile of a Profiler.' It didn't say much of anything new but I guess it gave Carl some credibility. I see his byline a lot. He left a message on my home phone to congratulate me after he saw me on *Larry King*. He'd also heard about my dad dying and wanting to send his condolences. I didn't call him back."

"How come?"

"I'm not a family-driven person. I don't have the need to sit around and trade stories of growing up with Cousin Carl."

"Is that because Cousin Carl's father reminded you of your own dad?"

"Oh, we're back to the psychological bullshit again, are we? Well, *no*. My uncle was the absolute opposite of my dad—passive as they come. Weak willed. Talked so quietly you could hardly hear him. He was also a hapless drunk, just like my father. Must run in the blood, eh? He crinked about ten years ago. Liver cancer."

"Deep-seated unresolved anger and guilt...." Kit replied.

"Huh?"

"Liver cancer. Your uncle must have buried some very deep and disturbing traumatic memories in his body."

"Well, he grew up with my father as his younger brother, so *anything* is possible!" Jane reported to Kit that she'd kept her cousin's phone number after he called and checked the area code out of curiosity. It turned out he lived thirty miles south of Las Vegas in the remote desert town of Jeffers. "I figure maybe I call him and ask to crash on his couch for the night."

"Crash on his couch...." Kit repeated with a twinkle in her eye. "It's been awhile since I 'crashed' on anyone's couch. Look forward to meeting your cousin."

"Yeah, right. You're just hoping to score some free pot!" Jane rummaged through her satchel and removed her address book. Finding Carl's name, she dialed his number.

He answered on the second ring. "This is Carl."

Jane was a bit uneasy. "Carl. Hi. It's Jane. Your cousin." The words staggered from her mouth in an uncomfortable rhythm.

"Well, *shit!* Jane Perry!" Carl replied, equally surprised. "What the fuck's up?"

Jane hated it when someone asked her *What's up?* "Oh, just life, you know."

"Yeah, I hear you!"

Jane surmised that given Carl's happy-go-lucky banter, he was probably tooting on a doobie as they spoke. "Listen, I know this is last minute and somewhat presumptuous on my part—"

"*Presumptuous?* Fuckin' big word!"

Yeah. Carl was stoned. Jane was sure of it. "Right. Look, I'm on the road and I'm going to be going through your neck of the woods tonight—"

"Nobody goes through my neck of the woods unless they're fuckin' lost! I live in Bum Fuck Egypt, cousin, and I like it that way. You can garden butt-ass naked in my front yard and nobody but a fuckin' coyote is gonna see you."

"Okay, you got me, Carl," Jane said, gritting her teeth. She hated conversing with people who were stoned. "I need to talk to

you about somebody you know." Jane hesitated but then revealed
Clinton's name.

"What the fuck do you want to know about him?"

"I'll tell you when I get there, which will be probably nine o'
clock tonight—"

"Say 10:30," Kit quickly interjected.

"Ah, how about 10:30? Is that too late?"

"Too late?" Carl guffawed. "Fuck! I don't get into my groove
until midnight! Sure! Look forward to it!"

Carl gave Jane directions to his remote desert house that included notations such as "Turn off the paved road" and "When
you see the rusty weather vane, you're about a mile from the
house." It appeared that "BFE" described his abode to a tee.

Jane said good-bye and clicked off her phone. "This should be
tedious," she remarked, musing over what to expect that evening.
"But I gotta do it."

Kit turned pensive. "We need to make one quick stop before
going to Carl's."

"Where's that?"

"Henderson, Nevada."

"Your daughter?"

Kit nodded. "It won't take long. I just need...." Kit took a deep,
meaningful breath. "I just need to do it. It's been over fourteen
years since I've seen her. I've talked to her on the phone maybe five
times. But the last call was a while back and it wasn't a good one.
She's just never forgiven me for what happened." Jane handed Kit
her cell phone and told her to call Barbara, but Kit pushed it away.
"No calls. If she knows we're coming, she'll leave. Trust me."

The two drove in contemplative silence for miles until Kit
squashed her buckwheat pillow against the side of the window
and drifted off to sleep. As they sped into Utah, the scenery drastically altered. It reminded Jane of what Mars might look like if
one could survive on that desolate planet. One monochromatic
landscape blended into another, only interrupted by patches of
snow that collected under the sagebrush. Fifty miles later, the

terrain turned magical as the ochre rocks rose like cathedrals intermingled with dustings of naturally-forming salt that powdered the territory as far the eye could see. Jane spotted the occasional crow perched on the highway guardrails, standing at attention like a sentinel. Ten miles later, another army of crows stood along the highway. Kit stirred just in time to see the gathering of black birds.

"Crows...." Kit muttered, half-asleep. "An omen of change," she whispered, shifting in the seat. "Forgive.... Don't fall into the darkness," she quietly said before drifting off to sleep again.

Jane regarded Kit with a questionable look. It was very odd. For the next sixty miles, there seemed to be a steady number of crows dotting the highway.

They passed Green River, Utah, and quickly rose in elevation, traveling across expansive mesas of striking red rock. There were more than 100 miles of nothing between Green River and Salina; a blur of high desert rock formations and the occasional Ranch Exit. After leaving Salina, Jane sped south on I-15 toward Richfield, and then fifty miles later ascended again in elevation toward Cove Fort, entering the land of pointy-tipped pines buried in three feet of snow. Jane and Kit ate a late lunch in Beaver, Utah, before powering on to St. George. Night fell too soon across the Utah landscape, with the accompanying glare of headlights as Jane tempted fate and topped speeds of over ninety-five miles per hour. The high speed allowed an arrival in Henderson, Nevada, thirty minutes earlier than expected. The bedroom community of Henderson had become a booming area to build mid-to-high-end development tracks so families could raise their children away from the steady din and bright lights of Sin City. But to Jane, it just seemed like another cluttered bastion of suburbia.

"It's changed a lot since I was here," Kit quietly said with an anxious edge.

"I thought you said you hadn't seen Barbara and Paul in over fourteen years."

"I haven't. But I came out here about seven years ago with a group of friends from Boulder who decided to fly out to Vegas for a long weekend. I rented a car and drove around Henderson by myself. I wanted to see where Paul worked and where they lived so I could have a better picture in my mind when I visualized them together. Do you mind if we go past Paul's automotive shop before going to the house?"

Jane agreed, turning the Mustang down a bustling street. They pulled up in the front lot of Automotive Specialists and parked the Mustang in the shadows, about thirty feet from the well-lit, glass-sided office that sat adjacent to the large vehicle facility. Jane and Kit could easily see Paul seated at his desk going over paperwork. Jane eyed the digital clock on the bank across the street. "Nine o' clock," Jane offered. "He keeps late hours."

Kit stared at Paul. "Yeah. Like I told you, Paul is a good provider. Always has been. But the late hours...I think it's worse than it used to be."

Jane took a gander at Paul. She figured he had to be in his early fifties, but the stark patches of gray that overtook his brown hair and swept across his weathered face made him look ten years older. Paul removed his eyeglasses and leaned back in his chair. After a moment, he fumbled under his desk and withdrew a bottle with an amber liquid inside. He poured a healthy quantity of the liquid into his coffee cup and took a meaningful sip. Jane was familiar with the MO. "That ain't apple juice."

"Shit," Kit whispered under her breath. "He was a teetotaler for as long as I knew him." Kit was desperate to reach out to Paul. "He's in such pain—"

"There's nothing you can do," Jane urged, but Kit already had her door open and one foot on the asphalt. The action caught Paul's attention. He stood up and strode his wiry frame to the door, opening it and squinting into the darkness.

"Who's there?" Paul yelled.

"It's me, Paul," Kit said tentatively. "Katherine."

Paul tightened his jaw just enough to produce a quick flex of muscle on his skin. "What in the hell are *you* doin' here?" The words were weak and slightly slow falling out of his mouth. But there was no mistaking the seething undercurrent of boiling anger in his voice. This was a weak-willed man, Jane surmised, but he was fueled right now by a tide of deep resentment.

"I...." Kit was uncharacteristically timid. "I'm just passing through town—"

"Then pass through!" Paul said, slurring his words a bit.

Jane put her hand on Kit's shoulder in a protective gesture. "Come on," she quietly instructed. "Close the door. Let's go."

Kit turned to Jane. Her face was etched with both shame and profound sadness. "I wanted to make amends," she whispered.

"Do I have to call the cops?" Paul yelled.

Kit turned back to Paul, heartbroken. She closed the door and Jane quickly backed the Mustang out of the lot. They drove to Barbara's house in silence until Jane spoke up. "Don't take what he said too much to heart."

"It's what he still feels that I heard back there."

They rounded the block and drove until they found the house, parking in front of it. Kit fussed in her purse in search of something. "By the way," she said, her attention focused on her purse, "they don't know about my cancer. And they're not going to. Understood?"

Jane was bewildered. "Okay."

Kit seemed satisfied with her search and carefully zipped up her purse. A wave of courage washed over her. "You stay here. I won't be long."

Jane directed Kit's attention toward the house. A portly, late fortyish woman, dressed in a sloppy pair of stained sweatpants, tennis shoes, and a heavy purple down jacket exited the house, slamming the front door behind her. Squinting toward the car and verifying the occupant in the passenger seat, the woman strode with angry purpose down the brick walkway. Kit got out of the car and met her just at the edge of the brown-tinged lawn as Jane emerged from the Mustang.

"I just got a call from Paul! He figured your next stop was here!"

"Barbara—"

"You got some nerve showing up like this!"

Kit appeared desperate. "Barbara, I know this is ill timed—"

"God, I thought after all these years, you'd get the message when I return your letters to you *unopened* and with 'Return to Sender. Will not accept' written across the envelope in *red ink!*" Even though it was dark, Jane could see waves of heat flushing Barbara's cheeks. "What does it take for you to understand that I don't want to see you, I don't want to talk to you, and I don't want to deal with you?"

Kit bowed her head in defeat. "I just wanted to see you. That's all."

Barbara moved closer to her mother, a look of pent-up rage spitting from her eyes. "I've got *nothing* to say to you. In my mind, *you are dead.*"

Kit looked Barbara in the eye. "Yes. I'm sure it makes it easier that way. I'm sorry you are so full of anger. Please...get help." Kit reached out to touch Barbara's shoulder, but Barbara backed away from her mother's touch.

"*I don't need help!* I need you to get the hell out of here and *never* come back!"

Kit nodded. "All right...but I need to use your bathroom before we go."

"There's a bathroom seven blocks down at the McDonald's," Barbara replied, her voice like burning vitriol.

"I *really* need to use your bathroom now," Kit said urgently.

Barbara stood back and shook her head. "This is the last time you will ever manipulate me! Go down the hallway to the left of the front door. It's the first door on the left. *And make it quick!*"

Kit quickly walked to the front door and went into the house.

Barbara looked over at Jane. "You a *friend* of hers?"

Jane took the question to mean, "Any friend of Kit's is an enemy of mine." Jane lit up a cigarette, took a long drag, and blew a plume of smoke into the air, never once taking her eyes off Barbara. "Yeah." Jane couldn't help but see that the bathroom light had never been turned on inside the house. Barbara kept her back to the house, but Jane's ever-observant eye didn't miss a beat. Jane casually turned to the side and then serendipitously caught sight of Kit's silhouette walking across the living room and then disappearing into a far corner.

"Do you know what happened?" Barbara asked, the words dripping like acid from her tongue.

Jane considered her answer carefully. "I know you lost your daughter—"

"*Lost?* No, we didn't *lose* her? She was *killed*. And it didn't have to happen!"

Another furtive glance to the living room and Jane noticed quick movement on Kit's part. Jane inhaled deeply on her cigarette.

Barbara took another few steps toward the Mustang. "You see, *somebody* fucked up badly. Somebody who was a fuckup her entire life. Somebody who chose to 'go with the flow' instead of paying attention and using common sense. Somebody who didn't understand that when you're put in charge of a child, it means you never let her out of your sight. It means you are on her ass from morning 'til night. Just like when she's home. That's the only way you can keep them safe from the sick fucks that roam the streets looking for their next conquest. I'm just telling you this because I think it's important to know about your 'friend' and all of her dark little secrets." Jane's ears perked up on the words *dark little secrets*. Barbara seemed to be baiting Jane and, oddly, Jane was intrigued. "Irresponsible doesn't even come close to describing her," Barbara added. "Her history should prove that!"

"For what it's worth, Barbara, not a day goes by that she doesn't blame herself for what happened to Ashlee."

"Oh, *spare me!*" Barbara's eyes were two piercing orbs of fire. "Don't you dare presume to tell me that shit! You remind me of the high and mighty minister at the funeral. He stood up there and said in his most self-righteous voice, 'If Christ could forgive those who killed Him, we could eventually forgive the man who sinned against Ashlee.' What a sanctimonious asshole! I wanted to choke the son of a bitch. Maybe if he lost his child...his *only* child, he'd feel differently. All he'd want is revenge. All he'd want to do is destroy the people who took the most precious thing from him." Barbara angrily wiped a tear from her face. She straightened her spine as rigidly as she could muster. "The monster who did this to my daughter got out last year on a technicality. He's going to get himself a new trial. And you know what? He'll probably walk!"

"That's not written in stone," Jane interjected.

"Oh, pull your head out of the sand! He *will* walk! That's the way it works! You do everything you can in this world to live right and treat others like you want to be treated and then you get fucked over!" Barbara shrugged her shoulders. "That asshole didn't just kill my daughter. He killed the whole family." She choked on the words, fighting back her ragged emotions. "Speaking of which, where in the hell is she, anyway?" Barbara turned to the house just as Kit opened the front door and crossed down the brick path toward the car.

Kit started to get into the Mustang when she turned back to Barbara. "Please take care of yourself, darling. I love you."

"Fuck you," Barbara said in an offhand, discarding manner before she turned and walked into the house, slamming the door with emphasis behind her.

Kit got into the Mustang. Jane squashed her cigarette into the asphalt before taking her seat. They sat in quiet contemplation before Jane broke the silence.

"You okay?"

"It hurts."

"Of course it hurts. To hear—"

"No. I don't care what she says to me. You can't hurt somebody unless they allow it. It hurts me to see her so torn up by her own hatred and grief. It's going to kill her. Mark my words, it's going to kill her." Kit stole a glance toward the house. "You know, Jane, I would have given my life to save Ashlee. It's my one regret. There's nothing original about death. People do it every day. But a death of purpose...of sacrifice...that would have made everything good in the end." She looked at Jane. "Carl's waiting for us. Let's go."

CHAPTER 15

Interstate 95 was clear sailing as Jane headed south for fifteen miles before connecting to Junction 165. The farther they drove, the more it became apparent that Cousin Carl lived in an extremely remote locale. The possibility that Carl liked the seclusion because he could grow pot with no intrusion from authorities crossed Jane's mind. Checking her low gas gauge, Jane took solace when she found a lonely Texaco gas station and the Black Crow Liquor Store in what appeared to be the dusty, forgotten town of Jeffers. Under the neon glow of the Black Crow sign, Jane pulled her jacket tightly around her chest and braced herself against the sudden icy wind. She removed the gas pump just as Kit exited the car and headed for the store.

"I need to use the bathroom!" Kit yelled back at Jane.

"I thought you went at Barbara's house," Jane replied.

"Her toilet was backed up! I won't be a second!"

Jane filled her tank and considered Kit's answer. The bathroom light had never gone on in Barbara's house. However, Kit had roamed freely in Barbara's living room. Gazing at family photos? Checking out the house? Stealing a small memento to remember Barbara? Whatever reason Kit needed to get into that house, it sure wasn't to use the bathroom. Jane's thought process was interrupted by the sound of her cell phone ringing. Ducking into the car, she retrieved the phone from her satchel and flicked it open to check the number.

It was Sergeant Weyler. Again.

Jane waited until voice mail rolled over before checking her messages. There were two, both from Weyler. The first was a simple "Call me." The second was longer.

"So, you're skipping town, are you? That's not like you, Jane. You don't run away from anything. What in the hell are you doing in Oakhurst, California? Do you need my help?" Weyler's voice softened on the last question. He sounded genuinely concerned for Jane. "Don't do anything stupid, Jane. You hear me? You know my number." With that, Weyler hung up. Jane dug her hand into her pocket and nervously rubbed the three sobriety chips and the snakestone. A queasy feeling of approaching angst enfolded her. The wind pressed hard against her face, stinging her checks. For a moment, she was hopelessly held in an unsettled limbo, unable to ascertain whether her feet were touching the pavement. No matter how much she tried to block out the sensation and bring herself back into her body, it persisted, smothering her senses in a disquieting pall. Jane's logical mind intruded, telling her that the feeling was due to being awake for than thirty hours with only coffee, a sugar cookie from Ingrid Bartosh, a tasteless spirulina ball, and a hurried lunch to fuel her spirit. But her gut told her this disturbing cloud of apprehension heralded something far more ominous.

"They have nuts!" Kit's voice rang out from the darkness, lifting Jane from her stupor. "Pumpkin seeds! I got you a bag and a bottle of wine for Cousin Carl. I hope he likes merlot." Kit started to get into the car but was taken by Jane's distant visage. "Are you okay?"

"Yeah," Jane replied unconvincingly.

They drove through the wintry darkness and finally came upon the significant rusty weather vane Carl had mentioned on the phone. Exactly one mile later on the left, they found Carl's single-story adobe abode. It was actually quite easy to spot, given the plethora of green and red chile lights that were strung around the house and atop the bevy of juniper bushes encircling the property. To Jane, it looked like White Trash Central, and she was almost certain that the lights were a permanent fixture rather than a once-a-year holiday display.

"How colorful!" Kit exclaimed. "It's like a landing pad for an aircraft. I like Cousin Carl already!"

An angular figure emerged from the front door, reflected in the glow of the red and green lights. "You found the place!" Carl yelled out as he walked toward the car. As he moved closer, Jane studied the man she had not seen in over fifteen years. Carl, who was pushing his late thirties, still had a shock of coal black hair that fell disheveled across his forehead and touched below his ears. While it seemed impossible, it looked as if Carl had actually grown taller than Jane remembered him. His slender six-foot five-inch frame appeared to be all legs as he ambled to Jane. Carl suddenly grabbed Jane, giving her a potent hug.

"How you doin', cousin!" Carl said with a happy clip to his voice. "Damn, girl! You looked whipped!" Jane was not prepared for such a gregarious show of affection. She automatically took a sniff of Carl's weather-beaten black canvas jacket. Nothing appeared to be there, but Jane speculated the cold winter air prevented the pot aroma from being detected. Carl turned to Kit. "Well, hello there! I'm Carl Perry!"

"So happy to meet you, Carl. My name's Kit." She extended her hand toward Carl, but he disregarded it and gave her a forceful hug.

"Shaking hands is for fucking dignitaries!" Carl said, patting Kit on the back.

They dragged the luggage into the house and Carl led them into the main room. The crisp sound of flamenco guitar issued from the four ceiling speakers. It was a spacious, Native American-themed room, with colorful native rugs on the walls, covering the two plush couches, and splayed erratically across the terracotta floor. On one wall, Carl displayed an impressive collection of Native artifacts, including peace pipes, arrows, tomahawks, and beaded leather bags that were securely framed behind clear glass. An oversized, open hearth with a roaring fire was the natural focal point for the inviting room as the intoxicating scent of piñon wafted through the air. Carl settled into a red rocking chair next to hearth. Kit melted into the couch closest to the fireside while Jane took a restrained seat in the center of the couch.

"Can I get you gals somethin' to wet your whistle?" Carl asked as he removed his black canvas jacket.

Kit brought out the bottle of merlot from her bag. "I hope you like red wine."

Carl took the bottle and admired the label. "Oh, I have a lot of memories of the burgundy and me."

"Excellent," Kit said, clasping her hands together.

"My cousin here will tell you there's not a whole lot of liquor in my life that I've turned down," Carl said with a soft smile and twinkle in his eye. "Thank you, Kit."

Jane was quickly reminded of Carl's penchant for knocking back five shots of tequila in one sitting and figured she'd better get on with the reason for her visit before he was too tanked. "So, about Clinton Fredericks—"

"Oh, that little fucker can wait!" Carl said as he got up and moved to the open kitchen area twenty feet away. "Can I pour you two a glass of wine?"

"Thank you, Carl," Kit said as she motioned to Jane to take it down a notch in her eager intensity.

"How 'bout you, cousin?" Carl asked, removing the cork from the bottle.

Jane wasn't in the mood to disclose her six months of sobriety. "No, thanks. I'm not a wine drinker."

"I got tequila. And I got a helluva expensive whiskey I snuck back from England last year," Carl offered, pouring a glass of wine.

An unexpected tension gripped Jane's body. Her tongue tingled with the fleeting suggestion. Her answer came too slowly to be convincing. "No, thanks."

Carl sauntered back to Kit, handing her the glass of wine. "How's Mike doin'?" he asked, shoving a loose piece of piñon back into the open hearth with his boot.

Family talk. Not something Jane was comfortable discussing. "He's fine. He's got a girlfriend. I think it's serious. He'll probably get married."

"Good for Mike!" Carl said earnestly, taking a seat. "I haven't seen him since he was...what? He's four years younger than Jane.

He must've been sixteen. *Damn!* Where does the time go? Glad to know he's in love. How 'bout you, Jane? You seein' anybody?"

For Jane, these kind of personal chats were more painful than a root canal. "No. I've got a pretty full plate right now, what with going out on my own and—"

"Shit, life ain't worth livin' if you ain't got someone to share it with." Carl leaned back in his rocker and snatched a framed photo from a side table. He handed the photo to Jane. "Her name's Kyoto. I met her in Japan when I was working on a story a few years ago. We've been together ever since." Jane handed the photo to Kit. "Ain't she a beauty? She's in Japan right now, seeing her family. *Jesus, I miss her!*" Carl's face softened as he thought about his lover. Kit handed the photo back to Carl. He traced Kyoto's face with his finger, lost in thought momentarily.

Jane wondered when and how she could turn the conversation back to Clinton Fredericks. She was just about to speak when Kit beat her to the punch.

"I guess you're not a merlot drinker, Carl?" Kit asked.

Carl gradually came out of his lovesick gaze and replaced Kyoto's photo on the table. "Well, the truth is, I stopped drinkin' about eight years ago. Stopped dope, too. I found somethin' else to fill in the blank spaces."

Jane was stunned. Her tequila drinking, doobie-tooting cousin was clean and sober. She felt an unexplained rush of resentment toward him. "Don't tell me you found God," Jane said, allowing her bite and bile to override her self-control. Kit flashed Jane a look of censure.

Carl broke into a toothy grin. "Good one, cousin!" he said completely unaffected by Jane's remark. He stretched his long, thin legs outward, clasping his narrow fingers behind his head. "I found my heart. So, yeah, I guess I found God." Kit smiled. "It wasn't about having this profound, enlightened moment of sobriety," Carl continued, "It was more like I was so tired of trying to control the outcome of everything. I found out that being vulnerable wasn't goin' to kill me after all. In fact, being vulnerable was the only way I was goin' to embrace the truth and move forward. I could sit around and blame everyone around me for my fucked-up life or I could forgive it all and find freedom for the first time ever." Kit snuck a meaningful glance at Jane, who shifted uncomfortably in the couch.

"If you're sober, why do you keep tequila and whiskey in the house?" Jane questioned him in her best detective voice.

"Just because I'm dry doesn't mean my friends have to be!" Carl stated with a mischievous tone. "I own the bottle but it doesn't own me." He rocked forward in his chair, clasping his hands together. "When I started trusting in what I couldn't see...but felt in here," he tapped on his heart, "instead of here," Carl motioned to his head, "everything became so clear to me." Carl glanced at the freestanding bookshelf next to his chair. Amid the crush of books, he located the one he wanted and handed a crimson-covered paperback to Jane. It was titled *The Occult Significance of Forgiveness* by Sergei Prokofieff, an obscure book Carl had found in a Russian bookstore. The book was a thought-provoking series of stories about people who had gone through hellish experiences and forgiven those who hurt them. "He doesn't preach the morality of forgiveness," Carl said, settling back in his rocking chair. "He presents spiritual awakenings that speak for themselves. What struck me was that the importance of forgiving was not just for one's personal redemption, but for the advancement of all humans. Just to repeat the same hatred again and again serves no country, no culture, no religion, no person." Carl recalled a story in the book about an attorney who lived in a concentration camp with his wife and five children. The Germans killed his wife and children in front of him. He begged them to kill him, but when they found out he could speak German, they decided to keep him as a translator. That night, he had a spiritual awakening; he realized that if he chose to hate the men who killed his family, it would destroy him. So he resolved that whether he lived another day or another fifty years, he would love every person he met. Years later, when the Germans were defeated and the camp was freed, this

man emerged looking the picture of radiant health, while everyone else looked near death. "The author says that forgiving can't
be a passive process," Carl stated. "It has to be done over and over
in a very conscious manner. The negative memory goes through
a spiritual death and leaves an empty space into which our God
self can work." Carl chuckled to himself. "I guess when the Bible-
thumpers talk about Jesus filling that empty space in their heart,
they're saying the same thing."

Jane's mind reeled with a million acerbic remarks. There had
to be a quantum of muscle left in holding on to resentment. "That
lawyer sounds like a modern day saint," Jane offered, handing the
book back to Carl.

"We're all saints, Jane, with varying degrees of tarnished ha-
los," Carl replied. "You keep the book. I know it by rote."

Jane reluctantly accepted the gift and set it on the couch. But
her impatience was growing. She expressed her urgency to learn
about Clinton and Carl finally acquiesced. He donned a black
canvas jacket and snagged another coat from the pegs by the front
door for Jane. Even with the garish glow of the red and green chile
lights outside the house, the clear sky shone with a brilliant palate
of sparkling stars. Jane lit a cigarette and took an eager drag of
painkilling nicotine into her lungs.

"So, what do you know about the asshole?" Jane asked with
pointed precision.

"Did you read my article about him in *Rolling Stone?*"

"Yeah. I want to know what you left out of the story."

"Why?"

"You following the news the last few days?"

Carl shook his head. Jane told him about Charlotte and how
Clinton was assuming the pseudo lead in the case. "Shit," Carl
said, nervously scuffing the hard dirt with the heel of his boot. A
bone-chilling, high desert wind whipped up, carrying the sweet
scent of sagebrush. "You involved in this kid's case?"

Jane eyed Carl with a reluctant gaze. "Maybe."

Carl considered the situation, motioning toward the house. "Is Kit involved?"

"I can't go into any details. Let's just say that this could turn out to be bigger than the Lawrence murder case." Carl arched his eyebrows at Jane's disclosure. "If it all plays out and my involvement turns out to be important, I will give you the exclusive interview." Jane waited for that proposal to sink in.

"It's taken me a long time to get the stories and the money and respect that go with them. If certain individuals found out I blabbed about stuff that didn't get put in the story, I'm seriously fucked."

"This conversation never happened, Carl. You have my word. And you'll have the biggest exclusive of your career if it goes down our way."

Carl dug his hands into the pockets of his jacket. "First off, you know as well as I do that there's really no such thing as a profiler. That's a manufactured Hollywood brand. The real term is 'Behavioral Analyst' and the only group that has a respectable B.A. program is the FBI. They have twelve psychologists, all FBI agents who got their Masters and PhDs in psychology. They're stuffed into a building in Quantico and analyze photos and case files from the comfort of their desk. They study victimology, they study crime scenes and the vic's background, and try to put together a best guess as to what happened and who did it. But you tell me, cousin, isn't that what any good detective does? The only thing you get from the Behavioral Analyst guy is the expert witness in court that comes on the stand and says 'I've got a PhD and here's what I feel.'

"Now, Clinton Fredericks, he calls himself a profiler, but he's just a guy with Nick Nolte hair and an ego the size of a Mack truck who uses the information from older cases to make assumptions about current ones."

"So why is Clinton Fredericks's name synonymous with crime solving?"

"Because he's got a good agent. He's also got a public relations firm that shores up his image and deflects the more compromising elements of his behavior."

"You're talking about Rudy Weiss and the killing of that bank teller?"

"That incident cost Fredericks pretty good bank with his PR gurus, but it paid off. He got a book deal and maybe a reality TV show down the road. I had to jump through fucking hoops when I wrote the article for *Rolling Stone*. One of the conditions was that I had to release the article to his PR man before the magazine got it. Anything they didn't like got censored. It was my first article for *Rolling Stone* and I was promised more work if they liked the piece on Fredericks. So I did what the PR guys asked and I never told the magazine about it."

"What'd you leave out of the story?" Jane asked, taking a drag on her cigarette.

Carl let out a long sigh. "Clinton sees himself as the resurrection of 'Gonzo' journalist Hunter S. Thompson. After Thompson committed suicide, I think Clinton felt he could match his idol's wildness and proclivity to *become* the story instead of report it. But Clinton's theater isn't journalism. It's hard-core life-and-death drama where average people can be used, bought, and manipulated to serve his higher purpose."

"What's his MO?"

"Clinton's not satisfied with the crumbs the cops throw him. He wants the whole loaf of bread he can get from a closer source: the family. He got cozy with that bank teller's family. That's how he knew so much about her when he was out there with the megaphone 'negotiating' for the TV cameras. Being close to the family also gives him the advantage of finding out some choice information that the cops may only divulge to the relatives. But he's also got a stalker mentality."

"How do you mean?"

"Basically, he leeches on to anyone and then steals that information for his own advancement. I spent three months with the prick. We drove from one fucking TV show to the next so he could promote his stupid book. But in between getting his makeup on for the next TV interview or doing book signings, he started opening up to me. All egomaniacs need a stage and another body to bounce their brilliance off of. I'm a good listener when I have to be, and so he talked and talked *and talked*. He wants to be super profiler, super negotiator, and super crime solver—"

"Clinton got that bank teller killed. How does that raise his image?"

"Didn't you see his stirring epilogue on live TV when he wept in front of America as he told of the brave sacrifice that poor woman made and how he was going to do whatever it took to have a park near the bank named after her. And he did it! And you better believe the fucker was there front and center on the day they cut the ribbon at that little park. Never mind that he was also quietly enjoying half of the $250,000 reward fund that the family of the dead woman *insisted* he receive."

"Are you serious?"

"As a heart attack. What's the reward up to for this girl from California?"

"I don't know."

"Well, I guarantee you he got cozy with the girl's mother and found out there was a reward fund. His presence on the case will fuel that fund and his personal involvement will deepen with each dollar that is added to the kitty. Clinton told me a lot of shit when I was out there on the road with him. He likes to drink and I know how to act drunk. He'd get loaded and I'd drink tonic and pretend to be fucked up so he'd feel comfortable talking to me. When Clinton's sober, he's a fucking asshole. When he's drunk, he's a Chatty Cathy doll with a psycho twist. For example, one night he gave me his 'recipe' for the perfect media crime event. Mix a child—preferably a girl—add a small town, pepper it with a high-profile mystery, get the parents to like you, spice it up with a large cash reward, and you've got the perfect showcase for Clinton Fredericks."

"Jesus...." Jane squashed her cigarette into the dirt.

Carl hesitated. "You know what else he told me?" Carl improvised a slurred, drunken voice. "'Bottom line, Carl, I don't give a fuck about the hostage. Do you have any idea how much pussy I get from what I do? Women want to fuck me from one side of the country to the next and I just stand back and take numbers.'" Carl pulled out of the drunken imitation. "So I say to him, 'But Clinton, what if the hostage gets killed?' And he says, 'We all gotta die sometime!' Then, he laughs like the fuckin' psychotic he is. Next day, he sobered up, but he's not like some drunks who forget what they tell you. He remembered everything. He pushed me up against my hotel room wall, held me by my throat and said, 'If you tell anyone what I said last night, I'll destroy you.' And that SOB has the connections to do it. So I did what I was told, knowing full well that somewhere down the road, some other victim was going to have a target on their forehead when Clinton got involved in their case."

"Clinton crossed the line with that statement. He went from being an asshole to being a physical threat to the victim! He needs to be exposed!"

"Not by me! Hey, I'm not proud of it, cousin. We all start out with this genuine desire to speak the truth. Then, if we're smart, we realize real quickly that the truth is not what matters when the lie is what you're selling."

Jane took a step toward Carl. "The truth still matters to me and it matters even more to that twelve-year-old girl." Jane weighed the circumstances. "Look, if it all pans out, you get the exclusive with me and *my quotes* annihilate Clinton in the story, not yours."

Carl considered the offer and nodded in agreement. "Okay." He smiled warmly. "You always had more guts than I did. We didn't see a lot of each other growing up, but when the families did get together, I always quietly envied your strength."

Jane lit another cigarette. "Appearances are often deceiving, Carl."

"Naw. You *are* strong. You're a survivor."

"You got the survivor part right," Jane said, taking a long drag on her cigarette.

A quizzical look came over Carl. "You mean surviving the media frenzy over that homicide case this past summer?"

Now it was Jane's turn to look puzzled. "No. I mean...*life.*" She waited for her response to sink in. "Growing up, you know?"

A pall fell over Carl. "I hear you." He cast his eyes downward, drawing circles in the dirt with the toe of his boot. "We turn eighteen, break free of the home, and spend the rest of our lives trying to right all the perceived wrongs against us. Along the way, we do too many drugs and drink a lot booze trying to suffocate the memories." Jane studied Carl's somber face. For the first time, she noticed an edge of sadness that hung close to this heart. "I hope your dad found peace in the end," Carl said. "I don't think mine ever did. Were you with him when he died?" Carl asked.

Jane's body stiffened. "No," Jane replied with a low flush of ire.

"I was with my dad." Carl let out a long exhalation. "It was good. After I learned about what happened between he and Uncle Dale, I started seeing him not so much as my dad but as a person who was still tortured by the fact that he couldn't forgive himself. I understood why he couldn't be there for me emotionally." Jane felt as if she were walking into a movie that was halfway done. "It's ironic, isn't it, how my dad was always so passive and quiet as an adult. He was always afraid of hurting someone." Carl's eyes were lost in the distance for a moment. "Always afraid he was going to be forced into doing something he didn't want to do. So he never tried. He kept it all inside. The only time he came out of his shell was when he drank. That's when he talked about the real stuff— the stuff that made him. He didn't want to feel. Because if he felt, he'd have to live with what he did over and over again." Carl looked at Jane "Every time I came to your house and saw Uncle Dale, I always felt so sorry for him."

"You felt *sorry* for my dad?" Her voice was shaky.

Carl furrowed his eyebrows. "Well, yeah. To go through what happened to him as a kid. It's just fuckin' evil."

Jane felt disoriented. "I don't know what the hell you're talking about." She tossed her cigarette into the darkness and walked inside the house. Carl followed.

Kit was still on the couch sound asleep. Jane's nerves sparked as she crossed to the breakfast bar in the kitchen.

"Your dad never told you what happened to him?" Carl asked quietly, so as not to wake up Kit.

"Nothing happened to *him!*"

Kit gradually awakened.

"Oh, God," Carl said softly, "You don't know, do you?"

Jane's gut twisted. "I don't need to know!" Her voice was low but forceful.

"Yeah. You do." Carl sat on a stool by the breakfast bar. "Starting from the time my dad was ten and Uncle Dale was six, and continuing for about eight years, Granddad Perry used to force the two of them to fight each other. And I'm not talking minor shit. I'm talking fight until you damn near kill the other one. Nothing was off limits. Punch, poke, kick. It was Granddad Perry's way of punishing them. The old man should've been put away in a mental ward for what he did to his sons."

"I don't know where you heard this bullshit, but it isn't true," Jane argued.

"It *is* true. My dad told me all these stories when he was drunk—"

"He was drunk!" Jane countered.

"That's when he spoke the truth, cousin!"

"This is *not* truth!" Jane jabbed her finger on the bar.

"*Your* dad was small and scrawny and four years younger. He never had a chance against my dad. He'd be bloodied and broken and begging for mercy and all Granddad Perry would do was yell out, 'Kick the little fucker!' My dad didn't want to do it, but he had no choice. If he didn't, Granddad Perry would whip the shit out of him with this belt that had metal studs on it. So my dad kicked your dad and prayed to God he would pass out so the fight could be over."

"I remember Granddad Perry! I liked him! And he always said *he* liked *me* because I reminded him of himself...." Jane nearly choked on those last words. The enormity of the startling revelation crashed around Jane.

"It's weird." Carl said. "All those years, my dad was the aggressor and then he turned into this weak, passive man. And your dad became a homicide detective."

Jane looked at Carl in a daze. "It's not true," she whispered. "It can't be!" She spun around, grabbed her satchel from the floor and stormed out the door.

She got into the Mustang and sped into the darkness.

CHAPTER 16

Kit nervously waited inside Carl's house for Jane to return. An hour passed and then another and there was no sign of her. Carl retreated to his bedroom to send an e-mail to Kyoto while Kit wore a worried path in the Native carpet. She looked up to check the time just as the sound of car wheels crunching gravel was heard outside. Peering out the front window, she saw the Mustang trolling to an uneasy stop inside Carl's front gate. The engine turned off, but the headlights remained on high beam. Kit watched as a lone figure emerged from the driver's seat, then disappeared behind the Mustang. She grabbed the warmest coat she could find on Carl's front pegs and walked outside. A biting wind swept across the front yard. Kit pulled the coat around her frame and squinted into the darkness. There was raw silence.

"Jane?" Kit's voice was full of apprehension. No response. "*Jane!*" Now there was more aggravation. Nothing.

Kit's ears perked up as she heard the distinct sound of metal clicking. Her heart raced. She took several steps toward the car. "Jane P.! What are you doing?"

The silence was broken by the clink of a piece of metal spinning into the air and landing in the hard dirt. Kit's hesitation faded, replaced by frustration. "Jane! Answer me!" She moved closer to the Mustang, standing in the blinding beam of light. Another piece of metal catapulted through the air, landing in front of Kit. She leaned down to retrieve the object. It was one of Jane's sobriety chips. "Jane!" Kit yelled into the darkness. "Where are you?"

Jane answered by tossing the snakestone toward Kit. Collecting the stone, Kit moved around to the rear of the Mustang.

Jane sat with her back supported by the bumper and her legs sprawled in front of her. In her hand, she clutched a half-empty bottle of Jack Daniels.

"Oh, dear God," Kit whispered. "Give me the bottle."

"I'm not done yet," Jane slurred as she ran her fingers through her stringy hair.

"Oh, you're done. You are beyond drunk!"

"No. I can still feel, so I'm not toasted yet."

"Jesus! You've drunk half a bottle!"

Jane unsteadily slid her body up the rear of the Mustang. "Oh, you know the AA saying, Kit: 'One bottle is too many. A hundred bottles aren't enough.'" She lifted the whiskey bottle to her lips just as Kit swiped it from her hand.

"You drove in this condition?" Kit yelled. "How dare you! You could have killed someone or yourself!"

"On *this* road? I might have nailed a jackrabbit or two, but aside from that, traffic was pretty clear. Give me the bottle!" Jane tried to snatch the whiskey, but Kit was too quick for her and hurled the sloshing bottle into the darkness and sagebrush. She took an angry step toward Kit. "Well, *fuck you!*"

Kit responded with a violent slap across Jane's face that sent her into the dirt. "Shame on you, Jane P.!" Kit stood over Jane's prone body in a menacing pose.

Jane shook off the rush of heat that stung her cheek and looked up at Kit. "Well, I've been here before! Why don't you start kicking? Kick me as hard as you can! Kick me until I bleed! Go on! Obviously, I bring that desire out in people!"

"How could you know as a kid that you reminded your dad of his own father?"

"And that gave him the right to do what he did to me?" Jane yelled.

"Of course not! But it finally gives the whole mess some kind of context."

"*Context?* This is not a fucking intellectual argument! *This is my life!*"

"Your dad was following an unconscious pattern—"

"Fuck you!" Jane screamed into the darkness.

"You triggered the anger in him." Kit refused to be cowed by Jane's drunken rage. "Maybe it was a word, or a look, or the shake of your head that was just like your grandfather—"

"Spare me the psychobabble—"

"Just like *he* probably triggered something in his own father's eyes. Don't we all just follow patterns our entire lives? Aren't you following an old pattern right now? Life gets too real and so you have to kill the pain with a whiskey bottle?"

Jane struggled to her feet. "My father is *not* a victim! He could have chosen not to do what he did to us! Carl's telling me all this shit about my dad and the voice starts in my head again. *His voice!* 'Get up, you stupid bitch! You're *nothing!*' That's what I've been trying to drown out of my head for the last two hours!" Jane's voice choked up with emotion as tears started falling down her face. "But then, there's his *other* voice. His *younger* voice! And it's screaming at his brother, begging him to stop kicking him in the balls. Which one of those voices am I supposed to listen to?"

"Both of them," Kit softly replied.

Jane wiped the tears from her face. "No! He can't be human. He *has* to be a monster! That's the shoe that fit him! He can't be both the victim *and* the perpetrator!"

"Sure he could. Lou Peters is both the victim and the perpetrator."

"What about responsibility? He never hung his head for what he did to us. Up until the second he died, he was a twisted asshole. He didn't pay enough!"

"That's not for you to say. That's between your father and God."

"I can't trust God to punish my father. God has too much mercy!"

"So, God's weak?" Kit asked with an incredulous smirk.

Jane searched for a snappy retort but came up blank. "All I know is how to hate my father."

"Let me tell you something, your hate is going to do *nothing* to him, but it'll suck the life out of you. Take a good, hard look at me, Jane P., because *this* is *you* in twenty years. Maybe ten, if you really let that vengeance swell up and eat away at your liver or your lungs. And when you're lying on your deathbed, dying of cancer, and staring at the ceiling and saying, 'Why God?' if you listen real closely you'll hear God reply, 'I didn't do it to you! You did it to *yourself!*' You with your unforgiving, single-minded hatred. Go on and hate yourself to death." Kit turned, lost in thought for a second. "There's a lot of sayings out there. One of them is 'Find the *middle ground* and you will find peace.' You really *can* live a life that doesn't drown in the extreme of hatred or rage if you stop self-destructing long enough! There's another saying: 'Sometimes the only cure for cancer is death.'" Kit let that one sink in. "I can handle that. Death is not a theory for me. It stares me down every goddamned day. But when I take my last breath, know this: my heart will be at peace and not at war with my past. I will die with redemption." Kit turned and headed back to the house.

"How do you stop the memories?" Jane asked.

Kit turned back to Jane. "You stop fighting."

"If I stopped fighting, I would die."

"Then you'll be reborn," Kit flicked the snakestone to Jane who caught it. "When you let go, you don't fall into the void. You can fall into the hand of God."

"When you close your eyes for the last time, are you gonna fall into the hand of God?"

"No, Jane. He's already holding me."

DECEMBER 30

Jane emerged from the bathroom, hair sopping wet and smartly dressed in a pair of dark denim jeans and a tan turtleneck.

"I'll fix you guys an omelet," Carl announced, "like none you've ever tasted. A midget in Morocco gave me the recipe. The only thing better than this omelet is sex."

Jane crossed to the breakfast bar as Kit walked into the steamy bathroom and closed the door. Carl opened the cupboard and brought out a bottle of vitamins. He took four large gelatin capsules out of the bottle and handed them to Jane.

"What's this?"

"Evening primrose oil. They shorten the duration of a hangover." Carl slid a glass of water to Jane. "They also make your skin soft and supple." He smiled and began breaking eggs into a large bowl.

"Is that what the midget in Morocco told you?" Jane downed the capsules.

Carl's eyes twinkled, happy to have someone to share his repartee. "We should have spent a lot more time together when we were growing up, cousin!" He added butter to a skillet and a dash of half-and-half to the eggs. "Just to know you weren't alone." He brought out a series of spices. "The one thing I've come to understand since getting sober is the concept that there is no good or bad in this world...there just 'is.' In that 'is'—that place of nothing— you find true peace."

"Jesus, you sound like Kit."

Carl poured the eggs into the skillet. "So, I checked on the Internet this morning about that kidnapped girl in California. You're gonna walk into a circus."

"It is what it is, Carl."

"I know you're keeping your role in this close to the vest, but my probing investigative journalistic penchant made me do a little checking."

"Checking what?"

"Katherine Clark."

Jane snuck a look toward the bathroom and heard the shower running. "What about her?"

Carl casually worked the omelet off the side of the pan. "I subscribe to a service that gives me access to reams of newspaper articles, old and new. I entered Katherine's name and found one with her photo on it from 1990. Had to do with her granddaughter who was kidnapped and killed."

"That's right."

"From what I read, she knew the guy who did it. Lou Peters?"

Jane wasn't sure whether her queasy stomach was due to her hangover or Carl's questions. "She knew him. Look, I really can't talk much about the case—"

"Did you do a background check on her?"

Jane glanced once again at the bathroom. The water was still running. "Where are you going with this?"

"I dug deeper and found that Katherine Clark is no stranger to the court system."

The queasiness truly set into Jane's gut. "Talk to me."

"She was arrested in 1985, along with a group of radicals, for taking part in the bombing of a shoe factory in Monterey, California. Four innocent people who worked at the factory were killed. She was charged with aiding and abetting the ringleader of the group with materials that were used to make the bomb that blew up the factory."

The shower water stopped running.

Jane leaned closer to Carl. "What was the upshot?"

"I'm not sure. I found that one article and the fact that she's in the system."

Jane tried to sort it all out and fight off an oncoming headache. "Five years later, her granddaughter's killed."

"What are you thinking?" Carl asked confidentially.

Jane said the first thing that came to mind. "Revenge...."

"The granddaughter was a revenge kill? By who?"

Kit opened the bathroom door, dressed in a pair of black pants and a blood-red, knit tunic. "Oh, Carl, the coffee smells divine!"

Thirty minutes later, Jane and Carl packed the last bags into the trunk of the Mustang. Kit settled into the front seat as Carl sidled closer to Jane.

"Remember, cousin," Carl said in confidence, "there are no accidents. Just a series of non sequitur events that all serve to solve the greater puzzle in the end."

Jane took a drag off her cigarette. "Sounds very Buddhist," she said warily.

Carl smiled as he embraced Jane with a hearty hug. He spoke in confidence to Jane. "Everybody in this world has something to hide, cousin. *Everybody.*" Jane considered Carl's portentous remark. "I'll light a stick of incense and ask that you be protected on your journey."

"Throw a penny in the pond and a dash of salt over your shoulder, too," Jane said, heading to the driver's seat and tossing the cigarette into the dirt.

"Will do!" Carl said brightly. He waved to Kit. "Take care of yourselves!"

As they drove away, Jane looked in the rearview mirror. Carl's hands were clasped in a prayer pose and pointed toward the car.

Jane figured it would take a little over eight hours to get to Oakhurst. Was it worth it to speed to a destination that might end up being a subterfuge? If she was being played by Kit, was it wiser for Jane to confront her now or hold back and wait to discover Kit's true purpose? But the question that spun endlessly in Jane's head as they neared Oakhurst was whether she was traveling with a woman who had more nefarious motives planned and was covertly using Jane to execute a criminal plan. The questions layered one on top of the other with no answers.

Jane turned on the radio so she could hear something else besides the sound of her own thoughts. She slowed the Mustang as she curved down the two-lane road that led into Oakhurst. It was the top of the hour and the local news station's headlining story only added to her growing trepidation.

There had been an arrest in the kidnapping of Charlotte Walker.

And the perp's name was *not* Lou Peters.

CHAPTER 17

The suspect's name was Trace Fagin. He was a married, thirty-eight-year-old father of two children from South Dakota. As was typical, the media referred to him as a "person of interest," which led Jane to believe they had some physical evidence that linked Fagin to Charlotte Walker. Immediately, Jane flashed on Charlotte's red leather jacket. Kit and Jane listened intently to the sheriff's voice on the radio as he gave the usual vague replies to reporters' questions, prefaced by the words, "At this time...."

"At this time, we can report that Mr. Fagin's vehicle has been impounded."

"At this time, Mr. Fagin is considered a person of interest and is cooperating with both detectives and the FBI."

"At this time, we are still considering this case open, but are very interested in any information Mr. Fagin may have regarding Charlotte Walker."

"So as not to jeopardize our case, at this time, we are not releasing whether we found any physical evidence that links Mr. Fagin to Charlotte Walker."

To Jane, it was your basic press conference—just enough information to appease the public, but not enough for an intelligent person to garner any useable data to determine Fagin's guilt or innocence.

"He didn't do it," Kit announced.

"That remains to be seen," Jane replied, turning off the radio and searching for a motel with a vacancy sign. A soft rain began to fall onto the water-swept streets.

"He didn't do it, Jane!"

"Maybe he did. Maybe Lou is absolutely innocent." There was a stinging tenor to Jane's voice as she kept her eyes focused on finding a motel along the main drag. Her suspicion was more firmly planted upon Kit Clark and her past nefarious dealings. Carl's unsettling disclosure of Kit's arrest three decades ago in relation to a shoe factory bombing that killed four people was beginning to seriously rankle Jane. The pervading thought that Kit was using her to instigate some kind of criminal objective was becoming more possible in Jane's mind. Perhaps Kit was bent on revenge for Ashlee's murder and this trip was a ploy for Jane to lead her right to Lou so Kit could kill him. She was dying of cancer and would never make it to trial for the murder. All that talk about forgiveness and compassion for Lou? Well, that was just New Age deception, as far as Jane was concerned.

"Look," Kit said with an irritated edge, "if the police and FBI are going to waste time with this Fagin guy, that just gives Lou more freedom to do whatever he wants with Charlotte and then kill her as he sees fit. If patterns serve, I feel that Charlotte must be found before January 5."

"Day twelve," Jane said offhandedly.

"So, you counted, too? That must mean you feel a similar urgency."

"No, it just means I counted days. And frankly, it doesn't mean anything."

"What are you talking about?" Kit said in disbelief. "He killed my fourteen-year-old granddaughter on day fourteen of her capture! Patterns, Jane! *Patterns!*"

"A pattern must be repeated at least once for it to count."

"I see. So, we wait until day twelve when Charlotte is found dead and then we can say, 'Ah, look. A *pattern.*'"

"I'll keep January 5 in mind," Jane said, building an emotional wall against Kit. The rain fell harder, creating puddles of neon reflections from the stores and restaurants.

Kit observed Jane carefully. "Something is different about you."

"Nothing's different."

Kit leaned closer to Jane. "Why are you lying to me?"

Jane came to a stoplight and turned to Kit, staring at her straight on. "I've got a lot on my mind, Kit. I've had a few things go wrong for me in the last twenty hours or so. If I'm coming off as deceitful...well, I guess that's your perception. Or maybe...

projection." Jane turned back to the road, letting that little gem sink in.

"Projection?" Kit asked bemused. "Are you saying that *I'm* being untruthful with you? Jane, I've told you everything that's necessary for you to solve this case!"

The words "everything that's necessary" weren't lost on Jane's cynical ears. She'd heard the same typical verbal dance from hundreds of perps over the years. They always answered questions with carefully placed words so as not to perjure themselves. The light turned green. Just as she passed The Bonanza Cabins, she saw the neon red NO VACANCY light change to VACANCY. Making a quick U-turn, Jane gunned the Mustang into the empty Bonanza parking lot. Driving to the front office, she parked the car in an area with a sign that read THE HITCHING POST. Jane let out a low groan, realizing she was about to enter not just a bad Western *kitsch* motel, but *kitsch* based on a television show that bowed off the air in the early 1970's. Not a good sign, Jane mused as she braced herself against the pelting rain and followed Kit into the front office.

The melodic sound of Roy Rogers singing "Happy Trails to You" played over the tinny front office speakers. It was another cheesy attempt to embrace the *Bonanza* theme. A balding, full-bellied man in his late forties stood at the front desk, eyes focused intently on a small TV screen that sat on a nearby shelf. "Hey, Marie!" the man yelled behind his shoulder. "I think I just saw the motel on the TV!"

"Use the TiVo and hit the pause button to be sure!" Marie yelled back.

"Hello," Kit interjected.

The guy looked up as if he were surprised to see the two women standing in his front office. His shirt proudly displayed a tag that read, HOWDY! I'M BARRY! He set down the remote control and turned on the charm. "Howdy!" he said with a big grin.

Jane hovered in the background, glancing over the racks of tourist brochures. The place smelled musty and old to her, like a dusty, antebellum attic.

"I see you have a vacancy," Kit asked in her most cordial voice.

"We *just* finished cleanin' the cabin." His eyes wandered over to Jane. "The crew from CBS vacated it less than an hour ago. They were here with Lesley Stahl to interview that girl from the barbeque place who saw Charlotte get into that guy's car. The interview's gonna be on TV *tonight!*" Barry yelled back to Marie. "What's her name again, Marie?"

"The chunky girl?" Marie hollered back.

"Yeah! Barbeque girl?"

"Leann Hamilton!"

"Leann Hamilton," Barry repeated.

"Did you get the TiVo to work?" Marie bellowed from the other room.

"In a second. We got customers!" Barry bellowed back.

"What network?" Marie screeched.

"Don't know yet!" Barry looked at Kit. "What network are you two with?"

"We're not with any network," Kit said. "Just two travelers looking for a place to rest our weary bones for a week or so."

Barry straightened up, looking unconvinced. "Christmas is over and last time I looked, Oakhurst ain't a destination spot for New Year's Eve festivities. Weather sucks outside and Yosemite is not exactly spectacular this time of year." Barry leaned across the counter. "This town is crawlin' with TV folks! It's like Fourth of July for us! Come on! You can tell me what network you're with. I promise I won't tell a soul!"

Jane looked at Barry. His demeanor was as sincere as an ex-con working the Tilt-A-Whirl carnival ride just so he could pick up underage girls.

Barry stared at Jane. "I *know* you're somebody. I've seen you on TV—"

Kit quickly laughed a hearty laugh and pointed at Jane. "Melody? My daughter?" Kit turned to Jane. "Sweetheart, isn't that something? He thinks he's seen you on television!" She turned back to Barry, still chuckling. "I just *wish* my Melody was a TV star. Wouldn't *that* be special?"

Jane wondered when her fifteen minutes of *Larry King* fame was going to end. Then she thought, *Melody?* God help her.

"So, you have a vacancy?" Kit said, desperately trying to change the subject.

"Yeah," Barry checked the register. "Hop Sing!"

"Excuse me?" Kit asked.

"The Hop Sing cabin."

"Hop Sing?" Kit repeated, not understanding.

Jane sidled next to Kit. "He was the Chinese cook on the Ponderosa," Jane said, feeling the walls of this cheesy, TV Western-themed motel closing in on her. Kit still didn't get it. "I'll explain later," Jane said, taking a gander at the rate card. The handful of cabins were named accordingly: Ben Cartwright, Little Joe, Hoss.... "So, it's $35 a night—"

"Ah, well, no," Barry said, sliding the stack of rate cards off to the side. "Normally, that's our winter rate. But, due to the current happening in town, we had to upgrade the cabins with satellite TV dish systems, TiVo, and high speed Internet for the press. So, we needed to raise our rates accordingly."

"And that would be?" Jane asked with a leery tone.

"$125 a night," Barry said without flinching.

"That's highway robbery!" Jane declared. "And your parking lot is empty."

"That's because all the TV people are down at the sheriff's office. He just finished a news conference about nabbing that Tad... Tom...." Barry spoke over his shoulder. "Marie! What's the name of that guy they picked up?"

"Trace. Trace Fagin!" Marie quickly yelled back.

"Trace Fagin," Barry repeated as if his wife hadn't prompted him. He leaned across the counter. "News is still fresh of course, but I heard a rumor that Alan from the gas station up on Highway 41 saw the cops nail this Fagin fellow right on the highway when he was takin' a piss." Barry arched his eyebrows. "*Takin' a piss....*" he repeated with an air of denunciation. In Barry's mind, Fagin might as well have been caught with a shovel in his hand burying Charlotte's body.

Jane pocketed one of the Cabins' business cards. "Back to the room. We'll be here for a week or so. How about a weekly rate?"

"No can do," Barry replied quickly. "And I advise you to lock in that price now. No tellin' how high our rates are gonna go when they find Charlotte. If all goes well, I might be able to build me another cabin. Hey, we treat you well here! You can mail letters here, have faxes sent to our front office, *and* there's a coffee maker *in* your cabin!"

"*In* the cabin?" Jane said with thick mockery. "Well, *that* explains the inflated price. I bet if we could upgrade to the Ben Cartwright suite, we'd get brand-new soap!"

"Honey, we're the only game in town, and there will be somebody walkin' through that door any second willin' to lay out cold cash for a room close to the action."

Jane was disgusted with Barry. This guy was worse than an ex-con at a carnival.

"We'll take it!" Kit interrupted.

"Your mama's a smart lady!" Barry retorted, handing Kit a registration form.

"Is there a place to eat nearby?" Kit asked as she wrote down her information.

"Sure. Lots of places. But your best bet for good food and gettin' a flavor for the whole event is The Circle 9 Diner half a mile down Main, then turn left on Buena Street." Barry made a point to pronounce "Buena" as "*Boo*-na," a fact that seemed curious to Jane. "It's right across from the Stop 'n' Save." Barry leaned closer to Kit, speaking in a pseudo-confidential manner. "The Circle 9's where Sheriff Golden and his deputies hang out in the back booths. Call it Charlotte Central." Barry winked. It was all Jane could do to not pound his head into the desk.

"Wonderful," Kit said, "Go down Main and turn on Buena—"

"*Boo*-na," Barry corrected. "Not *Bwaa*-na. Us locals have to always tell the tourists how to say the name of that street the right way." Barry slid two room keys toward Kit.

"I bet that gets *so* old for you, Barry," Jane said with a sarcastic tenor.

"Goes with the territory, little lady," Barry replied, blissfully unaware of Jane's derision. Jane and Kit headed for the door. "Oh, another little tip, Mrs... ." Barry checked the name on the registration, "*Clark*. You'll want to avoid the bottleneck of traffic around the grammar school where the cops have set up their command post, and also the area around Jenny's Hair Salon across from the KFC."

"Jenny's Hair Salon?" Kit asked.

"Jenny Walker. Charlotte's mama," Barry advised. "It's not like Jenny's there. She's holed up all day long at the house with that Clinton fella."

"Clinton Fredericks," Jane said to herself.

"Yeah, that's him! Clinton and Jenny do a live remote every night for all the TV stations from the front lawn of the Walker house."

"Well, Barry," Kit said with her most adulating smile, "you truly *are* a cornucopia of information!"

Barry checked the time. "If you get goin', you might be able to catch tonight's live TV update. But I warn you two, there are media trucks up and down that street."

"Where does the Walker family live?" Kit asked.

"Oh, it's just Charlotte and her mama. I don't think I've *ever* seen Daddy Walker." Kit stole a glance at Jane, who gave her an "I told you so," look. "To get there, go up Main Street, turn left on Spring, and then right on Raven Court."

Jane and Kit headed to the car. The rain slowed to a constant mist. As Jane backed out of the parking lot, she quietly repeated the name of the street. "Raven...." This was just too weird.

Raven Court was packed with media trucks and curious people gathered on the rain-slicked sidewalks. Jane crawled down the street in the Mustang, peering out at the barrage of satellite trucks, vans, and the occasional motorcycle cop whose job it was to maintain order amid the chaos.

"What a clusterfuck," Jane mumbled under her breath.

"That's gotta be the house up there," Kit said, pointing to a house on the right side of the street that was lit up like a football stadium.

There was barely enough room for Jane to maneuver the Mustang around the logjam of traffic that began forming three houses down from the Walker's modest home. The closer Jane got to the Walker's house, the more yellow ribbons she could see circling the oak trees along the sidewalk. Huge, hand-painted signs hung from the branches that read WE LOVE YOU CHARLOTTE! and BRING OUR ANGEL BACK TO US! Pockets of women and children stood in small circles near the Walker's house, holding candles and praying. Another band of women stood in the soft rain singing "Amazing Grace." It struck Jane that the whole thing looked like a sorrowful pageant; a tableau of tears that reeked of misplaced self-indulgence in the name of misery. Jane's cynical mind questioned whether these people felt a legitimate need to show up on the Walker's front lawn and mourn little Charlotte's kidnapping or whether they just knew when Clinton and Jenny Walker were scheduled to do their regular live evening update for the TV cameras and timed their appearance accordingly.

"Is that him?" Kit asked Jane, pointing toward the Walker's front lawn.

Jane peered into the high-intensity lights. "Yeah, that's the SOB," she replied. Sitting in a canvas chair, getting his trademark tangled blond locks combed, was Clinton Fredericks.

"Two minutes, Clinton!" a voice called out from behind the camera.

Jane shifted her focus to Jenny Walker, who sat in another canvas chair while a production assistant clipped a small microphone on her coat lapel. Another production assistant stood behind her, holding an umbrella over her head as the wind whipped up momentarily, sending a sudden surge of rain over the area. Jenny looked like a giant marshmallow to Jane. Dressed in an oversized white down coat, she appeared even plumper in person than she did in Charlotte's now-infamous birthday video. There was no mistaking the pained expression on her face, though. This was a woman who was deeply suffering. Clinton quickly joined Jenny in the chair next to her and clipped on his microphone.

"God help her," Jane said quietly. "She has no fucking clue how she's being used by that asshole."

"Maybe you could talk to her," Kit offered. "Tell her that—"

"I can't go anywhere near that woman. She's got a well-oiled fortress around her. Jenny Walker has become a commodity. Besides, I'm sure Clinton knows who I am. If I'm gonna work this case, I've got to do it as low-profile as possible."

"Well, you're registered back at the Bonanza as Melody Clark. So our friend Barry won't be barking Jane Perry's arrival around town."

Jane rubbed her face with anxiety. "God, this whole thing is getting too fucking complicated." She pulled the Mustang closer to a satellite truck, turned off the ignition, and grabbed a pack of cigarettes. Squeezing her lithe body between the Mustang and truck, she ducked under a tree and lit the cigarette. Across the street, the director asked the crowd to be quiet. Like a trained seal, Clinton assumed his character of the concerned ally as he tenderly grasped Jenny's arm and spoke to the camera.

It was too disgusting for Jane to watch. She pulled her jacket around her chest, took another deep drag on the cigarette, and sauntered twenty-five yards up the street. The farther away she got from the lights, the more Jane could blend into the wet darkness. Walking another twenty yards up the street, the pockets of onlookers started to diminish. That's what made the car so easy to spot.

It was a jacked-up older model white Firebird, complete with crimson racing stripes that stretched the length of the vehicle. Fancy chrome hubcaps hugged the wheels and glistened against the falling rain. Suddenly, Jane spotted movement in the driver's seat. Taking a step back, she slid behind a large oak tree. The driver—the lone person in the car—looked to be around eighteen years old. He flicked a cigarette lighter, caught a flame, and lit a cigarette. In that brief illumination, Jane saw his face. He was what girls call "cute," in a country kind of way. His jaw was well defined, his cheeks ruddy, and his eyes pensive. An aura of tension engulfed him as he blew a plume of smoke out the window and into the cold night air. Running his nervous fingers through his brown locks, the boy stared at the Walker house. Another drag on his cigarette and more smoke billowed from the car. The sound of a cell phone rang from inside his car. He flicked his cigarette outside onto the puddle-filled pavement and anxiously grappled for the phone in the darkness. He turned on the interior light, located the phone, and answered. Jane could easily see the boy now. His face was a map of fear.

"Hi," the boy answered with a familiar tone. "Yeah, I know. I'm at the pizza place getting somethin' to eat...." He fumbled with a loose thread on the steering wheel. "Okay. I'm leaving now. Bye." The boy turned off his phone and tossed it on the front seat. He sat back and let out a heavy sigh as he nervously bit his thumbnail.

Jane moved her foot ever so slightly, causing a crush of dead leaves to echo into the night. The boy instantly turned toward the sound. Jane stayed perfectly still as she watched the boy's paranoia take hold. He flicked off the interior light and started the ignition.

Gingerly, he edged out of the parking spot and drove up the street far away from the lights. As hard as Jane tried, she couldn't make out the license number.

By the time Jane got back to the Mustang, there was no point in trying to tail the boy's car. Looking around the area, she noted that most of the kids were under the age of thirteen and all of them were girls. That made sense—the missing girl was twelve. Twelve-year-olds attract twelve-year-olds, not eighteen-year-old boys who drive flashy Firebirds.

"Find anything interesting?" Kit asked as Jane got into the Mustang.

"No. Nothing," Jane said off handedly, inching the Mustang past the media trucks and heading back to town.

If the sound of clattering dishes and the steady hum of conversation under the strains of Kenny Chesney singing "She Thinks My Tractor's Sexy" was an indication of a successful, small-town restaurant, then The Circle 9 Diner would have won the grand prize. Kit and Jane waited while a waitress in her late twenties dressed in jeans, a white western shirt with snap buttons, a name tag that read DIANE, a red handkerchief tied around her throat, and a straw cowboy hat with a black 9 burned into the front cleaned the grease off the only available table in the joint. She slid the salt and pepper shakers across the wet Formica and motioned for Kit and Jane to take a seat.

"We're busier here than a one-legged man at a butt kickin' contest!" Diane cheerfully announced as she slapped two menus on the table. "Soon as that news conference broke up, it got thick as thieves in this place! Hell, you can't swing a dead cat in here without hittin' somebody!"

Jane had never heard three consecutive country clichés fired off with such rapid precision. She took a seat with her back to the door and opened the beer-splattered menu. "Yes, you're busy as a bee!"

"It's been like this ever since December 26!" Diane replied as the busboy placed two glasses of ice water shaped like a cowboy boots on the table. "Part of it's because we're just two doors down from The Barbeque Shack. Hey, 'Location, location, location!'"

"The Barbeque Shack?" Jane asked.

"Where Leann works?" Diane acted as if Jane was sadly uninformed. "Bein' it's the last place Charlotte was seen before gettin' into that Fagin guy's Chevy—"

"They matched Leann's description of the car to what Fagin's driving?" Jane asked.

"Well, yeah. A beat-up, four-door, Chevy—"

"How old is Leann?" Kit said, eyebrows furrowing.

"Gosh, ah, I don't know. Sixteen, I guess. I'm sure we'll learn more about her after we watch the interview tonight with Lesley Stahl."

"You don't know her?" Jane asked.

"Leann? No. I knew *Charlotte*." The waitress put a finger to her mouth. "Whoops! Guess I shouldn't say *knew*, huh? I *know* Charlotte and most all of the kids who live around here. The Circle 9 is *the* place to hang, ya know?"

"But you don't know Leann?" Jane pursued.

The waitress's back got a little stiff. "No. I don't."

"Why is that?" Jane said, treating the waitress like a suspect.

The waitress thought for a second and then shrugged her shoulders. "I guess she just sort of blends into the woodwork. If she were an inch taller, she'd be round," Diane said with catty flair, and then on review, recoiled. "Gosh, that's an awful thing to say about a kid, isn't it?"

"Charlotte doesn't blend into the woodwork, does she?" Jane stated.

Her mood quickly lightened "Hell, no! Charlotte likes to be seen and so...people see her." She leaned across the table, speaking in a loud whisper. "Hey, want to know somethin'? Lesley Stahl didn't actually come *in* here, but she had her people come in and get her a cola to go. Least that's what I heard from the girl who was workin' that shift. Isn't that *cool?*"

Kit scanned the menu, never looking up from it. "So, Leann is sixteen. How many sixteen-year-old girls can remember the make of a beat-up car in only a few seconds?"

The waitress looked confused. "Huh?"

"*I* don't know an old beat-up Chevy from an old beat-up Buick—"

"Well, you *should*," Jane smugly interjected. "You've *got* an old, beat-up Buick."

They ordered and Diane disappeared into the kitchen.

Kit leaned forward, speaking in a confidential tone. "Don't you think it's unusual for a sixteen-year-old *girl* to be able to properly identify the make of a car that she saw for, what? Less than half a minute? If she was so suspicious about the whole scenario, why didn't she get the license plate number?"

Jane privately agreed with Kit, but she wasn't about to give her any kudos. As far as Jane was concerned, she was going to remain skeptical for the time being. The front doors swung open. Every head in the place turned in unison, including Jane's. It was the portly Sheriff Golden and his four-manned, pot-bellied entourage. Behind them were two FBI suits. Like local rock stars, the group ambled to the back booths and squeezed into the seats.

Jane turned back to Kit. "Well, it's Sheriff Golden and his 'Yahoo Patrol.'"

"What *is* it with you tonight?" Kit asked, her voice edged with irritation.

"Oh, you know, I've just had a lot of time to think about my life and where I'm heading on my little journey." Jane's tone was sarcastic and somewhat self-abrasive.

"What are you? Thirty-four? Thirty-five?"

"I'll be thirty-six on January 11."

"*January 11?*" Kit said, slightly in awe. "Wow! One-one-one! It's a numerological code."

"*Riiiiight....*" Jane replied in a mocking manner.

Kit leaned across the table. "It's a unique number code that serves as a gateway to seek your highest potential. It offers you a Divine opportunity to surpass any limitations you have unknowingly set up for yourself. You should *embrace* this gift!"

"Anyone can find a message or a hidden meaning in any number to suit their private agenda—"

"One-one-one is *real*! It's a sign!"

"Sign? You sound like Dr. Bartosh!"

"January 11," Kit whispered, unaffected by Jane's comment. "What is the shamanic totem for number 11?" Kit titled her head toward the ceiling, searching for the answer. "Ah! Yes! The *hummingbird*!"

Jane felt her gut clench. In the Native American allegory of Pico Blanco, the hummingbird followed the raven.

"Hummingbird people are very powerful healers. They touch many people in their lifetime and leave indelible imprints on their souls—"

Jane leaned forward. "Are you making this up as you go along?"

"*Listen to me, Jane!* People with hummingbird medicine should learn to take note and back out of touchy situations before they get out of hand! Do I need to remind you that you didn't exactly heed that warning at The Red Tail Hawk Bar?"

"I think backing out of touchy situations before they get out of hand is good advice for anybody."

"Yes, but hummingbird people must—"

"Kit, how many criminals have used signs, symbols, or numbers to support their actions? You had the alphabet killer, the guy who always left the same color on his victims, another guy who carved symbols into his victims' backs...." Jane let out a tired sigh. "Bartosh told me he found the Lord at age thirty-three...the *same* age when Jesus was crucified. And let's not forget Lou's 'Power of Fourteen' theory! God! A person could go crazy with this shit!"

"Symbols are powerful motivators," Kit urged. "Look at the cross. Or the pentagram. We act and react according to what we viscerally associate with a symbol and *then* we give those symbols life. Play the Devil's advocate all you want! I know what I'm saying is true!"

Jane *was* purposely playing the Devil's advocate. Right now, it was the only way she knew how to operate with Kit. If Kit said the menu was dark blue, Jane would call it black, just to prove that she wasn't going to be anybody's patsy. She sat back in the vinyl booth and stared out the window. She half-hoped the kid in the Firebird would drive up so she could get a better look at him and grab his license plate number.

"So," Kit said with enthusiasm, "what's the first thing we do to find Lou?"

Jane turned back to Kit. There was a jagged impatience in the way Kit spoke that fueled Jane's mistrust. *"We?"*

"I hired you to find Lou, but I certainly want to be a part of the search as much as my energy allows—"

"I don't work that way." Her statement fell across the table with an abrupt echo.

"Jane, I have to do something!" Kit declared with authority.

"Read your books. Take a nap. Chat with Barry. Learn how to use the TiVo—"

"What in the hell is going on with you?" Kit whispered loudly with growing anger. "Suddenly I'm being discarded?"

Jane held her own. "You paid me to work this case and that's what I intend to do. If that doesn't set well with you, I'll refund half your money and let you sort it all out." She regarded Kit with a nonchalant glance, waiting to see if Kit would take the bait. Instead, she stared at Jane with a penetrating glare.

"Fine," Kit said tersely, but the underlying tone rang loudly that all was not fine.

Just then, the door to The Circle 9 Diner swung open with great gusto.

"Well, hello darlin'!" the booming voice rang out so that everybody in the place would hear him.

Jane didn't have to turn around. She knew that voice and the ass it belonged to. Diane appeared with the plates of food and Jane asked for "to go" boxes. Jane stole a glance behind her. Clinton had worked his way to where Sheriff Golden and his posse sat. Standing with one hand leaning on the wall and the other hand propped against his trademark camouflage pants, Clinton loudly complimented the men on nabbing Trace Fagin. He dragged a chair up to the booth and sat down and, as all good leeches do, launched into his real purpose for the impromptu tête-à-tête: *information*. Surprisingly, it seemed from Jane's vantage point that the sheriff, his deputies, and the FBI suits were starstruck enough to get hooked on Clinton's line.

"Jesus," Jane murmured under her breath. She turned back to Kit. "Meet me in the car. I can't risk him seeing me here." Jane successfully slipped out of the restaurant and secured herself in the shadows as she lit a cigarette.

She looked up just in time to see the red-striped Firebird speed up Main Street and disappear into the cold night air.

CHAPTER 18

"The show's going to start in less than a minute!" Kit alerted Jane.

Jane finished unpacking her toothbrush and blow-dryer in the bathroom. She took a troubled glance around the tiny, rust-painted room. Some idiot—possibly Barry—apparently didn't know that pastel colors make a small space look bigger. And you don't paint a bathroom all rust, *including* the door. Even with the door slightly ajar, Jane felt as if she were trapped in a clay tomb.

She walked into the cramped main room that held two twin beds with mattresses that groaned at the slightest touch. They were covered with paisley spreads, featuring *more* rust in the natty pattern. A teetering table sat between the beds with an old clock that told the time by flapping a new number down like a slow-moving card deck. Jane shook her head at that, figuring the clock was almost as old as she was. A cheap mirror hung above a three-drawer bureau opposite the beds. Atop the bureau sat a color TV that Jane gauged was over ten years old. The log cabin walls were painted with brown lacquer, forcing even more darkness into the sparse room. The only window was a mere six feet from Jane's bed and draped with heavy beige curtains rimmed with dust, grime, and cigarette burns. Jane sat on her bed, generating a painful squeak from the mattress springs. Punching her fist into the yellowed pillows to prop them upright, she took solace in the fact that at least she wasn't plugging down $125 a night for this shithole.

Kit fiddled with the remote control—the only thing in the room that smelled fresh and new. "There's too many buttons on this thing," Kit said, befuddled. "What's this TiVo, anyway?"

Jane reached over and took the remote from Kit, explaining as briefly as she could that TiVo was God's answer to instant recording while you watched television. If one missed what someone said or wanted to repeat a specific portion of a TV show, one simply pressed the REVERSE button and the program sped backward. Pressing the PLAY button, the show resumed. The handy PAUSE button allowed the viewer to freeze-frame the video. This came in handy, Jane explained, when the phone rang or one needed a bathroom break and didn't want to miss a moment of their show. Jane resumed playback of the news program.

The announcer's booming voice set the stage. "Tonight, see Lesley Stahl's exclusive interview with Leann Hamilton, the *sole* witness to the kidnapping of twelve-year-old Charlotte Walker." Leann's chubby face filled the screen as the picture dissolved into the angelic portrait of Charlotte Walker. Jane remembered the school photo from the *Denver Post*. She knew all too well how the media slants and creates bias based on camera angles, lighting, and careful editing. Her brief sortie into the limelight that past summer had confirmed how the media makes or breaks you by how they photograph your story. In Jane's case, they tended to shoot her with a harder, less forgiving light that made her look road-ravaged. The photo used to depict Charlotte Walker was one of innocence and prepubescent beauty. It looked especially softer in comparison to the more full-bodied shot of Leann Hamilton.

Lesley Stahl appeared on the screen, walking near the command post at the grammar school. A soft lens diffused the scene, giving it a comforting texture. The lens also did wonders for masking lines on the face—something most TV anchors demanded. "Oakhurst, California," Lesley stated with her trademark incisive tone. "A small town known as the 'Gateway to Yosemite.' But the day after Christmas, this tight-knit community was rocked by the brash, daylight kidnapping of one of their own, twelve-year-old Charlotte Walker. What made this crime so brazen is that it was done under the watchful eye of at least one person. Her name is Leann Hamilton, and at age sixteen, she carries the weight of the world on her shoulders...." The screen dissolved to The Barbeque Shack. As Stahl narrated, the camera followed a painfully aware Leann as she went about taking orders at the take-out window over her headset. Leann made frequent furtive glances toward the moving camera. Jane quickly noted a pervasive insecurity around Leann. She moved with hesitancy. Her actions were deliberate, as if she were terrified of making a mistake. The scene cut to Leann standing outside The Barbeque Shack with Lesley. Leann wore her uniform, a bright yellow shirt and striped hat that displayed the name of the fast-food joint in red embroidery. Leann pointed her fleshy hand toward the curb, acknowledging to Lesley that this was where she witnessed Charlotte getting into the car. A crowd of people could be seen gathered around the two of them, partly gawking, but mostly intrigued by the kid in the yellow shirt and striped hat talking to Lesley Stahl. Jane noticed that Leann stole a shy glance at the crowd surrounding them. She smiled a genuine grin at them and then turned back to Lesley.

The scene finally cut to a one-on-one interview between Lesley and Leann. Thankfully, Leann had changed into a navy blue, button front shirt and jeans, and sat nervously tapping her fingers on the armrest of the chair.

"This has been a big week for you, hasn't it?" Lesley asked.

"Yeah," Leann replied, letting out a burst of air and smiling momentarily.

"Take us back to that moment when you saw Charlotte getting into the car."

"Well...um...." Leann nervously looked off to the left, holding that glance as she continued. "It happened so fast. I saw her from the back. But I recognized her red leather jacket. She wears it a lot."

The show instantly cut to the birthday video that had been played ad nauseam for four straight days. As Lesley narrated, the screen once again showed Charlotte in her backyard, wearing the odd rainbow wig. The camera zoomed closer, filling the TV screen with Charlotte's face. Her hazel eyes, painted in thick black liner, stared at the camera in a provocative manner. "I *love* my new coat! It's *beautiful! Thank you!*" Charlotte squealed. The camera pulled back as Charlotte took off her jean jacket to reveal the tank top with the slithering snake image. Jane unexpectedly found herself sinking her hand into her pants pocket and rubbing the snakestone totem. Charlotte donned the red jacket and paraded for the camera. Jane grabbed the remote and pressed the PAUSE button just as Charlotte completed a modellike, runway twirl and faced the camera.

"Why'd you stop it?" Kit asked.

"Pretend you don't know she's twelve. How old does she look?" Jane asked, her eyes boring into the seductive face looking back at her.

Kit considered the question. "Maybe fifteen...fourteen at the youngest. Why?"

Jane resumed the playback of the show. "Just curious."

"Put it back on pause," Kit instructed. Jane obliged. "We know that Lou is attracted to victims who match his mother's looks: hazel eyes and brown hair. And then there's the age of fourteen—"

"And Charlotte is batting one out of three, based on that profile."

"But if she *looks* fourteen, then the only thing we're missing is the color of the hair."

"You're trying to fit a square peg of rationale into a round hole."

"Okay, forget the hair! Maybe Lou changed his MO!"

"So, *no* patterns? Lou just chose Charlotte for no reason?"

Kit let out a weary sigh. "Jane, it's like you're the Cheshire cat in Alice in Wonderland. I'm trying to make this—"

"Fit," Jane said, finishing Kit's sentence. "Because you hate Lou Peters. You told me so. You said you were so angry at him, that you gave yourself cancer—"

"I *did* hate him. But I don't anymore. In my heart, I have forgiven him. I see him for who he is: A desperately confused man who is still reacting to life because of the horrific abuse he suffered at the hands of his mother—"

"Cut the pabulum—"

"Lou was easily influenced. He *still* is. He could have become a charismatic, positive member of society. But the sexual deviancy he was subjected to at a young age somehow made him choose the darker path."

"You got one thing right: he *chose* it."

"Oh, Jane. Sometimes, there's a tender line between the good and the evil in a person. All it takes to fall either way is the perfect trigger." Kit leaned her body toward Jane. "You danced on that razor sharp edge. But *you* chose to live an honorable life."

Jane noted how Kit enjoyed turning the conversation back to Jane's troubled childhood. She wasn't going to take the bait. "Tell me something, Kit," Jane's tone was direct and unemotional, "how many times a day do you fantasize about killing Lou?"

"I don't," Kit replied without missing a beat.

Jane expected to hear a moment's hesitation to her question, but Kit's response was startlingly quick. From Jane's experience, a lie is found within the split second between the question and the answer. Based on that, Kit passed Jane's test. But she still wasn't sold on the fact that Kit's motive for tracking down Lou was completely altruistic. Jane pressed the PLAY button and the show resumed.

The camera cut to Lesley Stahl. "Did it look like Charlotte knew the man in the car?"

Leann looked right at Lesley. "From where I was sitting—"

"And where was that?"

"Um, I was on break. There's this area next to The Barbeque Shack with a bench where you can see the street and people walking by. That's where I was sitting." Jane noted that Leann's voice became stronger as she described the location.

"You were sitting on the bench and then you saw the car drive up?"

"Yeah, I just happened to be looking in that direction—"

"Describe the car," Lesley interrupted.

Leann appeared taken aback by Lesley's rapid question. "Um, like I told Sheriff Golden, it was an old, four-door Chevy. Blue. Grayish blue."

"Are you aware that the man who has been picked up, Mr. Trace Fagin, owns a vehicle matching that description, except that the color has more green than blue in it."

"Yeah, um," Leann became visibly nervous, anxiously rubbing the arms of the chair. "It was so quick. But there could have been more green than blue—"

"You told Sheriff Golden you were unable to discern the face of the driver?"

Leann looked down at the floor. "That's right," she replied with breathy worry.

Lesley reached over, placing her hand over Leann's trembling leg. "This is a lot of pressure for a sixteen-year-old."

"I'll be seventeen in a couple weeks," Leann weakly offered.

"It's obvious that this ordeal has been very traumatic for you. Hasn't it?" Lesley's voice was a mixture of genuine concern blended with high TV drama.

Leann's eyes filled with tears. "I just wanted to help. I saw her get into the car—"

"You saw Charlotte get in the car...." Lesley said, leading Leann.

There was a moment of hesitation from Leann. Her eyes strayed from the floor and wandered to the left, seemingly fixated. "Yes...I did."

The rest of the interview focused on the direction the Chevy took, any unusual markings on the car, and whether Leann and Charlotte were friendly. It was patently clear to Jane that Leann found the question of a friendship totally obscure. It wasn't just the age difference, Jane gauged, but the social clique that Charlotte rotated in. Jane imagined that Leann's life revolved around school, her job, and home, where she probably spent all her free time watching TV, gorging on food, and feeling the abject sting of loneliness engulf her.

The interview ended and the program went to a commercial. Jane pressed the MUTE button on the remote control. Kit unraveled her salt-and-pepper braid, letting her locks flow freely across her shoulders. She tentatively maneuvered her heavy frame off the bed, grabbed a pair of pajamas from her packed suitcase, and headed into the bathroom. Jane waited until Kit closed the door and turned on the shower before pressing the REVERSE button. Skimming the interview, she landed at the point where Lesley Stahl patted Leann's thigh. Pressing the PLAY button, the scene resumed.

"It's obvious that this ordeal has been very traumatic for you. Hasn't it?" Lesley said to Leann.

Leann's eyes filled with tears. "I just wanted to help.... I saw her get into the car—"

"You saw Charlotte get in the car...."

Jane leaned closer, eyeing Leann like a hawk. The girl hesitated and then her eyes moved from the floor to the left of where she was seated. "Yes...I did."

Jane pressed the PAUSE button and stared at Leann's tortured face. She kept staring at it until she heard Kit turn off the shower water.

DECEMBER 31

After a restless night of sleep, Jane awoke at six A.M. feeling a mix of apprehension and confusion taking hold. Kit lay sound asleep, her buckwheat pillow perfectly contoured under her neck. It seemed like an eternity to Jane since the last time she took a morning run. Deciding it was the best way to shake the cobwebs from her troubled mind, Jane quietly changed out of her Denver Broncos nightshirt and into running pants and a hooded sweatshirt. Coffee would have to wait. Jane wanted to make as little noise as possible so she didn't wake Kit and fend off questions such as "Where are you going?" She snagged a cigarette, a pack of matches, and her cell phone. One never knew when one may need to make a phone call, Jane reasoned as she slipped out the front door.

The sun was just cresting over the trees that framed the front office of The Bonanza Cabins, illuminating the barrage of media trucks that filled the parking lot. A handful of technicians were already outside, fiddling with equipment in their van and talking on their mobile phones. The sky was a dank, cloudy mess, and the air filled with a wet coldness that shook Jane to her core. She lit her cigarette and took several drags. As was her pattern, she gently squashed the cigarette out against the pavement before resting it on the window ledge. Jane judged that it was unlikely Clinton Fredericks would be out and about this early. However, there was always a chance he'd be cruising the main drag. With that in mind, Jane opted to jog around the remote, two-lane back road around the cabins.

Curving around the front office, Jane noted a stack of *Fresno Bee* newspapers outside the door. Too small a town to have a daily newspaper, Oakhurst relied upon the *Bee* to enlighten them on local and national news. The headline to the side of the center read, REWARD FUND FOR MISSING OAKHURST GIRL TOPS $50,000. Jane knew Clinton Fredericks would be tingling with anticipation when he read that newsflash.

She meandered around the cabins and started up the dirt road when she noted three navy sedans parked in the adjacent motel parking lot. Each had government plates that Jane identified as FBI. She felt a swell of anger as the pained memories of the not-so-pleasant dealings with the FBI came to mind. A few weeks prior to this, she had felt on top of the world, working with the Feds; now she was a very small fish in a very chaotic pond. Jane ran up the dirt road in an attempt to shake off the crush of bad memories. It suddenly struck her that tonight was New Year's Eve. A year ago, she spent it with her brother, both of them getting drunk in her home until they passed out at dawn. Since then, Mike had found a girlfriend, AA, and a new life of sobriety. Reflecting on her own last twelve months, Jane felt as if she had gone far and then fallen to a place even more desperate than when she began. *Six months*, she thought to herself with a sense of sadness. Six months of not picking up a drink. Six months worth of sobriety chips that lay strewn in her cousin Carl's gravel driveway. And now she had a little over thirty hours of sobriety under her ragged belt. An overwhelming sense of failure grabbed at her gut, suffocating her drive as she headed up a sharp incline. She ambled up the hill as a heavy mist blew across the road, signaling the onslaught of more inclement weather. Jane pulled the hood of her sweatshirt over her head, drawing the ties closer to protect herself from the bone-chilling climate. She considered turning back when the sound of someone hammering in the distance got her attention.

Jane crested the hill. Looking up the two-lane road less than a quarter mile, she spotted the white Firebird with the distinctive red stripe. It was parked on an unsteady angle off the right side of the road. She obscured herself in the shadows of the conifers and walked toward the car. The echoing sound of the hammer continued for another few seconds before abating. She spotted movement about 100 feet in front of the Firebird. Peering closely, she identified the boy walking back to his car carrying the hammer. It would be an easy sprint for Jane. She knew she could reach his car just about the time he got to it. She could strike up a conversation. Pretend she was lost. Anything, she reasoned, to draw him into her web.

Picking up the pace, Jane jogged with purpose toward the Firebird. The lonely road and the echoing of her feet slapping against the wet gravel attracted the boy's attention. He looked up, then resumed his gait with greater resolve toward his car. "Excuse me!" Jane yelled, waving her hand in the air. "I need directions! I'm lost!"

The boy reached the driver's door and hastily got into his car. He steered the Firebird back onto the road and drove away from the scene. It took Jane less than a minute to stand in the spot where the Firebird had been parked. The sound of paper flapping in the wet breeze caught her attention. Turning toward the fluttering noise, Jane discovered one missing child poster of Charlotte Walker after another, hammered to the trunks of trees along the road. The niggling idea crossed her mind that the best way for a criminal to cover his tracks and protect himself is to join the search effort for the missing victim. And what better way for that perp to feel the power of his crime than by driving a nail through his victim's head as he hammers her picture onto a tree?

Jane arrived back at the Cabins twenty minutes later. Jogging into the parking lot, she spotted an odd sight. There was Kit, dressed in her purple pants and heavy winter coat, walking backward in circles around the perimeter of the parking lot. And she was chanting. At least, it looked as if she were chanting from where Jane stood observing the disjointed scene. Kit's bizarre actions were attracting the attention of a few media technicians. Jane briefly considered corralling Kit and hauling her back into the room. But she weighed that option against the fact that Kit's momentary absence afforded Jane the opportunity to do some quick investigative work on her computer. She headed for the cabin, eager to retrieve her partial cigarette from the window ledge. However, the cigarette was gone. Jane checked the surrounding area, thinking the wind may have swept it away, but she found nothing. The morning was starting off on a bad note.

Inside the cabin, Jane hurriedly turned on her laptop computer. While she waited for it to boot up, she grabbed the local phone book from the top drawer of the bureau. It was a long shot that Lou would be listed in the white pages, but Jane had lucked out before by using the most obvious means of investigative know-how. It wouldn't work this time; there was no Lou Peters in the phone book. Jane quickly pulled out the voluminous files Kit gave her on Lou's case and searched specific pages where addresses were listed. All she found was Lou's prior address in Mariposa. Jane recalled Kit telling her that Lou dutifully called his bondsman to tell him he was moving to Oakhurst, but unfortunately, that address never made it into Kit's hands.

The computer beeped to alert Jane it was ready for action. Jane opened her Internet program and clicked on her bookmark "Favorites," opening one of her many subscription service Web sites. This particular site—sexcriminals.com—included a national directory that listed registered sex offenders by county within each state. Jane selected Madera County after checking the phone book cover for Oakhurst. She typed in her professional ID number and password to gain access. Within a few seconds, the page of names appeared. Scrolling down the page, Jane spotted Lou's name and address. Typing the address into MapQuest, Jane determined the location was about eight miles away on a rural road that skirted the edge of Oakhurst. Footsteps neared the cabin. Jane quickly jotted down the address before snapping her laptop shut.

Kit walked breathlessly into the cabin, closing the door behind her. "What an invigorating morning!" she gushed. "I trust your jog was as exhilarating?"

"Yeah," Jane guardedly replied.

Kit glanced toward the laptop. "Checking your e-mails?"

It was this sort of questioning that Jane hoped to avoid with Kit. "You got it," Jane said in a distant manner. Kit meandered around Jane toward her bed. "You have any idea what happened to the cigarette on the window ledge?"

Kit melted onto the bed, stretching like a cat. "Yes. I disposed of it."

Jane's ire swelled inside her chest. "I left it there for a reason! It's a ritual. I get dressed for my run, light a cigarette, take a few drags, crush out the tip, and leave it outside the door so I can re-light it when I get back and finish it!"

Kit regarded Jane as if she were insane. "Aren't you running to *improve* your health? Isn't cigarette smoking antagonistic to that endeavor?"

"I run when I need to think more clearly! *And* I like rituals—"

"Like all alcoholics do," Kit added matter-of-factly. "That's not a judgment, by the way. I love rituals. But some can be self-destructive. Case in point, the cigarette."

Jane moved toward Kit's bed. "That was *not* your cigarette to dispose of! If I want to smoke, go for a run, and then smoke the rest of it when I come back, *I will do it!*"

"That simply doesn't make any sense," Kit countered, twisting her body to the right until she successfully popped her spine.

"And walking backward in circles, chanting to yourself in front of television crews makes more sense?"

"Absolutely," Kit said casually. "I learned the technique from a Chinese acupuncturist. Walking backward in circles or in a straight line for twenty minutes every day relieves pressure in the low back. It's very common in China. They have walking backward breaks the same way we have coffee breaks. You should try it sometime. And I wasn't chanting. I was softly singing 'Me and Bobby McGee.' *God*, I still miss Janis—"

Jane took Kit's rambling as another attempt to conjure a sense of openness with her, whereby Jane would drop her guard. "*I* was under the impression that we're attempting to *not* draw any unnecessary attention to ourselves. Isn't that our agreed upon objective?"

"Of course."

"So don't you think that walking backward in circles singing 'Me and Bobby McGee' might contradict that objective?"

Kit furrowed her brow. "My goodness. You sound like a lawyer." Kit rolled off the bed, heading for the bathroom. "I intend to walk backward and sing whenever I want to. And you're welcome to join me anytime."

Kit closed the bathroom door, leaving Jane stewing. Locating her large stash of gourmet coffee, Jane set about to make her first strong brew of java. As the coffee percolated, she ducked outside, lit a cigarette, and stood in the softly falling rain sucking every drop of nicotine she could into her lungs.

When Kit emerged, Jane wasted no time. She grabbed a pair of jeans, wool socks, underwear, and a brown turtleneck and ensconced herself in the rust-colored box known as the Hop Sing bathroom. Fifteen minutes later, she reappeared, fully dressed, hair half wet, and eager to wrap her hands around a tall cup of coffee. However, there was less than six ounces remaining in the decanter. "What the hell?" Jane said out loud.

"Oh, I poured two cups off," Kit announced from her perch on the bed. "I hope that's all right. I need it for later. Since you'll be gone all day and not in need of my assistance, I figured I'd take advantage of my time alone and do a coffee enema. It's an old, natural protocol for cancer. Really *invigorates* you from the inside out!"

Jane stared at Kit. There was a self-righteous look on her face that Jane read as "Don't fuck with me, kiddo." It was the sort of passive-aggressive gaze that Jane took as far more aggressive than passive. First the cigarette and now the coffee. *Fine.* If it was a battle of wills Kit wanted, she'd picked the wrong woman to play her game. "You want the coffee? Take it!" Jane said, happy to call Kit's bluff. She dug in her duffel bag and retrieved her Glock. Strapping the shoulder holster over her turtleneck, Jane secured the Glock. And she did it all in plain view of Kit.

"You really feel you need a gun?" Kit asked quietly.

Jane looked at Kit. "You never know when someone's gonna try to fuck with you." She let the statement linger in the air purely for effect before donning her leather jacket and turning toward the door.

"One thing before you go," Kit said. Jane turned just as Kit tossed a metal disc in her direction. Jane awkwardly caught it. She looked at the object in disbelief. It was one of her sobriety chips. "Don't you get one for twenty-four hours?" Kit asked earnestly.

Jane didn't know what to make of Kit's bold gesture. As much as she wanted to thank her for saving the chip, she remained silent as she slipped the disc in her jeans pocket. Nobody was going to snare Jane in a trap under the ruse of altruism.

CHAPTER 19

You couldn't call it gourmet, but The Coffee Cabin certainly knew how to make a strong brew. Jane located the drive-through, log-cabinesque establishment on her way to Lou's house. The java tasted like the beans had been blackened, but the surge of caffeine made Jane feel more awake and alive than she had in days. The four-dollar jumbo cinnamon roll didn't hurt, either.

Jane lit a cigarette, feeling a sense of freedom that she was finally allowed to smoke in her own car. As she curved the Mustang down the two-lane highway toward the remote county road address, Jane did what she always did when she worked a case. She contemplated the various possibilities and what might go wrong. Then she systematically developed a loose contingency plan for every possible occurrence. First, she took the worst case scenario. What if she got to the house and found Lou and signs that Charlotte was there? She still wasn't sold on the idea that Lou had kidnapped Charlotte, but she knew she had to consider every conceivable option. If she found him there with the girl, she'd call for backup. But what if her mobile phone didn't work out in the boonies? Okay, Jane thought, she had her Glock and she had enough experience dealing with half-cocked psychos over the years to know how to save the victim.

Then Jane considered the absolute worst-worst case scenario: What if she had to kill Lou in order to save Charlotte? Jane felt a thud hit her solar plexus. She had killed one person in her entire career on the force and she had done it because she knew it was the only way to rescue the victim. There was no glory in it, nor was there a sense of relief. There was just the restless playback in her head that she did what she had to do. Jane knew one thing: As much as she hated pulling the trigger that day, she would pull it again if it meant that someone else would live.

The secluded county road popped up sooner than Jane expected. She pulled the Mustang off to the side of the main road and scanned the area. It was an undulating topography of dried grass and barbed wire fences that seemed to hold in nothing but endless acres of dead air. Jane clicked her cell phone on to check for a signal. There was coverage, but it was sketchy.

Turning onto the county road, Jane took her time winding around the paved road and checking the bars on her cell phone. She came to a rundown trailer on her left. Noting the address, Jane realized she had another half mile or so to go before reaching Lou's house. Driving farther, she came upon yet another trailer, this one painted bright pink. Rounding another turn, she arrived at Lou's address.

The house was a former, old-time schoolhouse that had been tenuously refurbished just enough to make it livable. Generous curls of gray paint coiled off the sides of the house. The front windows were missing drapes. From Jane's position, the front yard looked barren. A trio of large trash containers lined the road in front of the house. Each was stuffed so full of trash that the tops could not close. Jane checked her cell phone. There was only one bar. She backed the Mustang 100 feet down the road and parked it under a lone oak tree.

As she walked toward the house, the wind whipped around her body, driving the cold deeper into her bones. The clouds parted briefly, allowing a split second of sunshine to stream onto the road before being smothered by another bank of storm clouds. Jane reached the house and the trash bins. Opening the first one, she found several brown trash bags packed full. The second bin included assorted items that ranged from pieces of old carpeting to rusty tools. The third bin held a mix of old newspapers and plastic water bottles. Apparently, Lou was not into recycling. Out of curiosity, Jane pulled out several newspapers and checked the dates. They were all back issues of Oakhurst's local paper, *The Sierra Star.* The most recent one was from October, while the oldest dated back to May. Jane dropped the stack back into the bin. As they fell, the pages fluttered, exposing sections that had been carefully cut out with scissors. Jane retrieved one of the newspapers and flipped through it. The holes ranged from two inches square to half a page. Some of the missing pieces of newspaper were located in the section titled "Religion"; others were located everywhere from the front page to the color insert that featured the weekly specials at the market. Clearly, there was no rhyme or reason to what was cut out.

Jane tossed the paper back into the trash bin and closed the lid. She glanced up at the house and caught a glimpse of gleaming metal partially hidden around the left side of the house. She looked closer and realized it was the back end of a motorcycle. The hair raised on the back of Jane's neck. Detective Charles Sawyer had mentioned that Lou rode a motorcycle and used it, according to Sawyer, to entice Ashlee.

Okay, Jane thought, Lou is here. She carefully walked around the trash bins and turned into the front yard. The dead grass lay matted against the soaked earth, drowning in deep puddles of rainwater. Jane briefly considered knocking on the front door and being forthright. But she always preferred to silently case a house first before confronting a possible suspect. Jane gingerly slogged through the mud as she headed for the right side of the old house. Coming up to the first drapeless window, she peered into the room. It was a mudroom with stacks of loose boxes piled to the ceiling. Moving a few steps farther, Jane looked into the second window. The large main room lay stark in front of her. Across the thrashed wooden floor were several rolls of duct tape. A tangle of rope sat in the corner. The only other item in the room was a full-length mirror, propped up against the wall. Jane's heart started beating faster. Duct tape, rope, and a mirror. These were three of the items Sawyer said Lou had purchased prior to kidnapping Ashlee. Jane leaned in closer to the window when she heard a young girl's scream coming from the back of the property.

Instinctively, she reached for her Glock and turned toward the sound. The scream echoed into the wet morning air, lingered for a few seconds, and then quiet descended once again. Jane kept her right hand on the Glock and flattened her back against the house, cautiously moving toward the back of the property.

"Don't!" the girl screamed.

Jane's entire body stiffened. Quickly, she checked her cell phone. There was a shaky bar of coverage—not enough for clear transmission of a phone call. "Shit!" Jane whispered under her breath. She continued her methodical approach. The mud under her boots made a pronounced sucking sound with each step.

"That's gonna hurt!" the girl yelped.

Jane's mind raced as she picked up speed and finally hugged the corner of the house. She stealthily bent her head around the corner of the house just enough to get a clear view of the scene. A large, high-backed wicker chair stood in the middle of the muddy yard with its back to Jane. A young, preteen girl sat in the chair. The brief movement of another person could be seen sitting in front of the girl. From this angle, the whole scene looked depraved to Jane. She decided to make her move. Emerging from her safe cover, she kept one hand on the Glock and stood with her feet firmly planted on the wet ground. "Charlotte?" Jane yelled with authority.

The sound of a girl screaming in fright pierced the air, and was soon joined by a second screaming girl. An auburn-haired girl in her early teens leaped from in front of the chair. The younger girl, who looked to be around ten, jumped out of the wicker chair and stood next to the older girl. They stared at Jane in a state of confusion for a few long seconds. Jane noticed that the younger child held a frog in her hand. She released her grip on the Glock and quickly covered the gun with her jacket.

"Who are you?" the older girl asked.

"I'm—"

"What's going on here?" a booming voice yelled, coming at Jane from around the front of the house. Jane spun around. A large, mountain of a man in his early forties strode toward her with angry purpose. "Who the hell are you?" the man asked with impunity.

"Perry!" Jane said in an automatic response.

"Perry who?" the man asked, sneaking a quick glance to the girls and then looking back at Jane.

"Perry Grey." It was the first word that came to her mind as she looked at the drab sky.

"What can I do for you, Ms. Grey?"

"I'm looking for Lou Peters."

"I don't know anybody named Lou Peters," the man said, his voice calming down a few notches. "We're new in town. Just moved into the place two weeks ago."

"Not much furniture," Jane said, more as a leading question. She couldn't help it.

"Yeah, well, my wife's showing up in a few days with all our stuff. Good thing, too. This place was a mess. Had to rip up carpeting and pull all the trash—" The two girls gradually drifted toward Jane, interested in what she was saying. The man addressed them. "Hey! Aren't you two supposed to be cleaning out the back rooms? What in the hell have you got in your hand?"

The youngest held up the frog. "We saw him moving across the yard, Dad. He was limping. We were trying to make him feel better."

"Put him back where you found him, and hop to!" He clapped his hands together as added emphasis. "This place is not gonna clean itself!"

The girls dutifully returned the frog to the wet ground and went about their chores. The older girl, however, made a point of lingering close by.

"You gotta stay on 'em 24/7, you know?"

"Yeah," Jane replied. "So, you moved here two weeks ago?"

"We took ownership of the place then. We've been back and forth to Idaho several times during that period."

"Did it just come up vacant?"

"No. It's been empty at least a month. I know because I was out here around Thanksgiving to check out the place."

"I see...." Jane's mind temporarily drifted.

"Who's this Peters guy?"

"He's...bounced some checks around town. I'm from the collection agency. This was his last known address."

"They track you down in *person* now?"

"When you've bounced as many checks as Peters has, you get special treatment."

"I'm sorry I can't help you."

"Well, thanks for your time," Jane said as she sloshed through the muck and headed back to her car. The man went into the house, closing the door behind him. Jane was outside the front yard when she heard the sound of muddy footsteps behind her.

"Hey!" the voice said in a half whisper.

Jane turned to find the older girl running to catch up with her. The kid looked back at the house and then motioned for Jane to move farther down the road to move out of sight. When the girl felt she was at a safe distance, she stopped walking and turned to Jane in a friendly manner.

"So, his name is *Lou?*" The girl's hazel eyes danced with excitement.

"Yeah," Jane replied warily. "You know him?"

"*Weeelllll,*" the girl said with a coquettish tilt of her head, "I can't say I *know* him. But I met him. I just didn't know his name. *Lou,* huh?" It was obvious she was in love.

The girl melted into a flirtatious vixen. She spun her auburn hair around her index finger and used every ounce of charm to draw Jane into her confidence. Jane, however, was impervious to the kid's scheme. "How'd you meet him?"

"He stopped by a few days after we got here. I mean, I'm assuming it's the same guy. He picked up a box that he left. Said it was church stuff. But I didn't believe it."

"Why not?"

"He didn't exactly look like your typical Bible-thumper, if you know what I mean." The girl's hazel eyes twinkled with a mischievous sparkle.

"No, actually, I don't know what you mean," Jane asked, keeping her stoic persona engaged.

"He was absolutely drop-dead gorgeous! Blue eyes, brown hair that's all tangled by the breeze...." Her mind sensually remembered the face. "And a *really* cute ass," she added with a friendly cadence. "It didn't hurt that he had a motorcycle to go with his cute little body. *Tons* nicer than my dad's worthless piece of shit motorcycle. It was baby blue with this cool sticker of a white dove on the back. I mean, it just shows you how sensitive he is, ya know? *A dove!*"

"Uh-huh," Jane said, unimpressed.

The girl was getting irked that her playfulness was not working. Her tone became slightly forceful. "Well, it just doesn't make sense that a guy *that* good looking and *that* sensitive is bouncing checks all over town! Hey, like, people make mistakes, right? We're all human!"

Jane couldn't believe how desperate the girl was to apply as many worn-out clichés as she could muster to create the glowing image she wanted for Lou. In an instant, Jane understood the powerful effect Lou Peters still had on young girls. "Where was your dad when Lou came over here?"

The girl's face quickly changed into a pissed frown as she rolled her eyes with an overly dramatic flare. "He'd gone into town. It was like the *only* time he didn't have us in eyesight! God! It's like, I need a life, ya know? It's bad enough that he moves us to this shithole town so I can rot my life away! Like I'm supposed to... what? Do whatever he tells me, be a good girl, get good grades... blah, blah, blah. *Puhleeeeease*, spare me!"

"So, you only saw Lou once?"

"Yeah. To talk to him." The girl obviously had more to offer. As was her tried-and-true routine, she waited, arching her eyebrow in a provocative manner in hopes of eliciting more interest out of the adult. When Jane's steely eyes didn't give in to the kid's method, the girl quickly offered the information. "He drove by on his cool bike the next day. But my dad was in the front yard and yelling at us to rake the leaves. Lou just kept going down the road. Never saw him again. Thank you, *Daddy!*"

Like Jane said, the perpetrator always chooses the perfect victim. The only problem here was that *this* kid had a father who was big, loud, intrusive, and overprotective. "This all happened two weeks ago?" Jane asked, calculating the days. The girl nodded. "Okay," Jane said satisfied. She took a step closer to the girl. "How old are you?"

The tight proximity of Jane's body intimidated the kid. "Sixteen."

Jane heard her voice inflection rise up, signaling a lie. "If you're sixteen, I'm twenty-one." Jane put on her cop bravado and muscled her frame toward the kid in the most daunting pose she could muster. "I'm asking you again. *How old are you?*"

The girl was clearly nervous. "Fourteen," she managed to get out.

"You wanna see fifteen?"

The kid's eyes grew as big as two hazel saucers. "Yeah," she stuttered.

"Then stop trying to race the clock. Be fourteen. Do stuff that fourteen-year-olds do. Then be fifteen and do things that fifteen-year-olds do. If you don't fuck up your life, you'll make it to eighteen and you can leave this shithole town and strike out for greener pastures. And by the time you get to be twenty-five and the world's kicked you in the teeth, you can cry yourself to sleep at night, wishing you were fourteen again."

The girl stood in stunned silence. A hard pitter-patter of raindrops tapped against her face as she regarded Jane with bewilderment.

"Hey, where's your sister?" her father's voice rang out in the distance.

The girl rapidly turned toward the house. "I'm out here. The lady...." she hesitated, not sure what to say.

"Needed directions to the post office," Jane whispered, coaching her.

"Needed directions to the post office!" the kid yelled.

"Okay, make it quick!" her father yelled back.

"Go on," Jane said, turning around and heading to the Mustang.

The girl started back into her front yard, then stopped. "Hey, wait!" Jane reluctantly turned around. "You yelled out the name Charlotte when you saw us in the backyard. Isn't that the name of the missing girl in town?"

Jane considered the question before speaking. "Don't keep your dad waiting."

It's what wasn't spoken that sent the girl rushing back into the arms of her father.

Jane retraced the rural route back to the main road as the rain turned into a steady downpour. Buckets of water fell so fast that the Mustang's windshield wipers labored. The question rang in Jane's head: If Lou wasn't living where he was supposed to be living—where he was registered in the national database—where had he gone? Based upon what the father told her, the house had been vacant for at least one month. Lou's past MO, from what Kit told her, demonstrated that he dutifully checked in with his bondsman and probably the sheriff when he had a change of address. So how long did it take for the database to display that information? Furthermore, there was a missing kid in this town. That meant that every registered sexual predator had to be contacted by the sheriff's office and eliminated as a suspect as their alibis proved true. Law enforcement knew where Lou Peters lived. Somehow, the database had not reflected the address change. There were driver's license records, Jane thought to herself. She had access via a subscription service to all DMV records.

Jane's cell phone rang. Preoccupied with navigating the raging rainstorm, Jane flipped open the phone and answered with an aggravated clip. "Yeah! Hello!" Silence. *"Hello?"* Jane stressed. A distant click was heard.

Jane pulled the Mustang to the side of the road and checked the incoming number. All it read was RESTRICTED. Perhaps the call was dropped as Jane wound around the corners of the rural road in the rain. Or perhaps the storm caused her cell to not retrieve the data. These were the possibilities that quickly buzzed through Jane's mind just as the phone rang again. She checked the cell screen and this time a phone number registered. It was a "541" area code. If memory served, it was Charles Sawyer.

"Hello?"

"Hello, Jane. Charles Sawyer here. Did I catch you at a bad time?"

"No.... I'm good. Hey, did you just call me a second ago?"

"I'm sorry? We've got a dicey connection. What'd you say?"

"Did you just call me?"

"You're breaking up," Sawyer replied.

Jane pulled onto the road and crept toward the main highway in search of better cell coverage. "Never mind. What's up?"

"I don't want you to think I'm stealing your thunder, but you got my juices flowing after we talked. I did a little digging. Hope you don't mind."

"No, not at all. What'd you find out?"

"I still have some buddies from the job. I never mentioned your name when I made the calls, so they don't know the connection. Anyway, I found out the name of the lab where they're doing the DNA work on the condom they pulled from Ashlee's crime scene. It's all part of the groundwork for Lou's trial next year."

Jane continued driving through the pelting storm as the cell signal became stronger. Sawyer repeated that the condom was always a nagging loose end. That the greenish, "micalike" chip found on the condom pulled at his gut fourteen years ago and that he felt that there was possibly more to it. He got the name of the lab and the guy in charge and wanted Jane to contact him.

Jane let out a weary sigh. "I can't call the lab."

"But you're working the case, right?"

Jane wanted to be forthright, but knew she couldn't. "Yeah. But from a different angle. I just can't call the lab, Charles."

"Don't you have friends from the job you can trust who owe you a favor?" Sawyer wasn't going to let it die.

Jane only had one friend from the job who she could implicitly trust: Sergeant Weyler. But reconnecting with him meant burying her pride. And she wasn't ready to do that yet. "It's complicated," Jane replied evasively.

"Complicated?" Sawyer's voice became slightly irritated for the first time. "If you've got an inside connection, use it!"

Sawyer sounded like an annoyed father to Jane. "Look, I'm heading into a dead cell zone," Jane said, lying. "Is that all the information?"

There was a moment of thick silence. "Yeah. That's all," Sawyer said, dejected.

Jane knew that Sawyer was a guy who always played by the rules when he worked the job. He may have entertained thoughts that were outside the proverbial box, but he never had the nerve to act on them. Now he was off the job and living the good life. But there were those quiet moments of regret only a cop understands. One of those regrets was not following up on his gut instinct regarding the mysterious particles on the condom because he didn't feel anyone would listen to him. And here was Jane, doing the same thing to him. She usually didn't cave into sentimentality, but she did this time.

"What's the name of the lab and the contact?" she asked reluctantly.

Jane drove back into Oakhurst right before ten A.M. The rain stopped and the clouds parted toward the west, exposing slices of blue sky. She considered going back to the cabin to check Lou's DMV records, but the idea of dealing with Kit was not palatable at that moment.

Even though it was New Year's Eve day, the conclave of media trucks had not diminished. The morbid idea crossed Jane's mind that Oakhurst's loss of one was also Oakhurst's gain of many. And with that surge of warm bodies came across-the-board financial rewards. Just ask Barry at The Bonanza Cabins or Diane at The Circle 9 Diner. In fact, Jane was nearing The Circle 9 Diner when she happened to look to her right and see Oakhurst's latest celebrity, Leann Hamilton, getting out of her mother's older-model blue sedan in front of The Barbeque Shack. You couldn't really miss Leann dressed in her nauseating yellow striped uniform. Jane slowed the Mustang and pulled into a parking spot in front of the fast-food joint. She watched as Leann nodded a few times in response to her mother and then closed the passenger door before heading into work. Jane leaned forward on her steering wheel, straining to get a better look at Leann. The kid moved with such tentative steps, you would have thought she was dodging snakes. Part of that hesitation came from her pudgy frame, sadly accentuated by the unflattering uniform. Here was a kid, Jane reflected, who had just been featured on primetime TV the previous night. Where were her friends? Where were the backslappers? Where were the suffering users who suck onto anyone in the public eye? Some of her coworkers, all prettier and thinner than Leann, stood scattered in front of the restaurant. A few were on break, while a couple others wiped the rainwater off the plastic chairs and tables. None of them said a word to Leann as she trudged up the ramp. It was patently clear to Jane that Leann ached to be accepted. It was the way she slowed down as she passed her coworkers, hoping for a friendly glance or a word of encouragement. There was a sentient aura around the girl that cried out for attention.

If it was attention she wanted, it was attention she was going to get. That's the idea that ran through Jane's mind as she opened the car door with the intent of talking to Leann. But no sooner did Jane prop the door open than a black SUV with rental plates from Fresno zoomed up in the empty space beside her. Jane quickly pulled back the car door to avoid a collision.

"Fuck!" Jane half whispered, straining to get a look at the driver. She made out the face just as he turned toward her. "Shit!" she said to herself. It was Clinton Fredericks. Jane clumsily turned her body and pretended to be looking for something in her back-seat. Clinton emerged from the SUV and walked onto the curb. His prying eyes surveyed the Mustang and the lone driver in it. Jane could feel his presence but maintained her ruse. She decided to cheat a glance toward him and did so precisely as he turned away and jogged up the ramp toward Leann. Sloping as far down as she could in the front seat, Jane watched as the unthinkable took place. Clinton wrapped his arm around Leann's shoulder in a pseudo-compassionate show of appreciation. Leann looked at him in starstruck wonder. The bloodsucker had poached another victim.

Jane made an undetected exit from the restaurant, deciding that a brief trip back to the Cabins might be a good idea for the time being. But just before the turnoff for the cabins, she spotted the distinctive white Firebird in the left lane, two cars in front of her. Her heart jumped at the chance to finally track the car's movement.

She switched lanes and trailed the Firebird for less than a mile before he turned left into a residential district. At first, Jane wondered if the boy was headed back to Raven Court to observe Charlotte's house. But after she turned and followed him, she realized they were nowhere near Raven Court. Jane kept a safe distance between herself and the Firebird. She knew the boy was paranoid and she didn't want to screw up this golden opportunity.

They drove another block before the Firebird's brake lights glowed against the wet pavement. Jane hung back, trolling just enough to keep the car in sight. A delivery truck was parked in the center of the street, just ahead of where the Firebird slowed. Jane watched as the boy swung the Firebird into a driveway. She calculated the well-timed placement of the delivery truck and made her move. Without the boy noticing, Jane slid into a parking spot across the street obscured by the large truck. The truck prevented any clear view of the boy's actions. But it did offer adequate shielding of her body. Jane got out of the Mustang and circled back to the rear of the truck, where a five-foot stack of boxes stood on a wooden pallet. It was thankfully another source of coverage for Jane. Peeking around the side of the truck, Jane observed the boy methodically getting out of the Firebird and retrieving an empty legal-sized box.

The front door to the house opened. A sturdy woman in her late forties appeared. "Shane!" the woman yelled over to the boy.

"Yeah?" the boy replied in a faltering tone.

"We've got more posters coming! Your dad's bringin' 'em over. But I want you to eat something hot before you go out again in this weather!"

"I'll be right in, Mom," Shane acknowledged, deep in troubled thought.

His mother went back into the house. Jane observed the boy who now had a name. *Shane.* Instead of heading inside his house, however, Shane leaned against the side of his car. He looked cautiously around the area. Jane pulled back just enough so that she could still view the boy. Shane was troubled, but he was also terribly paranoid. The sound of tires rolling down the wet pavement could be heard coming from up the street. Shane saw the vehicle before Jane did. His visibly tense reaction to the car caused Jane to turn toward it. It was the sheriff's car. Realizing that Jane was in perfect visual contact with Sheriff Golden, she quickly grabbed a nearby stack of delivery papers that hung on the truck's back hook and pretended to be checking off the data.

Keeping her eyes fixated on the delivery papers, Jane heard the sheriff's car slow to a creaking halt in the middle of the road, directly in front of Shane's house. She snuck a quick glance to the car. She could see the sheriff observing the house momentarily before Jane shifted her focus to Shane. The boy straightened up and put on a determined face in an obvious attempt to shake off his inward struggle. Sheriff Golden opened his car door, worked his gut-heavy frame out of the car, hooked his black booted foot on the inside of the door frame, and looked over at Shane. Jane waited, sensing an Old West showdown.

"Day's turned to crap, hasn't it?" Sheriff Golden yelled over at Shane.

"Yeah," Shane replied in a halting manner as he moved to the rear of his Firebird.

"You puttin' posters around town?"

"Yeah.... I'm out."

Sheriff Golden ducked his head into the car. He emerged with a legal-sized box. "Well, son, I'm here to restock you!"

CHAPTER 20

So the mysterious boy was the sheriff's son. Jane let that little gem of family connections sink in as she drove back to the cabins. From all appearances, Shane was a boy who looked like he had something to hide; a boy who purposely parked on Charlotte's street, away from the action and watched. Just watched. Then when he got a phone call that night on his cell, he lied about his whereabouts to whomever was on the other end of the line. Jane's gut started twisting, a sign that her sixth sense was on to something. She wasn't certain if that "something" was part or all of the puzzle. Just the thought of the son of the sheriff involved in Charlotte's kidnapping raised a host of ethical issues Jane was too weary to consider at that moment.

Jane pulled into the Cabins just shy of eleven A.M. She had to look twice at the front of the Hop Sing cabin. Lined up in front of the wall were two glass mason jars filled with water and green rocks. A single cobalt blue bottle stood next to the one with rocks and, next to that, a green wine bottle. Upon entering the cabin, Jane's senses went on overwhelm. The musty scent of patchouli incense gripped her nostrils. Every inch of space was filled with bottles of herbs, bags of tea, and books that ranged from metaphysical to self-improvement. Kit sat cross-legged on her bed as the buzzing sound of Tibetan monks chanted a series of "Om" and "Ahhh" on her CD player. The TV was on, but the volume was muted. Hanging above the television were a string of colorful Buddhist prayer flags. Jane looked at the odd scene, mouth agape.

"Back from your morning constitutional?" Kit offered.

"What in the hell have you done to this room?"

"Well, after my coffee enema, I felt so *perky*. So with nothing else to do, I decided to unpack and make the place more homey."

"It's like a New Age nightmare. Do you mind turning off the monks and squashing the patchouli incense?" She grabbed a pillow from her bed—the only area of the room that didn't have an item on top of it—and wafted the cloying scent out the open door. Kit obliged Jane's requests. "Remember earlier when I mentioned the words 'low profile?' What part of that didn't you understand?"

"As strong as patchouli can be, I don't think the scent seeps through the walls."

"What about the bottles outside the door?"

"Oh, those. Well, I can't do anything about them. They're part of my regimen. I've got jade soaking in two bottles to make a gem elixir. Jade inspires wisdom during the assessment of one's problems. I've always loved the stone, as I lived in Jade Cove. The colored bottles are solar-charged water. Cobalt is for the nerves and green is an all-around excellent healer. You're more than welcome to try them. Might be the ticket to cure whatever's ailing you lately." The last sentence resonated with a defined cattiness. "I tell you, I have had one *exciting* morning. I watched a scintillating documentary on the Food Network that discussed the history of pudding. *Fascinating!* Then, we went right into 'Cook, Cook, Cooking with Kevin!' All I can say is thank God and Barry for TiVo!" If Kit's sarcasm got any thicker, Jane would need a shovel to wade across the room.

Jane glanced at the bureau where she left her laptop computer. It wasn't there. "Where's my laptop?" Jane asked with a suspicious edge.

"Here," Kit leaned down between the beds and picked up the computer from the floor. "I had to move it to accommodate my herbs."

Jane crossed to Kit, retrieved the laptop, and noted that it was turned off. She recalled that the last thing she looked up was the MapQuest directions to Lou's house. "You turn this off?"

Kit looked up at Jane's towering figure above her. It was done to intimidate, but there wasn't a bit of apprehension on Kit's face. "I had to unplug it in order to move it." Jane considered Kit's answer before placing the computer on her bed. Kit could have looked at the map. If the woman was computer savvy—something Jane was not sure of—she could have accessed the history of her web searches that morning and discovered the registry of sexual offenders with Lou's address. Jane's preoccupied facial expression caught Kit's eye. "Worried I saw something interesting on your computer?"

Jane turned to Kit. "I'm not having a pissing contest with you, Kit." Jane tried to act nonchalant as she maneuvered around the heaps of herbs scattered on the floor and opened her lone piece of luggage.

"For Christ's sake!" Kit angrily spouted, rotating her heavy frame off the bed. "*What* is going on with you? Ever since we left Cousin Carl's, you've been acting very distant with me. When I hired you, I made it clear that this was a partnership."

"I had a partner at DH. But it didn't work out. I found out I couldn't trust the son of a bitch. And I learned that the hard way—"

"Cut the crap, Jane! We have a finite amount of days to find Lou—"

"What about Trace Fagin? The cops obviously have reason to believe he's involved in this somehow." Jane wasn't sold on Trace Fagin's guilt, but she figured she would play the Devil's advocate.

"*Stop it!* Would you *please* just do your job and find Lou Peters?"

"I thought my job was to find Charlotte Walker."

Kit took an angry step closer to Jane. "Find Lou and you'll find Charlotte."

"But you're more interested in me finding Lou, right? Charlotte's just a bonus *if* he has her. And you want to be right next to me when I locate Lou. Why is that, Kit?"

Kit regarded Jane with a circumspect glare. There were a few moments of tense silence. "I'm hungry. I need lunch. Let's go."

Another evasion. And another reason Jane built a stronger wall against Kit.

They drove in silence to The Circle 9 Diner. On the way, Jane reflected on Kit's odd behavior over the last few days. There was the strange, disoriented wandering away from the car during Jane's visit with Dr. John Bartosh. Jane recalled that Kit said she thought she saw someone. And then there was the fact that after Kit insisted on using the bathroom at her daughter's house, she opted instead to wander around Barbara's living room. Top those off with her general shiftiness and the knowledge that Kit's name was in the system and Jane felt guarded as they entered the diner.

The only available table was toward the rear of the diner, one booth away from the reserved area set aside for the sheriff and his deputies. Kit and Jane took a seat. It was the last place Jane wanted to be at that moment. Given the option, she would be back at the cabin, searching the DMV records for Lou and Shane Golden, then following it up with a background check on Shane and Trace Fagin. But instead she was perusing the lunch specials while Brooks & Dunn belted out "You Can't Take the Honky Tonk Out of the Girl" over the diner's speakers.

"Well, howdy, again!"

Jane looked up and saw Diane, their waitress from the previous night. "Howdy," Jane replied with a soft undercurrent of big city disdain.

Diane delivered two boot-shaped glasses of water to Kit and Jane, then leaned down, resting her elbows on the Formica tabletop. "Well, what'd you think of that interview last night with Lesley Stahl?"

"Well, I...." Jane searched for the right words.

"You think Lesley colors her hair?" Diane asked with a serious tone.

Jane regarded Diane with a confused gaze. "Yes."

"Me too! And if I'd been Leann's mama, I'd have put her in another shirt! It made her face look wide. Didn't you think?"

Jane decided the conversation had reached the gossip stage. "I'll have the hamburger, medium."

Kit ordered the vegetarian quesadillas. Diane took the menus and turned to the front door. "Well, hey, Sheriff!"

Jane had a full view of the sheriff and his posse as they sauntered toward the empty booth behind Jane.

"Hey, Diane!" Sheriff Golden said in a familiar manner.

"Coffees all around?" she asked, entranced by the Sheriff's celebrity status.

"Yep," the Sheriff replied. "And maybe a plate of nachos for me and the boys."

Kit leaned across the table, speaking in a hushed tone. "Talk to him, Jane."

"I don't think so."

"Get the scoop on Mr. Fagin and the item that was found on his person. Don't mention Lou's name. Just find out more than what we're gleaning from TV!"

Jane found it interesting that Kit made a point of telling her to *not* mention anything about Lou. Why? If she was so sure he was connected to Charlotte's kidnapping, wouldn't she *want* to alert the sheriff to a possible suspect? "If I talk to the sheriff, there's a good chance my presence in this town is going to get back to Clinton. If that happens, any chance I have to work under the radar will be negatively affected."

"Well, then, how are you going to find out what's happening on the inside? For God's sake, Jane, time is ticking away!"

Jane agreed with Kit, but she wasn't ready to swallow her pride and call Sergeant Weyler. "I have web subscriptions to services for background checks and criminal—"

"You need access to the *inside!*" Kit spoke in an irritated whisper. Jane looked up as the front door of the diner opened and Shane Golden walked in. The look of interest on Jane's face piqued Kit's curiosity and she turned around. Returning to face Jane, Kit realized something was afoot. "What's going on?" Kit asked. "Who is that?"

"Shane!" Sheriff Golden called out.

Shane turned toward his father, obviously not comfortable with the attention.

"Come on over, son!" the sheriff insisted, waving Shane toward his table. Shane reluctantly obeyed. "Here, make room for my boy!" the sheriff instructed his deputies.

"Dad, I can't stay. Mom asked me to come down and tell you we've got a couple TV trucks parked outside our house. They wanted to interview her or me—"

"What'd you tell 'em?" the sheriff asked.

"I told them no," Shane replied, his voice sounding irritated for the first time.

"But you *do* have somethin' to tell 'em!" The sheriff eyed his deputies.

While Jane could not see what was going on behind her, she distinctly heard the catch in Shane's voice when he replied to his father's remark. "What do you mean?"

Diane appeared with a tray of coffees and a pitcher of cream.

"If I say it in front of Diane," Sheriff Golden remarked, "it'll be all over this town by two o'clock!"

"Tell me what?" Diane asked, always ready to hear gossip.

"We found out that Shane got a full scholarship to USC!" the Sheriff proudly announced. The deputies cheerfully offered a flurry of congratulations. "He's gonna be the first one in our family to go to university, let alone go there on a *full* scholarship!"

"What are you gonna study?" one of the deputies asked.

"Civil Engineering!" Sheriff Golden answered. "Just like we've been plannin' all these years! Shane is gonna be responsible for buildin' the roads of tomorrow."

"You got yourself a smart boy, Sheriff," Diane interjected.

"You betcha!" the sheriff agreed. "He's worked hard for it. He's had to give up a lot of holidays and amusements along the way so he could focus on his studies, but it's all been worth it when you open up a red and gold envelope from USC that says they want *your* son to head their way!"

Jane snuck a look to her left side. A full-length mirror hung against the opposite wall, allowing her to catch a glimpse of Shane's reflection. If this boy was happy about his university prospects, you'd never know it. Instead, a dark cloud of doom hung over him. How couldn't anyone else see it, she thought.

"I gotta get goin'," Shane said in a low-key manner. He started toward the door when his father called out to him.

"Tell your mom I'll send a deputy over to the house to shoo away those media boys!" Shane nodded and exited the diner.

Kit studied Jane's pensive face. "Tell me what's going on, Jane."

"I'm not sure," Jane replied honestly.

Kit leaned across the table, speaking in a confidential tone. "Are you still paying attention to the coincidences?"

Jane didn't want to admit it, but there did indeed seem to be one strange, dove-tailing fluke after another over the last few days. "I don't know—"

"Don't waste your time trying to explain or define any of it. Just *pay attention*."

Jane and Kit ate in silence, gaining no additional pertinent information from the conversations between the sheriff and his deputies. They headed back to the Cabins, hardly exchanging two words between them. Kit commented that even with the bevy of herbs she packed, she was getting low on a particular formula and she wished she could find an herb store in town. Jane listened with half an ear, more interested in logging on to her computer. Back at the cabin, while Kit strolled backward around the periphery of the property, Jane wasted no time with her Internet search.

First, Shane Golden. A speedy check of three different criminal investigation sites turned up nothing. Next, Trace Fagin. Zero findings on any criminal record. Jane logged onto the DMV records and first examined Shane Golden. A digital photo popped up of Shane. His driving record was as clean cut as he was. Jane jotted down his home address and then entered Trace Fagin's name. The DMV photo of the thirty-eight-year-old South Dakotan looked like a mug shot, but that could be said for most DMV photos. Fagin apparently liked to press the pedal to the metal, as he had two speeding tickets over the past twelve months. One was from California and one from Oregon. So he drives fast. If speeding were a felony, Jane mused, she'd be doing life without parole.

She entered Lou Peters's name in the DMV search engine. Within seconds, Lou's photo loaded onto the screen. Jane sat back and stared at his face. It was taken on the day of issue, less than a year ago. He would have been thirty-two at the time of the photo but he looked like he was in his late-twenties. He was fresh out of prison. Instead of aging and hardening him, it seemed prison had had no negative effect on his visage. Lou's piercing blue eyes stared at Jane in a captivating manner. The tousled brown hair—perhaps an intentional look—reminded Jane of the cover models on *GQ Magazine*. His clean-shaven face gave off a fresh, exuberant look that said, "I'm taking on the world!" Was this really the face of a killer, or a man whose only fault was drowning in religious fervor and taking young girls for rides on his motorcycle? Jane saw that the address on the DMV records matched the same remote county road notated on the sex offender's registry. A dead end, for now. She jotted down Lou's license plate number on a slip of paper and tucked it into the pocket of her satchel.

Glancing at the inside of her satchel, Jane spied the photo she'd stolen from the Bartoshs' house. Jane propped it up against her computer screen. Her eyes first locked on the two young girls in the front row with the expressionless faces. She then directed her attention to the lanky, longhaired, seventeen-year-old girl on the far left. From the way that part of the photo was purposely hidden on the Bartoshs' photo board, Jane was certain the girl was Mary Bartosh. Jane pulled the photo closer, brushing her index finger across Mary's no-nonsense appearance. "What happened to you, Mary?" Jane whispered. Out of curiosity, Jane entered Mary's name into the DMV search engine. Five entries appeared on the screen. She checked them all, but none of them looked anything like an older version of the snapshot in front of Jane.

Perhaps Mary was married and had gladly dropped the Bartosh name years ago? Still, Jane's suspicious nature couldn't help logging on to two of her criminal sites and doing a search for "Mary Bartosh." However, it proved fruitless. Maybe, Jane thought, the girl *was* dead. If so, what secrets did she take to her grave? Jane pulled a cigarette out of the pack just as Kit opened the front door.

"You're not smoking that in here!" Kit declared, breathless from her backward walk.

Without acknowledging Kit, Jane quit out of the Internet programs and shut down her computer. She grabbed her satchel and a pack of matches, slid past Kit, and walked outside. Overhead, the dark clouds merged together as a sudden crisp wind cut across the parking lot. Jane lit her cigarette and inhaled deeply. The cold, wet air felt invigorating at first, but quickly drove deep into her bones, causing Jane to brace her body against the repeated gusts of blustery weather. Rain fell quickly, and Jane took refuge in her Mustang. The clouds burst open with a relentless gush of water and wind. Jane sucked another few puffs on her cigarette, contemplating how she was going to do what she knew she had to do. She wasn't used to swallowing her pride for fear of choking on the sinew as it went down her throat. But the days *were* ticking away.

The storm continued unabated outside the Mustang as Jane flicked open her cell phone and dialed the number she knew by heart. The downpour seemed a fitting backdrop for her mood at that moment. She pushed the SEND button and let out a deep sigh of resignation. Two rings and no pickup. Three rings. Then four. Five rings and voice mail clicked on. Sergeant Weyler's voice sounded like warm honey poured into a steaming cup of tea. The recording beeped and Jane paused, swallowing hard. "Hey...Boss," As that single word struggled from her lips, Jane realized she was shaking. "I...ah...need your help. Call me."

Jane hung up and sucked the nicotine dry from her ash-heavy cigarette. The storm pounded violently on the roof of the Mustang as her father's voice reverberated in her head. "You're so *easy*. Now you've made yourself vulnerable."

CHAPTER 21

Jane sat in the Mustang, contemplating her next move. She would have to wait for Weyler's return call and the inevitable questions that had nothing to do with her case. Weyler probed people he cared about and he cared about few people. Sometimes he acted more like the den mother of his detectives back at DH, supporting them, allowing them free rein, but also checking in with them periodically to see how they were doing. It was an uncomfortable alliance for Jane during her drunken tenure at DH, but it was also oddly comforting.

Lighting a second cigarette from the dying one clenched in her mouth, Jane squashed the spent ember in the car's ashtray. The unrelenting rainstorm continued outside, drowning out her worried thoughts for a while. Pulling her satchel onto her lap, Jane rummaged through the contents and came across the generous stack of newsletters that Ingrid Bartosh had given her. Issues of *The Congregation Chronicle* ranged from the debut issue in January, 1989 to the most recent offering. Under the header of each issue was the proclamation in bold type, **WE ARE WARRIORS FOR JESUS!** Warriors, thought Jane. To her, that word implied a rabid individual who saw life as a continual fight. A "warrior for Jesus" was someone who was willing to give his own life for that of his Savior. Jane wondered how many of Bartosh's followers took that idea to heart and followed through with their own combative distortion.

Glancing at the 1989 debut issue, Jane read the first few paragraphs of the featured cover editorial by Dr. John Bartosh titled, "The Word Becomes Flesh." The article was Bartosh's personal mission statement for The Lamb of God Congregation. It compelled church members to study and commit to memory the book of John and especially the first chapter. In this chapter, Bartosh wrote, there were hidden messages and literal passages that the perceptive student of Jesus Christ would easily decipher. The entire King James Version of the chapter with its fifty-one verses could be found on page two of the newsletter. Bartosh made a point of bolding specific passages he felt were significant, such as verses six through nine.

"There was a man sent from God, whose name was John. The same came for a witness of the Light, that all men through him might believe. He was not that Light, but was sent to bear witness of that Light. That was the true Light, which lighteth every man that cometh into the world."

Jane reread the verses again. "There was a man sent from God, whose name was John." Was it a coincidence that Bartosh's first name was John? Was Bartosh implying that *he* was sent from God and that his word was filtered through God? That's the way it appeared to Jane. Bartosh could have chosen any book from the Bible as his manifesto for his Congregation, but he chose a book that cleverly insinuated a Divine connection. He was either an egotistical militant or a power monger or both, Jane decided. The next bolded text was verse twenty-three.

"He said, I am the voice of one crying in the wilderness, Make straight the way of the Lord, as said the prophet Isaiah."

An asterisk followed the word "Isaiah." When Jane checked the bottom of the page, Bartosh wrote a brief footnote: "Members must seriously study the book of Isaiah as it outlines the signs of the end times, especially chapters one and two."

Jane grabbed a pen from her visor and circled the footnote. It occurred to her that Bartosh had specifically quoted from Isaiah during their visit. Something about children rebelling and becoming corrupters. Searching through her satchel, she found the tape recorder with the cassette tape still inside it. Jane noticed that the ninety-minute tape had run nearly to the end of side one. She punched the REVERSE button, allowing the tape to spin midway through their conversation before hitting the PLAY button. Bartosh's booming voice seemed to reach out of the recorder.

"We are in the fight for our final redemption." Bartosh exclaimed, taking a deep breath. "If we lose this fight, the hammer of God will fall, Lucifer will rule, and darkness will engulf this earth, erasing the beloved blood sacrifice of our Lord, Jesus Christ."

Jane's ability to recall conversations and remember the pace of what was said convinced her to speed the tape forward. Taking another drag on her cigarette, she hit the PLAY button.

"I have nourished and brought up children, and they have rebelled against me." Bartosh recited, in midverse. "Ah sinful nation, a people laden with iniquity, a seed of evildoers, *children that are corrupters*: they have forsaken the *Lord*, they have provoked the Holy One of Israel unto anger, *they are gone away backward*." Bartosh took a deep breath. "Isaiah, Chapter one. Verses two and four, respectively."

Jane stopped the tape. Between the raging storm outside and the state of her mind at that moment, she didn't want to hear Dr. Bartosh's grating voice any longer. She noted the next three, bolded verses of John: twenty-nine, thirty-two, and fifty-one.

"The next day John seeth Jesus coming unto him, and saith, Behold the Lamb of God, which taketh away the sin of the world."

Aha! The origin of the name Bartosh's chose for his Congregation suddenly came to light.

"And John bare record, saying, I saw the Spirit descending from heaven like a dove, and it abode upon him."

Jane couldn't make any reasonable connection to why Bartosh bolded that verse. Then the final verse, number fifty-one.

"And he saith unto him, Verily, verily, I say unto you, Hereafter ye shall see heaven open, and the angels of God ascending and descending upon the Son of man."

Okay. Perhaps, Jane reasoned, this final bolded text served to stir the cockles of his follower's hearts. After all, just the visual promise of angels ascending and descending was enough to make true believers rise up and spread The Word.

The second featured article from the debut issue was titled "The Hammer of God Will Fall on All Sinners." Dr. John Bartosh was, once again, the author. A drawing of a hand holding a hammer in a striking pose framed the top of the article. Reading through it, Jane felt as if she were hearing a fire and brimstone speech, filled with castigating vitriol and dire warnings. "The hammer of God is swift and sure," Bartosh wrote. "Our Lord Jesus rebukes anyone who chooses to sin against Him. Understand that to sin against Jesus IS a choice we all make consciously. God made us perfect. It is WE who soil our souls and entrap our minds with the filth the secular world offers. While our Lord and Savior is a loving God, history has shown that He will only allow so much sin before He willingly allows his hammer to fall onto those who refuse The Word." Jane decided the text was extremely visual. She tried to imagine Jesus chasing sinners with a hammer in his hand, screaming that He was going to pound them into submission. Somehow, Jane concluded, it just didn't seem to fit Jesus' profile.

Peeling through the thick stack of newsletters, Jane chose another at random and read the back page. There was a large "Acknowledgements" box that referred to "our sisters" and "our brothers" and their achievements.

"Thank you to our sisters who baked the pies for the recent Brotherhood Council Conclave in Big Sur," read one posting. The date on the newsletter was May, 1992. Ah, yes. The Brotherhood Council. The group of men who, as Kit said, "didn't acknowledge the Goddess." It was the same bunch of men Bartosh had been visiting on the morning she contacted Ingrid. Jane mused that every organization she knew, whether it was a golf club or a church organization, made a point of creating a hierarchy that included a niche for those extra-special people. Golf clubs had the "Hole in One" Fraternity; churches such as The Lamb of God Congregation formed The Brotherhood Council. She pictured a group of stodgy old relics, their hair white and their body odor stale, sitting around in a private room in dusty wingback chairs, debating the future of their brethren. What power they must yield, Jane deduced. What blatant ego it must take to accept such a position. What secrets they must share. In Jane's mind, The Brotherhood Council sounded akin to the Masonic Temple with a Fundamentalist twist.

Jane located the most recent newsletter from December. Halfway down the Acknowledgments box on the back page, a word caught Jane's eye: Oakhurst. It read: "Many thanks to Rachel Hartly from Oakhurst, California. Our devoted sister in Christ single-handedly keeps the flame of God burning for all who need to hear The Word. Her tireless efforts have welcomed many to Jesus through her organization of our summer CYMC camp south of Yosemite. Because of the efforts of our sister, Rachel Hartly, many more children will know the Lord! May the Lord Jesus watch over you, sister Rachel, and hold you in His heart as you diligently prepare for another inspiring summer of hope for our young people!"

The rain slowed to a soft pitter-patter against the Mustang's front window. A glint of sun splashed across the hood, teasing Jane with the prospect of better weather. Before she had her plan fully formulated, Jane squashed out her cigarette in the ashtray and ran into the cabin. Thankfully, Kit was ensconced in the bathroom. Jane quickly located the phone book in the drawer of the bureau next to the Gideon Bible and looked up Rachel Hartly's name. She quickly found it and jotted down the address on a scrap of paper. The semi-rural address was another county road location that

Jane recalled passing earlier in the day on her way to Lou's former house. She started for the door, when Kit opened the bathroom door, drying her hands on a bath towel.

"Leaving again?" Kit asked, sounding deeply frustrated.

"I'll be back. Eventually," Jane hastily announced, heading out the door. As she pulled the Mustang out of the parking lot, she couldn't miss Kit's irritated face peering out from the curtains.

Jane's memory of the county road's location was impeccable. Turning onto the dirt road that sat just outside of town, she drove up one steep hill before plateauing on a stretch of rural developments. The single-story homes stood on several acres and were well kept. There was a section of raw land and then the tiny, blue home on the hill to her right that belonged to Rachel Hartly. A sturdy metal fence surrounded the house, creating the appearance of an unapproachable fortress. Jane parked the Mustang 100 feet up from the driveway. The rain had stopped, but the rural road stood saturated in deep, muddy puddles of gravel and silt. Navigating around the slosh, Jane walked to the metal gate. The butt of the Glock pressed against her chest, reminding her that she was carrying. She buttoned her jacket nearly all the way to conceal any sign of the gun.

Two intimidating metal signs greeted her at the gate. One read, KEEP OUT! in red letters. The other read, WHAT PART OF "NO TRESPASSING" DON'T YOU UNDERSTAND?! A large trash can sat to the left of the fence with a square plastic blue recycling box next to it. Jane propped open the trash can and found six neatly tied white trash bags stuffed into the bin. She lifted the lid of the recycling box with the toe of her boot. A stack of *The Sierra Star* newspapers filled the box. She pulled out the first paper on the stack and glanced through the pages. Every two to three pages, Jane found suspicious sections carefully cut out. She lifted ten issues of the town's thin, twice weekly offering out of the box and repeated her inspection. Each paper was missing sections that ranged from a few inches wide to half a page—identical to the newspapers she discovered buried in the bin at Lou's former residence. Jane stacked the ten papers together, unbuttoned her jacket, and flattened the stack around her torso. She rebuttoned her jacket, securing the papers underneath.

Jane headed for the front gate and stopped at the plain white and black mailbox. Yes, it was against the law. Technically. But laws sometimes have to be broken in order to solve crimes, she reasoned as she popped open the box and withdrew the contents. All the mail was addressed to Rachel Hartly. Much of it was a handful of cream-colored postcards from local return addresses. On the back of each postcard, it read: IF YOU ARE INTERESTED IN OUR SUMMER CYMC (CAMP FOR PRETEENS AND YOUNG ADULTS,) PLEASE RETURN THIS POSTCARD AND WE WILL SEND YOU INFORMATION. Jane assumed the CYMC stood for "Christian or Congregation Youth Ministry Camp." She took a gander around the area to make sure her illegal actions were not being observed. Returning to the contents of the box, everything else looked innocent. She replaced the mail in the box and took a good look at Rachel's house. The tiny blue residence stood on a slight hill at the top of the gravel driveway. A cluster of thirty-foot conifers hugged the rear of the property, cloistering what looked to be a workshop. There was no sign of a motorcycle or a car on the property.

Jane opened the metal gate and entered Rachel's property. The gravel crunched loudly under the soles of her boots. Jane noticed a separate garage to the right of the house with old-fashioned doors on the front of it that latched. From her point of view, Jane could not decipher whether a car was inside the garage. Between the house and garage was a small pen with young goats. A trio of hens and a single rooster filled another pen a few feet away. The closer Jane got to the house, the more the hairs on the back of her neck stood up. There was a decidedly unsettling feel to the property. She stopped and "felt" her way into the moment. When all else failed in her law enforcement career, she could always rely on her astute intuition and the unexplainable "creep factor" that usually signaled danger. Jane felt that creep factor very strongly as she turned to the left of the driveway and worked her way toward the stand of conifer trees in the rear of the house. When she was within fifty feet of the trees, she realized that the building secluded by the trees was a small, gray guesthouse. While Jane wasn't certain, the 600-square-foot guesthouse fit a certain MO for Lou in that he purposely sought out the guesthouse on Kit's property in Big Sur.

Jane skirted around the stand of conifers, keeping an eye out for any sign of life around the house. The closer she got to the guesthouse, the more her gut churned. In the distance, the rooster let out a loud "cock-a-doodle-doo" that echoed through the trees. Jane struggled through a thicket of wet branches before reemerging against the back wall of the guesthouse. There was a lone window a foot square on the back wall, covered by a white curtain. Jane waited momentarily, listening for any sign of music or conversation. Hearing nothing, she headed around the cabin and came upon a trio of two-foot-square windows. A thick white curtain cloaked the first window. Jane walked to the next one. It, too, was also obscured by a white curtain. She headed with greater purpose to the third window. As she approached it, she could see that there was no curtain across it. Jane was just about to peer into the window when the cold, hard business end of a rifle touched the side of her head.

She froze. Whoever was behind her proved to have greater covert ability than Jane. She held her hands away from her body, never once turning her head. Jane could feel the pressure of the Glock against her side, underneath the stack of newspapers beneath her jacket. However, there was no way she could get to her gun and defend herself against the person behind her; she would have to rely on tact and creative subterfuge. Frustrated, she uttered a faint "shit" under her breath. The person with the rifle piped up.

"'His mouth is full of cursing and deceit and fraud.'" The voice belonged to a woman. *"Psalms 10:7,"* the woman added with emphasis.

At that moment, Jane wished she knew the Bible better so she could rattle off an appropriate verse that would assuage the woman's desire to shoot her in the head. "Excuse my language,"

Jane offered, speaking quietly and keeping her face forward. "I just get a little nervous when a gun's pointed at my head."

"Who are you?" the woman asked with a menacing tone.

For some reason, the only name she could think of at that moment was her mother's. "Ann."

"Ann what?" the woman replied, forcing the cold steel into Jane's skull.

Jane traversed the ground with her eyes. "Stone. Ann Stone."

"Can you read, Ann Stone?"

"Yes."

"Then why are you standing on my property when my signs at the gate explain how I feel about trespassers?"

"'Forgive us our trespasses as we forgive those who trespass against us....'" Jane offered, hoping a verse from The Lord's Prayer would soften this woman's resolve.

"Is that your idea of humor?" the woman yelled. "Bastardizing our Lord's words to fit your immediate needs?"

Jane found the question oddly ironic, given the woman's knee-jerk, verse-spouting of Proverbs 10:7 just a minute earlier. Jane had had enough of the stalemate. "Look," she said quietly, "put the gun down. This is not what Jesus wants you to do."

The woman pulled the rifle point off Jane's head. "Turn around," she ordered.

Jane obeyed and looked into the emblazoned blue eyes of Rachel Hartly. She was a veritable mountain of a woman, nearing six feet tall. Rachel was the kind of woman people describe as big-boned and beefy. Her wavy, salt-and-pepper hair was cut in a no-nonsense style that brushed her earlobes. She wore no makeup, no earrings, no jewelry. Her boxy plaid wool barn jacket hid whatever size breasts God had given her. A pair of dark denim jeans fit loosely, scraping the tops of her well-worn, L.L. Bean gum boots. Instead of securing the rifle at her side, Rachel opted to simply take two steps back, continuing to hold Jane's head in the site.

"What do you want, Ann Stone?" Rachel asked with a sneer.

Jane found herself surprisingly calm for someone who was staring down the long barrel of a .22 rifle. "I assume you are Rachel Hartly?"

"That's right. What of it?"

"You greet everyone with your .22, Rachel?" Jane knew that one of the best ways to deal with someone who had you at gunpoint was to constantly repeat their name.

"No. Just those who come on my private property uninvited. Now, I'll ask you once again. *What do you want?*"

"I'm looking for someone, Rachel, and I have reason to believe he might be living in *this* guesthouse. His name is Lou Peters." Jane watched for any sign of falsehood crossing Rachel's face.

"No one by the name of Lou Peters lives here," Rachel steadily replied. Her cadence was strong and believable.

Jane stared into Rachel's eyes, searching for any sign of deception. There was something there. It was behind her eyes. It was like a word that lingered at the end of a sentence with no punctuation. Jane knew there were so many ways for the criminal mind to rationalize a lie by the way the question was asked and then carefully answered. "Do you know Lou Peters, Rachel?" Jane pressed.

"I do not."

"He's a member of the Lamb of God Congregation. Are you not a member of that organization, Rachel?"

"I am. And proud to be so! But I do *not* know anyone named Lou Peters."

"Well, that's curious," Jane continued very matter-of-factly, "because Lou does live in this community and the two of you are probably the only members of the Congregation from this area. Common sense says that you would know Lou."

Rachel slowly lowered the rifle, never taking her steely eyes off Jane. "I vaguely remember the name from long ago. But I assure you, he does not live here any longer."

Long ago? Lou had registered as a sex offender less than seven months ago. Certainly "long ago" did not usually imply less than a year. Jane decided to let that claim go. But she would not let

Rachel's second statement go unchallenged. "How can you assure me he's not living here if you don't know him?"

Rachel stiffened. "You attempt to manipulate my words. *So typical.*"

"So typical of what?"

"Your kind. You'd like to see all of us behind bars or dead. But we will not lie down and take your abuse any longer." Rachel held her index finger high in the air. "A Divine declaration has gone forth from on high to those who are true believers! The Great Commission of Christ demands that we ratchet up our ministry to a new level! We will no longer seek *tolerance* toward us. We are not weak! We are not passive! We have taken our rightful ownership of Jesus!"

Jane was certain that Bartosh used those same words during their conversation. It appeared that anyone outside of the Congregation was considered suspect and someone who wished to thwart the Great Cause. It also seemed in vogue to parrot Bartosh's words. Jane figured if you can't speak for yourself, mimic someone else who you respect. Jane shifted her stance and in doing so, the newspapers slid down her jacket. She grabbed the bottom seam of her jacket, pressing her hand against her body to prevent exposing the papers.

"What are you doing?" Rachel asked suspiciously.

Jane reacted quickly. "I haven't been feeling well lately. I ate some bad fish." Jane grimaced in pain and realized she had a clear way out. "You'll have to excuse me, but I need to go." She turned, placing both hands on her jacket to secure the papers as she walked. "Sorry for any misunderstanding," Jane said over her shoulder.

"If I see you near my property again, I'm contacting the authorities!"

Jane nodded and headed for the front gate. *The authorities*, she wondered. A woman like Rachel Hartly certainly didn't trust the secular world of law enforcement. She must be talking about God and His soldiers.

As she neared the Mustang, she heard the faint ring of her cell phone inside the car. Jane swung open the door and answered the phone. "This is Jane," she said. Silence. "Hello?" Jane said, irritated. It sounded like dead air, but then Jane realized there was the faint sound of someone breathing on the other end of the line. She quickly looked at the caller ID. Restricted. That was the same ID display from the caller who dialed her number after she left Lou's former address. "Goddammit! Stop fucking with me! Who the hell is this?" Jane yelled into the phone. There was a moment of silence before the line went dead.

A bolt of electricity sped up Jane's spine. Very few people had her cell phone number. Her brother, Mike, had it. A few of her connections at the FBI had it from the botched undercover job. Sergeant Weyler had it....

Just then, her cell phone rang again. Jane pressed the button to answer it without looking at the caller ID. "I don't know who the fuck you are, or how you got this number, but you better stop playing with me!"

"Well, I see you're still the same innocent, carefree young lass I grew to admire."

Jane didn't have to check the caller ID. She knew the sound of Sergeant Weyler's voice.

CHAPTER 22

"Oh, shit," Jane mumbled under her breath. She hadn't talked to Sergeant Weyler in nearly six months. She had outright avoided his incessant phone messages. And now, after all this time, she had answered his call with a misguided, profane greeting. She nervously lit a cigarette and took a drag. "Um...." Jane stumbled briefly, trying to salvage the conversation. "Sorry about that, Boss. I'm in the car. Somebody called me right before you did and I don't know who the fuck they are or how they got this number...." Jane suddenly realized that instead of feeling uncommunicative—the main reason she never returned Weyler's calls—she found herself rattling on to him about her problems just like in the old days. They had shared a deep bond of respect from the first day Jane went to work for DH in homicide. Jane could always be who she was, warts and all, and Weyler still liked her.

"Boss?" Weyler interjected, his smile reaching through the phone. "I thought I lost that title when you declined to return to our dysfunctional little family at DH." Weyler always had an elegant way of speaking. Jane chalked it up to his love of PBS.

"It just slipped out," Jane argued.

"You called me Boss on the voice mail message you left. One slip-up I can accept. But two?"

Jane let out a long sigh. "Look, you think it was easy for me to contact you?"

"Obviously not. They've had *five* pledge drives on PBS since I last talked to you. I didn't know if you were okay or if you'd—"

"I saw you on television," Jane interrupted, "with all the drugs and counterfeit money from the cartel bust. You were wearing your power suit and your red tie. And you looked pissed."

"I was irate. DH shagged that bust from *your* sweat and labor. We rode your coattails and I told them so."

Jane took a hard drag on her cigarette. "Told who?"

"Everyone who would listen!"

"Does that include your newest prick on the job, Sergeant Kenny Stephens? Was he the best you could get for that job?"

"No. The *best* turned me down. The *best* wouldn't return my phone calls."

Jane was touched by Weyler's words. For a moment, she didn't feel so inadequate as she had for the last few days. "That means a lot to me, Boss. But I don't think that I'm the best anymore."

"Tell that to your legions of fans who still call here on a regular basis! Not a week goes by that I don't screen calls from people asking for your help. Hell, I had a call from a woman today asking if you could speak at her son's graduation!"

Weyler's statement seemed incongruous. No one had ever asked Jane to speak at a graduation ceremony. "What the hell—"

"That's the price of fame, I guess."

"I think it says a lot about society when they get jacked up in 'worship mode.'" *Speak at her son's graduation,* Jane mused.

"Christ, Jane! What are you doing in Oakhurst?"

"If I tell you, you gotta promise that you won't say a word to anybody."

"Fine."

"There's this missing girl—"

"The national case?"

"Right."

"You working solo for the FBI?"

"I'm working solo, but not for the FBI. It's a long story and I don't have enough battery charged on my phone to get through it."

"Well, plug in the car charger, start driving, and talk to me!"

Jane had always appreciated Weyler's direct approach. She headed down the county road and back onto the highway that headed into town. Over the next thirty minutes, Jane revealed everything about the case to Weyler, including Kit Clark, her recent suspicions about Kit's motives, Ashlee's death, Lou Peters, Dr.

John Bartosh, The Lamb of God Congregation, the possibility of a January 5 deadline, the conversations with Detective Charles Sawyer, the strange, greenish, micalike particle on the condom, Clinton Fredericks's meddling, the suspicions she felt regarding Shane Golden's involvement, and her most recent escapade to Rachel Hartly's house. By the time she finished her rapid-fire chronicle of events, Jane had driven fifteen miles north on Highway 41 toward Yosemite.

"Jane, you got yourself mixed up in a job that requires a *team* of people!"

"Yeah, well if I could clone myself—"

"So, you need my help?" Weyler stated, cutting to the chase.

"Yes. You know a lot of people. I figured I'd take a chance and maybe you'd know somebody out here on the inside who can feed you information—"

"Maybe I do." Weyler said with an enticing tone.

"Is that a yes?"

"Possibly...." Weyler seemed to be dangling his help on the end of a stick.

"What's with all the caginess?" Jane nervously puffed on her cigarette.

"You're asking for one helluva favor. I'm going to have to pull a lot of rabbits out of a lot of hats!"

Jane sensed an oncoming bargain. "What's the bottom line? A donation to PBS?"

"No. That would just sweeten the deal. I'll agree to help you if you agree to come back to DH when it's over and take the position of sergeant in homicide." Jane pulled the Mustang over to the shoulder of the highway. Part of her felt insulted that Weyler didn't think she was up to forging a career as a private investigator. The other part felt great pride that he still wanted to upgrade her to sergeant in homicide—working alongside Weyler—after her months of evasiveness. "Did I lose you?" Weyler asked.

"No, I'm here, Boss."

"Do we have a deal?"

"What are you gonna tell Kenny Stephens?"

"If you agree, I'll tell him to get his pumped-up ass outta here! And I'll enjoy every second of it!"

Jane's heart pounded so hard she thought it would burst from her chest. She sucked on her cigarette. "Okay, Boss. You got a deal."

They discussed the most important things that Jane needed ASAP: more info about Trace Fagin, what item of Charlotte's he had in his possession, whether the sheriff's department had contacted Lou after Charlotte's abduction, any information from local sources on Shane Golden, and finally, to start a relationship with the DNA lab that was analyzing the condom found alongside Ashlee. For anyone else, the long list was an overwhelming request. For Weyler, it would occupy the better part of a morning.

Jane hung up. The tension in her body was beyond palpable. She felt a tightness in her chest and then remembered she had not removed the stack of *The Sierra Star* newspapers she'd stuffed inside her jacket. She removed them and turned the Mustang back onto Highway 41. Suddenly, her phone rang. This time, she checked the caller ID and found the mysterious RESTRICTED on the display. She quickly pulled over to the shoulder of Highway 41 again and answered her phone. "Who the fuck *is* this?"

There was silence and then a whisper. "Let me help you...." the voice said.

Jane pressed the phone closer to her ear. "What?"

"Let me help you," the voice still whispered, but there was a bit more definition to the cadence. Jane was sure it was a woman's voice.

Jane took a suspicious look around the immediate area where she was parked, wondering if the caller could be watching her. "Help me with what?"

"You're looking for Lou Peters?" the woman whispered.

"Yes," Jane replied cautiously.

"Let me help you."

"How?"

"Meet me in front of the Stop 'n' Save on Buena Street in thirty minutes."

"Okay."

With that, the caller hung up. Jane sat in the Mustang, playing back the confusing phone call. The words, "Let me help you," reverberated in her ears. The cadence was somehow vaguely familiar. Whoever was on the other end of the line was not a professional; a professional would have used an electronic disguiser to manipulate their voice and hide their identity. Anybody could buy the equipment on the Internet for a little over $100. But this particular person chose to simply whisper. The question that ran through Jane's mind was, did she whisper to disguise her voice or because she wanted to keep her conversation with Jane private. But the truly nagging question was, how did the woman get Jane's phone number? Checking the clock, Jane suddenly realized she had twenty minutes to speed back to Oakhurst in order to meet the mysterious woman.

As she gunned the Mustang south on Highway 41, she spotted Shane Golden's Firebird partially hidden by a stand of pine trees about a mile down the road on the opposite side of the Highway. "Shit!" Jane exclaimed, slowing down to get a better look. There was no way she was going to be able to get across to the opposite side of the highway with the amount of traffic going both ways. Even if she could, she barely had enough time to make it back to Oakhurst to meet the woman. Jane quickly jotted down the mile-marker—forty-four—and the location of the car, vowing to return later.

With only two minutes to spare, Jane screeched into the outside mall where the Stop 'n' Save was located. She buttoned her jacket with one hand to conceal the Glock, while she parked the Mustang. The clouds merged overhead, instantly darkening the afternoon sky. A gradual pitter-patter of rain pelted the concrete as Jane walked quickly but cautiously to the front of the store. She lit a cigarette and stood alone in the rain. Even if she had not been alone out there, her pensive look and constant glancing around the area would make her stand out to whomever wanted to meet her. A woman wearing dark glasses and a hooded jacket approached Jane. They made eye contact and Jane straightened up, ready for a confrontation. But the woman breezed past her and went into the market. Jane checked the time on her cell phone. It was two minutes past the designated meeting time. Maybe the mystery woman was late. Then again, Jane figured one would probably be on time for such a clandestine encounter. Jane took two more drags on her cigarette and let another three minutes pass. The rain slowed and then resumed its steady downpour. The wind sliced through the mall, forcing the rain sideways. But Jane stood firm, like a statue, impervious to the whims of the inclement weather. Fifteen minutes passed. The rainstorm dwindled to a steady mist, but the ire within Jane grew. What was the point of it? Was she being used? The realization that she could have checked out Shane's actions on the side of Highway 41 in lieu of this cancelled meeting further riled Jane. What purpose was there was in arranging a meeting and then not showing up? Jane took a final drag on her cigarette before flicking it into a puddle of water. She was only three steps from her Mustang when a booming voice called out her name. Jane spun around. A combination of heat and ice ran through her blood as she faced the beast standing in front of her. It was Clinton Fredericks, and he had a caustic smile across his face that could make paint curl. His trademark camouflage pants seemed to repel the softly falling rain, while his unkempt hair looked suspiciously molded, thanks to the tube of gel Jane figured he slathered on his head.

"Well, as I live and breathe!" Clinton exclaimed, moving closer to Jane. "What in the hell are *you* doing out here?" Jane tried to quickly sort through the strange series of events that had just taken place. She half-wondered if Clinton had made the unsettling phone call to her. But how would he know her private number? Jane had never met Clinton, but he obviously knew who she was from her recent summer foray into the media spotlight. "You workin' with the FBI?" Clinton asked, intensely interested.

Jane regained her tough girl vibe. "I'm just out here, Clinton."

"*Just out here?*" Clinton let out a guffaw that would've shaken the rafters if they'd been inside. "It's fuckin' hicksville! Don't blow smoke up my ass, girl."

Jane hated it when anyone called her "girl." She particularly hated it when someone as parasitic as Clinton sidled up next to her in an attempt to imply a professional kinship. His vibe felt oily; like the guy with slicked-back hair who sells tickets to nudie peep shows. "It's New Year's Eve. I got to go somewhere to celebrate. Why not Oakhurst?" Jane turned around and unlocked her car door. It was open a few inches when Clinton pushed it shut.

"Why did Denver PD send out their star girl to investigate the big story of the week?" Clinton asked in a trenchant cadence. "Is there a Colorado connection we should know about?"

Jane kept her back to Clinton. Somehow, with all his inside information, he didn't know that she was no longer working for DH. Jane needed to quickly use his ignorance to her advantage. She turned to Clinton, full of attitude. "You seem to be under the impression that this missing kid...ah...what's her name?"

"Come on, Jane. You're too smart to act so stupid."

Jane shook her head and rolled her eyes. "Clinton, this kid may be the reason *you* get up in the morning, but I'm here on different business."

"What could be more important than little Miss Charlotte?"

Jane started to answer when she spotted a dark sedan slow to a stop across the mall. A woman got out of the car, then leaned over to talk to the driver through the open passenger window. She was animated, pointing at a specific spot and seemingly giving directions before giving the driver the thumbs-up sign. Jane couldn't mistake the woman's bright purple trousers and long, salt-and-pepper braid. It was Kit Clark.

"What is it?" Clinton said, intrigued, as he turned around to look in the direction that was capturing Jane's attention.

Jane did her best to act nonchalant. "Nothing," she replied, attempting to get Clinton's attention drawn back to her.

Clinton turned to Jane. "You saw something...or someone."

Jane kept her eyes focused on Clinton, although she wanted more than anything to follow Kit. "I wasn't looking at anything. I get bored easily. My mind wanders."

Clinton turned with a great flourish. "You distinctly looked over *there*! Don't bullshit me!"

Jane allowed herself another glance, but Kit and the sedan had vanished. A growing anger welled up inside her gut. "Clinton, I don't have time for this crap." Jane opened her car door and got in, slamming the door shut.

Clinton leaned down, rapping his knuckles on Jane's window. "I'll see you around!" The statement sounded like a promise.

Jane made a determined exit from the parking spot.

Jane circled the mall's parking lot in search of Kit. Her brown hair was soaked from the storm and plastered across her cheek and neck. Lighting a cigarette, Jane took a meaningful drag and surveyed the immediate area. Being that it was New Year's Eve day, the lot was not very full. She pulled the Mustang to the side of the parking lot. The long line of stores included a video arcade, a beauty shop, a nail salon, and an electronics store. Jane considered going into every store in the mall to find Kit and tail her actions, but then her thoughts drifted to Shane Golden's Firebird on the side of Highway 41. Checking her clock, she figured he had been there for more than forty-five minutes. He could have left the area, which meant Jane could possibly go back to the spot and track his muddy footprints before the rain erased them. The idea captured Jane's imagination and she sped with conviction back onto Highway 41.

As she drove, an unresolved restlessness tugged at her gut. She sucked another drag of nicotine from the cigarette and flashed on Kit's energetic thumbs-up to the unknown driver who dropped her off at the mall. The thought suddenly occurred to Jane that

Kit had aligned with someone in Oakhurst prior to their visit and was waiting for the perfect opportunity to meet them. But for what purpose? Jane was certain that Kit was not being forthright. She *was* hiding something; something that held great significance. Something that involved finding Lou Peters. Jane felt stabs of betrayal the longer she drove up Highway 41. With each hot jab, a growing sense of resentment overwhelmed her ability to think rationally. Paranoia had been a constant companion when she used to drink herself into oblivion. Now that specious shadow of mistrust hovered next to Jane, goading her to act on the distant whispers that filled her head.

Clenching the cigarette tightly between her teeth, she changed lanes as she approached mile-marker forty-four, where she had spotted Shane's car. But as she checked traffic in her rearview mirror, Jane saw a black SUV behind her quickly follow suit. Jane purposely slowed, forcing the SUV to move closer to her. There was Clinton Fredericks in the driver's seat, an overeager grin pasted across his parasitical face. "Shit!" Jane exclaimed as she rolled within 100 feet of her destination. Looking to her right, Jane saw that Shane's Firebird was gone. It would have been a perfect opportunity to explore the woods and follow Shane's footprints. But thanks to Clinton's aggressive pursuit, Jane would have to pass up the opportunity and head back to town.

There was no point in trying to elude Clinton. Jane gave up any chance of keeping her local residence a secret as she turned into The Bonanza Cabins. Clinton hung back outside the property, closely eyeing Jane's Mustang as she parked in front of the Hop Sing cabin. Checking her side mirror, Jane saw Clinton's foreboding, black SUV semi-hidden in the line of trees on the main road. His red brake lights reflected against the wet pavement like a warning beacon. Jane knew that waiting him out was no use. He had her cornered. Her concern and calculated precautions regarding staying under Clinton's radar were now painfully validated.

Jane grabbed her satchel, let out a frustrated sigh, and got out of the Mustang. She half expected to see Kit when she entered the cabin. But, instead, she was met with a semidarkened room soaked in the lingering, musty aroma of patchouli and piquant odors of Kit's herbal cornucopia. Keeping the lights off, Jane charily peeked through the closed drapes. Clinton's SUV was in the same spot, looking more like a baleful sentinel. Knowing the way Clinton liked to operate, Jane figured he was scrutinizing her every move with a trusted pair of high-powered binoculars. At this point, Jane realized how paranoid she had become. But then again, she recalled a saying her ex-partner at DH used to repeat: "Just because people call you paranoid does not mean other people aren't out to get you." Jane closed the drapes. Checking the bedside clock, she saw that it was a few minutes past three P.M. Given Kit's tenuous health, Jane was surprised that she hadn't returned from her mysterious journey. The weather became more inclement as the afternoon pressed into New Year's Eve. Jane flopped onto her bed, splaying her arms to the sides. In doing so, she knocked a bag of herbs off the center table between the beds. She rolled over to recover the bag and her hand brushed the top of a paperback book. Turning on the bedside lamp, she found the local Oakhurst phone book face down on the floor and opened to a specific page. Jane turned the phone book upright. The page featured a variety of codes one could punch into the phone prior to or after making a call. Scanning the page, her eyes caught the word RESTRICTED.

*"If you wish to block your name and number on a per call basis, dial *67 before you dial. The caller ID of the party you are calling will register 'RESTRICTED'...."*

Jane picked up the receiver of the cabin's phone. She punched the REDIAL button to retrieve the last number dialed by Kit on their phone. A computer recorded voice replied, "I'm sorry, we were unable to determine the last number of the calling party...." While Jane was not certain, she seemed to recall that that specific recorded message was often triggered from calling a cell phone from a motel room. Her paranoia intensified.

Jane replayed the three instances where she received the Restricted message on her caller ID. Each time, she was alone and Kit had access to a phone. The woman's voice on the other end whispered to hide her identity. Somewhere in the back of Jane's mind, the voice felt familiar. *Very* familiar. A thicker layer of paranoia swept over Jane. She felt tangibly vulnerable. She also felt a surge of anger in her throat. Jane wanted to scream or beat the hell out of something or someone, but all she could do was wear a hard path across the carpet. She quickly turned off the bedside lamp, preferring the blanket of semi-darkness to hold her thoughts. The sun set quickly behind the far hills, cloaking the tiny cabin in a dusky shroud. Jane's heart raced as her mind tripped over a cascade of possibilities to explain Kit's behavior. At that moment, caught up in the daze of obsessed thoughts, all endpoints led to Kit using Jane for a nefarious purpose. Logic went out the window. The walls of the cabin closed in on her. This was what it felt like to be on the run and know that someone was out to get you. She was sure of it. Now her mind raced, one thought spiraling into another. Her thoughts turned to Clinton Fredericks—a known predator. The tension gained momentum. Jane crossed to the window, opened the drapes a half inch, and looked in the same spot where Clinton had parked. The fading light, accompanied by the streetlamps and the fact that Clinton drove a black SUV, complicated the search. From what she could see, Clinton was no longer parked in that spot. But that didn't mean he wasn't hidden somewhere else in the recesses of the parking lot. After all, once the large media trucks returned for the night, it would be easy for Clinton to slip next to one of them and hide from view.

The surging suspicion reached levels that Jane had never experienced. Not in all her years of heavy drinking had she felt this exposed. She paced around the cabin, feeling like a trapped animal in a small, log cage. When she looked at the bedside clock, it was nearly five P.M. Paranoia makes time fly, she thought. Jane paced to the rear of the cabin by the bathroom. Suddenly, she heard the distinctive sound of Kit's footsteps outside. The room was almost completely dark. Jane considered it an advantage. Having the upper hand would give her the edge she needed.

Kit unlocked the door, sending a gust of chilly night air into the cabin. She closed the door and carefully made her way around Jane's bed to turn on the bedside lamp. She turned the switch, screamed, and dropped a large brown bag to the floor. Standing six feet away was Jane, Glock extended and pointed at Kit's head.

CHAPTER 23

Jane's heart pounded as she steadied her Glock with both hands. The searing look in her eye was unmistakable to Kit.

"Jesus, Jane," Kit said, visibly shaken, "what in the hell's going on?"

"You tell me," Jane replied, all business.

"I had to go out...." Kit said, sounding like a confused child. "Tomorrow's a holiday."

"So what?"

"Stores are closed."

"You know, Kit. I really hate it when people think they can play me."

"Play you?" Kit's tone became more indignant.

"What is it you hoped to achieve by getting me to the Stop 'n' Save?"

"The Stop 'n' Save?"

"Don't act like a fucking idiot!"

"I'm not acting like a fucking idiot! I don't know what in the hell you're talking about!" It was obvious Kit was pissed. It didn't matter if a gun was pointed directly at her.

"You left the phone book turned to the number codes. The ones that tell you how to disguise your number when you call someone! And while it's hard to distinguish a voice from a whisper, I knew it was familiar. *'Let me help you....'"* Jane whispered those last words with a sarcastic twist.

Kit shook her head. "The phone book.... I used it to call a store.... I was getting ready to go and I think I knocked it off the table—"

"Give me a fucking break!"

"Somebody called you? Regarding Lou?" Kit interjected.

Jane reestablished her hard-line stance with the Glock. *"Stop playing me!"*

"For Christ's sake! I didn't call you!" Kit recalled something. "Look in the goddamned phone book! I circled the name of the store!"

Jane's head raced with possible strategies. Her back was up against the wall...literally. "I'm not checking the phone book, Kit."

"Then I'll show you," Kit said, turning to find the phone book. Jane quickly trained the Glock on Kit, waiting for her to make a sudden move. Kit nervously found the page in the Yellow Pages section and held it up so Jane could clearly see it. "Right there!" Kit said pointing to a one-inch ad at the bottom of the page. "Circled in blue ink." She cocked her head to the bedside table where a ballpoint pen lay. "There's the pen I used. You want to check it for the blue ink? The store is The Herbal Haven. They sell bulk herbs. I told you I was nearly out of one of my formulas this morning, but you didn't seem to care. You were too busy running off to your next...whatever. I didn't know when you were coming back. So I called Barry at the front desk and asked him if he was going to town. He said he was and he'd give me a ride. But it was going to take him four or five hours before he was done and he could pick me up. So I made do with the time I had. And, no, I didn't call you because I don't know your goddamned cell number!" Kit angrily threw the phone book across the room. She picked up the bag she dropped. "You want to see what I got at the store?" She pulled out one plastic baggie after another of herbs and tossed them on her bed. "And here's the last one!" Kit withdrew several packs of American Spirit cigarettes and tossed them with fervor on the bed. "Those are for you! I figured if you're going to smoke, you might as well smoke all natural tobacco! *You're welcome!"* Kit stared down Jane as an uneasy silence passed between them.

Jane still wasn't sold. She calmly kept the Glock on Kit. "You haven't been honest with me, Kit. I know you're in the system and I know why."

Kit's face sunk. She swallowed hard as her eyes traced the carpet. "I...I didn't know it was relevant."

"You didn't think that supplying the goods to a militant bomber who killed four innocent people was *relevant?*"

"Wait! Supplying the goods? Where'd you hear that?"

Jane recalled the single article that Cousin Carl had found on the shoe factory bombing. "That's how it was reported."

"In the *beginning*, yes. But that's before they knew all the facts of the case."

"So enlighten me!"

Kit took a shaky seat on Jane's bed. The memory clearly troubled her heart. "Please...put the gun down, Jane," Kit said, her eyes still focused on the floor. Her voice was weak and deeply distraught.

Jane gradually lowered the Glock. She wasn't about to drop her guard completely, so she braced her back against the wall.

"As you know, I've made a few bad judgments in my life. I believed that a group of dedicated people could make a big difference in this world. And I thought that anyone who wanted to make a difference was someone who had an honest heart. It never occurred to me that misinterpretations of what was said could lead an unstable person to commit acts that were never intended." Kit let out a hard sigh. "I belonged to a group of like-minded individuals in the mid-eighties. We called ourselves 'The Lightkeepers of Peace.' We met weekly at our various homes and talked about liberal causes. Migrant farm worker reform, decent wages for blue-collar work, the disgrace of the little man being usurped by the powerful corporate conglomerate. We were adamantly a pacifist organization and nonviolent to the core! We marched. We protested peacefully. We draped signs over highways to spread our message. We wanted people to be aware of how the corporate structure was destroying the fabric of our country. We'd been together as a group for five years when a man named Nelson Pudell started attending our meetings. In retrospect, Nelson was different from the get-go. He had an edge. A fever. When his eyes flared and his veins bulged, we encouraged what we took for passion. Looking back, it was so obvious that he wasn't like the rest of us...."

"You're stalling, Kit. What happened at the factory?"

Kit gathered her thoughts. "We received credible evidence from one of the Latino workers that the conditions inside the shoe factory were unsafe. We were told that a man on the assembly line lost the use of his hand; another lost a finger. The owners, Mr. and Mrs. Kapp, didn't care. We wanted the press and the community to know how this factory was treating its people. It was supposed to be a normal protest: stand at the gate with signs and let the owners know that what they were doing to their Latino employees was not acceptable. When we arrived, we noticed that Nelson wasn't there. We figured he'd overslept. We started our march and our chants. And then it happened. The explosion lifted us off our feet. It blew apart the front offices and started a huge fire. People ran out of the place screaming for their lives. Some of them were burned pretty badly. I saw body parts fall out of the sky. We thought it was a natural gas explosion. But then we saw Nelson emerge from the rubble, his fist in the air, yelling 'I am a savior for the Lightkeepers of Peace!' His rationale was that the Kapps had turned their back on two employees who had lost the use of a hand and were missing a finger. So he was going to place a bomb near the front offices where the owners worked and make them feel the suffering that they wouldn't acknowledge their employees had suffered. The old eye for an eye."

"Did he kill the Kapps?"

"He killed Mr. Kapp. The other three were Latino factory workers who happened to be in the front office when the bomb exploded."

"How did you get linked?"

"We were *all* linked by virtue of our association with Nelson. They booked every one of us and then did the sorting out later."

"The article said you provided Nelson with the materials for making the bomb."

Kit shook her head. "He came to my house a few times. Once he asked if I had any copper wire hanging around. I said I did and gave it to him. The next time, he asked me for a clock. Finally, he was at the house and asked to borrow some books from my library. I didn't know what he took. It turns out, he grabbed some pamphlets I'd picked up at an anti-war rally years before. I didn't know what was in them. But I found out! It was a bunch of articles written by angry, ex-military men from Vietnam that made a brief reference to how we should 'bomb the sons of bitches into oblivion who perpetrated the Vietnam War.' It was a single line, but to Nelson it was the trigger...the acknowledgement...the motivation he needed to validate his destruction." Kit looked at Jane, her eyes sad and weary. "I learned the hard way that the message you give someone may not be the message they hear. So in the end, the responsibility is equally shared between the one who gives that message and the one who acts on what he *thought* he heard. And most importantly, the responsibility of not recognizing the tenuous nature of someone's mind and heart *begins* with the one who incites." Kit let out a long sigh. "Whatever article you found, it must have been one that was written early in the case, because after they sorted everything out, the charges of aiding and abetting were dropped. My lawyer got it down that I was guilty of lack of judgment. Got a mug shot out of it and my name in the system... and memories that will haunt me forever." Kit got up and headed into the bathroom. She turned on the bathroom light. "You want to hear the sad irony?"

"What was that?"

"A month later we discovered that the credible evidence about the injuries to the Latino workers was false. No one lost a finger or the use of his hand. In fact, the factory's safety records were impeccable." Kit walked into the bathroom, closing the door behind her.

Jane holstered the Glock and stood silently for several minutes, the waves of paranoia extinguished. All that was left was a bone-tired ache. A half truth is as good as no truth, she thought. Half a story equaled none. Now with her senses back, she felt a sense of shame that she so readily jumped to misguided conclusions. To pull a gun on someone...Jane winced at her overreaction. She would have liked to blame her knee-jerk behavior on the lingering psychological aftereffects of her whiskey binge. But that argument seemed like a lame justification. She screwed up because she screwed up. No excuses. The only thing she craved now more than taking the last two hours back was a cigarette. She knocked gently on the bathroom door. "I'm going outside for a smoke."

Outside, the night air cut through Jane like an icy dagger. She lit her cigarette and hugged the side of the cabin to keep warm. The faint sound of New Year's Eve revelers starting their party early was heard in the distance. Jane had her own name for New Year's Eve: Amateur Night. Half in the bag before midnight and puking in the bushes. There was no style. No class. Just piss drunk, part-time party animals who waited all year to act insane when the clock struck midnight.

Her cell phone rang. Jane checked the number. It was Sergeant Weyler.

"Hey, Boss," Jane answered.

"There's that Boss word again. Hello, Jane." His voice was smooth and rich.

Jane couldn't help but smile. "I wasn't expecting you to call me back so soon. Being New Year's Eve...."

"I got the impression you were in a rush."

"What'd you find out?"

Weyler revealed that both Shane Golden and Trace Fagin were clean. Regarding Fagin, Weyler learned he was a sales rep for a restaurant equipment supplier. He was returning from the Ahwahnee Hotel when the cops picked him up on Highway 41. He'd parked his blue Chevy on the side of the road and walked into the woods to take a pee. Since the cops were on the lookout for his make of sedan based on the information from Leann Hamilton, they treated Fagin with greater suspicion. "They say Fagin acted suspiciously," Weyler noted, "and so they asked if they could pat him down. He said sure and that's when they found a girl's bracelet in his jacket pocket. It had silver hearts that spelled out CHARLOTTE.

"Oh, Christ."

"That was good enough for them to take him in. He swore up and down that he found the bracelet in the woods as he was walking to take his piss. Claims he thought it was pretty and that maybe his daughter would like it."

"Don't tell me he's got a daughter back home named Charlotte."

"No. But he *does* have a daughter named *Charlene* who he calls *Char*. He reasoned that he could remove the separate silver hearts that spelled LOTTE and she'd never be the wiser."

"The sheriff isn't buying that, is he?"

"He sure isn't. Fagin's got nobody to vouch for his whereabouts on December 25. He called his wife and kids once during the day, but said he was on the road alone the whole time. He claims he didn't even know about Charlotte's kidnapping. The sheriff finds that odd as the news was splashed across every news station. But Fagin maintains he doesn't watch TV. He reads books at night when he stops at a hotel. When he drives, he listens to books on tape instead of the radio. And these are inspirational books, by the way. Stuff like how to empower your life and think yourself rich. They're wearing Fagin down. *Hard.* My source tells me that Fagin can't take much more of it and he's probably going to cop to something soon."

Jane fell silent, feeling into her gut. "He didn't do it, Boss," she quietly stated. "His only crime was taking a piss in the wrong place at the wrong time."

"Driving the wrong car?"

"Are we hinging this guy's guilt on a sixteen-year-old girl's description of a car?"

"She's their only valid witness."

"Is she?"

"You want to tell me what you're thinking?"

"I got to ruminate on it. They've checked the woods where they found Fagin?"

"Yeah. Twice. But the rain is playing havoc with the job. They took bloodhounds out there with a piece of Charlotte's clothing. Supposedly, they picked up some kind of scent of the kid but lost it."

"They picked up her scent?" Jane let that information absorb for a second. "How'd the media not report that one?"

"The sheriff asked them not to talk about it in order to preserve the integrity of the scene."

"Where is this spot?"

Weyler fished through his notes. "Right near mile-marker forty-four."

Jane's throat stung. She contemplated mentioning that she saw Shane Golden parked in that same spot during the early afternoon of that day, but she wasn't ready to formulate any clear accusations of the boy yet.

"Now, this Lou Peters fellow?" Weyler continued. "Apparently, the sheriff's deputies didn't have to track him down. Peters showed up himself at the sheriff's office to declare his whereabouts on December 26."

Jane recalled Kit mentioning that Lou made a conscious point of following the stated rules. From checking in ahead of time with his bondsman to alerting the guards at Chino Prison that his cell door was not locking properly, Kit felt it was Lou's premeditated way of endearing himself to those in power. Look honest and people will treat you as an honest man. "How can Lou prove his whereabouts?"

"Receipts," Weyler stated. "One from a Shell gas station that is time coded and located about an hour north on Highway 41. The other two are receipts for later in the day from the dining room of a motel called...." Weyler shuffled his notes. "It's called The Hummingbird Motor Lodge."

"The *Hummingbird?*" Jane was stunned. "Holy shit." As much as Jane didn't want to believe it, the odd sequence of bird names that had followed her these last few days and mirrored the legend of Pico Blanco was uncanny and downright frightening.

"Is that significant?" Weyler asked.

"I don't know, Boss. Maybe it's just a...strange coincidence."

"Coincidence?" Weyler sounded intrigued. "You know how I feel about coincidences."

"Yeah. A coincidence is two steps away from a lucky break that solves the case," Jane said, repeating one of Weyler's many pithy sayings. "So, does the sheriff's office have a copy of these receipts?"

"Yes. And I just happen to have a fax copy of those receipts in my hand."

Jane stood dumbfounded. "Who do you know in this tiny town?"

"Can't tell you. I promised I'd keep their anonymity. You got a fax nearby?"

Jane remembered the business card she swiped from the front office and dug it out of her jacket. She rattled off the fax number to Weyler and told him to address it to "Melody Clark," the pseudonym Kit made up.

"One more thing," Weyler quickly added. "Charlotte went missing over Thanksgiving weekend. Friday to Saturday. Almost thirty-six hours."

"They have a police report on it?" Jane took a nervous drag on her cigarette.

"No. Her mother was about to call it in when Charlotte came home. The reason I'm telling you is the media got hold of it and they're going to report it tonight."

"Where does that lead us? She's a runaway?"

"Maybe. But she may be a dead runaway because of that bracelet Fagin's got."

"No, no, this is not adding up, Boss."

"What's your gut telling you?" Weyler asked respectfully.

"Layers. There are layers upon layers. It's not a straight shot. I can't say it any better way than that. All I know is Trace Fagin is innocent."

"You better figure it out soon because the way they're wearing Fagin down, he's about to cop to something he didn't do."

Jane knew that would be a death sentence for Charlotte. The authorities would curb their search for the girl, plodding along for a few weeks, hoping to find her body buried somewhere in the woods. The magic window of time had long since passed— those first forty-eight hours after a kid went missing. Statistics showed that the odds of finding a child alive after that initial forty-eight hours decreased substantially with each passing day. Her mind flashed to Rachel Hartly. Jane gave Weyler the condensed version of what occurred at Hartly's house that morning. The odd newspapers with the missing sections. The guesthouse. The rifle pointed at her head.

"You have to go back and check it out when she's not there," Weyler stressed.

"That's easier said than done, Boss."

"What if Rachel Hartly's hiding someone?"

"Lou?"

"Yeah. Or Charlotte." A chill went down Jane's spine. "Just go back and check around so you can rule out Rachel." Jane reluctantly agreed. That was going to be one tough assignment. "I don't have anything for you on the DNA from that condom. The lab's closed until January 2. But I got a good connection over there. The cousin of an ex-wife of a former desk sergeant heads the department."

Jane let out a soft chuckle at Weyler's convoluted connections. "You do get around, Boss." It felt good to talk to him. It was like home.

"How are you doing, in spite of all this?" Weyler asked, sounding paternal.

Jane opted to not mention the strange phone call she received with the whispered *"Let me help you."* She took a drag on her cigarette. A rare swell of vulnerability washed over her. In a sudden wave, the impact of her whiskey binge forty-eight hours ago grabbed at her throat. Tears unexpectedly welled and fell down her face. Jane tried to choke back the emotion, but it was useless. "I went out, Boss."

Weyler took a breath. "It happens. You're human. You keep forgetting that."

"I had six months," Jane softly said, tears still flowing.

"You'll get another six months. Then a year. Then a decade. And then a life."

"I'm a failure, Boss. I'll be thirty-six in twelve days. What do I have to show for it?"

"There's people alive today because of you."

"People are dead because of me, too."

"What do you want me to tell you, Jane? That you're a good person going through a bad patch? That there's a light at the end of the tunnel that isn't an oncoming train? That from this moment on you're never going to go out again? Maybe you will go out again. And if you do, you'll start over."

Jane winced at the thought. "I don't have the energy to keep that up, Boss."

"Then figure it out." Weyler's voice was hard for the first time. He knew that suffocating Jane in a sympathetic blanket would serve no purpose.

His tone worked. Jane drew in the rest of her resolve. She thought back on the trigger for her binge. "Boss? Do you believe that a person can be two polar opposites in the same life? A perpetrator *and* a victim?"

"A sinner and a saint? Of course."

"Does it make a difference if they were the saint first?"

"Yes. Because then their ending is tragic." There was a meaningful pause.

They ended their conversation just as the rain began to fall with greater fervor. Jane sprinted to the front office to retrieve Weyler's fax of Lou's receipts. One of the cable news channels played loudly in the foreground as Barry retrieved the fax. It was the same, worn-out loop of tape from Charlotte's birthday bash. Jane had the damn thing memorized. The kid's rainbow wig. The self-conscious giggle. The red leather jacket. The snake emblem on her tank top. Jane reached into her pocket and rubbed the snake-stone totem against the single sobriety chip. Clues, Jane thought as she stared blankly at the TV screen. What was she missing? Barry handed her the fax and insisted on ten minutes of idle gossip before Jane was able to duck out of the office.

The rain poured outside as she secured the fax under her jacket and ran back to the cabin. When she got to the door, it was slightly ajar. Jane poked her head inside and found the room empty. She turned and scanned the parking lot. Sheets of rain pelted the asphalt. Between the streetlights and shadows, Jane spotted Kit standing still near the far wall of the parking lot. She seemed to be staring intently at someone or something that Jane could not see. She yelled at Kit, but Kit remained unmoved. Jane raced across the parking lot, the deep puddles of rainwater splashing up to her knees. She yelled Kit's name again. Still no reaction. Jane was within twenty-five feet of Kit when she yelled at her once again. This time, Kit turned to Jane with an otherworldly expression accompanied by generous tears rolling down her face.

"What is it?" Jane asked Kit, out of breath and sopping wet.

Kit turned back to where her attention had been focused. She bent her head, defeated. "I need to get inside," Kit quietly replied as she walked back to the cabin.

Jane squinted into the shadows and the relentless rain in the direction Kit had been fixated. She saw nothing. But that didn't stop the icy shudder that raced up her spine.

CHAPTER 24
JANUARY 1

Sleep came hard for Jane. Every forty-five minutes, she woke with a restless jerk, her mind racing. As she watched the New Year's rising sun slip through the crack in the drapes, Jane felt old. Her lower back ached; partly from stress and partly from the cheap mattresses Barry had bought for the cabins. It had been her first sober New Year's Eve. But if her head was any indication, she might as well have drained a bottle of Jim Beam. A dull stupor overwhelmed her senses, mixed with a rock-tired throbbing behind her eyes. Even two cups of her special gourmet coffee did little to assuage the pain. Kit had gotten up early to walk outside and greet the rising sun, an apparent New Year's Day tradition. Fortunately, the storm clouds had abated overnight, transforming Oakhurst into a drier, yet still damp around the edges town.

Jane tiredly dressed in her running outfit, checking Kit's whereabouts outside every few minutes. Kit was finishing her second of five turns around the parking lot, walking backward and humming "Bobby McGee." From what Jane could decipher, Kit was back to her old, albeit eccentric, self. Nothing was said regarding Kit's strange journey across the parking lot the previous night. As much as Jane wanted to question her, she figured she'd already caused Kit enough grief by pulling a gun on the woman and accusing her of disreputable actions.

Jane grabbed her pack of Marlboros and then spied the American Spirits Kit bought for her. "What the hell," she thought as Jane tossed the Marlboros to the side and withdrew a cigarette from the all-natural tobacco pack. Outside, she lit the cigarette and sucked the smoke into her lungs. It was surprisingly strong and satisfying. After two more hard drags, Jane carefully extinguished the ember and rested the cigarette on the window ledge.

She waved to Kit and pantomimed that she was setting off on her run. Two days ago, Jane would have just taken off. But now she resolved to do whatever it took to reconnect with Kit and, hopefully, regain their old sense of camaraderie and shared purpose.

As Jane rounded the front office, she stopped to see the headline of the *Fresno Bee*. The reward fund for finding Charlotte Walker had jumped to $85,000. Jane knew that Clinton Fredericks was already planning how to spend the money. The night before, Kit and Jane had watched Clinton interview Leann Hamilton in front of the Walker's house. But Leann wasn't acting in the same manner as when she talked to Lesley Stahl. Her nerves were frayed. Dark circles lay under her eyes like ebony stains of smeared mascara. There was also a disturbing shell-shocked look that worried Jane. Leann spoke so quietly at times that Clinton had to repeatedly ask her to talk louder. She peppered too many "um's" and "ah's" throughout her answers. When Leann wasn't studying the ground with her eyes, she was biting the flesh off her thumbnail. Leann looked like a trapped rabbit right before the slaughter. It was god-awful, Jane decided. Just god-awful.

As an act of good faith to Kit, Jane tipped her off that Trace Fagin had Charlotte's bracelet in his possession. She also let Kit know that Clinton was shadowing her. Jane capped off the information dump with the fact that Charlotte had gone missing for thirty-six hours over the Thanksgiving holiday weekend and that the media planned to make it their New Year's Eve top story. When she revealed that Sergeant Weyler was her source for the inside information, Kit exclaimed, "How did you get your Sergeant Weyler to get involved in our good cause?"

"I promised I'd return to DH in the sergeant's position he offered."

Kit was clearly taken aback. "That's quite a compromise for you to make."

"I needed his help. Like you said, time is ticking away. I had no choice."

"You made that deal for me?" Kit asked.

"I made it for us," Jane said with a shrug of her shoulders.

"Thank you," Kit said, her opinion of Jane rising quickly.

Jane let out a long sigh, tracing the carpet with her eyes. "I watch over people, Kit. I protect them. I rescue them. That's my job." Jane's voice was detached. "That's *always* been my job. My mother died of cancer when I was ten. I was the only one with her when it happened. Right before she died, she told me to watch over Mike. I hated her for giving up on us. And I blamed her for making me responsible for Mike's safety. But after a while, I didn't do it because she asked me to. I did it because it's who I became." Jane looked Kit in the eye. "I may be a drunk. I may have a 'fuck you' attitude. I may jump to wild conclusions when I shouldn't. But no one can ever say I'm not responsible. When people ask me to help them, I do it. I knew you couldn't find Lou all alone. And I knew that if I didn't go with you and I found out later that something awful had happened to you, I'd never forgive myself."

Kit looked at Jane with deep compassion. "Jane, when you spend your life taking care of other people, you never get a chance to know yourself. The other people become convenient distractions because, deep down, examining who you are is too frightening."

"Knowing oneself is a luxury."

"Knowing oneself is freedom. Do you think we all need to be rescued by you, Jane?"

"Charlotte needs to be rescued."

"Yes, she does. But *I* don't. When you're told as a child that you must rescue others, you believe that everyone you come in contact with wants or needs *you* to liberate them. That's not always true. Some people just need to do what they have to do in order to make their lives right."

Jane was perplexed. The idea of allowing someone else to go about their life without her stellar judgment seemed patently careless. And what did Kit mean by "in order to make their lives right"? Jane stiffened. "What if something happens?"

"Something always *happens*, Jane."

"I'm talking something bad."

"What's considered bad to you, may not be bad to someone else. Bad is objective."

"I'm talking *death*. Death is not objective."

"In the end, Jane, it's all objective. My intention was never to be rescued by you. You're my ally. And besides, did you ever consider that, perhaps, our partnership exists so that *I* can rescue *you*?"

Jane jogged down the quiet back road behind the Cabins. "Rescue *me*?" she thought, her feet beating out a syncopated rhythm on the wet pavement. What an odd thing to say. She crested the far hill and passed the line of trees where Shane Golden had posted Charlotte's missing child flyers. The heavy rain had warped the posters, turning Charlotte's smiling face into a distorted visage. Jane stopped in front of one of the posters to catch her breath. She found herself fixating on the kid's face. She recalled a psychic DH had brought in years before to help locate a missing boy. The woman's eyes glazed over as she disappeared into the black-and-white photo of the child. She told everyone present that a part of her left the room and melted into the soul of the little boy. The tears that rolled down the psychic's cheeks signaled to Jane that she felt the boy was dead. Two days later, they found the torso of the boy buried in a sewage pond.

Jane stared into the weather-warped photograph of Charlotte in an attempt to feel into the girl's soul. "Where are you, Charlotte?" Jane whispered. Her meditative moment was interrupted by the approaching sound of an SUV. Jane quickly resumed her run. However, the SUV slowed to a crawl as it came within spitting distance. Jane glanced over and saw Clinton at the wheel, rolling down the electric window on the passenger side. He looked as if he'd spent the night in his clothes and partied until the wee hours of the morning.

"Damn, Jane! I never took you for being an exercise freak!" Jane continued to jog as Clinton rolled next to her. She hoped her silence would speak volumes, but the guy was as dense as the over-gelled lumps of uncombed hair that lay against his thick skull. "I did a little investigative research on you," Clinton said, his voice sounding like he swallowed a box of nails. "You're not working at Denver Headquarters anymore! *J.P.I.?* Isn't that what you call your new business?" Jane maintained her steady jog and silent loathing. "So, why are you involved in finding our little Miss Charlotte?"

Jane gathered her best acting skills. "I told you, I have no interest in her."

"Then how come you slowed down yesterday near the mile-marker where they picked up Fagin?"

Jane's ire boiled inside. "I don't know what the hell you're talking about. All I know is what I heard on the news last night. They said the kid went missing over the Thanksgiving holiday. So she's obviously a freakin' runaway who happens to chose holidays for her spontaneous getaways. No mystery there!"

"Don't you think there's a helluva difference between thirty-six hours and," Clinton checked his commando-style wristwatch, "going on 140 hours?" Jane shook her head with a blasé attitude. "Happy New Year to Jane Perry!" With that, Clinton purposely burned rubber, spitting gravel toward Jane, and sped down the lonely back road.

Jane turned and headed back to the Cabins. As she padded down the road, she reflected on her improvisational accounting of Charlotte's whereabouts to Clinton. The connection she quickly made up about Charlotte going missing on a holiday weekend and now during the Christmas break sparked her interest. Perhaps, she mused, this unexpected declaration was a plausible angle to follow.

Once back at the cabin, Jane discussed the idea with Kit. But it was clear that Kit did not care so much as to how or where Charlotte disappeared. Rather, Kit maintained that Lou had her and that Jane should focus on finding him. Period. It went against the way Jane worked. You started your quest for the suspect in an ocean, not a fishbowl. If you focused on one man, you might ignore the true predator or the accomplices. However, to draw in

Kit and tackle the Lou Peters angle, Jane explained what occurred
at Rachel Hartly's house the day before. Kit's reaction mirrored
Sergeant Weyler's: Rachel was covering for Lou or helping hide
Charlotte on the premises. In her typical reactive mode, Kit insisted they journey to Hartly's house to investigate. It took Jane a few
minutes to explain that any such exploratory trip to Hartly's house
would need to be well thought out to avoid being discovered.

Jane showered and changed into a pair of black jeans and a
tawny turtleneck. While Kit got ready in the bathroom, Jane fell
back on her bed and stretched in an attempt to reduce the pain in
her lower back. She thought back on the string of phone calls to
her cell and the whispered "Let me help you" before the setup at
the Stop 'n' Save. The calls had stopped, which signaled to Jane
that the caller had gotten whatever she wanted out of the ruse.
But that begged the question, what did the caller want? Was it
a bait and switch? Occupy Jane's attention long enough to momentarily take her focus away from where the real action was?
Jane considered all the options, but she kept coming up with more
unanswered questions.

Her restless spirit sent her mind traveling in vicious circles,
making it impossible to ease the tension in her lower back. Frustrated, she rolled over and stared briefly at the photo of Lou and
the campers at Pico Blanco. Her eye was always first drawn to the
two somber girls in the front row before meandering to the left side
of the photo and fixating on Mary Bartosh. Unfortunately, this
band of kids could no more talk to Jane than the weather-beaten,
back-road poster of Charlotte Walker.

Jane glanced at the stack of metaphysical books Kit had scattered on the floor between their beds. Jane spotted several books
on the power of gemstones, the tarot, numerology, and astrology.
One book titled, "The Beginner's Guide to Astrology" attracted
her attention. She found her January 11 birth date and read all
about the highs and lows of Capricorns. Jane skimmed until she
found a paragraph on the struggles all Capricorns must endure.
As she read the descriptive text, she couldn't believe its amazing

accuracy. Kit opened the bathroom door with a hurried flourish. Jane thought she had tossed the book down fast enough to avoid being discovered, but the action only drew more attention to her.

"What's this?" Kit said with a twinkle in her eye. "Did I catch you reading one of my books?"

Jane sat on the edge of the bed, wincing in slight discomfort from her back pain. "I was bored. It was there. No big deal. Ready?" She got up and grabbed her jacket.

"Does your back hurt?"

"It's felt better." Jane collected the stack of newspapers she'd stolen from Rachel's recycling box.

"You know, you should really try walking backward in circles. I can't tell how it relieves low back pain."

Jane shook her head in bemusement as she secured her Glock in her shoulder holster, snapping it across her turtleneck.

After a quick breakfast at The Circle 9 Diner, Jane drove by *The Sierra Star* newspaper offices. The New Year's holiday and closed offices afforded her the opportunity to fly under the radar with her plan. Luckily, Clinton and his big black SUV were nowhere to be seen. Driving around the back of the newspaper's offices, Jane located a large trash bin that read, NEWSPAPERS ONLY. She withdrew the stack of ten newspapers she had stolen from Rachel's house and instructed Kit to get out of the car.

"I'm going in the bin. You rattle off the various dates on these papers and I'll see if I can find them."

Kit's expression turned to an excited, almost mischievous one. Finally, she was getting to take part in the investigation. Although she had no idea how it was all connected. After twenty minutes, Jane was only able to unearth and match five of the ten newspapers. She hoisted her aching body out of the bin and laid the four papers on the hood of her Mustang along with their matching counterparts. Jane located the first mystery cut-out page and then flipped through the matching intact paper. The missing section was an ad for Henderson Chevrolet, "Your Friendly, Neighborhood Dealership." A portly man wearing a cowboy hat pointed his

finger at the camera. Above him, the ad said: COME TO HENDER-
SON CHEVROLET AND YOU CAN SAVE YOURSELF $2,500 ON A BRAND,
SPANKING NEW CAR!

Jane analyzed the ad but couldn't make any connection. She
turned the page to see what was printed on the back of the page
but just found a photo of a pumpkin. She tore out the ad and
placed it inside the missing square from the stripped paper.

Locating the next missing section, Jane found a smaller announcement that read: IT'S NOT TOO LATE TO SIGN UP FOR THE FALL
TOUR OF YOSEMITE. Again, nothing of note was on the opposite
side of the page.

The next section was found in the "About Town" pullout. It
read: SING! SING! SING! IT'S ALL YOU WANT TO DO AND THE CHORAL
CHORALE NEEDS YOUR VOICE FOR OUR HOLIDAY PAGEANT!

None of it made sense to Jane. It seemed like a random process, and yet each section had been meticulously cut out with scissors. She searched for a pattern that joined each section together,
but nothing sprung to mind.

The next one was an ad for wrinkle cream: WITH TRUE VAN-
ISH EYE CREAM, WHAT WILL YOU SEE WHEN YOU LOOK IN THE MIRROR
THE NEXT TIME?

Finally, there was a service ad that dealt with tax issues: YOU
MAY REDEEM YOUR SELF-EMPLOYMENT TAX EXEMPTION BY FOLLOWING
THESE STEPS.

Jane shook her head, feeling more frustrated than when she
started.

"Maybe it's a complicated code?" Kit offered.

"We're not in Paris and this ain't *The Da Vinci Code*, Kit."

"Well, it has to have some *meaning*."

Jane agreed, but right now the jumbled sections were just a
bleary mishmash. She stared up into the morning sky. The sun
slipped between two passing clouds, delivering a warm bath of
heat onto her face. "I look for patterns, Kit," Jane said, leaning
against the Mustang and digging out her pack of American Spirits. "If I'm going to tag this kidnapping on Lou, I need to start

seeing the established patterns that he used when he kidnapped and killed Ashlee."

"There was no sign of him at Rachel's house?"

"No. There was the guesthouse, but so what?"

"When he kidnapped my Ashlee, he didn't stay with her the entire time. That was the way he covered for himself. He went to work, then he'd drive to Pico Blanco, check on her, wait until she woke up from the Valium, torture her, and then dose her up with another pill so she'd fall asleep. Then he'd get on his motorcycle and come back to the house. *That's* his pattern."

Jane lit a cigarette and took a drag. "But what about the kind of kid he goes for? Fourteen, right? Doesn't that fit in with his 'Power of Fourteen' idea? And if he's doing all this because his mother raped him at age fourteen and he chooses girls who remind him of his mother—brunettes and hazel eyes—Charlotte's just got the hazel eyes. If we're going to look for patterns, the pattern has to follow through to be valid." Kit nodded. "Something's always bothered me. I can't understand why Lou chose you when he was looking for a place to live. Why does a rabid, Fundamentalist Christian agree to have a landlord who is delightfully Bohemian and decidedly off-center?"

Kit smiled as she propped her bottom on the Mustang's hood. "I've wondered that myself. He said he was looking for some place quiet and my little retreat in Jade Cove fit the bill. He liked to hear God's sounds—the rushing creek, the crickets—"

"But before he lived with you, didn't you say he lived with one family after another from the Lamb of God Congregation?"

"Yes, but he was nineteen. I think he probably wanted to strike out on his own—"

"And have a landlord who read the tarot, studied astrology, smoked pot, and painted zaftig models like your drugged out friend Genevieve?"

"She wasn't drugged! A little pot. Maybe a few downers to take off the edge—"

"You know what I mean. You would be the last person he'd want to be around."

"Maybe he looked on me as a Christian challenge! Someone he could convert. He was forever bugging Genevieve! Slipping little notes in her purse about how Jesus was watching her. Think about it. If he were able to convert a pagan like myself, he'd probably score big points with Bartosh. And trust me, he wanted to be seen as a good person in the eyes of Dr. John Bartosh. Actually, I think what Lou really wanted was for Bartosh to treat him like a son. Lou never knew his father. He told me that his mother conceived him on one of her many one-night stands. He never had any sense of identity, so he was always searching outside of himself for someone who could give him that."

"And Bartosh gave him an identity?"

"Yes. It's like you said about Charlotte and her AWOL father. It *does* make an impact on a child when there's no dad around. Lou wanted a strong, male presence in his life and Bartosh fit that need perfectly. He was stern but loving in his own peculiar way to Lou. And while I can't prove it, I know that Bartosh saw something in Lou."

"Saw what?" Jane asked, taking another two drags on her cigarette.

"The son he never had? That's an assumption, but they have a strong bond. Hell, Bartosh visited Lou in prison. He stood up for him in court. He was determined to defend Lou throughout everything. I'd look at Bartosh in court and there was this blind belief in Lou that overrode any measure of common sense. Lou conned everyone in the name of Jesus. At first, Lou was drawn to the Lamb of God Congregation because they took him in off the street and made him feel safe for the first time in his life. But he quickly used his good looks and charisma to endear himself to the Church members. And those naïve bastards fell for it. They treated him like a tiny God." Kit shifted her body on the hood of the Mustang. "You know, part of me wonders if Bartosh wants to pass the torch to Lou."

"Head the Church?" Jane asked with a stunned tone.

"Bartosh is getting up there. Even though he's old-fashioned, he's patently aware that he needs someone to carry on his work."

"Why not choose from the pool of the Brotherhood Council?"

"Maybe he wants someone younger. Someone who is charismatic, who can draw in more young people. Lou's proven to be a master at that."

"Excuse me, but how is having a convicted killer and rapist as the head of your church considered a *good* thing?"

"Jane, *I can't stress it enough.* Bartosh has never believed for one second that Lou is guilty of *anything*! Why do you think he posted bond for him? He trusts in his heart that Lou is being unjustly targeted and persecuted by the secular court system *because he's a Christian*! Bartosh won't give the evidence any examination! He's blinded by Lou's magnetism. *I* was blinded by Lou fourteen years ago! Between the story of his tortured childhood and his carefully constructed persona that ingratiates, I didn't want to see him as anything but a guy who needed to get past the hell and make a happy future for himself."

"Bartosh is an educated theologian. Narrow-minded, yes. But, he's no idiot."

"I didn't say he was an idiot. But there's that dichotomy again. That slice of two personas within one individual. He may be able to debate theology with the best of them. But there's a weakness buried just under his psyche. He may be exalted by his followers, but he's as human as the rest of us. He lacks discernment just as I did fourteen years ago. You've heard about being blinded by God? Dr. John Bartosh is blinded by God *and* by Lou Peters. Aren't all religious people looking for a savior in the flesh?"

"You think Bartosh believes *Lou* is the savior for his church?"

"Yes, I do." Kit turned away briefly, lost in thought. "You didn't see what I saw in court last year during the bond hearing. There was a distinct way Bartosh interacted with Lou. It made me queasy. It was like a meeting of two very twisted minds, both believing that they're working for the good of Jesus." Kit leaned forward. "There was this moment during the hearing I'll never forget. Bartosh was seated directly behind Lou. The judge ruled for a new trial and agreed that Lou could get out on bond. Bartosh immediately raised his fist in the air in a victory salute. Lou turned to him. They embraced and Bartosh said something to him. It was one sentence. If I read his lips correctly, Bartosh said, 'I told you Jesus wants you as our savior.'"

"What?" Jane replied, stunned.

"I'm a good lip reader. I have to make a leap and assume that Bartosh and Lou discussed his greater involvement in the Congregation during his prison visits. And since Bartosh believes that everything springs from what Jesus wants, it was a logical statement to make. If *Jesus* wants you to do this, and if I'm the middleman for Jesus, then it's as good as gold. The look that overcame Lou at that moment was one of great Divine entitlement. But it was cloaked in darkness. It has taken me years to have the courage to acknowledge evil when I feel it in my heart and not be clouded by the fact that I'm unfairly judging someone. That moment in court last year, I stared at Lou and all I saw was evil and his absolute intent to carry out his twisted agenda again."

Kit's revealing story gave Jane great pause. A prickly wave of electricity bolted up her spine. She might have considered the jolt a reaction to the cold weather, but the sun shone brightly overhead. Kit's statement felt true. She thought back to the past summer and how her own blindness had prevented her from seeing the devious criminal intent that nearly killed her and the victim she was charged with protecting. We're all blind at times, she thought, to things we simply do not want to see because it's comfortable to turn away. Facing the bitter truth is like plunging a hot knife into your heart and exposing all the pretty little stories we tell ourselves that make us feel safe or justified or blissfully ignorant.

They drove back into town. Jane skirted the main streets in town to avoid coming in contact with Clinton. She cut through the outdoor mall's parking lot and found herself stuck behind heavy traffic. Apparently, the New Year's Day sales at two of the mall's

stores were attracting a huge crowd. Jane waited impatiently behind a large minivan while the passengers got out and headed
toward one of the department stores. She did a double take when
she spied Rachel Hartly's boxy frame ambling across the parking
lot and into one of the crowded stores. Jane quickly pointed her
out to Kit.

"This is perfect!" Kit exclaimed. "She's not at the house. We
can check it out!"

"Are you nuts?" Jane replied. "She could be inside five minutes, then leave and head back home. It's fifteen minutes out there
and fifteen minutes back. Consider thirty minutes minimum for
finding something on her property. I'd need a solid hour at least!"

"Look at the crowd in there. She could easily be there an hour
or more—"

"No, Kit! I'm not setting myself up to be discovered out there
and ruin any chance I've got to work this case!"

"What if I stay here and follow her? She doesn't know who I
am. When I see her leaving, I'll engage her in stupid conversation.
Ask for directions—anything to stall her. Then when she leaves, I
call your cell and alert you. You'll have plenty of time to get out
before she arrives home." Jane's gut tensed up with the idea. She
did promise Weyler that she'd go back to Hartly's house and now
was as good a time as any. "Jane," Kit urged, "time's ticking away!
Come on! Let's do it!" Jane pointed out a lone pay phone by the
side of the store before jotting down her cell phone number. Kit
jumped with purpose out of the Mustang. "Go! Go!" Kit said,
waving Jane around the traffic.

Jane had nervously finished three cigarettes in a row by the
time she rolled her Mustang in front of Rachel's fenced property.
With an uneasy heart, she opened the front gate and started up the
long, gravel driveway toward the guesthouse.

CHAPTER 25

Kit stood in the store's entryway, overwhelmed by the crush of humanity. With a nervous eye, she scanned the crowd looking for Rachel. Not a sign of her. A moment of fear gripped Kit before she remembered the breathing technique she learned at the Boulder Yoga Festival. Drawing in a deep breath, she gently exhaled as she focused the energy around her solar plexus. She whispered an appropriate affirmation, "I am finding Rachel in this store," and calmly went about her search.

The first few aisles proved fruitless, but she hit pay dirt on aisle four. There was Rachel's broad frame hunkered over a bin of assorted half-price hardware. Kit nonchalantly moseyed down the aisle, trying to appear interested in hardware. Rachel turned and Kit quickly picked up a wrench, examining it with the kind of attention usually reserved for intricate surgery. Rachel pulled a hammer, a box of nails, and a roll of twine from the bargain bin and continued down the aisle. Kit felt a rush of suspicion. She tailed Rachel, allowing a good enough distance between them. Following her into the center of the store, Kit hid behind a fishing tackle display while she watched Rachel spend ten minutes picking out several shirts off a rack and proceed to the line outside the dressing rooms. Kit judged the line to be long enough to buy her some time. With great purpose, she made her way through the crowd and out the door. Arriving at the pay phone, she nervously dialed Jane's cell phone. Jane picked up on the first ring.

"*What?*" Jane answered with a nervous edge.

"She's buying a hammer, a box of nails, and twine!" Kit said quietly but with great emphasis.

"She's at the checkout counter already?"

"No. She's in line waiting to try on some shirts. Not attractive ones, either."

"Jesus, Kit! You scared the shit out of me! Call me when she's headed out to her car! I don't need a blow-by-blow account!"

"Isn't the fact that she's buying a hammer, nails, and twine important?"

"She could be building a tree house! *Only* call me back when she's leaving!"

Jane hung up and scanned Rachel's property for any sign of activity. She was alone, save for the cocking rooster and muted sound of the penned baby goats. The still soggy ground showed no signs of large footprints that might belong to a man. Jane rounded the rear of the guesthouse where she'd had her tense encounter with Rachel and noted a series of heavy-soled boot prints. She recalled the fact that Rachel wore a pair of L.L. Bean gum boots and realized the prints matched that type of boot. Jane sunk her hand into her pocket and nervously rubbed the snakestone against her lone sobriety chip. She looked up at the side of the house. The first two small windows were still covered with curtains. But the third side window, which had been exposed on her first visit to the property, was now obscured by a curtain. Someone had obviously gone inside and pulled the curtain after Jane's initial excursion. Jane discovered a sliver of space where the curtain was slightly parted. It was just big enough to see into the cabin and the edge of a bed. She strained to focus on the red-colored item that lay across the bed. The best she could decipher was that it was a sleeve. The heavy shading of the conifers around the cabin played tricks with the lighting. There was a definite sheen to the clothing that reminded Jane of leather. "Red leather jacket," Jane whispered to herself. She pulled back from the window, her heart and mind racing. The wind whipped up around her, causing the younger trees in the stand to bend almost to the point of breaking. A rush of pine needles swept toward her, wedging itself against the side of the cabin. Directly above Jane, a loose branch about three feet long shook loose and landed near the corner of the cabin. Jane formulated a plan.

She turned to the conifer that stood directly opposite the side window. Factoring what a realistic, weather-related accident would look like, she chose a thick branch on the tree and yanked it toward her. When that didn't release the branch, she hung on it, forcing it to break from her weight. Gauging the approximate angle that this branch would take when the ferocious wind caused it to break loose and crash through the window, Jane lifted it above her head and, with one swift swing, plunged the resinous branch into the window. Her calculated aim was perfect. Glass shards scattered inside the tiny house. Grabbing a small branch, Jane used it to pull the curtain to the side. Cautiously, she moved closer to the window, factoring in the possibility that someone was on the other side waiting for her. Jane unsnapped her holster. The window was far too small and too high up for her to crawl into the house. But the new view was good enough.

A twin bed sat across the room against the wall. Closer examination of the shiny red item on the bed proved to be a cherry red vinyl tablecloth. Around its edge was a defined, interlocking black-and-white pattern that Jane could not clearly identify. A modified kitchenette area filled the rest of that wall, including a white, apartment-size stove, a small refrigerator, and a sink. Across from the kitchen area, against the wall where Jane stood, sat a rough-hewn wooden table. Jane strained her neck to see the contents on the tabletop. There were stacks of books, a large Bible, and a closed laptop computer. A brown, stuffed armchair sat directly under the window. Particulate glass matter frosted the headrest. There was no sign of clothing, either men's or women's, anywhere in eyesight. Jane turned her attention to the closed door near the kitchenette area; she assumed it was the bathroom. Three feet to the right of the bathroom door was a smaller, closed door. Based on the distance to the outside wall, Jane figured that door must lead to a closet. She gave her next impulse a bit of thought before acting on it.

"Charlotte?" Jane yelled into the small house. The fact that she was even entertaining the idea that Charlotte was hidden in the house got Jane's gut twisting. She thought about the Valium Lou had given Ashlee and considered that a kid in a stupor might not respond to the sound of her voice. Jane wound around the backside of the house and stood facing the wall where the closet was located. She heaved her boot into the wall and gave it a solid kick. "Charlotte? Are you in there?" Nothing.

Jane stood back, feeling foolish. She turned, staring into the dense cluster of pine trees that cradled the back of the house. Her eyes dropped to the soggy soil and traced the outline of blurred footprints that led into the stand of trees. Jane followed the footprints, maneuvering her way around the low-hanging branches, laden with heavy droplets of moisture and threads of sap. Moving another twenty feet, Jane detected a distinct stench. Her heart pounded as she followed the footprints deeper into the stand of trees. The nauseating odor was familiar. It was the smell of a dead body. Instinctively, Jane moved her right hand to her Glock. The fetid aroma grew more intense. She turned to her right and saw nothing. Turning to her left, her eyes caught the glint of a metal shovel handle. As Jane moved closer, the stench turned from putrid to downright nauseating. Directly in front of the shovel, Jane noted a freshly dug grave, approximately four feet long. A heap of pine needles lay over the grave in what looked like an attempt to hide the burial place. The wind sent a hard, gushing current through the conifers. An uneasy chill raced up Jane's spine as she grabbed the shovel and started digging. But the muddy ground made the dig more difficult. Each scoop of water-soaked dirt felt as though it weighed 100 pounds. Jane punched the ground with the shovel and persevered. Five minutes passed and she'd only managed to remove less than four inches of ground. But the stench grew more intense, signaling that she wasn't far from hitting the body.

Suddenly, her cell phone rang, startling Jane. She stabbed the shovel in the ground and checked the number. It was local. "Hello?" Jane said, breathlessly.

"Jane!" Kit replied in an equally breathless and nervous manner. "I went back in and she was gone. I looked everywhere! Finally, I went outside and she was getting in her car and leaving. She turned right, heading toward the house. But I couldn't use the damn pay phone until now. Some kid was talking to his girlfriend—"

"How long ago did Rachel leave?" Jane yelled.

"Ten minutes!" Kit exclaimed. "She'll be there in five minutes or less!"

"Fuck!" Jane hung up and debated what to do. The smell of death intensified. She knew she was close. She resumed shoveling, plunging the shovel into the saturated ground and hitting a soft object. Tossing the shovel aside, Jane fell to the ground. She used her hands to push away the soil before working her right hand into the dirt and coming in contact with flesh. Jane was able to grab hold of the body with her right hand while using her left hand to scrape away the mud. Jane gasped and pulled back as a dead, hazel pupil stared back at her. Her racing mind attempted to make sense of it. She carefully moved both of her hands around the head and pulled the broken neck away from the suction of the mud. The disintegrating remains of a large goat emerged from the grave. Thousands of maggots covered the neck of the carcass, ingesting the pink flesh. Following the disturbed trail, a mass of ants slipped onto Jane's hands and eagerly began their journey up her sleeves.

"Jesus!" Jane exclaimed as she let go of the carcass and stood up. She peeled off her jacket, shaking it hard to release the insects. There was no time to replace the dirt on the grave. Donning her jacket, Jane figured she had less than two minutes to get to her Mustang and drive away from the house. She sprinted through the mass of conifers, heading for the far end of the front fence line where she'd parked her car. Thirty feet before the fence, she knew what she had to do. Making a bold, unstructured leap, Jane hurled her body over the fence and landed in front of the Mustang. Drawing the keys out of her jeans pocket, she opened the door, got in, and stabbed the keys into the ignition. Jane burned rubber and tore away from Rachel's house. As she crested the far hill, she looked in her rearview mirror. Rachel was pulling up to her front gate.

To be on the safe side, Jane continued to speed up the hill for another five minutes. She waited another ten minutes before turning around and heading back to Oakhurst. *What a mess.* That's all Jane could think about. In all her years of law enforcement, she had never been forced to operate in such a half-assed manner. She reasoned that everything she did was done for a good reason. Rachel might concede that the broken window was courtesy of the wind. But there was no getting around the obvious removal of the dead goat.

Kit stood waiting outside the store near the pay phone. Her eyes widened when she got into the Mustang and saw Jane's muddy clothes. Jane recounted everything to Kit, who was like a big kid as she interjected words like, "Wow!" and "Really?" throughout Jane's story. Kit let out an overwhelmed sigh. "Did you ever wake up on a Friday and think, 'Wow, if I'd known on Monday what would happen this week, I'd never have believed it!'" Kit dug in her large bag and pulled out a bottle of Arnica. "Here you go! You know how to use it! Those aches and pains will be history!"

They decided to grab a take-out meal at The Circle 9 Diner before heading back to the cabin. There was no parking in front of the Diner, so Jane let Kit out and parked three doors down in front of The Barbeque Shack. Jane's body began to ache from the trip she had taken over Rachel's fence. It was the kind of stunt a twenty-two-year-old rookie would pull; not a hardened cop who was turning thirty-six in ten days. "I'm getting too old for this shit," Jane mumbled to herself as she cracked the window and lit a cigarette.

Jane caught a quick glimpse of a black SUV pulling up behind her. The driver got out, not caring that his vehicle was blocking traffic. Jane knew what was coming next. Clinton rapped his knuckles on the driver's window and leaned down. Jane reluctantly rolled down the window, cigarette tightly clenched in the corner of her mouth. Between the pain in her body and her sheer disgust for Clinton, she couldn't repress her true feelings. She opened her jacket to reveal her Glock. "Clinton, if you don't get off my ass, I'm gonna shove this Glock—"

"Whoa!" Clinton said, backing off in a pseudo display of fear. "No need for threats! I'm on your side, Jane! Look, I got an idea. You and me band together to find Miss Charlotte—"

"I've already told you—"

"Spare me the bullshit," Clinton interrupted. "I've got access to a cameraman who can follow us and document our search! I'm thinking about the future—a crime documentary with the famous Jane Perry? It's solid fucking gold! Whether we find the kid alive or not, it's must-see TV. I've already sold my producers on the idea—"

Jane wanted to pull Clinton's throat out of his mouth. "What in the fuck are you doing talking about me to your producers?"

"Hey, this could make you a star!" Clinton said, puzzled by Jane's reaction. "You could have your own reality show on cable. Maybe *network* if you lose some weight and color your hair—"

"Clinton, you're blocking traffic! Get the fuck outta here!"

"I'll take that as a maybe," Clinton said as he gleefully turned and ran back to his SUV. Jane watched as he sped away, releasing the logjam of cars.

Now the tension was ratcheted up a few more levels for Jane. It wasn't enough that she was covertly attempting to track down Lou Peters. It wasn't enough that she was trying to quietly figure out Shane Golden's connection to this crime. It wasn't enough that there was a deadline date, however realistic, hovering just five days away. It wasn't enough that Leann Hamilton's behavior was becoming increasingly suspicious to Jane. *Now* she had to worry about Clinton following her with a camera crew. "Unfuckingbelievable!" Jane said to herself.

Two cars pulled out of their parking spaces to the left of the Mustang as a Chevy sedan pulled into the space farthest away from Jane. Leann Hamilton cracked open the passenger door and finished talking to her mother. Jane inconspicuously observed the girl. Kit returned with the food and plopped into the passenger seat.

"That's Leann," Jane whispered to Kit.

Kit took an immediate interest in the scene. Jane's eyes, however, focused on something more specific. Something that suddenly clicked. "Goddammit!"

"What is it?" Kit asked.

Leann got out of the car and closed the door.

"Want to know what guilt looks like?" Jane said before discreetly pointing her index finger at Leann. "It's wearing an ugly uniform and heading to work."

CHAPTER 26

Jane shared her sudden insight with Kit as they drove back to the cabin.

"Her mother drives a Chevy sedan.... Yes, it makes sense." Kit stared straight ahead, deep in thought. "I think you're right. I *know* you're right. This will change everything! This will finally make the cops look elsewhere!"

"Not necessarily. Fagin was still found with the bracelet—"

"But he obviously just saw it in the woods when he took a pee!" Kit insisted.

"Obvious to you and me, but not to the cops. The only thing that's going to help Fagin is if some reasonable doubt is cast over his guilt."

Kit thought for a second and then turned to Jane. "You have to talk to her, Jane."

"Kit.... It's just too risky. And what the hell am I going to say to her, anyway?"

"You can get her to confess! I know you can!"

"How? Hold her over The Barbeque Shack's grill and threaten her?"

"Use your powers of manipulation, Jane! Grab her by the psychological shorthairs. *You have to do this!* She's the lynchpin in this mess right now."

Jane turned into The Bonanza Cabins' parking lot and came to a quick stop in front of the Hop Sing cabin. Kit started to get out of the Mustang when Jane informed her of Clinton's plan to follow her with a camera. The news elicited a tart exclamation of *"That asshole!"* from Kit.

Jane took a shower to wipe off the grime and warm her muscles. She happily noted that while her back still hurt, the intensity had certainly diminished. Popping another few pellets of Arnica into her mouth, Jane started to change into jeans and a nondescript shirt. Then a thought crossed her mind—an idea so crazy that it might just work. She glanced briefly again at a few pages in the astrology book she'd been reading that morning before turning to Kit.

The individual who left the Hop Sing cabin alone in the Mustang bared no resemblance to Jane Perry. This woman wore a diaphanous purple jacket that covered a white cotton turtleneck with iridescent beads around the collar. Since Jane was slimmer than Kit, she opted to wear a pair of stonewashed jeans and a pair of tennis shoes she had thrown into her bag. The finishing touches, however, were the large crystal necklace and the short, blond wig atop her head. It was the same wig Jane had donned at The Red Tail Hawk Bar except, this time, it didn't reek of smoke or look as if it had been dragged behind a truck.

Jane kept an eye out for Clinton as she drove closer to The Barbeque Shack. Checking the time on the bank clock across the street, Jane factored that her timing was perfect. Moving closer to The Barbeque Shack, she glanced to a side area behind a short wall where the employees took their breaks. There was the kid, seated alone at a table, reading a newspaper. Jane briefly closed her eyes as she slipped into character and walked toward the table.

"Excuse me," Jane said to Leann, affecting a soft, southern accent.

Leann looked up from her newspaper. Her doe eyes took in the spectacle. "Yes?"

"I assume you live in this town?" Jane asked, touching the oversized crystal that hung from her necklace.

Leann was still in awe of Jane's appearance. "Yes, ma'am. Can I help you?"

Jane moved closer to the table. "I'm afraid I'm all turned around. I'm looking for the sheriff's office. Do you know where that is?"

There was a moment of palpable concern on Leann's face before she gave Jane precise directions. "Thank you, darlin'," Jane replied as she stared above Leann's head with glazed eyes.

"What is it?" Leann asked tentatively. Jane continued to stare, seemingly in a daze. "Ma'am?" Leann said, her voice becoming more concerned.

Jane let a look of gravity fall across her face before speaking. "I'm sorry. Sometimes I can't control my gift. I really need to get going—"

Leann stood up. "Why are you going to see the sheriff?"

Jane looked around with a faux sense of secrecy. "I can't tell you, darlin'."

"They hired you, didn't they?"

Jane moved closer to Leann and spoke confidentially. "Well, which one of us is the psychic? Yes, they hired me. But I can't tell you—"

"They want to know where Charlotte is," Leann said quietly but emphatically.

Jane made a point to look troubled. "Yes. But my appearance in this town is meant to be very hush-hush. You understand, darlin'?"

Leann sat down, nervously biting her lower lip. "You were looking at me. What...what were you seeing?"

Jane sat across from the girl. "I've had the gift of clear seeing since I was a child. I was looking at your aura."

"What'd you see?" Leann asked with great trepidation.

Jane gave a dramatic pause for effect. "I see distortions around your head."

"*Distortions?*"

"Yes. It indicates great stress and...well...how can I put this? You feel great concern over something that you've done. Something that was misunderstood?" Leann's chin began to tremble.

"May I see your hands, darlin'?" Leann reluctantly held out her palms. Jane studied them with great precision. Leann's nails were bitten to the quick. The flesh around the nails had been chewed until it bled. Jane quickly recalled that Leann stated during her interview with Lesley Stahl that she would turn seventeen within the week. Calculating the dates, Jane proceeded. "You're a Capricorn."

"Yeah!" Leann was shocked. "You can tell that by looking at my hands?"

"Oh, I can tell a lot of things by looking at a person's hands. Your Capricorn nature makes you hardworking, diligent, and determined." Jane stared into Leann's eyes and spoke from her heart. "You need a purpose in life in order to feel useful. You have a stubborn streak that is admirable. You do things because, deep down, you want to make this world a better place. You want to help your fellow man. You're a hard worker and you take your responsibility *very* seriously. You work on holidays—even Christmas Day. Family's important to you. So is your pride. You like to feel a certain amount of acknowledgment. You don't want your name in lights. In fact, too much attention to your good deeds makes you feel *very* uncomfortable. The downside is that you feel as if you must suffer in order to feel alive. You think that all your good deeds carry a heavy price. Because, while you truly want to help people, sometimes you want to help them too much...what starts out as an admirable plan can easily turn into a cloak of deception." Jane paused briefly, realizing how close her words hit home for her. "Then there's that pessimism. You worry you're not strong enough to make it to the next day. You want to give up because you don't want to be wrong...you don't want to fail because you don't just fail yourself. Your failures are reflected in everyone around you. And your pride is too strong to handle that kind of failure. You're too hard on yourself." Jane felt as though she was stepping back into her body. "My advice to you? Don't beat yourself up so much. You're human. Forgive yourself and do the right thing." Jane held Leann's palms together.

Leann tried to speak but she was choking on tears. "You can see...what I did?"

Jane talked to Leann as herself, albeit, a softer version. "You thought you saw something...or someone...but it was so fast that you weren't sure." Leann nodded, tears streaming down her face. "And then you heard news about a terrible crime. You wanted to help." Leann nodded. "You convinced yourself that what you witnessed was correct. That strong pride of yours overrode your clear memory. You figured you could make it fit if you tried hard enough. Because you just want to help...you want people to think you're a good person."

Leann burst into tears, burying her head in her arms on the table. "But they still won't talk to me!" She sobbed uncontrollably. "What does it take?"

Jane felt deep compassion for the kid. She softly stroked Leann's hair. "It's okay."

Leann lifted her head. "No! It's not! I told the sheriff it was a Chevrolet sedan because that's what my mom drives."

"What did you see?"

"I was standing outside over there on break," Leann said, weakly pointing toward the street. "I happened to look over by the curb. There were a lot of people walking by on the street. I looked up again and I saw a girl get into this car. She had short blond hair."

"Charlotte's got long blond hair."

"I told myself her hair was tucked down her jacket."

"What color was the jacket?"

"Pink. But I told myself it was red. Just like Charlotte's jacket."

"How old was the girl you saw?"

"Eighteen...but I told myself she could have been younger."

"How many people were in the car?"

"Three. But I told myself I could have been wrong."

"Because you wanted to help."

Leann looked Jane in the eye. "I *never* thought they'd arrest somebody just 'cause of the car description. I feel so bad for that man. But then they said on the news that he had something on him that belonged to Charlotte. So maybe the cops just lucked out!"

"How many times have you told yourself that over the last week?"

The tears flowed again. "A lot!" Leann sat back, a look of real discouragement crossing her face. "*Please don't hate me.* I mean, that's the messed up part of this, isn't it? I just wanted people to talk to me and now, if they find out what really happened, they're gonna hate me!" Leann started to hyperventilate. "I won't be able to go to school. I'll have to move! I've never lived anywhere else but here—"

"Calm down!" Jane patted Leann's hand. "You're getting ahead of yourself."

Leann got control of her thoughts. "You're the psychic. Can you look in the future and tell me what I should do to make it right?"

Jane calmly closed her eyes and took a deep breath. She opened her eyes and gazed above Leann's head. "Go to the sheriff. Tell him you have thought long and hard about that day and that you are no longer positive that you saw Charlotte get into any car. Insist that all your testimony be erased from the record and that you would feel more comfortable if they explored other angles."

Leann looked at Jane in stunned silence. "Are you *serious*?"

"You have to do this. If you let this mess fester, trust me, by the time you're in your thirties, you're going to be self-medicating with drugs or alcohol. You'll always be looking over your shoulder, wondering if someone's going to figure it out and come get you. That's no way to live." Jane leaned forward. *"Do it."*

Leann nodded in reluctant agreement. "Okay."

"I need to go now. I'm glad we could talk. It seems like it was destined, doesn't it?" Jane thought of something. "By the way, when you talk to the sheriff, there's no use mentioning me to him. He'll tell you that he didn't hire a psychic. Law enforcement never recognizes our valuable work, *especially* in a small town like this."

Jane started to walk away when Leann spoke up. "Wait. Since you can see in the future, where's Charlotte?"

Jane wasn't prepared for that question. "It's still in God's hands."

"Is that what you're going to tell the sheriff?" Jane nodded. "Can I ask you one more question?"

"Sure."

"Am I ever going to be somebody?"

Jane stared at Leann. "Yes. You're going to keep doing well in school. Then one day, you're going to leave this town and discover that there's a world of people who can't wait to know you. Don't mess up that good future of yours. Okay?"

Leann choked on her tears. "Thank you."

Back at the cabin, Jane revealed to Kit what she had learned from Leann. Kit was more impressed by Jane's ability to pull off a New Age persona. "I knew she was lying," Kit declared. "Now, we can focus on the *real* criminal!"

Jane wolfed down her late lunch and changed out of her psychic garb and into a comfortable pair of sweat pants and a long-sleeved T-shirt. She clipped her cell phone to her waistband to keep it close at hand. While Kit busily went about changing the colorful water jugs outside the cabin and rinsing the pieces of jade that soaked in the water, Jane went online to check out the Bartoshs' Ministry Forum. She'd never participated in an Internet Forum but Jane quickly figured out how to navigate around the long list of individual threads. Their titles ranged from "A discussion of God and family" to "Prayer needed for a Member in Oregon." The third thread on the list showed a lot of activity—over 2,000 hits—and was titled "The Power of Sacrifice." Jane selected the thread. Unlike many of the others, this particular thread was started by Dr. Bartosh in early November. His initial posting read like a sermon with the usual fist-pounding cadence.

There is great power in sacrifice. Without understanding sacrifice, how do we learn the true meaning of what our Savior went through on the cross? Sacrifice cleans our bodies, spirits, and minds. It makes us pure again. Look around you and you will see that there is nothing truly pure in this world anymore. Man has turned away from God. Children have been drawn into the dark hole of temptation. They know nothing of real sacrifice. They only know what feels good to them. Ask yourself this: Did Jesus ask what felt good to Him or did He do what his Father asked without question? Did Jesus fight his Father when He was told of the sacrifice he needed to make for Mankind? No! He bore His suffering with dignity, knowing that His Divine sacrifice would save the souls of Mankind for eternity.

Bartosh's rambling continued on for another page. Jane sat back, letting out a long, tired breath. She could literally feel Bartosh's fist coming through the screen. How could anyone live with this man, she wondered. With that, her thoughts turned to Mary Bartosh. So what if she got pregnant fourteen years ago? If that was her only way out of her father's house, Jane reasoned it was a good trade-off.

Jane scanned the following posters—almost all with Biblical names—who were more than happy to discuss what sacrifice meant to them in relationship to God. Each post was equally dry until she came upon two posters who engaged in a heartfelt repartee. One called himself Luke.D.61, the other Manul.Crst.123. Their passionate, written exchange began in early November and continued up to the present, with the last posts dated December 30. Jane scrolled down and read those posts.

Luke.D.61 wrote:

I know without sacrifice in my own life, I would not be able to appreciate the glory of God. When you start to understand that sacrifice is not a punishment but a gift that continues to give you greater understanding of what it feels like to be alive and drinking in the wonder of this world, you seek it out with greater gusto.

Manul.Crst.123 responded:

I feel your enthusiasm, Luke.D.61! Thank you again, Dr. Bartosh, for coming up with this all-important message! I have preached the power of sacrifice to everyone who would listen! We MUST be willing to feel the pain of Christ in order to move closer to HIS heart. I have suffered at the hands of society, but I have suffered with dignity. But when I think of my pain, I know it's nothing but a pinch on the arm to what He suffered for us. I have sacrificed everything for God, but I love him SO VERY MUCH that I want the world to understand His pain so that they can come to Him and be saved. The Great Commission of Christ demands that we do it! We will ratchet up our ministry to a new level! Wouldn't it be wonderful, Luke.D.61, if all God's children understood this?? As Dr. Bartosh has said for years, it's the children who are in harm's way. We must do everything we can to bring them to God!!
GOD WITH US

Manul.Crst.123 signed off all his postings with those three words: "God with us." It seemed an odd fragment of words that strangely hung in limbo. Jane reread two sentences in the last post: "The Great Commission of Christ demands that we do it! We will ratchet up our ministry to a new level!" She was almost positive that Dr. Bartosh used those *exact words* during their interview. Jane sat back and entertained the notion that perhaps Bartosh was masquerading on the Forum as Manul.Crst.123. But why would he do it? There were at least forty posts by Manul.Crst.123 over the past two months, and many of them were long-winded. Did Bartosh have the kind of time it took to write this much passionate banter? Furthermore, Jane got the distinct impression during their visit that Bartosh knew little about the verbiage used in the Forum. She recalled how Ingrid gently corrected him when he used the word "print" instead of "post" when talking about the Forum. And yet, Manul.Crst.123 seemed to be a cutout version of Dr. Bartosh.

Jane sat back, letting out another tired sigh. Didn't these people have anything better to do than write ad nauseam about sacrifice? Perhaps it was Jane's naturally instigating personality, or just something to momentarily entertain her, but she decided to put in her two cents. In order to do so, she needed to create a name and an e-mail address that would not be shown on the discussion board. Requiring an e-mail address for such Forums always separated the true-blue seekers from the lookie-loos. She set up a fictitious e-mail account and then decided on her name. What better name than Mary, mother of God, she thought. Thus, she became known as "Mary.mog" on the Forum. Jane couldn't help but smile as she logged onto the Forum with her new moniker. She hit the POST REPLY button and wrote a brief response meant to goad the faithful.

> Sacrifice? I know the beast all too well. If sacrifice is such a great thing, then why do I still feel let down? How much sacrifice am I supposed to endure before I feel as good as all of you?

Jane reread her post and decided it had just the right venomous twist to rile the troops. She gleefully hit the POST button and watched as her strident words were added to the thread.

Kit entered the cabin, holding a piece of jade in her hand and a jug of water in another. "Weather's turning bad again." Kit situated herself on her bed, poured water from the jug into a glass, took a few sips, and then lay flat on her back with her head slightly propped up. Jane watched askance as Kit placed the piece of jade over her forehead, closed her eyes, and took several deep breaths, exhaling each time with great gusto. Kit let out a mellow sigh, opened her eyes, and reviewed the stack of newspaper clippings that Jane and she had collected earlier that day.

"What are you doing?" Jane asked, a bit afraid to hear the answer.

"I need insight," Kit replied matter-of-factly, the piece of jade wobbling precariously on her forehead. "Jade brings to light that which is hidden."

"*Right.* Of course. I figured that's what you were doing." Jane's tenor was obviously sarcastic, but in a gentle way. She pulled out the bottle of Arnica and popped another four pellets under her tongue before sprawling on her bed.

"You really should try walking backward," Kit advised, never taking her eyes off the newspaper clippings.

"Uh-huh," Jane tiredly replied.

Kit balanced the clippings on her belly and stared straight ahead. "The strange calls," she said, slightly preoccupied. "The ones you got on your cell with the restricted ID? Have they stopped?"

"Yeah." Jane was close to relaxed until Kit brought up the disturbing and mysterious caller.

"You never told me what the person said."

"She whispered to hide her voice. She said, "*Let me help you*' three times during the short conversation. Then she said, *'You're looking for Lou Peters?'*"

"She said his name?" Kit replied, stunned.

"Yeah. I said I was and asked how she was supposed to help me. She told me to meet her in front of the Stop 'n' Save on Buena Street in thirty minutes—"

"Wait a second," Kit said, turning her head. The piece of jade dropped next to her shoulder. "How did she pronounce 'Buena?'"

"Like it sounds," Jane said offhandedly. "*Bwaa*-na."

"But don't you remember what Barry said to us when we checked in? He made a dramatic point of informing us how the locals were always correcting tourists when they called the street '*Bwaa*-na' instead of the local pronunciation, '*Boo*-na.'"

"So what?"

"You're certain the caller pronounced the street '*Bwaa*-na?'"

Jane reflected on the memory of the call. "Yes. I'm positive."

"So that means the caller is not a local resident," Kit enthusiastically responded, sitting up and facing Jane.

"Or they are local and they're just pronouncing the street name the way the rest of world says it."

"I'm telling you, small-town locals have a covetous mentality. If they choose to refer to something by an odd-sounding name, they will continue to do so quite unconsciously. Whoever called you is *not* a local."

Jane considered Kit's theory. It felt right to her. "Okay. So they're visiting and, for some reason, they want to meet me. But they didn't show up."

"Maybe they did. Maybe their ultimate goal wasn't to meet you. Maybe they just wanted to see you from afar. Or perhaps, it was the ol' bait and switch. Put you one place while the real action's going on somewhere else." Jane had already entertained both options. But somehow, hearing them from someone else lent a plausible credence to them. If the latter was true, did that mean that the actions of Shane Golden at mile-marker forty-four during that time were what the caller wished to push Jane away from? Then again, how could the caller know that Jane would be anywhere near mile-marker forty-four and spot Shane's Firebird? The bait and switch theory didn't make plausible sense to Jane. So perhaps the former was true. Maybe Jane's presence was demanded so the person could view her actions from afar. But what actions, she thought. All she did was stand in front of the market.

"I think this person wanted to see you," Kit said, seeming to read Jane's mind at that moment. "Observe you. Identify you." Kit shuddered. "I just got a chill. And goose bumps. That's confirmation, kiddo." Kit recovered the piece of jade from the bed and reclined back on her pillow. "What did I tell you about this jade? *Encourages insight and brings to light that which is hidden*! You *really* should give it a try." Kit exhaled a deep breath and replaced the jade on her forehead before closing her eyes.

"I gotta do some thinking," Jane said, getting up and grabbing her jacket.

"Which means you need a smoke," Kit said softly, her eyes still closed.

Jane grinned at Kit's perceptive deduction. "Wow. There really *is* something to that jade." Kit opened one eye to look at Jane and they exchanged soft smiles before Jane walked outside.

Jane no sooner lit her cigarette than her cell phone rang. It was Weyler. "Hey, Boss," Jane answered.

"Happy New Year, Sergeant Perry," Weyler proclaimed.

"I'm not your sergeant yet," Jane retorted.

"For the amount of background favors I'm doing for you, you damn well better be!" Weyler's voice was easy as usual.

"I wasn't expecting to hear from you today." Jane took a drag on her cigarette.

"Mrs. Weyler had me tied to the snow shovel this morning until my back went out. I had to sit down to relieve the pain. But while I was sitting, I figured I'd do some intelligence snooping for you on my computer."

"Hey, Boss. If you want to get pain relief, you have *got* to get yourself some homeopathic Arnica. This stuff rocks."

"Arnica," Weyler said with obvious skepticism. "I'll look into it. Here's what I found out. The Bible-thumper, Rachel Hartly?" Jane took another nervous drag on the cigarette, not sure what was coming next. "That's not her real first name. It's *Linda* Hartly. And she's got a criminal record. Ten years ago she was arrested for taking part in an abortion clinic bombing. No one was killed, but a doctor from the clinic was injured and forced to quit his practice."

"Was the group the Lamb of God Congregation?"

"No relation at all. But it was shortly after that episode that Linda Hartly became Rachel Hartly and joined the Lamb of God."

"Yeah, that goes with the territory. Bartosh told me all about it. It's part of being born again. A lot of them choose a Biblical name that resonates with their new identity."

"I see. Well, Rachel, Linda whatever, is as right-wing militant as they come. In her deposition after the clinic bombing, she wrote in great detail what she believes. She's against the government, calling them 'pawns of Lucifer.' She staunchly reiterated that Christians are continually persecuted by secular society and must do whatever it takes to protect themselves from being victimized by a world gone mad. She stressed that she follows the rules of God and not the rules of man. She believes in self-sufficiency, grows her own food, and raises her own animals because she thinks that the secular world is poisoning us so they can weaken our resolve to seek the Lord."

Jane halfheartedly wondered if Rachel gave her dead goat a Christian burial before launching into the *Reader's Digest* version of her trip to Hartly's house that morning. "I can't tell if Lou Peters lives in her guesthouse."

"I hear doubt in your voice."

Jane sucked another drag on her cigarette. "When Lou checked in with the sheriff, he never mentioned his change of address. At that time, he'd already vacated his old house and moved on. From what Kit tells me, the guy's very premeditated with his actions. I think he went to the sheriff so they wouldn't come looking for him. They probably assumed he had the same address and were impressed by his receipts that proved his whereabouts. I'm sure they checked his name off the list. The thing is, Boss, if Peters did kidnap Charlotte, and if he's following his pattern from before, he's moving back and forth between where he lives and where he's

got the kid. It's apparently the way he covers for himself. He kept
Ashlee drugged the whole time so there was no chance she'd yell
out or escape when he wasn't there."

"How do you account for the receipts from the Shell gas station and The Hummingbird Motor Lodge? They're time coded
and an hour's drive from Oakhurst."

Jane felt an icy shiver speed up her spine when Weyler said
hummingbird. "Time frames don't matter anymore," Jane declared
as she told him of her confrontation with Leann Hamilton.

"How'd you get her to confess?" Weyler said.

"You wouldn't believe me if I told you. The point is, Charlotte
could have disappeared anytime and anywhere."

"The dogs picked up her scent at mile-marker forty-four. Maybe that's where it happened. It's where they nabbed Trace Fagin."

"Fagin has nothing to do with this! Leann promised she'd go
to the sheriff and do whatever she could to take the heat off him.
Can you do anything from your end?"

"I can throw out some deflectors to my contact, but that's
about it. Fagin was still found with the bracelet—"

"I don't give a shit if he was found with her fucking jewelry
box! He's innocent!"

"I've got a call in to the lab regarding the DNA on the condom. Keep an eye on Hartly's house. See if you can catch sight
of Peters."

"I'm afraid my Mustang is too much of a marker. I can't be
scoping the place 24/7 in a big blue target. If she's as paranoid
as you say she is, she's gonna recognize me and report me to the
sheriff. I can't risk that, Boss."

"Then check out her place occasionally."

Jane halfheartedly agreed. She was about to say good-bye
when a thought crossed her mind. "Hey, Boss. I need another favor. Can you check into a woman named Mary Bartosh? She lived
in the Big Sur, Carmel area fourteen years ago. She'd be thirty-one
or thirty-two now if she's still alive."

"How does Mary tie in with Charlotte Walker?"

"She doesn't." The photo of Mary with the tough girl attitude flashed in Jane's mind. "But there's something there. I just don't know what."

Weyler agreed to Jane's request before bidding her goodnight. A wave of cold air blew across the parking lot, sending Jane back into the cabin.

Kit lay sound asleep on her bed, the piece of jade perched on her forehead. Jane quietly closed the door and crossed to her computer. Her enquiring mind needed to be satisfied regarding Rachel's choice of her pseudonym. If you're going to change your name, Jane deduced, you choose one that creates the identity you wish to project. She typed "Meaning of Biblical name Rachel" into the search engine. A long list of Web sites appeared on the page. Jane chose the first site and scrolled down until she found "Rachel." The text read: *"Rachel (Hebrew) One who chooses to follow; An innocent lamb."*

Jane considered the irony before closing her computer. Kit stirred, knocking the piece of jade off her forehead. Jane crossed to Kit and picked up the gemstone. She sat on her bed, her mind preoccupied, rubbing the surface of the jade. Jane popped four more pellets of Arnica in her mouth before falling back on her bed. For the first time in almost a week, Jane realized how desperately tired she was. She closed her eyes and let out a long-winded exhalation. Her fingers gently caressed the piece of jade as she quickly slipped into a deep sleep.

There was a moment of peace before she felt the panic rip into her gut.

CHAPTER 27

Jane spun around. Breathlessly, she took in the scene. A sparse forest of conifers surrounded her; at her feet lay a cushion of dead leaves. Fear engulfed her. Her rational mind told her this was a nightmare. She pinched her arm and felt pain. It wasn't a dream, she said to herself. The panic set in far more deeply. She'd been running through the woods for what seemed like hours. Everything felt severely disjointed.

Without warning, an eagle flew in front of her. The heavy flutter of wings echoed in the cold air long after it settled on the ground. It stared at her before flying off into the woods. Suddenly, she heard the sound of a motorcycle revving its engine. Jane turned toward the resonance and caught a glimpse of a wheel just as it slipped behind a stand of trees. Instinctively, she ran toward the motorcycle, but the rider heard her boots crunching on the dry leaves. He revved his engine and sped into a clearing, revealing only his back. Jane caught sight of the motorcycle—a baby blue motorcycle with a decal of a white dove on the fender. Jane recalled the description of the motorcycle from the girl where Lou used to live. It was Lou. Somehow, she was standing in a forest, and there he was on his baby blue motorcycle with the dove decal.

Lou never looked back at Jane as he wound around the trees. Jane ran after him, the smell of exhaust from the motorcycle stinging her throat. He knew she was behind him; she felt him loving every minute of it. As she approached a stand of pine trees, she noticed a sleek, black crow perched on a low branch. He cawed loudly, flaring his eyes wildly at Jane. Racing past the crow, she continued her pursuit.

She heard a quiver of wings above her head and momentarily stopped to look up. A coal black raven circled above her head before disappearing into the winter horizon. The motorcycle's engine slowed. Jane peered into the distance and saw Lou 200 feet in front with his back still facing her...waiting...baiting Jane to continue the foot chase. He flashed the headlight on his motorcycle several times in a teasing gesture. Jane pressed onward, her boots suddenly thick with mud. She was within fifty feet of Lou when he zoomed forward, spitting dirt and fumes into the icy air.

Jane's breathing became labored. She wasn't sure how much more she could take. Just then, a spirited hummingbird dashed in front of her, nearly touching her cheek with its rapid wing movement. It was just enough to send her backward in mid-run and cause her to fall off balance. She landed awkwardly in a tangle of dirt and dead branches, feeling a sharp pain in her already aching back as she hit the ground. Lou brought the motorcycle to a stop far in the distance, as if he had reached his destination. Jane gingerly stood up and peered through the trees. There seemed to suddenly be someone else there with Lou; someone who felt familiar to Jane.

She moved toward them, each step pushing a knifelike pain down her legs. Yet the closer she got, the more her eyesight clouded. It was as though she were walking in a thickening fog bank. She heard the motorcycle's engine rev loudly in the distance, but her clouded perspective couldn't determine where it was headed. Jane kept moving, sensing a darkness closing in around her. Within seconds, her foggy vision dispersed and she took in the frightening scene.

Lou and his motorcycle were gone. Instead, another male stood twenty-five feet in front of Jane with his back to her and his head bowed forward. A jolt of terror pierced her gut. Jane grabbed for her Glock but found the holster empty. She traced his body with her eyes. That's when she saw the crimson blood dripping from the tips of his fingers.

"Shane?" Jane half whispered, her voice cracking in terror.

Shane turned to Jane. His eyes were dead, his face pale and sweaty. "What have I done?" he said to Jane in an eerie monotone cadence.

With that, he pointed a bloody finger to a nearby outcropping of rocks. Sprawled naked on the rock was Charlotte Walker. Her deathly, hazel eyes stared skyward. But there was no sign of blood. Her ivory skin shone spotless. Shane began to sob, choking on his grief. Jane moved closer to Charlotte. She looked dead, but then quite strangely, her torso moved. Jane took a few more deliberate steps toward the naked child. Charlotte's torso moved again, but the movement came from *within* her body. Jane held her breath as she watched a growing ripple of energy begin to wave under the child's belly. The once-silent forest filled with the deafening sounds of birds. Jane covered her ears to stifle the strident cacophony, but it penetrated her senses. The wave of movement grew angrier under Charlotte's belly until her skin protruded six, seven, then eight inches upward. The discordant dissonance of birds grew as Charlotte's belly split open. Blood poured from a deep gash that sliced from the girl's navel to her chest. Suddenly, a red-tipped wing punched through her skin. Then another wing. Jane stood by helplessly and watched as the head of a red-tailed hawk broke through Charlotte's belly and leaped onto her body. Jane turned back to Shane and realized he was gone. But his voice could still be heard in the wind.

"It's no use...."

"No!" Jane yelled into the air. It was the bloodcurdling sound of her own terrified voice that awakened her. She sat up, flinging the piece of jade onto the floor beside her bed. Darkness enveloped the cabin. She turned to Kit's bed, expecting to see her there, but she was gone. Checking the clock, Jane realized that two hours had passed since she lay her head on the pillow. She slid off the right side of the bed and peered out the draped window into the parking lot. There was just enough light from the streetlamps to see that Clinton's SUV was gone. Her Mustang was still there. Perhaps Kit was talking to Barry. With that thought, the cabin's front door opened. Jane stood frozen in the darkness. Kit entered the cabin, closing the door behind her.

"Hey," Jane said softly, so as not to startle Kit. But Kit didn't react. She moved to her bed in a dazed and somewhat drugged manner. Jane turned on the light switch, illuminating the room. Kit lay on her bed, tears streaming down her cheeks, and closed her eyes. "Kit?" Jane said in a concerned voice. Kit's breathing became deep; the kind of breathing associated with deep sleep. Jane approached Kit's bed and stood observing her for several seconds before saying her name again. No response. Jane placed her hand on Kit's arm. She jumped, startled out of her stony sleep.

"What? Who?" Kit quickly said, not recognizing Jane at first.

"It's me! Jane!"

Kit focused and her usual soft expression replaced the disoriented, frightened visage. A lone tear drifted down her cheek. Jane gently reached down and brushed it off her face with her index finger. "I think you were sleepwalking," Jane offered.

Kit's eyes drifted to the cabin door. "Was I?"

"You've done it before."

"Here?" Kit said, turning back to Jane.

Jane nodded. "What do you see...that makes you cry?"

Kit shook her head, but her eyes revealed the edge of an otherworldly secret to Jane.

JANUARY 2

Jane woke several times during the night. When she wasn't mentally wrestling with the disjointed, violent dream she'd had concerning Charlotte, she was attempting to digest the three-cheese pizza they'd ordered for dinner. By three A.M., Jane decided it was better to get up than battle her head and belly. She crossed toward her laptop, stepping on the piece of jade she'd flung onto the floor. Picking up the stone and carrying her computer into the bathroom, Jane shut the door behind her so as not to awaken Kit. She sat down on the toilet and waited for the computer to boot up, giving the jade a cursory examination. The laptop toned, signaling it was ready. Perhaps it was the early hour or just Jane's normal probing self, but she logged on to the Internet and typed the words: "Jade Metaphysical properties" into the search engine. A cavalcade of Web sites appeared. She selected one and scrolled past the drier information that discussed the mineral components. Under the header, Metaphysical Properties, it read: "Jade is the dream stone. Meditating with this stone can bring the realization of one's life purpose. If one remembers their dreams when using this stone, the information they receive can solve problems in their life." Jane nearly fell off the toilet as she read the words. Her logical mind screamed that it was some kind of odd coincidence. But there was no denying the unearthly visions her subconscious mind concocted.

Jane opted to log on to the Ministry Forum, figuring a dose of good ol' fashioned hellfire and brimstone would ground her troubled thoughts. She was surprised to see that the thread, "The Power of Sacrifice" had an additional five postings since she'd left her acerbic response the day before. Jane selected the thread and scrolled down to the new posts. Posters with the names Daniel, Matthew, Joshua, and Timothy had responded to Jane's posting, continuing the Lamb of God's penchant for Biblical monikers. Each of them offered their own treacle-rich retort. However, the final poster—the ever-loquacious Manul.Crst.123—spoke more personally to "Mary.mog."

> Dear Mary.mog,
> I hear your pain. You ask "How much sacrifice am I supposed to endure before I feel as good as all of you?" I KNOW where you're coming from. I've asked the SAME questions.
> Dear sister, who hurt you so deeply when you were younger? I know someone did—someone close to you who should have loved and taken good care of you. My father rejected me, leaving a giant hole in my life. Did YOUR father abandon you? Please write. I feel we are kindred spirits.

Manul.Crst.123
GOD WITH US

Jane stared at the screen dumbfounded. She started to log off the Forum, but then stopped. For some odd reason, this person seemed to truly care. While Jane wasn't one for bearing her soul, it was late and she couldn't sleep, so she figured "What the hell."

> Dear Manul.Crst.123,
> My father was always there. That was the problem. He was a larger-than-life figure who was respected by everyone who worked with him. But they didn't know the man he became when he came home every night. Maybe it was his pride that became his downfall. Or maybe it was an inborn sickness that took over and corrupted his ability to think clearly. But it took nothing for him to become obsessively enraged. There was no reasoning with him at that point. In order to protect myself and those I cared about, I had to sacrifice any kind of normal childhood. I couldn't go to my mother, because she was weak. She should have stopped it. But instead, she took the easy way out. There are no soft memories for me.

Jane read back her post. She was startled by her words and the lingering hatred that entangled them. Yet there was a certain therapeutic freedom in exposing herself under an assumed name. The catharsis served its purpose, but she wasn't ready to reveal her raw emotions to the faceless masses of the Ministry Forum. She scrolled up to the DELETE TEXT button but, in her tiredness, she mistakenly hit the POST button. Within seconds, her vulnerable declaration scrolled onto the screen for all to read. Jane felt a stunned, sinking sensation take hold. There was nothing left to do but close her computer and go back to bed.

She awoke as the morning light cut through the sliver of curtain. Her stomach still felt dicey from the pizza. Kit lay sound asleep. Jane started a strong brew of coffee and checked the cloudy weather outside before changing into her jogging outfit. The first few sips of coffee jolted her back into her body, quelling the queasiness. She was lacing her running shoes when the wind kicked up and the sky gave way outside, dumping a flood of rain against the cabin. Jane lay on her bed, feeling thwarted by the inclement weather. She withdrew a few issues of *The Congregation Chronicle* from her satchel and flipped through the 1989 issue that featured "The Hammer of God Will Fall on All Sinners" article. Jane noted her circled footnote on one page that read: "Members must seriously study the book of Isaiah as it outlines the signs of the end times...." She opened the top drawer of the bed table and found the ubiquitous Gideon Bible. Turning on the table lamp, she located Isaiah and started reading.

"You're not getting religious on me, are you?"

Jane looked up to find Kit peering at her with sleepy eyes. "It's just research," Jane said with a coy smile.

Kit yawned. "Learning anything?"

"I'm learning that if you're a member of the Lamb of God Congregation, you're taught that the road to redemption is fraught with pain, suffering, and sacrifice."

"Oh, yeah," Kit said, still in a sleepy stupor. "It's all about struggle, denial of carnal needs, infusing the person with guilt if they feel human desires...."

"You mean sexual desires?"

Kit jokingly put her finger to her mouth. "Shhhh. Just saying such a thing could bring a beefy young man with a lovely package right to our door...and I'm not dressed properly for such an occasion."

Jane chuckled at Kit's mischievous comeback. "Why did Bartosh chose the name 'Lamb of God'?"

Kit rolled on her back. "The Lamb of God is the Messiah. I think Bartosh wanted to personify the Messiah, or Jesus, through his Congregation. But the lamb is also mentioned throughout the Bible as a sacrifice." Jane's ears perked up when Kit mentioned the word "sacrifice." "While I'm not a Biblical scholar, I remember bits and pieces from Sunday School. Lambs are sacrificed throughout the Bible. Jesus, the Lamb of God, would one day be sacrificed. It's a metaphor. It's all prophesized in Genesis. Abraham was told by God to sacrifice his son, Isaac 'on the mount of the Lord.'"

"Yeah, I remember that one. Cut his throat. Nice visual."

"One can't look at these things literally. Those who believe in the more literal Word of God argue that God was willing to sacrifice His own Son to save the world. Thus, we should be willing to make sacrifices of equal proportion. With Abraham, it was a test to prove his love for God, but God stopped him before he sacrificed his beloved son. The irony, of course, was that on that same mountain outside Jerusalem, 2,000 years later, God allowed *His* beloved Son to be sacrificed for Mankind. So, you see? The mountain was Divinely connected between one Father and another."

"God, Kit, you sound like you buy into all this."

"I think the connection of the mountains is intriguing. I like stories that come full circle." Kit thought for a moment. "And really, sacrifice is misunderstood. To sacrifice your life for Mankind...there's beauty in that. To sacrifice your life to save another, even one...there must be some honor in that." Kit looked deeply into Jane's eyes. "You understand that feeling, don't you? You were willing to protect your brother as a child at the expense of your own safety or life. There was no question, was there? You would have sacrificed your life for him."

Jane's memory flashed back to that dark, defining day. "I almost did."

Kit cradled Jane's hands. "You *understand*. That's very important to me."

The rain stopped falling. "I'm going for a run. We should get moving soon."

"I'll let you ride solo today," Kit said, rubbing the back of her neck.

Jane felt her gut pinch. "What's wrong?"

A smile creased across Kit's face. "Oh, please. Get that worried look off your face. I have good days and bad days. Today feels like it's not going to be a good one. Pizza is not on my holistic cancer diet. I need to rest, take some herbs, and meditate. Which reminds me, where's my jade?"

Jane recovered the gemstone from the bureau and handed it to Kit. "You know where I got this?" Kit asked, holding up the green stone. Jane shook her head. "I found it in the cove near my house in Big Sur. Well, I *did* live in Jade Cove! There's pockets of it all along the ridge and down by the creek. It's a powerful stone."

Jane agreed with the "powerful" description, but she wasn't about to share her disturbing dream with Kit. She ran her usual circle, keeping a sharp eye out for Clinton and his SUV. Before coming up on the Cabins, a thought crossed Jane's mind. She couldn't believe she was entertaining the notion. Looking around to make sure nobody could see her, Jane turned and proceeded to walk backward for the remaining part of her morning constitutional. By the time she got back to the cabin, she felt pain-free.

Jane popped the cassette tape from her interview with Bartosh into her car's player and headed out of the Cabins's parking lot.

"Do you believe in signs, Mrs. Lightjoy?"

Hearing Bartosh's voice again was strangely unsettling for Jane.

"Of course," Jane said on the tape.

"They are all around us. At no other time in history have the signs been so unmistakable that we are on the eve of Armageddon...."

The dark clouds pulled together overhead as Jane turned onto the main road. Her first stop would be a furtive drive past Rachel Hartly's house to see if there was any sign of Lou or his motorcycle.

"Our children have forsaken Him because the secular elitists in power have allowed darkness, disparity, paganism, occultism...."

Jane drowned out Bartosh's voice as she cruised down the road. She factored what she would do if she found Lou or his motorcycle at Rachel's house.

"Christians have become the most persecuted people on this earth. The wonder-working power of Jesus is defiled. His sacrifice is spit upon. We cannot depend upon the sideliners to bring the children back to Him...."

Jane turned down the volume, unable to take anymore of Bartosh's dogma. Within minutes, she was in eyesight of Rachel's house. The weather decided her next course of action, as another onslaught of precipitation poured down on the Mustang. She squinted through the windswept rainstorm, trying to focus on the hillside house. From what she could tell, there was no sign of a baby blue motorcycle.

Jane headed back down the road and onto the main drag. Traffic was thick. Jane surmised it had to be the tourists heading back home after the New Year's holiday. She turned up the volume on the tape.

"*... the change must take place with our children.* If they are not taught to fear God and worship His name, we are destined to live in the abyss and subsist on the pustules of Lucifer for eternity...."

Jane changed lanes in an attempt to make better time, but traffic moved at a snail's pace. A soft rain fell against her windshield as the wipers swept back and forth in a syncopated beat. Bartosh's voice seemed to draw her into a slight stupor.

"Do you have any daughters?" Bartosh asked Jane.

"No. Two sons."

"God has blessed you."

The rain pelted the windshield with greater conviction.

"Were you and your wife so blessed?"

"Yes. A daughter.... But she's no longer with us.... She's in Lucifer's hands now."

Jane's focused on the mass of traffic in front of her. She glanced at the bumper sticker on the truck in front of her, trying to read the faded words. Her eyes traveled across the blur of vehicles until they rested on a white dove bumper decal peeking out from the vehicle two cars ahead in the next lane over.

Bartosh's voice resonated in the background. "The Lord will knock on the door of your heart and all you need to do is answer and obey His Law. Those who refuse will experience the hammer of God and live forever in the pit of darkness."

White dove. Her mind felt as though it was falling into a trance. Jane stopped the tape and rolled down her window to force in the cold air. Still not able to move in the stalled traffic, she lit a cigarette and took a generous drag. It grounded her. Her eyes traveled again to the white dove decal. The vehicle gradually moved forward a foot in the next lane. That's when she saw the baby blue paint and the motorcycle. The rider wore a black helmet that obscured his face, but the body matched that of a man in his early thirties. She dug her hand into her satchel, searching for the scrap of paper that held the specific license plate number. She found it and compared the number with the motorcycle in front of her. This wasn't a dream. She was within spitting distance of Lou Peters.

Jane checked her side mirror in an attempt to change lanes. The driver of the vehicle beside her allowed her to cut in. Glancing back at the courteous driver, she saw Clinton Fredericks's beaming face smiling back at her. Seated next to him was another man. And he was pointing a video camera directly at Jane's car.

CHAPTER 28

"For God's sake!" Jane yelled with frustration. The traffic started to move and Jane made a knee-jerk decision. Seeing an open slot in the oncoming traffic, she barreled around the car in front of her, forcing the Mustang directly behind Lou. Not to be outdone, Clinton swerved his black SUV in the same manner and tried to cut in behind Jane. It was a move that Jane was sure would attract attention, and the last thing she wanted right now was for Lou to be aware of her subterfuge. "Fuck you, Clinton!" Jane exclaimed, slamming her hand on the steering wheel. Traffic suddenly opened up. Lou slipped into the right lane and expertly wove a forward path between the cars. Jane gunned the Mustang into the right-hand lane, enduring the vocal wrath of more than one unhappy driver. Lou made good progress up the main drag, but Jane still had him in clear sight. The bottleneck cleared up and Lou gunned his engine. Jane forced her way into the left lane and back again into the right, at one point riding the curb to get around vehicles. This enticed Clinton, who indiscriminately followed Jane's erratic actions with his SUV.

Jane perched her cigarette in the corner of her mouth and pressed her foot on the pedal. She wasn't about to be this close to Lou and lose him. Charging forward, she came within a comfortable distance of the baby blue motorcycle. Lou accelerated onto Highway 41 heading north. Jane pursued him, making sure to hang back far enough. Thankfully, the rain abated. They traveled at sixty miles per hour for another five miles before Jane caught Clinton's SUV in her rearview mirror. The guy with the camera held the lens tightly on Jane's Mustang, obviously enjoying the chase. They were out in the open now with little traffic impeding them. There was no way Jane was going to allow Clinton to make any connection with Lou Peters. Eight miles later, she noted a stream of orange traffic cones in the right-hand land about a half-mile up. Several heavy equipment trucks moaned under the weight of the fallen rock and thick mud they had retrieved from a fallen hillside. Cars and trucks quickly started to slow to accommodate a single lane ahead. Due to the distance Jane had allowed between Lou and the Mustang, three cars pressed between them, blocking her clear view of the motorcycle. "Shit!" Jane said. She attempted to repeat the risky maneuver she had successfully performed on the main drag, but the opposing traffic never allowed leeway for the bold move. Clinton hung tight to her rear bumper as though he were attached by an invisible chain.

They approached the rock slide as traffic compacted into the single lane. Jane lowered her window to tip the ash from her cigarette. She could hear the rumble of Lou's motorcycle and leaned her head outside in an attempt to get a visual of Lou, but the traffic prevented a clear view. Lou revved the motorcycle's engine again, this time with more determination. Jane's impatience grew with every passing second. Suddenly, up ahead, she spotted Lou bolting into an empty patch of oncoming traffic, easily moving around the slowed cars and trucks and circling around the mudslide. His adept circumventing allowed him to easily surface on the other side of the mudslide and speed north. Traffic finally eased around the slide. Once Jane cleared the area and two lanes opened up again, she gunned the Mustang in an attempt to catch Lou. Clinton barreled down the highway behind Jane. But Lou was nowhere to be seen. If he turned on one of the many side dirt roads, there was no way to find him. Jane's only solace from this aborted pursuit was that Lou was indeed still in town and that, for whatever reason, he had reason to head north on Highway 41.

Jane checked her rearview mirror. Clinton still hung close. Checking the right shoulder of the highway, Jane noticed obscure side roads. There was only one way to ditch Clinton. Jane continued north on Highway 41 for another few miles, deftly zooming in and out of traffic. Her driving skill allowed greater distance between her and Clinton. Once Jane managed a quarter mile of space between the Mustang and the SUV, she looked for a large truck traveling in the right-hand lane. As she wound around the next corner, she found one. Speeding forward, Jane buzzed past the truck before carefully shifting the Mustang in front of it. The truck's size was the perfect cover Jane needed as she located the nearest side road. Winding around another bend in the road, Jane quickly spied a sheltered dirt road 100 feet ahead. She slowed enough to make the tight turn, spraying a cloud of dust and debris as she screeched onto the road and descended down a shallow embankment shadowed by pine trees. Jane waited, her eyes locked on the highway. In less than a minute, Clinton's SUV sped north, unaware of Jane's stealth tactic.

Jane shifted into first gear and ripped the Mustang up the embankment. Back on Highway 41 heading south, she took a much-needed drag on her cigarette. After traveling ten miles, she was certain she successfully ditched Clinton. Jane let out a welcome exhalation and was just starting to calm down when she spotted Shane Golden's Firebird hidden under a stand of trees on the left side of the road, near the infamous mile-marker forty-four. Jane quickly made an illegal turn across two lanes and parked the Mustang under an adjoining group of trees. Jane got out of the car, securing the Glock under her jacket. She cautiously approached Shane's Firebird and peered into the car. Empty. The heat from the engine could be felt from a couple feet away, indicating to Jane that the Firebird had been parked for less than fifteen minutes.

Jane turned and scanned the dense forest for any sign of Shane. A sense of déjà vu came over her. She moved into the conclave of trees, her boots sucking against the muddy ground. Fifty feet in, Jane entered a small clearing. She turned back toward the highway, noting that the trees acted as a buffer against the sound of traffic. She once again scanned the immediate area for any sign of the boy, but she couldn't detect a footprint. Suddenly, Jane heard the roar of an engine. An image flashed before her eyes; a split-second visual from her violent dream. Jane spun around to source the persistent motor. Seconds later, a passenger jet flew high overhead, heading north. She let out an edgy sigh. Taking a step forward, she felt the crunch of an aluminum can under her boot. Kicking the can over, Jane identified a cheap brand of beer; the kind teenagers drink. She walked another thirty feet and found a matching empty can of beer. Peering closer into the leaf-strewn ground, Jane made out the distinct sole prints of what looked like a man's work boots.

Ten steps farther, Jane located another empty beer can and footprints leading deeper into the densely wooded area. An ominous perception pressed against her chest. Her breathing became rapid, as if she'd run a marathon. Jane unbuttoned her jacket, unsnapping her holster. With one hand on her Glock, she quietly followed the path of prints as they led around a thick stand of scrub oak and juniper. For a moment, she felt as if she were walking in a fog and unable to decipher anything in front of her. But with the bend of a large branch, she entered a small clearing.

At first, she didn't see him because he was on bended knees and turned away from her. But the image quickly registered when she saw the glint of steel from the .38's barrel inserted in his mouth. She drew her Glock and pointed it at the boy. "Shane!"

Shane turned toward Jane. His face was pale and ghostlike, his cheeks ruddy. He appeared to be discombobulated at first, a possible side effect of the alcohol. But when he caught sight of Jane, he staggered onto his feet and pointed his .38 at her. "Get away from me!" he screamed, his voice breaking in a high squeak.

"Put down the gun, Shane!" Jane moved several steps closer, Glock outstretched.

"What the fuck—" Shane kept his .38 trained on Jane. "I'll shoot you! Get away!"

"I can't do that, Shane." Jane stood still, never taking her eyes off the boy.

Shane's hand shook violently. He grasped the .38 with both hands, keeping a steadier bead on Jane. "Goddammit! Did my dad send you?"

"No! I don't know your dad!"

"*Everybody* knows my dad!" Shane's voice turned bitter. "I know who he is but he doesn't know me."

"And who is that?"

"Jane Perry. I'm a detective. A private investigator. I work in Colorado. I'm out here to find Charlotte."

Shane's face screwed into a confused glare. "Why would you come all the way out here to find her?"

"It's a long story. Put the gun down, Shane."

"You're gonna play me!"

"No, I won't! I just work better when I don't have a gun pointed at me." It took the boy several minutes before he reluctantly laid down the .38 on the wet earth. "Kick it toward me, Shane." He did as Jane asked. Jane holstered her Glock and retrieved the .38. Keeping one eye on Shane, she unloaded the revolver. The impact of the scene overwhelmed Shane and he broke down, heaving hard sobs. "You don't get it!" Shane whined through his grief. He held up his hands in an act of surrender. "I've got blood on my hands, lady!"

Jane slid the ammo and .38 into her jacket pocket as Shane's words echoed eerily in her head. "Why?"

"It's all my fault. If I had...." Shane's mind drifted. "But I couldn't, you see? They would have called me a fucking pervert!"

"Tell me what you should have done and maybe I can fix it."

Shane shook his head. "No, it's too late."

"It's not too late."

"*She's dead!*" Shane screamed, his cheeks flushing bright red. "That Trace Fagin guy is innocent. And if I tell my dad the truth, I'm fucked. The town will lose respect for him because of me, my dad will hate me, and I'll lose my scholarship and the future that he's so jacked up about. The truth would destroy everything."

"And killing yourself is *not* gonna destroy your family?"

"It's the lesser of two evils."

"No, Shane. It's the evil of two lesser plans." Jane pulled her pack of American Spirits out of her jacket pocket, knocking out a

cigarette. She walked calmly toward the boy, extending the cigarette to him. "Here."

Shane looked at Jane with a nervous glance. "I don't smoke."

Jane flashed on the boy sitting in his Firebird on Charlotte's
street sucking the life out of a cigarette. "Yeah, I don't either. I just
like to keep my fingers occupied while I think. Go on." Jane jerked
the pack toward Shane. Shane pulled the cigarette out of the pack.
Jane withdrew her lighter from her pants pocket and lit his cigarette
before lighting her own. The boy took a long drag which seemed
to calm him down. "I'm intrigued," Jane said, crossing over to a
stone outcropping and sitting down. "When suicide is a better option than the truth, the truth must be loaded." Shane remained silent, taking two more quick drags on the cigarette. "There are only
a few things that people decide they can't reveal because of society's judgment—things they've done that they think would ruin
them if anyone found out. One is committing a crime. Embezzle-
ment. Rape. Murder. Another is sexual orientation." Jane's manner was matter-of-fact. "Small towns don't embrace homosexuals,
especially the sons of law enforcement officers. There's also sexual
perversions. You get off on bestiality...or tying up your partners, or
you like to be tied up and—"

"It's none of that!" Shane's expression was pained.

Jane took a drag. "You're eighteen. Charlotte's twelve. A six-
year age difference is no big deal when you're in your twenties or
older—"

"Jesus Christ! I didn't know she was twelve!" Shane sucked
hard on his cigarette, pacing in circles. "I met her at the mall.
She told me she was fifteen, almost sixteen. I thought she looked
younger, but I figured some girls just naturally look like that—"

"And you liked her," Jane stated.

Shane nodded, his face softening. "Yeah. I did. She had a lot
of personality. She was fun to be around. I felt really...." Shane
searched for the right word, "content around her. She made me
forget all my problems when we were together. No one else could

do that for me. But I told her we had to keep our relationship quiet."

"If you thought she was almost sixteen, what was the problem?"

"A lot's expected of me. Always has been. Anything that might *distract* me is no good. I'm the first one in my family to go to a university. I got a scholarship. I'm expected to be more than I want to be. But I just want to have a life. I never felt carefree, you know? But I did when I was with Charlotte. She's a free spirit."

Jane recalled Kit using the same term to describe Ashlee. "So you want to live someone else's dream the rest of your life?"

"It takes guts to stand up to my dad and walk away from the scholarship. That's my problem. I don't have any guts. I just do what I'm told." Shane looked resigned to his fate. "If I had guts...." The emotion caught in his throat. "Charlotte wouldn't be dead. I would have said 'fuck it' and told them everything, and then they wouldn't be fucking around with false leads—"

"So, what happened?" Jane's tone was direct.

Shane sucked another long drag on the cigarette and stared at the wet earth. "I wanted to hang out with Charlotte, but we had to do it secretively. She was cool with it. Hell, she *liked* sneaking around. We arranged to meet at mile-marker forty-four each time. She'd take the bus out of town. There's a stop a few hundred feet from here. She'd wait for me by the road. Sometimes she had to wait longer because the old man would corral me into doing something at the last minute. But she'd always be here when I showed up and she was never pissed that I was late."

"What would you do together?"

"Sometimes we'd hang here or go for a drive. We *never* had sex. I swear to God! We messed around a little...." Shane winced. "Jesus, I messed around with a twelve-year-old. Fuck, I'm going to hell."

"Chill out, Shane. Tell me some of the stuff you'd do together."

Shane took a drag. "We talked a lot. She actually listened to me. Imagine that! Somebody *listening* to *me* instead of lecturing me." Shane smiled at a good memory. "I had to go down to L.A. for an interview at USC. I was able to steal away for an hour on my own and I found this bracelet that had her named spelled out on the charms."

"*You* gave her that bracelet?"

"Yeah. I know it was cheesy. But she really loved it—"

"Didn't her mother notice the bracelet and ask where she got it?"

"It wasn't unusual. Charlotte's got the kind of personality that makes people want to give her stuff. She's got this magnetic quality."

Magnetic. Free spirit. Jane figured Ashlee and Charlotte were cut from the same fabric. "How'd the bracelet get dropped here?"

"She lost it on Thanksgiving weekend. It fell off her wrist. We arranged to meet the day after Thanksgiving in the morning. My folks were out of town visiting family."

"Why didn't you go with them? It was Thanksgiving weekend—"

"I had midterms coming up," Shane's voice spiked with anger, "and my dad wasn't satisfied that I was prepared enough. So I had to stay home alone and study."

"But you decided you had better things to do."

"*Damn straight!* Charlotte told her mom she was going early Christmas shopping on Friday. I picked her up at the usual spot, but she just wanted to hang here. I moved my car off the road so nobody could see us. We talked, made out for awhile, drank beer." His anxiety peaked. "Jesus, I got her drunk! I got a *twelve-year-old* drunk!"

"You didn't force it down her throat—"

"Well, she got wasted and she didn't want to go home and have her mom smell the booze. She asked if she could just stay with me the rest of the night. I was cool with it. We slept in my car—*just slept.* Next morning, we went for a walk and that's when she lost her bracelet. The clasp came loose. We looked all over but we couldn't find it."

"So when Charlotte went missing for thirty-six hours, she was with you?"

"Yeah," Shane said with a sense of shame.

Jane took a good drag. "You said you had blood on your hands. Why?"

Shane grimaced. "We arranged to meet here on Christmas Day, but...."

"But what?"

"I was goin' through the newspaper that morning and I saw a photo of the kids from the grammar school Christmas pageant. There was Charlotte, dressed up in her costume, playing the Mother of Jesus in the play. The caption read, 'Charlotte Walker, twelve years old,'" Shane said, slightly disgusted. He buried his head in his hands. "Shit! My world collapsed around me. That's fucking illegal! I freaked!

"What would people think—" Jane asked rhetorically.

"Exactly!" Shane began to pace again.

"But you didn't have the guts to face her."

Shane spun around. "I didn't know what to say to her!"

"So you left her waiting on the side of the highway on Christmas Day."

"Yeah," Shane's voice choked up. "Next day, it's all over the place. Charlotte went missing. Then the TV's got it and it was just too much."

Jane took a moment of thoughtful contemplation. "I know how you can redeem yourself, Shane."

The boy slightly perked up. "How?"

Jane stood up. "Tell your dad everything you know."

"Are you crazy?"

"You could save Charlotte's life!"

"Charlotte's dead."

"You don't know that!"

"Statistics! I heard my dad talking about it on the phone. Most missing kids are killed by their captors within the first forty-eight hours. *She's dead.*"

"You *want* her to be dead?" Jane ire was clearly sparked. "Would that make it easier for you in the end?"

"No, I—"

"You can drag your sorry ass down to USC, do what your daddy wants and hope that one day you can drink her memory away." Shane looked like a trapped rabbit. "That's how you've learned to live because you don't have any guts, right?"

"Maybe—"

"You can't bullshit another drunk!" Shane was taken aback by Jane's pronouncement. "You're trying to drown out your dad's voice. But it doesn't matter how much you drink. He *still* finds a way to needle his way into your head. And *trust me*, Shane, you can drink a fuckin' keg and you'll never get his voice out of your head."

"How do I do it?"

Jane flicked her dying cigarette on the ground, snuffing the ember into the dirt. "You gather up your guts and you talk to him. It doesn't matter what he says or what he thinks of you. You're doing this for *you*. You're doing this so you don't waste twenty years drowning him out in booze." Jane realized the irony of her own advice.

"I don't know." Shane paced back and forth. "He just wants the best for me. Maybe I should just go along with what he wants. I made a mistake. I should never have liked Charlotte—"

"You didn't like her, Shane. You *loved* her."

Shane stared at Jane and broke into tears. "I *did*," he murmured though his sobs.

"Help me find her."

"I don't know where she is!"

"If you tell your dad everything, then he can stop focusing his investigation on a guy who innocently picked up a bracelet—"

"No!" Shane's face clouded with panic. "I am not telling my dad anything! And if *you* tell him, I *will* kill myself and it'll be on *your* head!" Shane stared down Jane with a fierce, impenetrable stance.

"So your reputation is more important than someone else's life?"

"*All I got is my reputation!* My future is locked in if I keep my mouth shut."

Jane looked at Shane. He was frighteningly ignorant of how guilt works its way into one's marrow and corrupts one's future happiness. Standing there in that clearing, Jane felt as if she were watching a human train wreck. She knew he would kill himself if she leaked his information to the sheriff, and she wasn't willing to have another suicide victim to mourn. The one she loved so long ago still haunted her. "Okay, Shane. I won't say a word. But you gotta help me. Does the name Lou Peters ring a bell?"

"No. Why?"

"You're positive you never heard Charlotte talk about a guy named *Lou Peters?*"

"I'm positive. Who is he?"

"He's this good-looking guy who lives around here. People say he looks like Brad Pitt. Drives a baby blue motorcycle. He has a history of picking up girls who are...*magnetic.*"

Shane's eyes widened. "You think he took Charlotte?"

"I don't know." Jane pulled a pen from her pocket and crossed to Shane. "If you think of anything, here's my cell number." She wrote the number on the palm of his hand and looked at him. He stared behind her with a gaze of abject horror. Jane turned. Crouched fifty feet away in the stand of scrub oaks was Clinton. Next to him was his cameraman recording the entire scene. Jane turned to Shane and whispered. "Go hide in the bushes!" Shane immediately did as he was told.

Clinton emerged from the stand of oaks. The cameraman followed, never moving the camera off Jane. It was all she could do to not rip him a new one as she rapidly walked toward him. "Give me the fucking tape, asshole!"

The cameraman continued filming, smiling at Jane's feverish reaction. Clinton leisurely pulled a plastic water bottle from the deep pockets of his camouflage pants and swallowed a refreshing slug. "Hey, cool your jets, Jane!" Clinton said in a singsong manner. "We didn't see anything. Just you talking to the kid for two minutes. And writing on his hand. He's kind of young for you, isn't he?"

Jane slapped her hand against the lens, forcing the cameraman to stop filming. *"Give me the fucking tape!"*

Clinton rested his water bottle on the ground. "Jane, let's talk about this—"

Jane withdrew her Glock and pressed the butt dead center against the cameraman's forehead. "Shut up, Clinton! Give me the fucking tape!"

"Jesus Christ!" The cameraman's smirk dissolved into fright. "Here!" He fumbled with the camera until he ejected the tape.

Jane snapped it from his hands and threw it on the ground. Keeping the Glock pressed to his skull, she smashed the tape with her boot heel. "Give me your press pass."

Clinton kept a cool eye on Jane as the cameraman nervously searched through his pockets before locating the plastic card and handing it to Jane. He was a freelancer for the *Fresno Bee*. She glanced at his name. "*Buddy*, is it? Let me tell you, Buddy," Jane said, tightening her body against him while keeping the Glock hard on his flesh, "if you tell anybody what you saw out here, I'll make sure you never work again."

"You can't do that," Buddy said in a weak show of bravado.

"Isn't it hard to be a cameraman if you're missing a foot?" Jane countered.

"I'm not missing a foot."

"You will be when I track you down and shoot the fucker off!"

The color drained out of Buddy's face. His eyes turned to Clinton. "Is she serious?"

Jane kept her eyes on Buddy but casually aimed the gun on the dirt next to Clinton. She fired one shot and blew his water bottle into the air, spraying a stream of water over Clinton's pants. Jane pressed the Glock back against Buddy's forehead. "I've got a perfect aim, Buddy." Jane let her action sink in before standing back, still training her Glock on both the men. "That goes for you, too, Clinton. Now, walk back to your car and get the fuck outta here."

Buddy took off but Clinton remained in place. "Man, Jane, that was raw!" He exclaimed with an oblivious sense of the moment. "You are *so* fuckin' real!" Clinton spun around and followed Buddy.

Jane waited until she heard their vehicle drive away before holstering her gun and collecting the shattered videotape. "All clear, Shane!"

Shane cautiously crept from behind the stand of oaks. "They got me on *tape*," he said, hyperventilating.

"And I've got what's left of it," she said, holding up the pieces of plastic.

"But they can put two and two together, who my dad is—"

"Stop it! They don't know the connection. Besides, I think I sufficiently scared the shit out of Buddy." She stuffed Buddy's press pass into her jacket pocket. "He's not gonna talk. At least not now."

Shane gave a thoughtful pause. "Would you *really* shoot off his foot?" he said in a confidential tone, intrigued.

Jane eyed Shane with the best cop look she could muster. "If I find out he leaked a word about you and me out here, I'll shoot off his foot and deliver it to your doorstep in a gift-wrapped box." Shane's eyebrows arched. Jane pulled Shane's revolver from her jacket pocket. "I'm giving this back to you because I gave you my word that I won't tell anyone about what happened here. You gotta give me your word that you're not gonna use this on yourself. Agreed?" Shane nodded and took the .38. "Are you okay to drive?"

"I think the conversation sobered me up."

"Go home. Take a deep breath and a hot shower. And call me any time, day or night, if you think of something else that you forgot to tell me.

Shane nodded and started to head out of the woods. He stopped and turned to Jane, tears welling in his eyes. "You really think Charlotte's still alive?"

"She's alive, Shane. And I'm gonna bring her home." Shane let out a relieved sigh and walked back to his Firebird. Jane stared into the overcast sky.

"Please God, don't make me a liar."

CHAPTER 29

It took Jane thirty minutes to speed back to Oakhurst, but it took her less than five minutes to devise a plan of attack. The scheme didn't exactly have what she'd call *flow* since each step depended upon a lot of "what-ifs?" But with four days looming until her self-imposed deadline of January 5, Jane knew she had to crank up the intensity of her investigation. However, with the likes of Clinton Fredericks hanging around, Jane also knew that she needed help if she was going to pull off her complicated plan. With that in mind, Jane ducked into The Circle 9 Diner and placed an order. While she waited, she looked up the address of the Shell station where Lou had purchased fuel and furnished the receipt to the Sheriff. The location was fifty miles north on Highway 41.

Jane returned to the cabin to find Kit propped up in bed, the piece of jade resting on her forehead. *The Congregation Chronicle* newsletters were spread out across her bedspread, as were the sundry clippings from *The Sierra Star* newspaper. A steaming brew of foul-smelling herbal tea sat on the bedside table while a tape of discordant sounds played on Kit's recorder.

"What the hell is that?" Jane asked, setting down one large plastic bag after another on her bed.

"Whales. Their voices are thought to be soothing." Kit stared in puzzlement at the large number of plastic bags.

"Soothing?" The cacophonous timbre suddenly rose with a jarring underwater scream. "Jesus! What are they doing? Fucking?" Kit regarded Jane's comment with a look of admonishment. "Spare me the schoolteacher look. Turn off the tape. We've got to talk." Kit clicked off the tape as Jane sat on her bed. "I saw Lou."

Kit's mouth dropped open. "At Hartly's house?"

"No. On the main drag." Jane proceeded to give Kit a blow-by-blow account of the morning's pursuit and how Clinton trailed her.

When Jane finished, Kit sat up straighter in bed, allowing the jade to drop off her forehead. "You have to go back!"

"I know. I'm not sure where he went. Maybe he works up there. You said he did maintenance jobs?"

"Yes."

"We have to assume he's still doing that. Perps usually don't change the kind of work they do when they get out."

"You can't stop at every lodge between here and Yosemite."

"No. But I can ask around at places where I know he's been." Jane revealed the copy of Lou's receipts that Weyler had faxed her. Kit appeared genuinely impressed by Weyler's adroit ability to gather information. "But I need your help to do it." Kit's eyes danced with eagerness as Jane explained her plan in detail. "Think you can handle it?"

"Of course. I'll do whatever I have to do. But I don't have the strength today—"

"I'm five steps ahead of you," Jane said, standing up and unloading the plastic bags. "I've got two different kinds of chicken, four cartons of beef stew, a half pound of hash browns.... Fish. You like fish, right? I got you salmon with mustard sauce.... Salad. And *no iceberg lettuce.* I made a point of that. All romaine, with little radishes and tomatoes. *And* I made them put tons of orange slices in there to jack up your vitamin C. You like noodles?" Jane turned to find Kit staring at her with a sweet smile.

"Thank you," Kit quietly said. "We're okay again, you and I, huh?"

"We're okay," Jane replied, feeling an unexpected catch of emotion. "You can live a lot longer than the doctors told you. You just got to take care of yourself—"

"You're afraid I'm going to die on your watch."

Jane sat on her bed, collecting her emotions. "I just want you to be strong."

"I'm stronger than you realize, Jane P." Kit's tone rang resolute.

Jane had wanted to ask Kit the question before but didn't know how. "How do you...." Jane struggled with the question, "live every day knowing...."

"Your days are numbered?" Jane solemnly nodded. "All of our days are numbered. I just have a better idea of my personal timeframe."

"How do you not go crazy? *I* would."

Kit leaned her head back on the wall in a moment of contemplation. "When they first tell you, your world suddenly becomes very small and precarious. The walls tighten around you. You perceive everything from a tiny box. Your steps become measured. The finite aspect of life stares at you. You feel your freedom being caged. You're living in the same world as you were before you got the news. But once you hear those words, you swear the world has changed. First, the world's a fearful place because you're so full of fear. Then it becomes an angry, vengeful world because you're so full of hate that you've lost control of your life and your body has turned on you. For some, it stays an angry world because they can't get past the rage. But if you do move beyond that...which I did...the world suddenly becomes beautiful. You notice the texture of a flower. You breathe in the sweet scent of the season. You take time to watch a bird fly above your head and see the reflection of its wings against the sun. When the wind moans, you feel its pain. You hold on to every moment you're given and drink it in because tomorrow is a gift. If you're smart, you finally figure out that your destiny was never about what you accomplished, but rather, who you loved and who loved you." Kit sat up and grasped Jane's hand. "Have you ever been in love, Jane?"

Jane's throat tightened as her eyes welled with tears. "Once. But it was a lifetime ago. And it ended...badly."

"You got your heart broken?"

"More like destroyed."

"But you discovered you had the capacity for profound love?"

"I wouldn't put it that way—"

"No. You prefer to say you were destroyed. That's the glass half empty. For you to love him so much, there must have been more than one cathartic, orgasmic, breathtaking moment between the two of you."

"Yeah. But that's all colored by how it ended."

"How it ended shouldn't darken the love. You've mourned long enough. It's time to risk again—time to break down that wall, expose your vulnerability and press your body against another. Even if it doesn't work out—even if you only have a beautiful night together—it's a night that will feed your heart." Kit sat back against her pillow. "You can catch all the bad guys in the world, Jane. It doesn't matter in the end. When you take your last few breaths, you should rest your eyes on the one you love and let that love carry you to the other side."

Jane felt a twinge of sadness for Kit. "Who will you be looking at?"

Kit glanced off to the side. A distant smile crossed her face. "I won't be alone."

JANUARY 3

Jane knew it was only a matter of time before Clinton showed up at the cabin. Earlier that morning, he'd made an unexpected satellite appearance on one of the cable news shows. Standing in the not-so-far-background, Clinton did his best job of comforting Jenny Walker while Sheriff Golden announced that there had been a "sudden shift" in the Walker case. Thanks to a witness' declaration the day before, the sheriff was "cautiously exploring other avenues." Jane shook her head at the carefully framed words—bureaucracy at its finest. She deduced that while the overwhelmed sheriff was cautiously exploring, Lou might be carefully carrying out the murder of Charlotte. As Jane shut off the TV, she realized that her mind had firmly gelled around the idea that Lou either had kidnapped Charlotte or knew where the girl was hidden.

Jane surveyed the parking lot for Clinton's black SUV. She wasn't venturing outside. Everything that was to follow depended upon perfect timing and deception.

Kit emerged from the bathroom. "What do you think?" she asked Jane.

Jane turned and examined Kit's appearance. Her salt-and-pepper braid was hidden under her bouclé hat; her heavy, multi-colored winter coat closed tightly around her body with dark pants peeking out underneath. A thick scarf wrapped around her neck. "Wrap the scarf more around your face and lower the hat to cover up." Kit obliged. "Good. We need something memorable so he identifies you right away."

Kit fished a cherry red scarf out of her suitcase and stashed it in her jacket pocket so that it generously hung over the flap. "Will that work?"

"Red flag. I like it!" Jane glanced out the window just in time to see Clinton's SUV discreetly pull into the parking lot and hide behind the dumpster. "Take off your clothes. It's showtime!"

A round figure emerged from the Hop Sing cabin wearing the multicolored coat, bouclé hat, and red scarf. She sauntered down the parking lot so that Clinton would have a good view. Pulling the scarf away from her mouth, Jane lit a cigarette and took a deep drag. Jane pretended to act unaware of Clinton's presence as she paraded in view of him several times before walking back inside the cabin.

Several minutes later, Jane emerged again. This time she carried a bag of trash and ambled toward the dumpster. She discarded the trash, then walked up to the driver's side of the SUV. Clinton sat with a generous smirk across his face. Jane moved within inches of the window and pulled down her scarf. "I'm getting a restraining order against you! If you don't stay 100 feet from me, your ass is in jail!" Jane turned and headed back to the cabin.

Clinton rolled down his window. "Let's work together!" he yelled.

Jane opened the front door of the cabin and flipped Clinton the bird before slamming the door behind her.

Thirty minutes later, the wintry-dressed figure emerged from the Hop Sing cabin again. In her hand, she held a burning cigarette. As was the custom, she squashed the ember gently and placed the cigarette on the window ledge. The figure turned her back to Clinton and performed several perfunctory stretching moves before quickly walking around the cabin and heading toward the back road. Clinton waited a couple minutes before starting his engine and following the figure on her usual morning route.

When she was positive that Clinton was gone, Jane quickly emerged from the cabin. The well-worn blond wig was a last-minute idea of Kit's. Jane tossed her satchel in the front seat of the Mustang and carefully drove out of the parking lot and onto the main drag, heading north. There was no time to check out Rachel Hartly's house; Jane couldn't risk doubling back through town and allowing Clinton to spot her car.

Fifteen minutes later, Jane was certain the ruse had worked. She was powering north on Highway 41 and, if all was going according to plan, Clinton was keeping 100 feet of distance behind Kit, who was leading Fredericks on the greatest bait and switch goose chase of his life.

Jane turned on the radio and suddenly heard Bartosh's booming voice.

"We are a powerful, unified group of people with a common cause!"

Jane realized she hadn't removed the tape from her interview with Bartosh.

"I was telling the Brotherhood Council this morning that *we have to ratchet up our ministry to a new level*! We will no longer seek *tolerance* toward us...."

She lit a cigarette and listened to the interview with Bartosh for another twenty minutes, making a point to interject lots of sarcastic comments. Every time she heard his imperious tenor, Jane felt an odd pang of compassion for Mary Bartosh. She intimately understood Mary; it was like they were twins born of different mothers. Jane rounded a bend of highway where particulate dirt lined the asphalt. The sloppy weather looked as if it had affected another waterlogged hillside. Finally, after hearing Bartosh prattle on about the battle for Mankind's soul, Lucifer's stranglehold on the children, and how the Congregation members are "motivators for Jesus," Jane turned off the tape.

Thirty minutes later, she pulled into the infamous Shell station just off the highway. Inside, the place was empty save for the teenage girl seated behind the counter watching MTV. "Is the manager around?" Jane asked the girl.

The girl smiled and stood up. "Is there a problem with the pump?"

"No. My name is Jane Perry. I'm a police detective. I need to find out—"

"What's this?" The voice belonged to an obese, red-haired woman who surfaced from a side office. Her nametag simply read, MANAGER.

Jane introduced herself and regarded the woman with the kind of attitude she reserved for bums and drug addicts. "You keep videotapes of the pumps outside?"

"Yeah," the woman answered warily. The teenager turned the TV on mute and gawked at Jane with an admiring stare.

"Would you still have them from December 25?"

"Hell, probably not." She eyed Jane up and down. "Oakhurst don't have a lot of detectives—"

"I'm not with Oakhurst PD. I work independently." Jane pulled out her wallet and showed the woman her official identification.

"*Colorado?*"

"Yeah," Jane said, snapping her wallet shut. "Can you check to see if you still have that Christmas Day videotape?"

"What's this got to do with?" The woman's tone was unnecessarily confrontational.

Jane wasn't sure how much information she wanted to spill. "It's a side investigation for that missing Oakhurst girl."

The teenager promptly moved closer. "Charlotte?" she asked with great interest.

"You know her?" Jane replied.

"No. But I look at her poster every day," the girl said, sliding a display of chewing gum off the counter to reveal Charlotte's well-worn flyer taped onto the glass.

"You finish stockin' the soda?" the woman asked the girl with a brusque tone.

"Not yet, Mom," the kid responded in a deflated manner.

"Well, get to it!" the woman said, angrily gesturing to the back of the store. "I don't pay you five bucks an hour to sit on your ass and watch MTV!"

The girl stole one final lingering look at Jane. Jane returned the kid's glance with a sympathetic smile before turning back to the abrasive woman. "Can you check to see if you still have the tape?"

"I'm sure it's copied over," she said, not budging. "And anyway, I'd have to get me written approval from the police department 'fore I let you see anything."

"Written approval?" Jane's tone went up a notch. "I'm trying to find a missing kid. All I want to do is review the tape. I've shown you my ID—"

"And you're not from Oakhurst. Bring me back some written approval on Oakhurst's PD's letterhead and I'll see if we still have the tape!" The woman waddled her broad beam back into her office.

Jane stood dumbfounded. *Another great example of one more ego-inflated minion wielding their sliver of power.* She turned and saw the teenager across the store staring at her with a sorrowful look. Jane waved good-bye to the kid and walked outside. She lit a cigarette and headed toward her car when she glanced north on the highway. About 1,000 feet up the road on the left-hand side, the word "bird" caught her attention. It was part of another word on a bright red neon sign. Jane drove onto the highway to get a closer look. It quickly became clear: The Hummingbird Motor Lodge.

Jane pulled over to the side of the road and riffled through her satchel to find the faxed copy of receipts Lou presented to the Sheriff's department. There were two receipts from The Hummingbird Motor Lodge, both from the dining room. They were time-stamped five hours apart and were both for sodas. Jane slid the fax back into her satchel and took a drag. Casually, she turned to the Lodge—your run-of-the-mill, two star motel—and stared at the flickering white hummingbird on the red neon sign. Her eyes traveled to the parking lot and the sparse collection of vehicles. The baby blue motorcycle easily stood out of the pack.

Jane turned off the engine. She flashed on an idea and checked her jacket pocket to make sure she still had her handy prop. Looking in the rearview mirror, Jane adjusted the blond wig and solidified her next con....

Kit snuck a glance backward. Clinton trolled his SUV 100 feet behind her on the road behind The Bonanza Cabins. With the agreed-upon battle strategy in mind, Kit took a purposeful, sharp turn to the right and diverged into the muddy conifer forest. As expected, Clinton sped up to monitor her actions. The glaring red scarf tucked into Kit's coat pocket acted as the perfect beacon to keep her in Clinton's sight. When Kit was sure Clinton could easily observe her, she ducked behind a waist-high pile of deadwood and dug into the dirt. She took a moment to stand up, peer around with a false sense of apprehension, and then bend down again to repeat the identical maneuver. After ten minutes of this ruse, Kit secretly removed a small mason jar from her coat pocket with a rolled up paper inside and placed it in the hole. It took five minutes to pack the dirt back into the hole. Kit made sure the area was easy to find by disturbing the ground. She gave a bogus worried look around the spate of trees before walking deeper into the forest....

The inside of the Hummingbird's dining room smelled musty. The sign above the bar read, A PROUD PART OF THE VALLEY SINCE 1944. From the looks of it, Jane figured the owners hadn't redecorated or dusted since they opened the joint.

"We don't start serving for another hour."

Jane turned to find a sweet-faced girl in her early twenties approaching. There was a deafening vacancy to the place that Jane hoped would work to her advantage. "Is the manager here?" Jane asked in a cloying manner.

"Uh, no. He and his wife are still on vacation. They'll be back in two days—"

"Oh, shoot," Jane replied. Score one in her favor, she thought.

"Is there something *I* can do for you?" the girl asked.

Jane withdrew the press pass she took from Buddy the day before. "I'm with the *Fresno Bee*." Jane carefully covered up Buddy's name, flashing the pass in front of the girl's excited eyes. "I interviewed one of your employees last week when I was doing a human interest story about the classic lodges in the Valley. His name is Lou Peters. Works maintenance?"

"I wouldn't know. I'm just temping during the Christmas break. You're featuring *this* Lodge in the *Bee*?"

Jane wasn't sure if the girl thought the idea was absurd or intriguing. "That's the plan. But Mr. Peters said I could come up and mosey around to infuse the story with a more 'been there' feeling. You know what I mean?"

"Absolutely!" The girl replied, not having a clue what Jane meant.

"You think I could walk around and drink up the atmosphere?" Jane asked, her tone so sugary-sweet she thought she'd choke.

"Sure!" The girl said, happy to feel that she had a modicum of power to allow Jane roaming privileges.

Jane meandered around the empty dining room as the girl disappeared into the kitchen. She walked past the wooden bar with its swivel seats, each engraved with a series of hummingbirds across the backrest. Jane felt her gut tug. It was her personal form of radar; an indication that she was close to something significant. She surveyed the back of the bar. It was seriously disorganized. Stacks of newspapers sat precariously next to the cash register, next to a metal stake loaded thick with paid table checks, next to pitchers of water, next to a garbage can piled high with debris. She turned to face the dining room and contemplate her next move when the fresh-faced girl walked back into the dining room carrying a stack of red tablecloths.

"Drinking in our atmosphere?" she said with a happy cadence.

"You betcha!" Jane responded. "I'm just gonna mosey around the motel."

"Have fun!" the girl exclaimed as she shook open one of the tablecloths.

Jane's eyes locked on the tablecloth. It was shiny and vinyl and looked like a red leather jacket from a distance. She flashed on Rachel's guesthouse and the shiny red material she couldn't identify from outside the house. She recalled a specific black-and-white design that bordered the material; something tiny and repetitive. The girl spread the cloth on the table and walked to the next station. Jane moved closer and identified the pattern as interlocking hummingbirds. It seemed that Lou broke at least one commandment: Thou shall not steal.

Outside, Jane rounded the dining room and crept around the corner. Lou's inimitable baby blue motorcycle with the white dove decal on the rear fender was still there. She strolled near the motorcycle, getting a closer look before sauntering down the walkway. Jane approached a narrow cement entryway, where she located a single door with a placard that read: EMPLOYEES ONLY. She pressed her ear to the metal door and, after hearing no one, turned the knob and walked inside....

Kit took a sip of herbal tea and stared out the window of The Circle 9 Diner. It had been an hour since she'd spied on Clinton as he hungrily took her bait and dug up the mason jar with the handwritten note inside. Kit waited for what she hoped would be his stunned reaction to the words. She wasn't disappointed as he read the note.

> Jasper,
> Thank you for agreeing to help me. I trust you will find this message so that we can move forward. Please meet me in this same spot tomorrow between ten a.m. and noon. We will proceed from there. So I know you got this message, please remove it and leave the mason jar in plain view.
> Jane

Clinton looked as if he'd just uncovered the map to the Holy Grail. Kit observed him slide the note back into the jar, secure the lid, and return it to the hole. After replacing the dirt and tamping the soil, Clinton arranged the loose deadwood into a ridiculous pattern that resembled an arrow pointing at the freshly dug ground.

Kit smiled at the irony of the whole thing. Jasper was the name of a former, passionate lover Kit used to covertly meet forty years ago. She figured he'd be proud to have his name used for another kind of misguided tryst. The waitress brought the check as Kit debated her next move. She knew Clinton would be hovering near the forested area to catch a glimpse of "Jasper." However, she also knew he couldn't spend his entire time there. Most likely, he would steal away and return frequently to check the status of the note. The trick was to make sure he was occupied long enough somewhere else so Kit would have enough time to return to the forest a half-mile away from the diner and remove the note in order to give Clinton the impression that "Jasper" had discovered it. As if someone above heard her prayer, Kit glanced outside and found

Clinton parking his SUV in the diner's parking lot and immediately being corralled by Sheriff Golden into an impromptu media interview. Kit removed her hat, letting her salt-and-pepper braid fall across her chest, folded her distinctive coat over her arm, and walked right past Clinton without so much as a glance from him.

It took Kit twenty minutes to hike back to the forest and successfully complete the deception. Her job was done, according to the detailed outline of Jane's plan. However, Kit wasn't ready to journey back to the cabin. She'd gotten a good serving of sleuthing and she liked the tingling aftertaste. And there was someone she really wanted to talk to....

Jane surveyed the small space. The cramped, mustard-yellow room was barely big enough to hold the row of lockers, a center bench, a small table shoved against the wall, four folding chairs, and a coffeemaker. About the only thing that stood out in the windowless room was the trademark low-hanging red vinyl tablecloth with the interlocking hummingbird motif. Jane crossed to the bank of numbered lockers. None of them had locks securing them, and they also didn't have nameplates to identify them. Jane glanced above the lockers and noted individual numbered plastic baskets lined up with each locker. She dragged a folding chair away from the table and stood on the seat to get a better view of the baskets. The container in the middle with the number "3" held a motorcycle helmet. Jane jumped off the chair and opened locker number three. A seven-inch square mirror hung on the inside of the door with a three-inch-wide "Jesus Lives!" decal taped over the top portion of it. To Jane, it seemed like an odd location to put a decal that size since it obscured almost half of the mirror. She heard voices passing outside and felt her heart race momentarily before the sound faded into the distance. Resuming her search, Jane found a neatly folded denim shirt sitting on top of a compacted black leather bomber jacket. On top of the clothing lay a thick leather wallet. Jane looked inside and found forty-two dollars and Lou's driver's license. It was the same license Jane had retrieved during her Internet DMV search; the same clean-cut mug with those piercing blue eyes. She replaced the wallet and noticed a white, leather-bound Bible under the clothing. She gingerly inched it out of the locker. The cover stated that it was the "red letter" version of the King James Bible. Handwritten at the top of the cover in red ink was, MY SPECIAL WORDS. Jane carefully flipped through the pages. Throughout the various chapters, she saw long and short passages highlighted in yellow. A thought crossed Jane's mind and she turned to Isaiah. As she expected, Lou had highlighted the entire chapter in yellow. Of course he did, she mused; Bartosh told his devotees to memorize Isaiah because of its supposed significance to the coming Armageddon. A long bookmark in the shape of a cross was tightly wedged in another section of the Bible. Jane turned to that section to find the beginning of The New Testament and the Gospel according to St. Matthew. The entire first chapter was highlighted in bright yellow. Alongside the narrow margins, Lou had written a series of exclamation points. They seemed to correspond to specific verses within chapter one.

Jane would have gladly spent another five hours going through Lou's Bible, but she knew it was only a matter of time before somebody walked through the door. She quickly stashed the Bible back exactly the way she found it and focused on a black backpack stuffed deep into the locker. She knew she couldn't safely remove it without disturbing the appearance of the locker. So instead, Jane unzipped the backpack and sunk her hand into it. Feeling around, she came upon something metal and sharp. Withdrawing the object, Jane noted a portable razor. She returned the razor to the backpack. Fishing around in the bag, her fingers brushed against a small, plastic cylinder about three inches in length. Jane was just about to remove it when she heard the sound of echoing footsteps heading through the outside entryway. Her heart pounding, she pulled her hand out of the backpack, leaving it unzipped, quietly closed the locker door, and spotted the only place in the room to take refuge....

Kit walked into Jenny's Hair Salon at the stroke of eleven A.M. She expected to find a horde of media holed up in the bubblegum-colored establishment, but the place was eerily vacant. A row of hair dryers lined up against the left wall of the tiny salon. Across from them were four shelves, all holding Styrofoam molded heads and every kind of wig a woman could desire. Kit meandered over to the display. Underneath each wig was a label describing the celebrity style of the coiffure. There was the "Bo Derek from *10*"—alluding to the corn-rowed hairstyle she wore in the classic 80's flick—sitting next to the "Bo Derek 2000", a more up-to-date blond wig. The names of the celebrities ranged from those Kit recognized to those she never heard of. She noted that there were two Styrofoam molds that were missing wigs. One placard under a missing wig read OLD LADY. The other missing wig placard read CHRISTINA AGUILERA/MTV 2003 VIDEO LOOK. Her eye briefly caught sight of a long strand of purple and red from a wig tucked in the corner. She moved two hairpieces out of the way and saw the familiar rainbow-colored wig Charlotte wore in the birthday video. Kit removed the wig from the Styrofoam mold and held it with great reverence. She lifted the wig to her face, her mind momentarily drifting far away.

"Hello?"

Kit turned around. She immediately identified the woman standing across from her as Aunt Donna, *also* infamous from the birthday video. "Hi. My name's Katherine." Kit held out her hand to Donna, who remained stoic.

"Are you with the press?" Her voice was weary, her attitude guarded.

"Oh, heavens no!" Kit turned around to face the wigs and hatched an excuse. "I'm heading to Fresno with my daughter to have chemo. The doctors suggested I find a wig so that I'll have something ready to go when my hair falls out."

Donna's face sunk. "I'm so sorry. Forgive me. I'm just exhausted and not thinking straight." She halfheartedly crossed to the shelves of wigs. "I honestly doubt you'll find anything here that you want. None of them are new. We rent them out for costume parties, community theater, and school plays."

"Ah, I see," Kit replied, still tenderly stroking the rainbow wig.

"Why don't you cut off your long hair before you lose it and have a wig made out of it?"

Kit was genuinely impressed with Donna's creative suggestion. "What a wonderful idea!" She handed the rainbow wig back to Donna.

Although she tried to hide it, the portly woman started to choke up as she placed the multicolored hairpiece back on the mold. "I'm sorry," Donna stammered.

"Don't apologize," Kit countered with her trademark empathy. "Come here." With that, Kit drew Donna toward her and hugged her tightly. The woman lost control and uncontrollably sobbed against Kit's shoulder.

"I'm sorry," Donna uttered though her sobs. "You have enough troubles of your own, what with your chemo."

"Forget about that. Come on. Let's sit down." Kit led Donna to the row of pink-vinyl hair dryers and sat next to her. "Talk to me," Kit said, like a mother to a child.

Donna dried her eyes. "I assume you've heard about the little girl who went missing here in town?"

Kit furrowed her brow, looking confused. "Ah, I think I did. Charlene?"

"Charlotte. She's my niece." Donna melted into another puddle of tears.

"Oh, darling. I had no idea." Kit carefully weighed what she was about to say. "I know people say they understand, when they don't have any idea what you're going through. But I can honestly tell you that I truly do know what you're feeling right now." Donna wiped her nose and looked at Kit with sad, doe eyes. "My grand-daughter went missing fourteen years ago when I lived in Big Sur."

"How long was she gone?" Donna asked, feeling an immediate kinship with Kit.

"Fourteen days."

"Charlotte's been gone nine. May I ask what happened to your granddaughter?"

Kit considered the question. "She was found...alive."

Donna smiled as tears streamed down her face. "*Really?* After fourteen days? You know what they say, don't you? You have to find them in the first forty-eight hours or—"

"Oh, that's just rubbish! They found my girl alive and safe. She's twenty-eight now." Tears welled in Kit's eyes. "She's still strong and still as beautiful as she was at fourteen. And she visits her ol' grandmother all the time. She's worried about my cancer, but I tell her I'm going to be fine."

"I can't tell you what it means to me to hear this. I'm going to tell Jenny. That's my sister.... Charlotte's mother. She hasn't been in here since Charlotte went missing."

"Has Jenny got good people around her?" Kit asked, arriving at the critical core of her improvised visit.

"She's taking advantage of the media's interest in order to keep Charlotte's disappearance on the minds of the public."

"One thing I learned when my granddaughter disappeared is that you have to be very careful who you allow into your circle. You wouldn't want...oh...what's that awful man's name...." Kit pretended to struggle with her memory. "Clinton! Clinton Fredericks! You would never want that terrible man near your sister!"

Donna's eyes showed immediate concern. "Why?"

"Didn't you hear what happened to that lovely bank teller woman in Arkansas two years ago?" Donna shook her head, obviously getting more worried. Kit gently informed Donna how Clinton's actions had led to the death of the bank teller. Donna put a hand to her shocked mouth. "And what's more," Kit said with a disapproving glare, "the bastard manipulated the family into giving him half the reward fund! Where there's money, there's Clinton Fredericks!"

Donna let the information sink in. "Thank you so much, Katherine! I'm going to let my sister know about this immediately!" Kit got up as Donna headed to the front counter. A stack of flyers with Charlotte's photo were prominently displayed. "Maybe you could take a few of these to Fresno when you go for your chemo treatment," Donna said, handing Kit a small stack of flyers. "It doesn't hurt to spread the word, right?" Donna stared at Charlotte's photo. "*Nine days!* She's never been away from home that long. Not when she went to visit Disneyland, or her class trip to Yosemite, or that stupid local youth camp...."

Kit's ears perked up. "What youth camp?"

"She was only there two days because she hated it and made the woman who ran the camp drive her home early. I happened to be at Jenny's house when she dropped Charlotte off. She was pissed that Charlotte wouldn't do what she was told. But if you know Charlotte, she's an independent kid. I remember the woman turned to my sister and said something like, 'Your daughter does not appreciate what it means to have clean Christian values!' She basically suggested that Charlotte was a slut!"

Kit leaned toward Donna. "You should report that woman to her church. Do you remember her name?"

"Jenny said her name was Rachel."

Jane heard the door open and close. She pressed her back against the wall and tightly drew her legs up to her pounding chest. If she was lucky, the red vinyl tablecloth was long enough to obscure her body. For some peculiar reason, she recalled Kit's advice about "hummingbird people," of whom Jane was a card-carrying member thanks to being born on the 11 of the month. *"People with hummingbird medicine should learn to take note and back out of touchy situations before they get out of hand!"* Maybe that woo-woo warning was not so crazy after all.

The individual in the room cleared their throat, signaling the presence of a male. Jane cautiously leaned her head down to see if she could identify him. The man stood dead center of the lockers and was wearing black motorcycle boots. She wanted nothing more at that moment than to charge out from under the table and hold Lou at gunpoint, demanding that he take her to where Charlotte was hidden. However, that kind of stunt was only played out in action films and bad murder mysteries. If Lou was smart—and Jane knew he was—he would plead ignorance regarding Charlotte Walker and the kid would most likely die before anyone located her. There was only one way Jane knew of to connect Lou to Charlotte, and that was to somehow tail him and hope he would lead her to the girl.

Jane spotted a cigarette burn in the overhang of the vinyl tablecloth. She leaned forward and peered through the minuscule opening. Jane caught sight of Lou just as he was securing his helmet over his head. With his back to her, he donned his black leather bomber jacket and quickly checked his appearance in the locker's mirror. Lou made what looked like an acknowledging nod into the mirror before quietly closing the door, wrapping his pack around his back, and heading out the door.

When she was sure he was far enough away, Jane crawled out from under the table. But halfway to the door, she heard the echoing sounds of voices heading into the employee room. "Fuck!" she whispered as she dove back under the table.

Two Mexican women entered the room, speaking rapidly in their native tongue. Precious seconds ticked away as Jane listened to their banter. Peering through the hole in the tablecloth, she realized that they were planning an extended stay in the break room. She had only choice. She cleared her throat loudly, hoping this would prevent a loud, startled reaction. The women immediately stopped talking. Jane purposely pounded the underside of the table with her fist and crawled out from underneath it. She stood up, brushing off the dust from her pants and looked at the women. They stood expressionless. Jane grabbed the table from both sides, appearing to check its integrity. "Table was wobbling!" Jane announced to the women. "But don't worry. I fixed it!" She leisurely strolled to the door. The women continued to regard Jane with impassive stares as she exited the room.

Jane dashed into the parking lot. Lou's motorcycle was gone. "Shit!" She pounded her boots down the concrete walkway and onto the sidewalk. Looking both ways, there was no sign of him. Jane drew a cigarette from her pack, lit it, and made her way across the highway to her Mustang. Slamming the door shut, she took a hard drag and drew the nicotine into her lungs. The blond wig began to irritate her scalp, provoking Jane to brusquely remove it. She released the pinned tendrils of her brown hair, combing them out with her fingers. Checking her appearance in the rearview mirror, she let out a sudden, stifled gasp. Lou Peters sat on his motorcycle behind the Mustang, staring directly at Jane through his darkened helmet. How long had he been there, she wondered? Had he seen her remove the wig? It took every ounce of discipline for Jane to nonchalantly act disinterested. His attention moved to the Mustang, lingering momentarily on her license plate before leaning his head toward the driver's side mirror. Jane clandestinely slid her hand inside her jacket, unfastening the holster on her Glock. He revved the motor several times. Jane wondered if that action was meant to intimidate her. She stole a glance in the side mirror. His only movement was the slight turn of his darkened helmet toward the road. Another nerve-racking rev of his engine cut through the tension. Jane felt her frustration turn to anger. She wanted to jump out of the car, turn the Glock on Lou, rip off his helmet to expose the pretty-boy face underneath, and terrorize him into disclosing what he knew about Charlotte. But instead, she'd stay still, waiting for him to make the next move. A painfully heavy minute passed before Lou revved the engine and sped onto Highway 41, heading north.

CHAPTER 30

Jane knew it was too risky to follow Lou. His strong interest in her Mustang made Jane wonder if he had been expecting her. But how could that be? Had he caught sight of her classic vehicle during the chase up Highway 41 the day before and become suspicious? Paranoia did seem to run rampant in the bloodstream of all Lamb of God Congregation members. Whatever the reason, there was no way Jane could trail Lou now without giving herself up. All she could do was watch him speed up the ribbon of highway and into the distance. Thankfully, the road remained straight for another half mile and the traffic was light, affording Jane the opportunity to trail Lou's movement. He nearly approached the point where the highway curled to the right when he made a sudden turn to the left and disappeared.

Jane couldn't help herself. She gunned the Mustang up Highway 41. She approached the area where she thought he'd turned, but there was no road to the left; just a solid, mud-slicked hillside. The distance between them, while not great, had deceived Jane. "It was before the bend," Jane told herself. She made a U-turn and slowly came up on what appeared to be a single faint tire track that led up a steep gravel road. She turned onto the road and rolled down her window to listen for the sound of a motorcycle engine. Nothing. The sky darkened overhead and the wind whipped a violent gale around the Mustang, signaling that another heavy storm was about to hit. She started to crest the road when a series of rocks cascaded down a nearby embankment. Within seconds, a slow slurry of mud roamed down the slope, covering the loose cushion of gravel. The Mustang's wheels slightly sunk into the water-soaked ground. Jane weighed her options. She wasn't certain Lou had even taken this road. Mother Nature bellowed, pelting the car with a wave of water, forcing Jane to turn around.

The weather abated by the time she got back to Oakhurst. Once back in town, Jane drove past Rachel's house. There was no sign of her car or Lou's motorcycle. Jane wanted to raid the guesthouse and turn it upside down in an attempt to prove Lou lived there. Sure, he could have given the distinctive red vinyl tablecloth to Rachel to use in her guesthouse. It didn't prove he lived there. But it *did* mean Rachel had lied to Jane when she said she didn't know anyone named Lou Peters.

Jane took the long way back to the cabin, skirting the command post at Charlotte's grammar school. There were significantly fewer people sitting at the tables and milling around. From Jane's perspective, it seemed as if the glimmer of hope had faded from the handful of stalwart folks who still gathered. Now, a heavy sadness and acceptance of how things had turned out set into their faces. She could almost hear their words…. "Common sense tells you it's over…." Jane curved around the block and came upon four teenagers seated on a picnic bench. Shane happened to turn his head and catch sight of Jane as she rolled by his group. She could see a sudden look of apprehension cross his face. If he thought for a moment that Jane was going to renege on her deal and attack him in front of his friends, the boy didn't really know her. Instead, Jane coolly continued down the road and drove back toward the cabin.

But a few blocks before her turnoff, she spied Rachel's car pulling into the supermarket parking lot. Jane's curiosity got the better of her. She parked in the farthest corner of the lot and followed Rachel into the store. Jane trailed the broad-shouldered woman down the center aisle on what appeared to be a very deliberate mission. Rachel strode to the pharmacy counter's pick-up window. Jane viewed the scene from one aisle over, hiding behind a tall display of humidifiers. Rachel collected her prescription, turned, and headed back down the center aisle. Jane furtively paralleled her movement from the next aisle over. The surreptitious plan was going well until Rachel made an unexpected left-hand turn at the end of the center aisle and ran straight into Jane. The contents of her prescription bag rolled against the endcap of the aisle. Jane leaned down and retrieved the two orange, plastic containers. One was high blood pressure medication, the other a prescription for Ambien, an insomnia medication. Jane's immediate thought was that Rachel's religion was doing nothing to relieve her stress if she had to rely on these drugs.

Rachel's face hardened; her square jaw turned rigid. She grabbed the drugs from Jane's hand and stared down with rage and conviction. "He that worketh *deceit* shall not dwell within my house; he that telleth lies shall not tarry in my sight," Rachel recited. "Psalms 101:7," she quickly added before turning and heading back down the aisle.

"You know," Jane said, her voice at full volume, "anybody can find a Bible verse to validate their actions." Rachel stopped. "The *real* trick is thinking for yourself. But you stopped doing that a long time ago. Didn't you...*Linda*?" Rachel's broad shoulders tightened. "Why else would you pick a name that means 'one who chooses to follow?'"

After a moment of hesitation, Rachel turned. Her countenance was a mix of vehemence edged with uneasiness. "God hates the lie as well as the liar."

Jane took a step toward Rachel, lowering her voice, "Let he who is without sin cast the first stone." It was the only Bible saying she could remember at that moment, but it fit. "The question is, Linda, which one of us is the bigger liar?" Jane let that jewel sink in as she brazenly crossed in front of Rachel and exited the store.

"I thought you'd never get back!" Kit exclaimed the second Jane entered the cabin.

An animated account of Kit's morning adventures continued for thirty minutes, with the telling announcement that Rachel Hartly had met Charlotte during the child's brief stay at the summer youth camp. "There's got to be a connection!"

"You think Rachel kidnapped Charlotte?" Jane asked, feeling a sense of utter confusion.

"I don't know. She expressed irritation against Charlotte because the child demanded to leave the youth camp and made Rachel drive her all the way home!"

"That's not enough motive to make somebody kidnap a kid—"

"Rachel *has* to know Lou!"

Jane revealed the sighting of the red hummingbird tablecloth, a comment that elicited a gasp from Kit. "Of course they know each other. But until I can place either Lou Peters or his motorcycle on her property, it's a fucking cat and mouse game. If I didn't have the restraints of Clinton Fredericks on my ass, I could drive around more freely and not be afraid of tipping my hand."

"He took the bait this morning. That'll buy you a couple free hours tomorrow."

"Clinton's not the only one who knows what the Mustang looks like." Jane disclosed the unexpected encounter with Lou, eliciting another dramatic gasp from Kit. "Any further chance of anonymity is looking dicey." Jane sat on the bed, dejected.

"It's very simple how to solve this," Kit declared offhandedly. "Rent a nondescript car and park it around the block so Clinton can't see it." Jane was staggered at how simple a solution that was. "By the way," Kit added, "who's Christina Aguilera?"

"Huh?" Jane was considering what type of car to rent.

"I suppose she's a singer. They had a spot at the shop for a wig style she must have worn on the 2003 MTV Awards."

Jane half listened to Kit. "Hell if I know. Check her out on the Internet."

"Ah," Kit said, waving Jane off, "I'm not Internet savvy. Besides, there's better things I'd like to investigate on the Internet."

"Like what?" Jane asked, pouring the last of the morning's coffee into a cup.

"I still have a soft spot in my heart for Big Sur. I'd look up photos of Point Lobos, The Ventana Inn, maybe Jade Cove."

Jane sat down in front of her computer. "Pull up a chair and I'll show you how to go down memory lane."

For the next half hour, Jane gave Kit a quick lesson in surfing the net. Jane let her loose on the computer while she checked the phone book for rental cars. It took Jane a half hour to walk into town and five minutes to choose the most ironic, nondescript vehicle: a blue, Buick sedan that looked as if it could be the kissing cousin of Kit's old jalopy. Jane picked up lunch at The Circle 9 Diner and returned to the cabin, parking the Buick behind The Bonanza Cabins in a vacant area.

"You're gonna laugh when you see the rental car!" Jane exclaimed as she entered the cabin. Kit sat motionless in front of the computer, staring at the screen in a pensive manner. Jane set down the food and peered over Kit's shoulder at an aerial view of Jade Cove. The panoramic photo took in the sweeping Pacific Ocean and jagged rocks along Highway 1. "What is it?" Jane asked tentatively.

"My house was right there," Kit quietly said, pointing to a minute spot on the screen." Jane leaned closer to get a better look. "The guesthouse sat back in the trees, overlooking the creek which ran along this way." Kit traced her index finger along the narrow gulch. "I just remembered something I saw."

"What?"

"It was the day before Ashlee was killed. He'd come back to the house like he did the whole time she was missing, so he'd have an alibi. I was beside myself with grief and worry. I went outside at twilight to smoke a joint and calm down. I happened to look up toward the guesthouse and saw Lou. He was standing on the rim that overlooked the creek. He was focused intently on something below. I snuck around quietly from the other side and stood in the conifers looking down into the gulch. There were two kids, teenagers, lying on the side of the creek, having sex. I looked over at Lou." Kit paused for a moment, flashing back on the scene. "There was just enough light to see his face. He had this look of pure rage. And he was masturbating. It didn't feel right to me. Not the kids having sex or Lou masturbating...it was that look on his face." Kit turned away from the computer. "About an hour later, I went outside again and I saw him coming up from the gulch in the dark with a flashlight. He walked by me carrying a plastic bag. The look of rage was gone, but he had a frenzied edge. He said something like, 'Kids don't have any self-respect any longer. It's bad enough what they do down there, but they don't have to litter the gulch with beer cans and condoms!'" Kit stood up and crossed to her bed. "Looking back, I think that was the trigger he needed to kill Ashlee, because he took her life less than twelve hours later."

"I thought he planned all along to kill her on day fourteen, in keeping with his whole 'Power of Fourteen' theory," Jane gently asked.

"He did. But don't you see? I could have stopped him. I saw that rage—"

"You didn't know Lou kidnapped her! You can only make that rage connection with hindsight."

Kit buried her head in her hands, sobbing. "I could have saved my girl. I would have given anything to save my precious girl. I would have given myself!"

Jane grasped Kit's hand. "I know you would have."

"We have two days! Two days and that bastard will do it again!"

"I'm gonna find Charlotte," Jane said with confidence.

"Dead doesn't count!" Kit's tone was edged with fury. "This trip will have been worthless if she's not found alive!"

"I'll find her alive." Jane passed the bag of food to Kit and crossed to her computer. She searched for half an hour looking for an adequate map of the northern stretch of Highway 41 where she saw Lou turn, but all she found were nameless roads that seemingly led nowhere. While Kit picked at her food and skimmed through the stack of *The Congregation Chronicle* newsletters, Jane checked out the Ministry Forum. There were several new discussion threads since her last visit, with one titled "The Age of Un-Reason, Part II" started by Dr. John Bartosh. Jane scrolled down the page and found that "The Power of Sacrifice" thread had one addition. It was a reply from Manul.Crst.123 to Jane's vulnerable, early morning retort from the day before.

> Dear Mary.mog,
> A girl's father should be her guardian. Without the strength of a father, a girl is left helpless and at the whim of evil in the world. I see so many girls today in the same boat as you were in. Their fathers might be living in the home but they are not truly THERE for them. Sadly, so many fathers LEAVE, as mine did, and they don't care if their children are left to suffer in a sadistic home. My mother, like yours, was weak. She let Lucifer into her heart. The weak always do. She drowned in darkness and dragged me with her. I still hear the voices in my head. "You're no good!" "You'll never be anything." Do you still hear the voices, Mary.mog?
> Manul.Crst.123
> GOD WITH US

Jane felt paralyzed as she read the last sentence. The whole thing felt far too invasive and yet...it seemed that someone else shared the same endless tape of admonitions in their head. Jane started to close out the Forum when she reconsidered and posted a quick response.

> Manul.Crst.123,
> Sometimes. But the voice has taken on a different tone lately.
> Mary.mog

"Oh my God...." Kit quietly whispered.

Jane turned around. Kit was staring at one of the newsletters, her mouth agape.

"What is it?"

"It's an obituary from fourteen and a half years ago. For...for Donald Kapp."

"Kapp?" Jane searched her memory. "The guy who died in the shoe factory explosion you were linked to?"

Kit nodded in a slight daze. "I didn't know he was a member of the Lamb of God Congregation." Kit scanned the obituary. "He was very involved in the Congregation. Member of The Brotherhood Council—"

Jane crossed to the bed. "Let me see that." Kit handed her the newsletter. Jane read through the glowing memorial. "On this day, five years ago, our brother in God was taken from us so callously...." framed the second paragraph. "His wife was thankfully unharmed in the blast, but she still suffers his loss greatly. Please pray for her...." Jane turned the page and found a series of grainy photographs of Donald Kapp and his family. "Wait a minute...." Jane stared at one of the photos. "That looks like...." Jane searched the room for another photo. She located it in her satchel and held it next to the newsletter. "You tell me," Jane asked Kit, showing her the photo she'd stolen from Bartosh's hallway. "Is Kapp's daughter one of the two sad-looking girls in the front row?"

Kit closely analyzed the photos. "Yes. She is."

Jane sat down on her bed. "You said Lou lived with various families within the Brotherhood Council, right?"

"Yes."

"Is it possible that Lou could have briefly lived with the Kapps after Donald's death to help out the family?"

"It's more than possible," Kit said, feeling a mysterious piece of her past click into place. "It's *highly* probable. Lou told me how he filled in for the various families whenever they needed a man around the house. He seemed quite proud of that fact."

Jane stood up and started to pace, fleshing out a plausible premise. "So, let's say one of those families was the Kapps. From the tone of this article, there was a lot of unresolved anger because of the way Donald Kapp was killed. They're dredging it up in the newsletter five years later... Look here," Jane pointed to a paragraph. "'It is always sad when someone we love passes into our Lord's hands. But the pain is even harder to bear when the death was easily prevented.' You know what I read between those lines? Mrs. Kapp is angry. She can't let it go. And she's gonna tell everybody in earshot exactly how much those who were responsible for her dear husband's death should suffer. And what do you know? Less than six months later, who's showing up on Kit Clark's doorstep asking to rent the guesthouse?"

An uneasy pallor colored Kit's face. "I...I don't understand—"

"Remember when I asked you why someone like Lou Peters would be interested in renting a guesthouse from a Bohemian like yourself? It didn't fit. But now it does."

"Wait...." Kit struggled with the diabolical concept. "The Kapps suggested he—"

"No. It was Lou's idea. You said he's easily influenced by what he hears? So he's living with Mrs. Kapp and her sad little daughter and all he hears is 'Katherine Clark took part in my husband's death.' Here's a guy who admittedly believes in the *literal* translation of the Bible. Vengeance may be mine, sayeth the Lord but there's also an eye for an eye—a life for a life."

Kit's eyes widened. *"I was his target?"*

Jane took a step back to consider the vile possibility. "If everything else plays out, then yes, I think you were."

"Then why didn't he kill me?"

"He got to know you and he found out that—as you've said to me—even the Devil speaks the truth sometimes. But just because she's the Devil, it doesn't mean that she doesn't say things that make impressionable nineteen-year-old boys vacillate from their original intention. Lou opened up to you and you listened with your heart. You offered him compassion for his tortured childhood. You were probably the only person in his life who *genuinely* befriended him with no motives...no judgment. The thing you regret the most—your lack of judgment—may have been the one thing that saved your life."

Kit let it all filter through. "But if there must be an eye for an eye, then that means Ashlee was the sacrifice for me."

Jane recalled Detective Charles Sawyer's vivid description of Ashlee's naked body baking on the limestone rock in Pico Blanco. "It looked like a sacrifice to the gods of Pico Blanco," Sawyer commented. "Ashlee showed up that summer," Jane offered, "and Lou made her fit into his warped 'Power of Fourteen' theory. It was the dark union of a twisted mind and a Biblical bullet." Kit sunk back onto her bed, struggling with Jane's haunting scenario. Jane's mind raced with a million possible connections. "There's nothing you can do about what happened fourteen years ago. Don't waste the energy. I need you to stay mentally strong so you can help throw Clinton off the track tomorrow."

Kit looked up at Jane. "I won't let you down. Don't worry."

Jane clicked on the TV, skimming through the cable news channels. CNN promised a live link to Oakhurst's command post with Clinton Fredericks within the next half hour. The time window afforded Jane the opportunity to drive the rental car to the cabin and transfer items from the Mustang without worrying about Clinton's prying eyes. Jane muted the sound and instructed Kit to keep an eye on the upcoming story before heading around the block to get the Buick.

As Jane rounded the Cabins's front office, she glanced into the parking lot of the adjacent motel. The suits from the FBI were packing their sedans and heading out of town. It was obvious to Jane that the powers that be believed Charlotte was dead and the manpower to find her alive was no longer necessary. She stopped to check the *Fresno Bee* headlines. There was nothing about Charlotte. Both the child and the headlining story had sunk into the void.

Barry stepped out of the office carrying a large newspaper recycling box. "Sad thing about them not finding Charlotte, isn't it?" Barry said, dropping the heavy box on the concrete.

Jane was surprised to hear Barry waxing with such melancholia. "Yeah."

"Yep," he replied, collecting outgoing mail from the postal box by the office's front door. "The action's slowin' down! I'm losin' media folks every day! *Damn!* There go my big plans for building the Virginia City DE-luxe cabin!" Barry shook his head in disgust and went inside.

Jane's initial impression hadn't changed—Barry was still the same sentimental bastard. She drove the Buick into the lot, parking it next to the Mustang. A soft rain fell as the afternoon light sunk under a blanket of dark clouds. Jane smiled at the Buick and how it resembled Kit's old clunker. After transferring items, Jane opened the trunk to check it out. She heard the cabin's door open and Kit's footsteps. "Well?" Jane asked, partially hidden behind the open trunk. "What do you think of my rental choice?"

There was a heavy pause before Kit spoke. "Is that you?" she whispered.

Jane heard a remote sound in Kit's voice. She poked her head around the trunk's lid. "Of course it's me—" Jane caught herself. The misty rain softly collected on Kit's hair, forming a delicate halo around her head. Her eyes looked vacant, like two hovering orbs with no clear direction. Jane realized Kit was sleepwalking. "Hey, we better get inside," Jane gently suggested taking a few steps toward Kit.

As she moved closer, Kit stared at Jane in a disconnected, yet intense manner. Her eyes welled with tears. "Oh, sweetheart...." Kit said with a catch in her throat. "How's my girl?" Jane stared into Kit's loving eyes. It was a look Kit reserved for only one person. Kit took a few steps closer to Jane as tears streamed down her face. She extended her hand to Jane's face, tenderly stroking her cheek. "You're whole again, baby." She grabbed Jane and hugged her tightly. "God, I miss you." Kit sobbed hard as she pressed Jane tightly to her body. "I'll be with you soon."

Jane felt a wellspring of sadness overcome her. She couldn't hold back her emotion as she wrapped her arms around Kit. This is what it felt like to be Ashlee. This is what it felt like to be deeply loved forever.

Kit pulled back just far enough to study the face in front of her. Her brow furrowed as she watched a tear fall from Jane's eye, though Jane knew that Kit was still seeing Ashlee. "Why are you crying, sweetie?"

"It's okay," Jane whispered. At the sound of Jane's voice, Kit fell back into her body. The shock of waking up forced her forward into Jane's arms. "You were sleepwalking again."

Kit ran her hand across her face, trying to sort out her thoughts. "But...she was...wasn't she?"

"Come on," Jane said, holding Kit steady as she maneuvered her toward the cabin's open door. Kit moved uncertainly. As she approached the gem- and water-filled glass jars lined outside the cabin, she caught her heel on the pavement. In steadying herself, Kit accidentally toppled a jar, shattering the contents onto the ground. A large chunk of jade broke loose inside the jar and came to rest atop splinters of glass.

"My jade water!" Kit exclaimed

Jane settled Kit inside the cabin before returning with a bag and towel to tend to the broken glass. Overhead, the clouds parted, sending a warm shaft of sunlight across the parking lot. Jane lifted the small chunk of rough jade but immediately felt a shard of glass cut her finger. Without thinking, she let the jade fall to the concrete. It struck the pavement, cracking into two pieces. "Shit," Jane said as she stared at the broken stone. Drops of water glistened on the jade, reflecting a radiant sparkle thanks to the sun's appearance. Jane's attention was drawn to one of the broken pieces. At first she thought it was a stray piece of glass stuck to the stone. But upon closer examination, she realized the pinpoint of shiny particulate matter was part of the stone. "Damn," Jane whispered, "that's it."

CHAPTER 31
JANUARY 4

It had been another restless night of sleep for Jane. Her head raced with the intricate connections of events that had occurred fourteen years ago and the probable links that proved Lou killed Ashlee and that he cleverly used a prop to cast doubt on his guilt. If he indeed was solely responsible for kidnapping Charlotte Walker, Jane wondered if he planned to frame someone else for this crime. The pieces of the puzzle slowly took shape as the wee hours of the morning crept forth. Jane was painfully aware of the date. If patterns served, Charlotte would be killed the following day.

The weight of that overwhelming thought forced Jane out of bed and outside to smoke a cigarette. She scanned the parking lot with a mindful eye. A third of the media trucks had indeed vacated the premises, off to hunt and shoot fresher prey. There was no sign of Clinton's SUV. Jane surmised he was getting a few good winks so he'd be in tip-top shape for his stakeout in the woods later that morning. The Buick was safely secured once again behind the Cabins. All seemed peaceful. And yet, Jane knew that somewhere out there, Charlotte was going through a living hell.

Back inside the cabin, Jane turned on her computer and searched in vain again for a map of the rural roads around The Hummingbird Motor Lodge. She picked up the snakestone totem stone from where she'd set it on the table after emptying her pockets. Rubbing the vertical snake etching with her left hand, Jane selected the Ministry Forum Web site. There were a few new topics that lead the page. She focused on the most recent offering from Dr. John Bartosh titled "The Age of Un-Reason, Part II." She'd noticed it the day before and pondered what boring drivel Bartosh was regurgitating now. Clicking on the thread, Jane read through a long-winded posting by Bartosh in which he relentlessly continued a discussion on the state of our children that he had apparently begun in "The Age of Un-Reason, Part I" back in mid-November. Bartosh's posting read like a manifesto. The gist of the post was that our youth are now exposed to more hardcore, secular garbage and that, by doing this, "a world has been created where innocence no longer exists." He continued, "The eleven-year-old of twenty years ago still had a chance to drink from a virtuous cup. An eleven-year-old in today's society sips the slop from the cup they are given and is drunk on the swill by age twelve. They are lost by that age as they choose to degrade themselves and turn against God Almighty!"

Jane exited the post, finding Bartosh's strident words abrasive and disturbing. She scrolled down the Forum page and noted that there were two replies to Jane's quick posting. Selecting "The Power of Sacrifice" thread, Jane scrolled down until she came to the last two. The first one was from Manul.Crst.123.

> I hear you, Mary.mog! I now hear the voice of my true Father in Heaven! You know what He says? He says that it's time to forgive your mother, Mary.mog. Forgive your father. Only through forgiveness can we find God in our hearts! I forgave all those who hurt me. I found who I was born to be and my life changed forever! DO IT, Mary.mog!
> Manul.Crst.123
> GOD WITH US

Jane found it ironic that a faceless person on a Forum was advocating the same pat answer of forgiveness Kit espoused. Was there really that kind of freedom waiting for her? Was forgiveness, as Kit told her, truly a gift you give yourself when you release the person who hurt you? Jane ran her fingers around the edge of the snakestone. A welcome sense of tiredness drifted over her as she slipped back into bed.

"I think we're in the clear for a bit."

Jane stirred and quickly blocked the fierce ray of morning sunlight that streamed through the parted drapes. "Close the drapes," she said, still half asleep.

"I don't see Clinton parked out there," Kit continued, closing the drapery. "It's almost seven thirty. Shouldn't you be getting up?" Jane moaned, trying to wake up. Kit crossed around Jane's bed. "What's this on your computer?"

Jane opened one eye. "It's Bartosh's Ministry Forum.... I was checking it out last night." Even in Jane's dog-tired state, she decided it was best to keep her postings a secret. Jane heard Kit clicking on the computer's mouse, scrolling through the text.

"My goodness," Kit said as she read the postings, "people really let their hair down...." Kit continued to scroll. "What does this last post mean?"

"Huh?" Jane yawned.

"It just says, 'Mary Rose? Is that you?'"

It took several seconds for Jane to process Kit's statement. She flung back the covers and stared at her computer screen. The words, "Mary Rose???? Is that you????" hung like a neon sign in the posting box. Jane scrolled down to the bottom of the box to identify the poster's screen name. It read: "Ingrid/Forum Moderator." Jane's stunned expression concerned Kit, but it was too complicated to explain. "It's a misunderstanding...an ironic misunderstanding...."

Jane decided to forego her morning run. Instead, she showered and dressed in black jeans, a green pullover, and her trademark cowboy boots. Just in case she ran into Clinton, Jane donned the same cap and multicolored coat with the red scarf hanging out of the pocket. She set out in the Mustang to snag a take-out breakfast from The Circle 9 Diner. If the diner was any indication, the crowd of people spawned by Charlotte's disappearance had thinned to a handful. Thankfully, Clinton wasn't one of them. She returned to the cabin with a hearty breakfast.

"I want you to drive the Mustang when you go to meet Clinton," Jane stated between bites of hash browns. "You gotta conserve your strength."

Kit nodded. She took a bite of eggs and glanced at Jane's computer screen. "I read through the 'Power of Sacrifice' thread. That person named Mary.mog sounds a lot like you." Kit gazed at Jane with a knowing look; Jane's hesitation confirmed Kit's suspicions. "You opened your heart for the first time. Good for you." Kit took a sip of herb tea. "What did you mean that the voice has taken on a different tone?"

Jane tried to formulate her thoughts. "I still hear him. But now I hear a little bit more pain when he speaks."

Kit considered Jane's words. "Tell me a happy memory about your dad."

Jane gulped down her coffee. "They don't exist," she said with a shrug.

"No one is pure evil, Jane. Think about it. You need to start holding good memories in your heart."

Nine-thirty came quickly. It was time for Kit to get in the Mustang and arrive in the woods before Clinton made his scheduled appearance. Jane holstered her Glock, donned her jacket, and snuck around the Cabins to get the Buick. No sooner had Jane cleared town than her cell rang. It was Sergeant Weyler. "Boss! I thought you'd forgotten about me!"

"How does anyone forget *you*?"

"We're getting down to the wire here." Jane lit a cigarette. "If this whole pattern plays out, I've got less than one day to find Charlotte—"

"One thing at a time. I just got information back from the lab on the condom. There is a more than a high probability that the particulate matter matches—"

"Matches jade," Jane interrupted.

Weyler was clearly taken aback. "Yes."

"If you check the semen, you probably won't get a DNA match. Unless the poor SOB who used and discarded it in the Cove fourteen years ago ended up with a record."

"Cove?"

"Jade Cove. I figured it out in theory based on a story Kit told me and then breaking a piece of jade." Jane took a drag. "Just call it a coincidence."

"I like those."

"I'm gonna need a lot more of them in order to find this kid alive." Jane gunned the Buick north on Highway 41. "I can prove that Lou took the condom out of the gulch and placed it next to Ashlee's body in order to cast reasonable doubt. But I think he also did it to defile her reputation. He considered her a tramp, like his mother. He wanted to degrade her as much as he could to teach her a lesson."

"You got inside his head."

"I'm getting there, boss. I just wish I had more time."

"You'll figure it out. You're too smart and stubborn not to. You know, Jane, your dad would be proud of you...."

Weyler's statement caught her off guard. "You really think so?"

"I *know* so. You're not a failure, Jane."

"I'll try to keep that in mind," Jane replied, holding back her emotions.

"You keep moving. I'll keep my ear to the ground on this end."

Jane hung up and took another hard draw of nicotine. She turned on the radio, but all she got was static as she wound the Buick between the hillsides. Jane pulled the Bartosh tape out of her satchel and popped it into the player.

"I came to know Jesus as my devout Savior and Lord when I was thirty-three," Bartosh said, "the same age that our Lord was crucified. Divine Irony, I always tell my Congregation. He died for me at thirty-three and I was reborn at that same age...."

Kit parked the Mustang so Clinton could easily see it. Wearing the same getup from the day before, she waited at the assigned spot in the forest. The sky was clear, but standing in the shadows of the conifers, Kit's legs felt heavy. It was just after ten A.M. and there was no sign of Clinton. She kicked a pile of leaves and pine needles into a neat cushion and then lowered her frame down onto the ground. Ten minutes later, she heard Clinton's SUV park in the shelter of the trees behind her. The game was on. She checked her watch. 10:25. It felt longer to her. She gave a cursory glance both ways to give the impression she was looking for the fictitious Jasper.

Another hour passed. The chill from the damp earth made Kit's bones ache. Figuring there must be a blanket in Jane's car, she tried to get up. But a wave of temporary numbness enveloped her legs as she struggled to get control. The sound of Clinton's car door opening echoed behind her. "Jane?"

A fit of panic hit Kit. This would ruin everything. "Jasper?" Kit called out, attempting to sound like Jane and failing miserably.

Clinton stood on the side of the road looking into the wooded area. *"Jane?"*

Kit tried to mimic Jane's impatient tone. "Clinton? What are you doing here?"

Clinton strode with angry resolve into the woods. Kit battled to stand up, finally using a large rock as leverage. If she could keep her back to Clinton and get to the Mustang, she might be able to save face. But she no sooner stood up than Clinton grabbed her by the arm and spun her around.

"Who the fuck are you, lady?"

Jane pulled into the Shell station that sat catty-corner from The Hummingbird Motor Lodge. After filling her tank, she walked inside to pay.

The same sweet-faced teenage girl sat behind the counter watching MTV. She gave Jane a puzzled look. "Hi!" she said, getting up. "Weren't you blond yesterday?"

Jane realized she'd been caught. "Yeah," she said, leaning forward and whispering, "I was working undercover."

"Really?" The kid was impressed. Jane nodded. "You must have *such* a cool life!"

"I have my days." Jane peered at the folded maps by the cash register. "Do these maps show the highway and the roads that go off to the side?"

The girl leaned forward, talking to Jane in a highly confidential manner. "You need a map for your undercover work?"

Jane had to hold back a smile. "It wouldn't hurt."

The girl pushed a map toward Jane. "No charge." Jane folded the map into her jacket pocket. The girl rang up the pump sale as the blare of "The Best of MTV" played on the TV. She handed Jane her receipt with a preoccupied mind. Jane thanked her for the map and started out the door when the kid spoke up. "Hey...." Jane turned. "You still looking for this girl?" She pointed to the ragged flyer taped to the glass counter.

Jane sensed a loaded question and returned to the counter. "Why?"

"There's this camera in the corner behind me and it's recording everything we do. So walk over by the corn chips and act natural. I'll follow you in a second."

Jane realized she was dealing with a kid who had watched too many thriller films. She nodded and sauntered toward the corn chips. The girl followed and tilted her head toward the office, encouraging Jane to follow her. Once inside the office, the girl quickly closed the door and crossed to the corner of the room.

"You said you were looking for the tape from Christmas Day?"

Jane's interest immediately peaked. "Yes. You have it?"

The girl uncovered a videotape from under a pile of folders. "I ran across it yesterday afternoon and hid it. I was hoping you'd show up again." She slid the tape into a player on the desk. "My mom'll be back in less than an hour."

Jane dashed out to the car to retrieve her satchel and the faxed copy of receipts that Lou gave the sheriff's office as proof of his whereabouts. While the kid returned to the counter to watch MTV, Jane fast-forwarded the tape to the time code on the receipt. The TV screen split into four equal squares with each square focused on an individual pump station. When the time code neared that on the receipt, Jane pushed the PLAY button. Her attention centered on the bottom right quadrant that monitored pump number eight. A truck pulled away from the pump as the time code rotated within seven minutes of the one on the receipt. Jane waited for the appearance of Lou's blue motorcycle. Another minute passed and a woman pulled up to pump number eight in a sedan. She slid her card into the reader and put a few gallons in her tank. Jane watched as the time code on the screen neared the exact number on the fax. The woman replaced the pump handle, which coded the sale. Jane paused the tape. The time code numbers matched at the moment the sale was complete. The woman returned to her car and drove away.

Jane pressed the FAST FORWARD button and sat back, her attention still on pump number eight. Five minutes later, she pushed the PLAY button. The sweet-faced kid appeared on the screen with a broom and dustpan. Jane observed her walk around each pump, sweeping discarded trash into the dustpan. The kid checked each pump, performing a quick visual maintenance. When she reached pump number eight, she checked inside the receipt receptacle and collected a leftover receipt, dropping it into the large, nearby trashcan. Another piece of the puzzle began to fall into place for Jane and she hit the FAST FORWARD button, keeping a rabid eye on the bottom right quadrant. Her deduction was played out as the tape sped forward to nearly midnight. Lou's motorcycle rolled into the frame by pump number eight. The helmeted figure got off his motorcycle and did a visual scan of the vacant area before reaching into the receipt receptacle on pump number eight. Coming up empty, he pulled out a small flashlight and aimed it into the trash can. He pulled out several soda cans before removing a curled, white piece of paper and placing it into his pocket.

"I got you, you sly son of a bitch," Jane said under her breath. She ejected the tape, dropped it into her satchel, and walked out to the counter. The sound of Madonna singing "Hollywood. Hollywood. How could it hurt you when it looks so good?" played on the TV. "I need to take the tape with me as evidence," Jane told the girl.

"You found something?" she said, turning away from the TV momentarily.

"Yeah. Thanks for your help." Jane looked at the TV screen. Three women sang and strutted across the stage. "What's that?"

The girl turned back to the TV. "It's the best of the MTV Music Video Awards. This is the one from 2003 where Madonna kisses Britney! It's coming up right here!"

Jane watched Madonna lean over and share a passionate kiss with Britney Spears. "Lovely," Jane said derisively. "The other girl looks pissed she's not getting a wet one."

The girl smiled at Jane's comment. "That's Christina Aguilera."

Jane started out the door when the name "Christina Aguilera" rang a bell. She turned back to the TV and watched as the camera flashed on Christina's ass-high, skintight white shorts, pouting lips, and long, brunette locks. It was an image Jane placed in the back of her mind before leaving the store.

She flattened the road map across the hood of the Buick, tracing her fingers across the northbound stretch of Highway 41 where she had seen Lou turn the day before. The series of side roads, many unnamed, appeared to end abruptly and were less than two miles in distance. Some looked to be forest service roads that extended far into the mountainous topography. The only differentiating marker between the unidentified roads was a small body of water that curved gracefully within a valley that sat approximately three miles off of Highway 41. Jane folded the map so that the section of nameless roads was prominent. She patted the hood of the Buick like a worried mother. "Let's hope you're strong enough to pull me up there," Jane said, returning to the driver's seat. She lit a cigarette and was heading out of the parking lot when her cell rang. It was Sergeant Weyler. "Boss!" Jane said, her voice rising in inflection, "I found out how the bastard accounted for his time! The Hummingbird receipts are a no-brainer 'cause he works there. I'm headed north on Highway 41—"

"Jane, hold on! You told me to keep an eye out for a Mary Bartosh?"

Jane's gut clenched. "Yeah. What about her?"

"I've been doing sporadic searches in the system on Mary Bartosh. I just got a hit on a Mary Rose Bartosh, age thirty-one, who was arrested last night traveling in a stolen car with $5,000 cash, heading south on Highway 5." Jane recalled Ingrid's posting on the Ministry Forum and her reference to "Mary Rose." How many thirty-one-year-old Mary Rose Bartoshs could there be out there? "They're holding her in at the Fresno PD."

Jane's head spun. "That's a good two hours from where I am right now."

"I can't say how much longer she's gonna be held there."

Jane looked down at the map. She wished somebody could split her in half and send part of her up the highway and the other half down to Fresno. It didn't make logical sense to drive all the way to Fresno with the clock ticking. And yet, there was something about Mary Bartosh that pried on Jane's intuitive gut. "Call them and let them know Sergeant Perry will be down to talk to Mary by 1:30."

CHAPTER 32

Jane peeled into the Fresno PD parking lot just shy of 1:30. Inside, an officer led her down a hallway and up a flight of stairs. She walked through a large, teal-green room that housed detectives. Jane noticed a black Labrador puppy tethered to a desk.

"You let detectives bring their dogs to work?" Jane asked the officer.

"No. He belongs to the gal you're here to talk to."

The puppy eagerly jumped in the air as Jane approached. She leaned down and scratched his chin as a long-ago memory suddenly flashed back.

"She's in room two," the officer stated. He escorted Jane into an adjacent observation room with a two-way mirror. A blunt-shaped, dark-haired detective walked across the small room to shake Jane's hand. "Sergeant Perry?" he asked.

It was going to take Jane awhile to get used to that moniker. "Yeah." Jane turned to the two-way mirror and stared at the woman seated alone at the tiny metal table. Her long brown hair, narrow face, penetrating hazel eyes, and thin frame matched the girl in the photo. She may have been fourteen years older, but she still had the same irrepressible attitude that bled through the snapshot. Jane immediately liked her.

"She hasn't got a record," the detective declared. "She admits the car is in her boyfriend's name but says she didn't steal it; just took it to get away from him. Claims the five grand is hers. Said she was tired of his abuse and feared for her kid's life."

Jane's interest sparked. "Her *kid?*"

"Yeah. A girl. She's down the hall with an officer."

Jane studied Mary's face. Maybe she did leave home because of the baby. She'd be around fourteen. Dr. Bartosh had a granddaughter and didn't even know it.

"Can I ask why you're interested in this woman? Your jurisdiction is in Denver?"

Jane turned to the detective. "She's a piece of a very complicated puzzle." Jane noted Mary's increasing edginess. "I'd like to talk to her privately."

The detective shrugged. "I'll take lunch," he said, walking out of the room.

No sooner did Jane enter the interrogation room than Mary stood up. She was dressed in old jeans, a long-sleeved T-shirt, and a ratty sweater.

"Who the fuck are you?" Mary yelled with a nervous edge.

Jane extended her hand, undaunted. "Jane Perry."

"Where's my daughter?" Mary intolerantly asked, ignoring Jane's gesture.

"She's being well taken care of by an officer down the hall. Why don't you have a seat?" Jane sat down across from Mary.

"*I want my daughter!*" Mary stood defiantly, looking down at Jane.

"She's okay," Jane assured her.

"She's too young to be alone! If you don't bring her to me, I'm not saying a fuckin' word to you!"

Mary was everything Jane thought she would be and more. "I'd rather she didn't hear a lot of the stuff I need to ask you."

Mary regarded Jane with a baffled look. "What are you talkin' about? She won't understand any of it! Stop fuckin' around and bring her to me?"

It was Jane's turn to look perplexed. Why wouldn't a fourteen-year-old understand? "Okay," Jane agreed, getting up. She asked a passing officer in the hallway if he could get Mary's daughter. Returning to her seat, Jane pulled out her pack of cigarettes, offering one to Mary.

"I don't smoke anymore," she said with steel resolve. "Besides, there's signs all over this place sayin' you can't smoke inside."

Jane glanced at the no smoking sign on the wall. "Who pays attention to signs?" she said with a shrug, knocking a cigarette out of the pack for herself.

"*I do!*"

For a moment, it was unclear which one of these women was in law enforcement. Jane slid the cigarette back into the pack. She noticed a tattoo of two words burned across Mary's right wrist. "Carpe Diem?"

"What about it?" Mary retorted with an angry edge.

"Seize the day. It's not your typical tattoo."

"Right. White trash like me should have a fuckin' tat of a black widow spider or a red rose next to my pierced nipples. Is that what you're sayin'?"

The door opened. Jane turned to see the officer carrying in a baby no more than nine months old. "Here you go, ma'am."

Mary melted into a flood of tears as she quickly got up and cradled her daughter. "Oh, Christina! Mommy was so worried about you!" She sat down, offering her index finger to the girl, who happily sucked on it.

Jane sat dumbfounded. "Wait a second. Is that your only kid?"

"Yes," Mary replied. "What's it to you?"

"Your name is Mary Rose Bartosh. You're thirty-one. Your father's name is Dr. John Bartosh and your mother's name is Ingrid. You grew up in Big Sur, California, and beat feet out of town fourteen years ago."

"I don't know what you're talkin' about," Mary replied evasively.

Jane opened her satchel and whipped out the photograph of Mary taken at Pico Blanco. Slapping the photo on the table, Jane pointed to the lanky girl at the edge of the photo. "*Is that you?*" Jane asked with an intimidating tone.

An emotional paralysis took over Mary as she fixated on the photo. "Where did you get that?" she whispered.

"It was tacked up on a photo board in your parents' house."

"What's goin' on here?" Mary said with trepidation. "I thought I was in here 'cause they think I was driving a stolen car... *which I wasn't*—" Mary suddenly looked like a deer in the headlights. "Shit! Are they gonna walk through that door?"

"They're not outside," Jane said. "They're sitting in Grand Junction as we speak."

"Colorado?" Mary asked incredulously.

"Yeah. Got a new Lamb of God Congregation going there."

Mary was visibly staggered. "My mother hates snow." She let the information settle. "How long have they been there?"

"I'm not sure. Couple years." Mary continued to try to make sense of what she had just heard. "You want to know how they're doing?" Mary shrugged. "Your father's still the same old religious blowhard. Age hasn't slowed him down. Your mother's still sweet, dutiful, caring—"

"Weak," Mary quietly interjected.

"She misses you terribly. She thinks that you call the house and stay on the line without saying anything before hanging up."

"I've never called," Mary honestly replied softly.

"It makes her feel good to think you do. It makes her feel good to think you're trying to get in contact with them, even on the Internet."

"I don't have a computer." Mary pulled herself together. "Look, am I bein' arrested 'cause my boyfriend reported the car stolen? 'Cause that's all bullshit. I work more than that asshole does. My waitress money paid for that car. I just went along and didn't put my name on the registration. I should have, but old patterns die hard."

"Old patterns of doing what you're told?"

Mary stared at Jane as if she were psychic. "Yeah. But I'm workin' to change all that! That's why I got this tat!" Mary held up her right wrist. "I wanted to always remember to seize the day! I bought some Tony Robbins tapes when I was pregnant. They're all about awakenin' the giant within yourself. I quit smokin' cold turkey. Decided I didn't want a cigarette havin' that kind of control over me." Mary started to choke up. "It probably sounds corny to someone like you who's got her shit together. But it worked. I got my courage up. I started sneakin' my tip money away in a jar. That bastard wasn't gonna beat on me any longer, and he sure as hell wasn't gonna touch Christina! I knew I needed five grand to make it on my own. Once I had the money, I split. I swear that's the truth! I may be white trash to you, but I wasn't raised to steal!"

"Mary, I don't think you're white trash. I think you're one of the most resilient people I've ever met. And I know you weren't raised to steal. You were raised in a place that couldn't hold you. And the tighter they tried to shove you in their Godly box, the harder you kicked until you finally said 'Enough' and left."

Mary's mind drifted. "It was a little more complicated than that—"

"You got pregnant."

Mary looked at Jane in shock. "Fuck! How did you know that?"

"Your mother told me she found a positive home pregnancy test in the trash."

Mary's mouth dropped open. "Oh my God! She *knew*?" Mary sat back, shaking her head. *"Oh my God...."*

"What happened to the baby?" Jane asked with uncommon restraint.

Mary rocked Christina, her mind traveling to dark places. She shifted her eyes away from Jane with a shameful gaze. "This is my worst fucking nightmare."

"You got pregnant. Everybody makes mistakes when they're younger."

"It wasn't *my* mistake!" Mary recoiled, taking a moment to sort through her thoughts. "Look, part of taking back my power is not allowing my past to dictate my future."

"It looks like your past is still affecting how you operate. You can empower yourself all you want. But I think whatever happened back then still drives you."

"There's no point in rehashing it—"

"You can't pretend away your past."

Mary dissolved into tears. "I always get stuck at this point. It's so...*hard*, you know?" She looked at Jane like a terrified child.

Jane dropped the cop attitude. "Yeah. I *do* know."

Mary began to shake. "I've never told anybody what happened. I couldn't. I called a cop once. But I was *so* scared. I told him about these two girls who got raped, but he wanted me to come down to the station and write it out. I told him to fuck himself and hung up."

Jane instantly made the connection. It was Mary Bartosh who had frantically called Detective Charles Sawyer fourteen years ago. "You know for a fact that two girls got raped?"

"Yeah, and don't ask me why I didn't do somethin' about it! I tried! God knows I tried! But I wasn't ready to die for tellin' what I knew!"

"*Die?*"

"Look, I've got a fresh start now. I've got $5,000. I've got Christina. And I'm going someplace where nobody knows me and where I'll be safe."

"Safe from your boyfriend?"

"Yeah...." Mary replied with an unresolved tone.

"Who else?"

Mary wrapped a hard wall around herself. "I'm not telling you any more!"

"Goddammit, Mary! You want me to stick you in jail!"

Mary let out a contemptuous laugh. "Oh, I get it! 'Fuck you, Mary! Do my bidding or I'm gonna put your ass in jail on some trumped up car theft charge!' Well, you know what? *Fuck you!* I've done everybody's bidding but my own for my entire life. I swore when I left Seattle that I was startin' fresh and livin' life on my own terms. And I'm holding to it. I'm not making any deals with you! *My life is not a fucking deal anymore!* I've got a little girl to protect now!"

"Who are you afraid of, Mary?" Mary didn't budge. Jane jabbed her index finger onto the photo. "Is that who you're afraid of? Is that who's got a hold of your head?"

Mary briefly looked at Lou's smiling countenance. "No...."

Jane heard the lie reverberate across the tiny room. "You found out he's free on bond, didn't you?"

"I don't know what you're talking about," Mary said, skirting her eyes to the left.

"And you're sure he's gonna go free because assholes like him have better luck than you and me." Jane sorted through her satchel. "You think that if you tell me something about what he did fourteen years ago to a little brunette, hazel-eyed girl named Ashlee...." Jane pushed the snapshot of Ashlee and Kit toward Mary, "something bad will happen to you or, maybe, *your* little hazel-eyed girl."

Mary's fear dissolved. "If he went anywhere near her, I'd kill him." She glanced down at Ashlee's photo and turned it over. Jane started to turn the photo upright when Mary laid her shaking hand on Jane's arm. "Don't...please."

Jane sat back. "How long did you know Ashlee?"

Mary rocked Christina. "Not long."

"How long did you know Lou?"

"Too long." She turned away, a mournful sob gripping her throat. "I wanted to save her. But I was too scared."

"You knew Lou had her?"

"Don't hate me. I already hate myself enough for what I didn't do."

"Mary, listen to me," Jane said gravely. "Lou kidnapped another little girl. She's twelve. He's still got her...somewhere. Every minute counts, because since he killed Ashlee on day fourteen, I'm assuming he's gonna kill this little girl on day twelve. That's tomorrow."

"My God.... I don't get it.... Why—"

"I'm sure you heard him talk about his 'Power of Fourteen' theory back then, right?"

Mary furrowed her brow. "What?"

"'The Power of Fourteen'? When a girl or boy turns fourteen, it signifies a pivotal moment in his or her development. The kid is highly impressionable and can be easily—"

"Molded spiritually, mentally, physically, and emotionally," Mary said, as if reciting an old proverb. "Whatever occurs in your fourteenth year defines who you will become as an adult."

"How'd you know that?"

"Because I heard it almost every day of my life from my father. 'The Power of Fourteen' was *his* theory!" Jane sat back, speechless. "That's so fuckin' typical of Lou. He's such a poser. If you can't think for yourself, let somebody else fill your mouth with words." Mary thought for a moment. "My dad was fond of a lot of sayings. 'We need to ratchet up our ministry to a new level.' God, I heard that one constantly! And then there was 'Redemption only comes through intervention.' That was a big one. He'd say, 'Those who are evil need to experience a deep, one-on-one intervention that shows the evil one what he or she is setting themselves up for.' It was just mindless words to me, but it jacked up his Congregation. It made them want to go out and force their narrow-minded views onto the world! Remember, Armageddon was starin' us in the face! You had to save as many people as you could so they could be taken up by Jesus in the Rapture." Mary stared at the photo from Pico Blanco. "We'd be at Pico Blanco, in the cabin, talkin' about God in our little Christian circle. And Lou would start talkin' about all this stuff that my dad had said during a sermon. But he always twisted it. He's like a...what's that word? Fanatic. Yeah. *Fanatic.* He always took what he heard *literally*. He memorized whole chapters. Isaiah and Matthew were his favorites. He'd recite the chapters to us like he'd written the words himself. It was fuckin' weird. Then he'd make these connections that were just so out there."

"Give me an example."

"Apples."

"Apples?"

"Because Eve ate the apple, Lou said God was telling us it was sinful. So, that meant that if you craved an apple, you were *purposely* allowing yourself to be tempted by the Devil. He'd get seriously pissed if somebody showed up at camp with an apple. I mean, he'd just flip out! One minute he's fine, and the next he's a fuckin' crazy person."

"Why didn't his actions disturb other people?"

"Most of the girls were in love with him. He looked like a movie star. A lot of girls let shit slide that they shouldn't let slide when they like a guy—"

"You said 'most of the girls?'"

"Karen and Annette figured out real quick what kind of a guy he really was."

"Are those the two girls he raped?"

Mary nodded and then realized the link. "They were fourteen when it happened!"

"How did you find out about them?"

"They told me. Maybe they figured I could do something because of who my dad was. But I told them my dad wouldn't believe me if I told him because, as far as he was concerned, Lou was perfect. Lou lived with us off and on so I knew him real well. Got to watch how he and my dad interacted. My dad was so fuckin' blind. He always defended Lou and protected him. Lou brings that out in people. They find out about his childhood and they want to help him."

Jane thought how perfectly both Kit and Rachel fit that description. "You knew about his childhood?"

"All I know is his mother sat at the right hand of Lucifer," Mary said, sarcastically repeating what she'd been told. "So I guess she was fucked up." She arched an eyebrow. "I don't know what happened to Lou, but I do know that he used whatever happened to make my dad feel for him. And it worked. Dad treated Lou better than anyone else in our household. He was the Golden Boy. 'He came from hell but he preached about heaven.' Lou did whatever my dad asked him to do. He was everything my dad wanted in me but couldn't get. Lou was sent from God and I was going to hell because I questioned everything."

"Why didn't Karen and Annette's parents press charges?"

"The girls never told their parents what happened. They knew nobody would believe them. Especially members of The Brotherhood Council."

"The girls' fathers were in The Brotherhood Council?"

"Yeah." Mary's eyes drifted to the Pico Blanco photo.

Jane observed Mary. "Is that Karen and Annette?" Jane asked, pointing to the two sad girls in the front row. Mary nodded. "Which one's the Kapp's daughter?"

"Karen," Mary replied with a wistful tone.

"Lou lived with the Kapp family, didn't he?"

"Yeah. He stayed with Annette's family too. He raped them when he lived with them. I don't know what Annette did to make him do it. But all Karen did was eat one apple too many. She had to be taught a lesson, I guess."

"Is there any way I can get in contact with these girls?"

"Annette moved away years ago. Karen killed herself. Overdosed on pills. I found her obituary when I was in the Seattle library and readin' the hometown paper."

Jane sat back. "How did you know Lou took Ashlee?"

Mary braced herself before allowing the memories to flood back. "I'd only met Ashlee a couple times. She was with her grandmother. I'd see them down by the beach collecting seashells. Ashlee would throw off her shoes and run into the water and laugh this great laugh. I remember thinkin' how amazing it must be to feel that kind of freedom. She was *so innocent*, though. She was perfect prey for Lou. When I found out Lou was livin' in their guesthouse, I got this real sick feelin' in my stomach."

"Why?"

"I knew he was plannin' somethin'."

"How?"

"My dad had been talkin' a lot about sacrifice in his sermons. He'd say 'You have to feel the power of sacrifice in order to get closer to God.' Then he'd talk about how we're in the fight for our final redemption and if we lose the fight, the hammer of God will fall. He was always preachin' about saving children from Lucifer. 'Redemption only comes through a deep, one-on-one intervention.' 'We have to ratchet up our Ministry to a new level.' Lou would hear all that and he'd repeat it to us over and over at Pico Blanco. I'd listen to him and I just felt like he was gettin' ready to go on his own weird crusade. I think he wanted to put my dad's words to the test. But in order to do that, he needed to find the perfect child who he thought needed deep, one-on-one intervention. Then Ashlee went missing, and I knew he took her. I didn't know where he took her. For two weeks when she was gone, I wracked my brain tryin' to figure out what to do. But it was hard to prove he did it when he was makin' a point to hang around town and act normal the whole time." Mary held Christina tighter to her chest. "So I figured if I can't go to somebody and report it, I'd go to the source."

"You went to *Lou?*"

Mary turned away, obviously battling the memory. "Yeah."

Jane leaned forward. "What happened?" she asked cautiously.

"He'd come over to my parents' house to pick up Bibles for the youth group. They weren't home. I took him out to the garage where we kept the extra Bibles. Lou was real calm. I'd never seen him so relaxed. His hair was wet and he smelled clean; like he just took a long shower to clean off what he'd done. I said to him, 'You took Ashlee, didn't you?' My voice was strong when I said it, too. And that was my first mistake, because he thinks strong women are dangerous. He turned around and his face was flushed with heat...rage...it was like something took him over...He grabbed me by the throat and said that he had to destroy me in order to save me. But I pried his fingers off of me and screamed, 'Where is she?' He slapped me across the face and started quoting scripture." The blood drained out of Mary's face. "Then he threw me on the garage floor and raped me...while reciting Isaiah verbatim, chapter and verse. When he was done, he reached over and grabbed a hammer that was lying on the table. He held it over my head and said 'The hammer of God will fall!' He aimed that fuckin' hammer at my head, but I moved just enough that it missed me. Somehow, I was able to get up and I kicked him in the balls. It hurt him enough that he let me go for a second and I was able to run like hell out of that house. I hid out all night down at the beach. Washed myself off in the water. The next morning, I went home and I found out that Ashlee's body had been found at Pico Blanco. I can't remember much after that except that I didn't sleep through the night until the cops arrested Lou. But my dad went to bat for him, told the cops they had the wrong guy, and I was so afraid that my dad's blindness was gonna set Lou free. I knew if Lou got out, he would find me and kill me, too." Mary floated away from herself, disconnecting. "Then my period was late. And I knew I had to run."

Jane felt her gut churn. "Jesus...."

"I packed a bag, got on a bus, and never looked back."

"And the baby?"

Mary's vacant eyes stared at Jane. "You think I would let something that spawned from evil grow inside me?" A tear drifted down Mary's cheek. "I lost part of my soul back there. So I keep moving. I keep looking for that missing part of me. But it's always in the next town." Mary came back into herself. "Want to hear the strange part? I still believe in God. But he's not a hateful God like the one I heard about growing up. My God is a loving God who gave me the courage to leave that hell, then and now. Dad always talked about being reborn. That's what I want for myself. But not in the same way he talked about it. I want to be like a snake when it sheds its skin and becomes new again. So I got this to remind me." Mary lifted her left sleeve to reveal a two-inch slithering snake running vertically up her arm. Jane stared in disbelief at the snake tattoo. It was a perfect match to her stone totem. "Dad always said that Jesus died at thirty-three, the same age he found God and was reborn." Mary said, pulling down her sleeve. "As corny as it sounds, I liked that idea. So, I got two years 'til I'm thirty-three. Two years to shed my snakeskin and be reborn."

Jane turned away to clear her thoughts. "Would you be willing to tell a jury what Lou did to you and what you know about Ashlee?"

Mary's face turned pale. "I can't do that."

"I'll make sure Lou can't ever get to you."

"What about my parents? You gonna keep them away from me?"

"You hate them that much?"

"I don't hate them. How do you hate the ignorant?"

"Then why are you afraid to see them? Don't you think they'd like to know about Christina?" Jane considered the situation. "You keep looking for the piece of your soul that you lost. Maybe you need to face the one person who scares you the most before you can find it." Jane slid her chair away from the table and got up. "I'll do whatever I can to make sure the charges against you are dropped."

"Then I'm free?"

"Well, free to go...." Mary looked at Jane, understanding the irony of her statement. Jane placed her business card on the table. "If you're ever in Colorado...for any reason at all...give me a call." She picked up her satchel and headed for the door.

"You know what I figured out when I was drivin' south?" Mary declared. "There's three kinds of people in this world. There are those who want to control you because they can't control themselves. What they don't get is that the more control you go for, the less control you have. Then there are those who are looking for someone to love them because they feel empty by themselves. What they don't get is that if you don't love yourself, you'll always feel as if you're lacking. The third kind of person is looking for redemption. They see themselves as dirty sinners who can never get clean enough. What they don't get is that they've been told a lie. God made them perfect. It's life that made them forget that."

Jane considered Mary's observation. "Which one of the three are you?"

"I don't want to control anyone, because I know what it feels like to be controlled. I'm not looking for love. I have it, right here in my arms. And I'm not looking for redemption anymore. I'm waiting for resurrection. So maybe there are four kinds of people. And the fourth one's me."

Before Jane left, she convinced the Fresno cops to scrutinize Mary's boyfriend more closely. A quick search found that he had a long rap sheet that included numerous assault and battery charges, along with filing two false crime reports. They agreed to drop all charges against Mary.

Back in the Buick, Jane looked at the clock. 2:30. Jane checked her cell for messages. Nothing. She started to turn the ignition key when her cell rang. "Hello?"

"Hey...it's me...Shane?" His voice was tentative. "You said to call if I ever thought of something?"

"What is it?"

"You mentioned about a baby blue motorcycle?"

"What about it?"

"You know how I told you Charlotte would wait for me and sometimes I was late? Well, a couple days before Christmas, I was late getting there. When I drove up, she was talking to this guy on a blue motorcycle. It had a dove decal on the fender."

"That's him, Shane!"

"You said he looked like Brad Pitt? This guy didn't look anything like him. He had a beard and a mustache and long hair past his shoulders. If he was trying to look like anybody, I'd say he looked more like Jesus Christ."

The hair on the back of Jane's neck stood up. "Oh, my God...."

"Wait. His name wasn't Lou Peters.

"How do you know?"

"When Charlotte got in the car, I asked her about the guy. She said he was just this nice guy who pulled over to talk to her. Said his name was Emmanuel, but that she could call him 'Manuel' for short. The only time I ever heard that name before is in that Christmas song we sing in church. You know? 'Oh, Come, Oh, Come Emmanuel'?"

"Emmanuel is Jesus," Jane whispered to herself. "Did Charlotte say why Emmanuel stopped to talk to her?"

"He said something about how she looked lost. But if you want my opinion, I think he was probably attracted to her red leather jacket and her long hair."

"Her blond hair?"

"Ah, no. I forgot to tell you. She'd always disguise herself just in case someone she knew came by and saw her waiting there on the highway."

Another piece clicked for Jane. "She'd wear a wig."

"Yeah. The Christina Aguilera one from her mom's beauty parlor. The look Christina had on the MTV Video Awards. You know? When she was a brunette?"

CHAPTER 33

The pieces of a very complicated mystery were coming together for Jane. Looking at the major players—Lou, Bartosh, Mary, Charlotte, and Ashlee—Jane recognized that there was a complex congealing of warped perspectives and ironic misunderstandings. Lou's deeply traumatic childhood and mental disconnect bonded with the powerfully persuasive fear of God. Every encounter for Lou was Biblical. He attached signs and distorted perceptions to everything. Brunette, hazel-eyed girls became miniature versions of his mother; versions he could subdue and torture until the evil was crushed out of them. The only problem was that he could never pound the life out of enough girls.

Dr. John Bartosh blindly preached his narrow dogma at the expense of clearly seeing what took shape in his own home. When one has tunnel vision, Jane mused, you can't see the enemies that are standing on either side of you. Without realizing it, Bartosh had continued to feed Lou the words he needed to commit monstrous acts. Detective Charles Sawyer had shrewdly intuited this behavior when he said that Lou was "intelligent by proxy." Jane deduced that as far as Lou was concerned, Bartosh granted him Divine permission through his words and actions to continue his reign of terror. How else could Lou interpret it? Bartosh treated him like a son, defended him in court, visited him in prison, and made it possible, as a character witness, for Lou to now be out on bond. They were two souls with very different missions; each one believing that the other was working toward the same objective: redemption. Salvation of a soul for one was the acceptance of God as the greatest power; salvation for the other was the destruction of that body so that the soul could be saved.

The question still remained, Why Charlotte Walker? Was it enough that she looked "lost," needed Lou's brand of salvation, and mirrored his mother's image? What was the trigger for Lou? There always had to be a trigger. Jane's mind flashed on the Ministry Forum. There was the odd thread started by Bartosh titled "The Age of Un-Reason." Jane did her best to recall some of the more compelling messages in his long-winded discourse. She remembered a section where Bartosh wrote that an eleven-year-old today drinks the slop from the secular world and is drunk by age twelve. Was that enough, she wondered? To the best of her memory, part one of his discussion began in November. Jane mused that Lou may have been reading the thread since that time, building more fortitude and validation as it progressed. A collision of thoughts rocketed through her head. There was the interest in the girls who lived in his old house, but whose father was overly protective of his children. Jane knew all too well that child predators like Lou often stalk their victims, always searching for the "perfect" child that fits their necessary profile.

If it was important to find a child who was twelve, how could Lou determine this? Unless he outright asked the girl—which was possible—there was no way to judge age except by appearance. With Charlotte Walker, a visual judgment of her age would be difficult. Even Shane was shocked to uncover the truth. The question kept coming back, Why Charlotte? What was the defining trigger for Lou that meshed the age of twelve with the desire to engage her in his own one-on-one ministry intervention? The only way to solve any of this, Jane decided, was to get back to Oakhurst as fast as possible.

She sped out of the parking lot and onto the highway. The tape of Bartosh automatically resumed playing.

"One is only as strong as his faith," Bartosh said. "It defines you. It motivates you. It narrows your perception...."

"You insulated son of a bitch," Jane shouted at the tape.

Ingrid's soft voice broke in. "It looks like you need a refill on your coffee, Jackie."

Jane lit a cigarette. There was the muffled sound of Jane mis-
judging Ingrid's aim with the coffee pot and the subsequent spill
of java onto her skirt.

"Oh, my goodness, Jackie!" Ingrid exclaimed on the tape.
"I'm so sorry! It's my fault! Let me help you!"

Jane turned toward the tape. "Holy shit!" She rewound the
tape.

"It's my fault. *Let me help you....*"

"Jesus!" Jane exclaimed. It was the same cadence as the whispered voice who called Jane, barring her phone number from her
caller ID. "What in the hell?" Jane yelled, changing lanes and
speeding past two trucks. The tape continued turning as Jane's
mind spun with possible motives. There were the muted sounds
of Ingrid's voice directing Jane to the bathroom. Then, on the
tape, a telephone rang in the background. The sound of footsteps
trod into an adjacent room. Jane heard Bartosh's booming voice
answer. She turned up the volume as high as it would go.

"Well, hello!" Bartosh replied to the caller with a familiar tone.
"No, no, it's a fine time to talk. How are you doing, Manuel?"

Jane nearly lost control of the Buick. She leaned closer to the
speakers, but all she could hear was the occasional "God" or "Jesus" interspersed in the conversation. Jane counted back the days
in her head. She had met with Bartosh on December 29. Lou kidnapped Charlotte just days before. Their conversation suddenly
took on an unsettling quality. Was Lou calling to fish for further
justification from Bartosh? Lou had certainly figured out by that
date that Charlotte was wearing a brunette wig. Had that discovery changed his plans and, if so, where was his twisted mind taking
the scenario?

Jane put a call into Sergeant Weyler as she reached speeds over
ninety miles per hour. She got his voice mail and left a brief, urgent
message to return her call. Less than an hour later, Jane tore into
Oakhurst. Checking her gas gauge, she made a quick stop at a local station. As she stood at the pump, her mind continued to race.
Suddenly, the reason Lou used a hammer to rape Ashlee fourteen

years ago made sense. It was his interpretation of "The Hammer of God" Bartosh wrote about in the Congregation's newsletter. Jane's thoughts turned to Rachel. Her comment that she did not know anyone by the name of Lou Peters was correct; she only knew a man named Emmanuel. She thought of Rachel's guest-house. The red vinyl tablecloth from The Hummingbird Motor Lodge where Lou worked, the Bibles, the computer. He *was* living there.

She arrived at The Bonanza Cabins and parked the Buick next to the Mustang. Turning to the front office, Jane noticed the recycling bin of newspapers that Barry had brought out earlier that day. She collected the bin and brought it back to the cabin.

"I'm in here, Jane," Kit answered brightly from inside the bathroom. Jane turned on her computer. "Were you successful today?"

"Yeah." Hearing her computer signal, she went online and logged on to the Ministry Forum. Locating "The Age of Un-Reason" thread, Jane quickly scrolled through it to source any further clues. Jane reread the section that mentioned the age of twelve, but beyond that, all she could deduce was that the rest served to stir Lou's emotional pot. Jane started to log off when she noted a single reply to "The Power of Sacrifice" thread. She selected it and scrolled down to read the last entry. It was from Manul. Crst.123.

> I have only a few minutes to write, Mary.mog. Have you been reborn? I feel that you have. When I met my new father on earth, Dr. Bartosh, my life changed. He taught me to watch for the signs and he has always been right! But my life took on a whole new meaning, when I became truly reborn this year... when I realized who I REALLY am and what my TRUE calling is, I was able to forgive everyone who has hurt me because of who I AM now. I AM MANUEL.
>
> I have felt SO close to you since we began our

heartfelt discussion. You share the name of my Virgin Mother in Heaven. But I must continue with the mission that my Father in Heaven has asked of me. I am of the age in which it has been prophesized. There will be a great sacrifice on my part, but it is a sacrifice I will joyfully make! I KNOW my Judas will appear. The signs have told me that. But the Glory of God will shine forth at the mountain and they will all know ME. GOD incarnate will be known to the masses and the children will finally see how they have sinned against ME. The mount is in sight. I have my lamb ready, although she has greatly deceived me. GOD WITH US.

Jane stared at the name, Manul.Crst.123. How could she not have seen it? She checked the time code of when the last entry was sent. *Eleven a.m.* She reread the posting several times, trying to read between the lines. Jane looked again at the handle, Manul. Crst.123. "Manual, Christ," Jane whispered to herself. But the meaning of "123" evaded her. The "God With Us" salute always seemed strange. Jane entered those three words into an Internet search engine. She scrolled through an endless list of matches until she came on one that mentioned "Emmanuel." Jane selected the Web site. Seconds later, a banner of block words in black peeled across her computer screen:

"Behold, a virgin shall be with child, and shall bring forth a son, and they shall call his name Emmanuel, which being interpreted is, God with us."

Matthew, 1:23

The "123" finally clicked.

Kit emerged from the bathroom. "So what did you find out?"

Jane turned to her. As much as Kit tried to hide it, Jane easily saw the scratches on the side of her face. "What in the hell happened to you?"

"I lost my balance and fell against a thicket in the woods." Kit settled onto her bed, obviously in some physical discomfort.

Jane easily sensed deception in Kit's voice. "You're lying. *What happened?*" Jane asked, her voice shaking.

Kit finally admitted that Clinton had discovered the deception. "When he grabbed my arm—"

"*He grabbed you?*" Jane's blood boiled. "That fucking asshole!"

"*I'm fine.* Now, please, tell me what happened!" Jane calmed down and delivered the day's events, interjecting the connections as she told the story. She finished by showing Kit the postings on the Ministry Forum. "He thinks he's *Jesus?*" Kit yelled.

"He's thirty-three. Bartosh made reference on many occasions to being reborn at the age of thirty-three, the same age when Jesus died. Lou obviously attached great significance to that."

"Wait a second. If Lou's energy is poured into literally *being* Jesus, then he can't live past the age of thirty-three!"

Jane realized Kit was correct. Criminals add to their patterns each time, and their plans often become more intricate. She quickly reread his last posting on the Forum. "*I am of the age in which it has been prophesized. There will be a great sacrifice on my part, but it is a sacrifice I will joyfully make! I KNOW my Judas will appear shortly*" stood out to Jane. "He's going to take himself out with her," Jane said.

"Who's his Judas?"

"With any luck, I am."

"There's got to be some sign of where he's holding her, Jane!" Kit declared.

"I'm sure there is, Kit. But short of reading his favorite books of Isaiah and Matthew all the way through for a clue—"

"What do we know for certain? What words resonate with Lou?"

"Jesus, Emmanuel...sacrifice—"

"Sacrifice! Isn't that what he did to Ashlee? Isn't that what he's planning to do to Charlotte?"

Jane grabbed the Gideon Bible. "There's gotta be hundreds of references to sacrifice in here."

"Start with Isaiah and Matthew."

Jane set the recycling bin on the floor between the beds and instructed Kit to search through the papers for any further clues to the mysterious cutout sections from *The Sierra Star* newspapers.

They went about their projects with a dual sense of impending doom. Jane ran her finger down the pages of Matthew, but quickly realized that with nearly thirty pages of text and time ticking away, there had to be a faster way to mine out what she needed. Crossing to her computer, she located an online Bible concordance. Entering the words "sacrifice" and "Matthew" into the search engine, she located two verses. But after reading them, they clearly spoke against sacrifice. She changed her search to include Isaiah and found three verses. The first one didn't form any connection. The second spoke of "the Lord hath a sacrifice in Bozrah, and a great slaughter in the land of Idumea." While it seemed to portend a clue, Jane felt that it was too obscure for Lou. She didn't know everything about how Lou's mind worked, but she did know he was literal. Obscure references weren't his style. That left the third matching verse in Isaiah; a verse that was as literal as they come:

Upon a lofty and high mountain hast thou set thy bed: even thither wentest thou up to offer sacrifice.

Jane turned her attention back to the Ministry Forum. There were two references to mountains: "The Glory of God will shine forth at the mountain and they will all know ME" and "The mount is in sight." Jane recovered the map she got at the Shell station, laying it across her bed. She assumed he wrote these words seated at the computer in Rachel's guesthouse. But the guesthouse was surrounded by thick conifers. How could the mount be in sight? Jane checked the area on the map around Rachel's house. No mountains. Jane continued to search. The only remote connection to a mountain or mount was Pinoche Peak, located within the Sierra

National Forest and skirting Yosemite National Park. She ran a quick search on the name Pinoche and uncovered nothing of significance. Jane reread the references to mountains again. "The Glory of God will shine forth at the mountain...." Why "at the mountain" and not "on" the mountain, Jane wondered. She worried that her detective's eye might be reading things in that weren't there; an ironic twist when dealing with a psychotic who does the same thing to validate his crimes.

Jane watched the top rim of the sun quickly set outside the cabin. Any chance of searching for Charlotte in daylight had passed.

"Hey, look at this," Kit said, "I didn't know Charlotte was in the school pageant?" Jane turned to Kit.

Jane recalled that Shane mentioned he had found Charlotte's Christmas pageant photo in the Christmas Day paper before he was set to meet her. "Holy shit," Jane said. "Let me see that!" Jane grabbed the paper and stared at the photo. There was a group of schoolchildren, dressed in manger garb and circling a wooden cradle. It was the standard crèche scene, with the three wise men, the angels, Joseph, the baby Jesus, and Mary. And front and center was Charlotte's smiling face looking back at Jane, wearing the identical brunette wig from her mother's salon. The caption read, "Charlotte Walker, age twelve, played Mary...."

That's how Shane knew how old she was and that's how Lou found out. Jane knew it was also his final trigger. In his mind, brunette-haired Charlotte was defacing the name of his heavenly mother.

It was only a matter of one day before Lou played out the finale to his distorted drama. Jane figured she could continue to find a needle in a haystack or she could make a bold move and call the only person who might know where Lou had taken Charlotte.

She opted for the bold move.

CHAPTER 34

Jane would need to use a pay phone to make the call. She knew if they saw her number on their caller ID—the way they accessed her number when she called to set up the interview—they would not pick up. After informing Kit of her plans, Jane drove the Buick to the Shop 'n' Save, a seemingly appropriate location, and crossed to the pay phone. She lit a cigarette and dialed the number she'd jotted on a piece of paper.

"Hello?" the kindhearted voice answered.

"Ingrid!" Jane said with an affected, syrupy tone. "How are you?"

"I'm fine," she replied with an uncertain sound to her voice.

"Checking the caller ID?"

There was a pause. "Ah...yes—"

"You should know this area code pretty well since you get regular calls from Rachel Hartly checking in."

"Who is this?"

"Feeling paranoid?" Jane's tone hardened as she sucked a drag on her cigarette. "That's all in a day's work for you and John, isn't it? It's kinda the way I felt when I was standing about twenty feet from where I am right now at the ol' Shop 'n' Save four days ago! Here's a little local trivia: they pronounce the street *Boo*-na and not *Bwaa*-na." Jane heard a slight catch in Ingrid's throat. "It's a pisser getting caught lying, isn't it? Especially when God hates liars so much."

"Now, wait one second, Miss Perry." Ingrid did her best to gather her righteous indignation. "If we are speaking of liars, you must admit your own attempt to fabricate your identity as well as misrepresenting yourself as a writer for *Christian Parenting Today*. My husband checked with the magazine's editors. That's when he discovered that there was so such person as 'Jackie Lightjoy' on their staff. I also recognized Miss Clark from a distance when she got into your Mustang after you left our house."

"From her many appearances in court, no doubt?"

"That's correct."

"So you called my cell to find out who I was and I was dumb enough to answer with my name."

"It was simply to confirm our suspicions. My husband remembered you from your appearance on Larry King's program. He's got a *very* good memory. I called the Denver Police to talk to you, but I was informed by your sergeant that you were no longer employed there and that you were working independently in Oakhurst."

Jane recalled Weyler mentioning a woman who called DH to request Jane as a speaker at her son's graduation. It had seemed an obscure invitation to Jane when Weyler first told her. But it was the kind of innocent-sounding ruse she now knew Ingrid used to get the information she needed. Weyler innocently passed along the information to Ingrid that Jane was no longer at DH and out of the state working in Oakhurst. "I get it. You've got Jane Perry and you've got Katherine Clark; a detective and a woman whose mission in life it is to keep a certain criminal off the street. Then you find out that I'm in Oakhurst, *exactly* where Lou Peters lives... or should I say *Emmanuel?* And since you and your husband protect Emmanuel from all the bad people who want to punish him, you were making damn sure my presence was known by your local disciple, Rachel Hartly. What was that conversation like when she obediently called you to report that she observed me in the parking lot and that she'd keep an eye on me? Did she promise she'd alert Emmanuel to my presence? Maybe tell him the kind of car I drove, so he could be on the lookout for me?"

"You don't understand Emmanuel's plight. He's been—"

"You said your husband has a very good memory? I suppose his memory overcompensates for his blindness?"

Jane heard another voice in the background and Ingrid's muffled voice saying, "It's her...."

"Is that the King of the manor house, Ingrid? Tell him to pick up the other line!"

Ingrid whispered to her husband.

"*Miss Perry?*" Bartosh said with a booming, fearsome voice.

"Save the attitude for someone else! I want you to listen to me. And if you hang up, I will send the police down on you so hard, it'll make Armageddon look like an insignificant event! I know you like to feel power. I also know you like that word. The *Power* of Fourteen? The *Power* of Sacrifice? You can be very persuasive, Doctor. You have the ability to make a lot of people follow your every word without question. Well, let me tell you *exactly* how persuasive you are. A guy named Lou Peters used *your* 'Power of Fourteen' theory to validate kidnapping a fourteen-year-old girl named Ashlee. You remember her? He held her for fourteen days before he crushed her head with a rock at Pico Blanco."

"You are mistaken. He was wrongfully convicted by the secular—"

"Stop hiding behind the cross! It *is* true! He also raped three girls in your Congregation. One of them he raped *after* he killed Ashlee. She got pregnant. And she left town because she was scared she'd be his next victim. You know this girl. You like to think of her as dead. But she's very much alive. You think she calls home and hangs up. You think she's baring her soul on your Ministry Forum—"

"Dear God," Ingrid gasped, bursting into tears. "Where is she?"

"It's up to her to contact you."

"Is she all right?" Bartosh asked, his voice suddenly weakening.

"She's beautiful! But there's not a day that goes by when she's not haunted by what your 'Golden Boy' did to her."

"There must be some mistake," Bartosh stammered.

"You know, 'There are none so blind as those who will not see.' Didn't it bother you when Lou Peters chose the name *Emmanuel?* It's one thing to choose the name of a disciple; it's another thing when you pick the name of your Savior!"

"I never told him he was Jesus!"

"Yes, you did! When you were in court with him, after the judge let him out on bond, you said to Lou, 'Jesus wants you as our Savior.' Kit Clark witnessed it!"

"I certainly didn't mean that literally!"

"Isn't it *all* literal, Bartosh? Isn't that what you preach?" Jane took a hard drag on her cigarette. "Walk with the phone to your computer. Log on to the Ministry Forum and look at the last entry in 'The Power of Sacrifice' thread." Jane heard Bartosh's footsteps walking across the room and the beep of the computer. "I want you to see with your own eyes what the guy you supported, loved, and helped get out on bond is planning to do with another little girl named Charlotte Walker."

"Charlotte Walker?" Ingrid repeated. "Why is that name familiar?"

"She's been plastered across the TV for the last eleven days!"

"We haven't watched television in weeks. No, I've heard that girl's name somewhere else," Ingrid insisted with a nervous tone. "I remember! It was from Rachel. That was the child who requested to leave the youth camp early."

"Did Lou meet Charlotte at the ministry camp?"

"He's not allowed around children while he's out on bond. All I know is that Rachel was upset by Charlotte's strong-willed behavior and shared it with us—"

"And I bet she didn't mind sharing her disapproval of Charlotte with Lou," Jane added with a sting. Suddenly, another connection formed. There was an eerie parallel between Donald Kapp's widow verbally disapproving of Kit and Rachel Hartly's verbal disapproval of Charlotte—both in the presence of Lou Peters. "How you doing with that posting, Doctor?"

"Dear Lord...." Bartosh uttered as he finished reading. "I don't understand."

"He's going to kill himself after he kills Charlotte! Your dream of the Golden Boy taking over the Congregation is never going to happen!"

"He *loves* God. We've discussed his passion for the Lord on so many occasions."

"What you see as passion, Dr. Bartosh, is mania. *Psychotic* mania. And with every phone call you've shared with Lou, you have involuntarily helped him plan and strategize Charlotte's abduction and torture—"

"I would *never* do that!" Bartosh replied with great fear.

"*But you did!* Read the posting! He credits you, 'his father on earth,' for changing his life. I'll admit that as evidence in court and you and your church will be ruined. I will also pin you as an accessory to the kidnapping, rape, torture, and murder in Ashlee's case. He raped Ashlee with a hammer—"The Hammer of God." Sound familiar? He got the idea reading your article in the newsletter. After I prove your indirect involvement in Ashlee's murder, I'll do the same for Charlotte Walker when they find her dead body next to Lou's—"

"Please, you must believe me. It was never intentional!"

"You want to save Charlotte Walker?"

"Of course I do!"

"Then throw out your narrow, predigested perspective and start figuring out where he's holding her! The way I see it, she'll be dead before tomorrow ends."

"Good Lord," Ingrid whispered. "*John, think!* Please!"

"What has he said to you over the last eleven days?" Jane demanded.

"We've talked about a lot of things—"

"*Sacrifice?*"

"Yes."

"What about mountains?"

"Mountains? I don't think so—"

"*Think, dammit!*" Jane shouted.

"*I don't know!*" Bartosh's voice cracked in distress.

"You still have my cell number?"

"Yes," Ingrid acknowledged.

"You have three hours to figure it out. If I don't receive a phone call from you with something substantial by then, I'll make sure that everything you cherish—your freedom, your peace of mind, your beloved church—is taken from you. I'll let every media outlet know your name. The public will despise you for your ignorance! Are you afraid of the wrath of God, Bartosh? Well I can meet Him in spades!"

Jane slammed down the phone. She checked the time. 5:30 P.M. A soft rain began to fall. By the time she got back to her car, the skies opened and sent a thundering downpour across Oakhurst. She pulled out of the parking lot, passing Clinton's infamous black SUV parked in the lot. He'd obviously been watching her the entire time. She'd planned to drive past Rachel's house to check for any sign of Lou but, thanks to Clinton, she'd have to abandon those plans now. Clinton continued to trail Jane back to the Cabins, parking in direct sight of their cabin.

"Make sure the curtain's drawn tight!" Jane exclaimed when she walked in the cabin. "Clinton's lying in wait."

Kit was seated on the bed, balancing a book on her knee and writing on what looked like a journal. Jane repeated the entire conversation with Bartosh. "What if he can't make any solid connections?"

Jane tossed the keys to the Buick on the table and sat down on her bed. Her body was bone-tired, but she knew if she fell asleep, she'd be out for hours. "I don't know, Kit." She plugged her cell phone into the charger. "It's a crapshoot. But it's all we've got right now." Jane stretched her legs out on the bed. "What are you writing?"

"Oh, just thoughts and feelings." Kit smiled, covering the page with a book.

The rain fell hard outside, pelting heavy drops against the lone window in the cabin. "I wonder if she can hear the rain right now?" Jane said to herself.

"She can," Kit solemnly replied.

"I'm sorry," Jane said with a sigh of resignation. "I'm sorry for not believing you. Not trusting you. Wasting your time—"

"You never wasted my time, Jane P.!"

Jane stared blankly. "I could have done more."

"There are just so many hours in a day and you've used them well. Why don't you get some rest—"

"No. I can't sleep."

"I'll put on my whale music. It deeply relaxes the subconscious mind—"

"He may call. I gotta be sharp."

The sound of rain outside mixed with the drone of truck engines pulling into the parking lot. Jane got up and peered through the drapes. Four large freight and delivery trucks parked at the far end of the lot. One of the drivers jumped out of his rig and ran toward the front office. Jane opened the cabin door.

"What's going on?" she yelled to the driver.

"There's been another mud slide on 41," he said, sheltering his face from the rain with his jacket. "We're stuck here 'til the road opens. Hopefully before dawn!"

Jane closed the door and retreated back to bed. "What else can happen?" There was a thick silence before Jane spoke. "You asked about good memories with my dad?"

"Yes?"

"Mary Bartosh has a black lab puppy. It triggered a memory. I was about ten or eleven. I know my mom was dead. One night, Dad brought home this black lab puppy. It belonged to his sergeant, who was on a two-week vacation, and Dad, for some reason, said he'd take care of the dog. My first impression was fear. Fear for the dog. But the strangest thing happened. Dad built him a pen outside where he could run during the day. Then at night, he let him come inside. The first night, after Mike and I went to bed, I came downstairs for a glass of water. Dad didn't see me but I saw him. He was sitting at the kitchen table, drinking his whiskey, cradling the puppy in his arms and rocking him like a baby. I sat on the steps and watched him for over an hour. Finally, I got up because I knew the dog would be safe." Kit reached out between the beds. Jane turned to her and took her hand. Jane's cell rang. She sprung out of bed and answered.

"It's John," Bartosh replied. "I've wracked my brain. There's nothing I can point to that Emman—" Bartosh stopped, "*Lou* said that alludes to where he's holding the child."

"He *had* to have said something to you!"

"I'm telling you the God's truth! We talked about the things we always talk about. Salvation, our love of God, the future—"

Jane ran her fingers through her hair. She went through the basics in her head. Criminals follow patterns; patterns with victims, patterns with crimes, patterns with locations. She thought of Ashlee and Pico Blanco. *"Pico Blanco. White Peak,"* she muttered to herself as she grabbed the large map. "A peak could be a mountain. His Forum post made a strong reference to mountains. It was within a thread about 'The Power of Sacrifice.' Sacrifice and mountains! How do they interconnect?"

"Biblically?"

"Of course, *Biblically!*" Jane yelled impatiently.

"Sacrifice...mountains...." Bartosh repeated.

"Abraham," Ingrid said in the background.

"Yes! Abraham was told by God to *sacrifice* his son on the *mount* of the Lord!"

Jane recalled Kit telling her the story. "Right. It was a metaphor for the Lamb of God...*Jesus*...who would be sacrificed on the *same* mountain 2,000 years later."

"Exactly!"

"Well, he's not headed back to Pico Blanco!" Jane stared at the map. "Wait a second, there's a Pinoche *Peak*. It skirts the outside of Yosemite."

"Ingrid's bringing me the atlas." There were a few moments of page turning before Bartosh returned to the phone. "I see it. I don't know of its relevance—"

"I saw Lou drive north on Highway 41 and turn left. Based on approximately where I was that day, Pinoche Peak would still be miles away from where he turned."

"Wait! He was driving *north* on Highway 41?"

"Yes!"

"That's in the direction of our youth camp—"

Jane recalled the letters of the camp: CCYM. "Congregation Christian Youth Ministry—"

"No, the Congregation Christian Youth *Mountain* Camp—"

"*Mountain?*"

"My God...."

"That's gotta be it! It's not the same mountain, but it's an offshoot of the same camp where there's a peak of a mountain named Pinoche in sight. Where's the camp?"

"It's almost impossible to find in the winter. All of our signage is taken down."

"You gotta give me *something*! *Anything*! A landmark?"

Bartosh struggled under pressure. "We...we have a large lake on the property where we do baptisms. Look on the map and you'll see it. It wraps around a valley that's about three miles off the highway."

Jane remembered the distinctive body of water Bartosh referred to. She quickly located it on the map and marked it with a pen and arrow. "Got it!"

"Three cabins surround the lake—"

"*Cabins?* Shit! He's copying exactly what he did to Ashlee!"

"I just realized something. The lake doesn't have a name. But we refer to it as 'The lake of sacrifice and resurrection.' I think that's your connection, Miss Perry."

Bartosh told Jane of a gate that led to the property and gave her the combination. They said their good-byes as Jane focused on the map.

"What's this about the camp?" Kit asked Jane. Jane traced her finger on the map, along the nameless roads, and toward the lake of sacrifice and resurrection. "That seems like an easy enough trip for you," Kit offered.

"Shit!" Jane exclaimed. "The highway is shut down!"

"When the truckers leave, you'll know it's open and you can go."

"What about Clinton?"

"I'm sure you can evade him in that Mustang." Jane paced. "Lie down, Jane. You've got to conserve your energy for whatever lies ahead."

"I can't sleep. I have to focus."

"I'll wake you when the trucks leave. Get some rest. Do it for me. Please?"

Jane tiredly agreed. Indeed, she was too exhausted to fight Kit. Kicking off her boots and removing her Glock and holster, she crawled into bed fully clothed.

"Goodnight," Kit whispered as she slid into bed and turned off the light.

JANUARY 5

Somewhere in Jane's dreams, she felt herself falling. But each time, before she hit the ground, a wave of ocean water lifted her up. She could almost smell the sea air and feel the sting of salt-water on her face. The monotonous drone of whales whined in the distance. It was so deeply seductive. So soothing. So perfectly planned.

Jane opened her eyes. The room was dark, but she could see whispers of daybreak creeping through the crack in the drapery. Still half asleep, she realized the sounds of her dream still vibrated. She turned to the side table to see Kit's tape recorder and the circling tape of whale sounds. Jane turned on the light. The covers were pulled back on Kit's bed; there was the sound of water running in the bathroom behind the closed door. "Kit! What time is it?" Jane leaped out of bed and threw open the drapes. The last freight truck was preparing to leave the lot. Across the way,

Clinton stood outside his SUV, talking feverishly on the phone and making frantic hand gestures. Jane looked closer at his car. His front tires were completely flattened. She spun around and grabbed her Glock and holster, securing it around her chest. "Kit! You said you were going to wake me!" No answer. "You'll never guess what happened to Clinton's SUV!" Jane grabbed her coat, cell phone, and the map. Out of the corner of her eye, she spotted a note on her computer in Kit's handwriting.

> Jane,
> T.S. Eliot wrote that: "And the end of all our exploring will be to arrive where we started and know the place for the first time." Wise words.
> I know you won't be far behind me. Don't worry about Clinton. I took care of him.
> Kit

Jane ran across the room, bursting open the bathroom door. Kit had left the faucet running. The full impact hit Jane. "Oh God, Kit," she whispered to herself. "Don't do it."

CHAPTER 35

Jane flung open the cabin door. Her earlier interest in the trucks and Clinton's car trouble had prevented her from seeing that the Buick was gone. Clinton was still on his cell phone screaming for someone to get him alternate transportation when he saw Jane bolt to her Mustang. He wasted no time and sprinted to a delivery truck just as it was about to leave the parking lot. Jane peeled the Mustang around the truck and burned rubber onto Highway 41. She laced the car in and out of traffic, keeping an eye out for the blue Buick. Running the timeline through her head based on when the trucks left the parking lot, she hoped that Kit was only five minutes ahead of her. If that was the case, she figured she could make up the time by speeding. The only problem was the road. The rain had finally stopped, but there were sporadic stretches of soupy mud slicks that had to be maneuvered around carefully. Jane's cell rang. Checking the number, she saw that it was Weyler.

"Boss! I need your help! I'm pretty sure I know where the kid is!" Jane ran down the details of the location, giving as many references as she could. "I need backup! You gotta call it—" With that, Jane lost cell phone service. "Shit!" Checking the rearview mirror, she saw the delivery truck Clinton had nabbed bearing down fast. Knowing Clinton, he probably used his name and the promise of celebrity if the driver did whatever it took to follow her up the highway. Jane pressed the pedal to the metal.

Forty-five minutes later, there was still no sign of Kit. The morning sun crested over the farthest peak, illuminating the puddles on the asphalt with a golden luminescence. The seeming peacefulness and staggering beauty belied what was taking place on the other side of the ridge.

Jane sped past the Shell station and The Hummingbird Motor Lodge. She'd successfully created distance between she and Clinton. The thought occurred to Jane that there was a gate with a combination lock. She had memorized the combination but not given it to Kit. That was sure to slow Kit down. Checking the map, Jane slowed down and kept an eye out for several mile-markers she used for reference. Locating them, she approached three separate dirt roads on the left and came to a screeching halt. Jane scanned the map again, trying to determine which road led to the camp. Each road had crisscrossing tire tracks. None of the three roads showed a speck of disturbed debris left from the Buick tearing up the gravel. Jane was about to abandon the area when her eye caught the edge of a wooden sign that had been placed behind a large rock. She swung the Mustang into the middle road and got out to check the sign. In large, yellow, hand-painted letters, it simply read CCYM with an arrow. Jane ran back to the Mustang. In the distance, she heard the fast approaching rumble of the delivery truck. Jane gunned the Mustang up the narrow, steep hill, but her tires began to shift and sink into the wet earth and gravel road. Pockets of dirt and pebbles spewed from the rear of the Mustang as Jane shifted gears and fishtailed farther up the hill. The field of debris gave the trucker an easy heads-up to Jane's destination. She snuck a glance in her side mirror. About 500 feet behind her, the truck began the tricky ascent. Jane spotted a patch of flat ground and turned onto it. She gained immediate traction and was able to speed forward with greater resolve. Behind her, the truck moaned. There was a loud clank of shifting gears, then the sound of tires losing their grip against the gravel. She was almost certain she heard Clinton screaming a stream of expletives as she gunned the Mustang up the hill.

Jane pressed forward another half-mile. About 1,000 feet ahead, she saw what looked like a gate. She figured Kit would have to be stalled somewhere at that point. However, as she moved closer, the image became clearer. The gate had been smashed and driven through, leaving only the remnants of blue paint against the twisted metal. This was a woman on a mission, Jane realized.

She gunned the Mustang through the broken gate and quickly came to a flat clearing. The Buick stood alone with the driver's door wide open. Jane sped toward the car, sliding to a stop. Grabbing her cell phone, she noted only one bar of service. Hoping for the best, she dialed 911 and purposely didn't disconnect the call. If Weyler couldn't send help from his end, Jane figured the cell would have to function as a GPS beacon.

She raced around the Mustang, eyeing the Buick, and then scanned the immediate area. A stone-cold stillness descended over the landscape. The only sound was Jane's pounding heart and rapid breathing. She spotted a footpath that led down into a thick stand of pine trees. Jane pulled out her Glock and steadily made her way down the slippery trail. The silence was heavy and held a tortured tremor. Two hundred feet in front of her, Jane spotted a cabin. She sprinted off the footpath and into the woods in order to make a stealth approach to the cabin. Coming up on the side window, Jane peered into the place. She saw nothing. Racing around to the front door, she held the Glock forward and kicked in the weather-beaten door. Inside, Jane spun around the large room lined with bunk beds. Nobody.

She ran outside, searching the dark woods for the other two cabins. Her gut twisted as a pervading sense of death hung in the air. Suddenly, the trees swayed slightly in the wind, allowing a splinter of sunshine to touch the forest floor. It was just enough to shine a spark of light against a metal stovepipe that sat atop a cabin roof. Jane headed toward the cabin at full speed, sliding across wet, matted pine needles. As she neared the tiny bungalow, she could see the front door swung open. A cold chill darted down her spine. Jane moved to the edge of the front door and then rotated into the cabin, Glock extended. The stench quickly gripped her senses. It was the fetid smell of sweat, blood, vomit, shit, and piss merging together. The main room held three single beds, a wood stove, and small table. It was typical camp counselor lodging. Visually inspecting the room, nothing seemed amiss. But the stench grew stronger the closer Jane crept to the far corner, where a door stood slightly ajar. With Glock outstretched and holding her breath, Jane inched open the door with the toe of her boot.

A narrow, cedar-walled closet stretched in front of Jane. Dangling from a chain, a dusty light bulb dimly illuminated the psychotic scene. Dried vomit crusted the corners of the closet while urine soaked the floorboards. Streaks of blood and feces spattered across a bedsheet bunched in the center of the closet. Next to it lay discarded pieces of duct tape and cut strands of twine. The infamous red leather jacket lay in a shredded clump, presumably for the child to use as a pillow. Taped across the main wall were the remains of the mysterious missing newspaper sections. Their significance quickly made sense to Jane. Lou had clipped the strings of words he wanted from each headline. YOU CAN SAVE YOURSELF and YOU MAY REDEEM YOUR SELF were taped low on the wall, eye level for someone prone on the floor. The word "sing" was shortened to "sin" in the banner that read, SIN! SIN! SIN! IT'S ALL YOU WANT TO DO. A slender mirror hung on the inside of the closet door. Taped along the side was the headline, WHAT WILL YOU SEE WHEN YOU LOOK IN THE MIRROR THE NEXT TIME? As expected, Jane spotted the newspaper photo of Charlotte from her Christmas pageant pinned to the opposite wall.

She spied the same black backpack she had found in Lou's locker at the Motor Lodge and dumped the contents onto the cabin floor. Two hunting knives slammed against the wooden planks, along with a full roll of twine, duct tape, and an orange plastic prescription bottle. Jane picked up the bottle. The prescription was made out to Rachel Hartly and the drug was Ambien. Patterns, Jane thought to herself. He was recreating what he did to Ashlee.

"The lake," she whispered. No sooner did Jane take a step around the cabin than she heard Kit's screaming voice echo across the valley.

"*Stop!*" Kit wailed.

Jane reeled toward the sound of Kit's terrified scream. She tore through the slick woods, her heart pounding in fear. Breaking through the dense forest, Jane emerged into a shallow valley that gently sloped toward the glistening lake. The scene 200 feet in front of her momentarily halted her movement. Kit stood at the rim of the lake. Lou, naked except for a loincloth, hovered with a hunting knife over Charlotte's nude, unconscious body, which he'd placed faceup over a large rock outcropping in the shallow end of the lake. The brunette wig sat askew on Charlotte's head. Lou's countenance was driven, and yet disconcerted by Kit's appearance.

"Lou, don't do it!" Kit screamed.

"I know not of whom you speak, woman!" he yelled back.

Jane aimed the Glock at Lou's head. But given the distance, pulling the trigger was a dicey proposition. "Let her go!" Jane bellowed.

Kit spun around, stunned. Lou scooped Charlotte into his arms and, still clutching the knife in his right hand, moved backward toward the deeper water. "My Judas has appeared, Lord!"

"Lou, stop!" Kit demanded as she slogged into the chilling lake.

"Kit!" Jane screamed, running to the edge of the lake. "Stay away from him!"

Lou lifted Charlotte over his head. Her limp arms dangled across his crazed face. "My lamb will be sacrificed and we will be resurrected in my Kingdom together!"

Jane lowered the Glock to Lou's head, but Charlotte's torso and arms prevented a clean shot. "Kit!" Jane screamed, "Get back!"

Kit continued to trudge through the frigid water toward Lou. "Lou! It's me! *Kit!*" Lou's maniacal eyes stared at Kit. A split second of clarity bled through the madness. "Don't do to her what you did to my Ashlee! I forgive you, Lou! But the world won't!" In that moment, he briefly came back into himself and lowered the child's body from above his head. "Let this child go, Lou! Give her to me!" Kit stood within five feet of Lou, her arms outstretched. *"Give her to me!"*

Jane trained the Glock on Lou, taking measured steps into the lake. There was a tenuous pause between Kit and Lou. And then, the blink of clarity dissolved and the darkness descended once again.

"Lord, why hast thou forsaken me?" Lou bellowed into the wind. Suddenly, a cascade of small rocks tumbled down the slope behind Jane. She turned for only a second toward the sound. *"It is finished!"* Lou screamed.

Jane reeled back around just as Lou plunged Charlotte into the water and thrust the knife with deadly aim toward Kit's heart. Kit staggered several feet, falling backward into the icy water.

"No!" Jane screamed and fired off a round into Lou. He let out a bloodcurdling cry as he grabbed his bleeding side and thrashed through the lake to the shore. Charlotte surfaced, floating slowly on her back toward the deeper end of the lake. Jane ran to Kit. Her grey face was just above the lapping water; her eyes heavy as they stared skyward. "Kit!" Jane screamed, holstering her Glock and dragging her onto a bed of pebbles.

"Save her," Kit whispered, a gurgle of death rattling in her throat.

Jane threw her jacket onto the rocks and strode toward Charlotte's floating body. Lou collapsed on the ground, writhing in agony as blood gushed from his bullet wound. Jane reached Charlotte just before her porcelain face sunk into the chest-high water. Lou's painful wails echoed across the valley as Jane carried Charlotte to shore. She covered the child with her jacket and checked for vital signs. "Charlotte? Can you hear me?"

The child turned her head slightly and whispered, "Mommy?"

Lou let out another scream of agony as he staggered back onto his feet. "Forgive them Father!" Lou howled. "They know not what they do!"

Jane spun around, rage seeping from her pores. She made sure Charlotte was secure before she pulled out her Glock and headed the few yards to where Lou teetered upright against the sand and rock. Pointing the gun at his head, she screamed, "You want to feel pain, motherfucker?"

He looked at Jane, his eyes half open. "Do it," he whispered.

Jane slammed the butt of the gun against Lou's forehead. "I'm not afraid to kill you!"

The insanity suddenly drained from Lou's face. In its place, torment and anguish lay etched. "Please...*make it stop*," he gasped, "*kill me.*"

Jane stared into Lou's desperate eyes. "Dying is what you want," Jane said, "so I'll let you live."

Lou's eyes rolled back into his head as he grabbed his bleeding wound and, falling unconscious, collapsed backward onto the rocks.

Jane holstered the Glock and darted back to Kit, kneeling next to her soaked body. The hunting knife was lodged too deeply in her chest for Jane to remove it. She grabbed Kit's hand, holding it tightly. "Kit, I—"

"Charlotte...." she whispered.

"She's fine. She's drugged but she's alive."

A victorious smile swept across Kit's ashen face. "Good...."

Jane leaned closer to Kit. "Why did you take off?"

"You'll understand...."

"I'll understand?"

"Soon...." Kit's voice drifted, "you'll understand." She turned her head, focusing on the knife handle.

Jane felt a wave of helplessness overcome her. "I can't pull it out, Kit. It's in your heart."

"Aah," Kit said, weakly arching an eyebrow. "That's a supreme metaphor...."

Jane wasn't giving up. "I dialed 911. Help should be here any second."

Kit managed a feeble smile. "Suddenly you're an optimist?"

Jane grabbed Kit's hand. "Hold on, Kit."

"It's okay, Jane. It's...what I...." Kit moaned. Her eyes glazed over briefly as she tried to focus on Jane's face. "I...." She rolled her head to the other side and fixated on a face. Her eyes brightened as she held her hand outward. Jane knew the look. She stared into the void and saw nothing. But she could feel her presence. She was kneeling beside her grandmother and holding her hand, waiting to catch her spirit and take it home. "I'm ready," she whispered before she took her final breath and passed between the shadows and into the light.

Jane rested her head on Kit's chest and felt the life slip from her body. As much as she wanted to grieve her death, the grace of that last moment was too profound.

Charlotte let out a shallow cry. Jane crawled to the child, drawing her onto her lap and covering her tightly with the jacket. The sound of police sirens blared in the distance, converging on the lake. Jane shielded Charlotte's face from the penetrating sun and stared into the distant sky. The sirens grew louder as a solitary red-tailed hawk circled above their heads.

For Jane, the next few days fell like lead around her heart. Sergeant Weyler offered to come out and assist, but Jane declined his offer, preferring to get the formalities over with and leave. She carried on professionally, debriefing the FBI and Sheriff Golden on her involvement with the case; she turned over all the evidence she had that linked Lou Peters to Ashlee's murder.

However, a dull ache had gradually engulfed her senses. After the reward fund was awarded to Jane, she quietly gave the money to Mary Bartosh. The act did nothing to buoy her flagging spirit.

It didn't feel like a conquest to her when she successfully barred Clinton from capitalizing on Charlotte's story and exposed him as a corrupt opportunist.

When Trace Fagin walked free into the arms of his wife and children, the moment was short of victorious.

When she passed Shane Golden on the street with his father and realized that the boy had no intention of ever telling anyone of his relationship with Charlotte, she regarded him with an inert expression.

As the final pieces of the puzzle started to fit—the connection between Lou stealing the Valium from Genevieve's purse fourteen years prior and repeating the same theft of Rachel's sleeping pills—the realizations lacked profound impact for Jane. When it was firmly established that Rachel Hartly's only crime was suffering the same blindness as her mentor, Jane didn't feel a need to contact Rachel and strong-arm her into compunction.

As for Dr. John Bartosh, it didn't take investigators long to link him with Lou Peters. The news media grabbed onto the story like a leech. Satellite trucks from every cable news station lined up in front of his house in Grand Junction, monitoring each move he made and turning his controlled life into a living hell. The story was just too good. "Respected head of Christian Congregation linked to murderer and child rapist." It was guilt by association for Bartosh as news programs encouraged the public to call in their votes on whether Bartosh should be liable and face prison for his ignorance. As the months unraveled, Bartosh would eventually escape time behind bars. But his reputation would be burned forever.

As for Lou Peters, he would stand trial for the murder of Kit Clark and her granddaughter as well as the kidnapping, rape, torture, and imprisonment of Charlotte Walker. With her testimony and indisputable evidence, Jane would make sure that Lou would never see the outside of a prison wall again.

But that was all to come. As she wrapped up the loose ends before leaving Oakhurst, she couldn't shake off the deadness she felt inside her heart. It was as if Jane's entire soul had been stripped bare and all that remained was a raw, blank canvas. She made final arrangements to have Kit's body cremated and the remains sent to her. On January 9, Jane packed Kit's possessions into her trunk and headed out of town. But there was one stop she had to make before she left.

Jane considered it an obligation that she'd rather forego. She'd received the handwritten message that Charlotte wanted to talk to her in person. From Jane's observations of Charlotte in the infamous birthday video, she surmised that the girl usually got what she wanted.

Jenny Walker greeted Jane at the door with an effusive hug and teary welcome. The living room of the Walker house was filled with flowers and colorful foil balloons that sported WELCOME HOME, CHARLOTTE! messages. To Jane, it seemed odd. From what she knew the girl had gone through, the celebratory atmosphere felt irreverent.

"Charlotte's in her bedroom," Jenny offered in a breathy, nervous voice. It was clear that the woman was in awe of Jane and the vaunted reputation that followed her. For Jane, it made the whole visit that much more uncomfortable. After offering Jane an array of beverages and Jane settling on coffee, Jenny rapidly reported their plans. "Charlotte wants to be homeschooled, at least for this year." Jane privately wondered why a social butterfly would opt for such an austere educational option. "But the doctors want to give her another month or so to decompress before we launch into any of that." Jane nodded politely and took a sip of coffee, knowing full well the decompression would take a helluva lot longer than a couple months. "And we've made another decision," Jenny declared with anxious enthusiasm. "We're going to church every Sunday from now on!"

"Really?" Jane replied, showing no emotion.

"I think it's a good idea," Jenny said, searching for approval. "Comforting, you know?"

"Yeah. Comforting." Jane could have said more, but the solution seemed absurd, given the ironic religious bent of Charlotte's abductor. Jenny led Jane down a cheerful yellow hallway lined with one photograph after another of Charlotte smiling playfully for the camera. Upon reaching the closed door, Jenny softly knocked and announced Jane's visit. To Jane, it sounded as if she were being introduced to the royal gallery.

"I'm coming." Jane immediately noted that the child's voice was restrained.

Jenny self-consciously addressed Jane with a whisper. "She locks the door now."

Charlotte unlocked the door and slowly opened it. She wore no makeup and, to Jane, the kid suddenly looked younger than twelve. A baggy, brown plaid, long-sleeved flannel shirt hung loosely on her body, obscuring any sign of her large breasts, while a pair of gray sweat pants, also a size too large, completed the drab façade. "Hi...." Charlotte said, obviously self-conscious and tense. "Come in."

Jane slid past Charlotte and stood at the foot of her bed. Charlotte quietly closed the door and locked it. The yellow shades on the three windows were pulled down. Jane noted that wooden dowels had been placed within each window as an extra safety precaution. While the sun shone brightly outside, the room felt dim and painfully claustrophobic. Charlotte's bed was covered with clothes from her closet. A large plastic trash bag lay against a near chair, bursting with additional clothing.

"You can sit on the bed if you want," Charlotte said in a weak voice. "Sorry it's a mess."

"Don't worry about it." Jane took a seat on the edge of the bed, resting her leather satchel on the floor. An unexpected wave of compassion rushed over her. The kid she had privately judged at times was as much an empty shell as she was. Several moments of hard silence passed as their unspoken bond solidified.

"I wanted to...." Charlotte struggled with her words as she fidgeted with the seam of her flannel shirt. "To...say...." Her eyes filled with fat tears. "To say thank you." Her voice caught as the tears rolled down her pale cheeks. There was a raw fear behind her eyes, smothered in a dark nightmare she couldn't quite recollect.

Jane did everything she could to control her emotions. "I'm glad I was there." Charlotte looked smaller to Jane than she had when she dragged her limp body to safety by the lake. *Fragile.*

Charlotte continued to roll the edge of the shirt seam between her thumb and first finger. "I don't remember anything," she quickly said. "The last thing I remember is walking into the cabin with him...." Her voice drifted far away.

"It's okay, Charlotte," Jane leaned forward and touched the kid's arm. "You don't need to dredge it up."

Charlotte looked at Jane, her hazel eyes glistening with tears. "But it's right there." Her young mind desperately tried to reconcile it. "...on the edge of my head." She looked down at the cluttered carpet, not focusing on anything in particular. "I used to love the smell of cedar. But it makes me throw up now." Charlotte turned to Jane, searching her face for answers. "Is that crazy?"

Jane recalled the cedar-walled closet that served as Charlotte's prison for twelve days. "You're not crazy, Charlotte," Jane gently replied.

"Are you gonna go to court and tell them what you saw happen to me?"

"Yes," Jane said with authority. "And you have my word that he will never get out of prison again."

"I...I heard the sheriff talking to my mom when I was in the hospital. He said I might have to get up in court and...tell them... things. Is that true?"

Jane tried to hide her disgust for a system that insisted on re-violating the victim in court. "If you don't want to do it, there's no law that's gonna make you."

A look of abject shame fell over Charlotte as tears streamed down her face. "They took pictures of me in the hospital. Pictures of my body. Here and down there." Charlotte sheepishly pointed to her breasts and groin area. "People I don't know are gonna see those pictures and that's not right." She broke down, choking on fear and humiliation.

Jane pulled Charlotte toward her, holding her tightly against her chest. The free-spirited child that had posed for the camera in the birthday video was dead. Jane knew the predictable cycle had begun. The traumatic event occurs and you're never the same again. Your world closes tightly around you. Your perspective of every experience is viewed through victim's eyes. The pain and shame grow into festering anger and then unbridled rage. You approach each day like a battle and fasten your emotional armor tightly to deflect vulnerability. Emotional detachment quickly takes hold so you don't have to feel. Numbness sets in and life becomes flat. You feel you have to do it to protect yourself against a world that has become evil and intent on violating those who can't defend themselves. Then the self-destruction begins.

Charlotte hysterically sobbed into Jane's shoulder. "I want to—"

"Disappear," Jane stated in a simpatico tone.

Charlotte lifted her head from Jane's shoulder and stared at her. "Yeah...." Someone understood her. "People saw me naked...." She fell into Jane's shoulder, softly crying.

The same damn pattern was forming, Jane thought. She tenderly lifted Charlotte's head away from her body. "Tell me why you're throwing out all this stuff."

The child scanned the heap of clothes on the bed and the plastic trash bag on the floor. "Because...." she offered weakly, "they're too...bright."

"They draw attention to you," Jane stated.

"Yeah."

Jane turned around and sorted though the pile on the bed. She pulled out a red spandex top that looked to be two sizes too small for Charlotte's chest. "Well, this one's probably not the best choice for you." She unearthed an orange vest with a diamond pattern. "But this is colorful. Nothing wrong with color—"

Charlotte snatched the vest away from Jane and quickly buried it in the trash bag. "No! People will look at me!"

Jane reached up and stroked Charlotte's cheek. "Oh, God, Charlotte. Don't do this to yourself. Take my word for it. You're walking down a rocky pathway. There's something called 'the middle path.' This is not it," Jane held up the red spandex top. "But this is," she uncovered a bright green sweater. Jane collected her thoughts. "Ever heard of Buddhism?" Charlotte shook her head. "It's not a religion. It's a philosophy," she said, recalling a bittersweet memory from only twelve days ago. "They believe in that middle path, among other things. The path between this," she held up the spandex top, "and this." She pointed to Charlotte's oversized brown plaid shirt. "You don't want to be bold and brazen anymore. I understand that. So this one goes." Jane tossed the spandex top into the trash bag. "But if you choose this one," she softly stroked the flannel shirt, "you choose an equally bad extreme. You choose to hide your spirit. And your spirit is why good people love you." Jane pulled Charlotte close to her. "If you drown your spirit, he wins...and you lose everything."

Tears rolled down Charlotte's cheeks. "But I'm scared," she whispered.

"I know. Believe me, *I know*. But it takes more courage to live strong than die slowly."

Charlotte nodded. "You know what I told my mom about you? I said you were the angel who saved me."

Jane lowered her head. "But I'm not." She withdrew her wallet from the leather satchel and removed a photograph. Fondly, she looked at the photo before handing it to Charlotte. "You have two angels right there." Charlotte stared at the photo of Ashlee reposed in Kit's arms. "They're the ones who made sure you were found safely."

The child was in awe. "Can I talk to them and tell them 'thank you?'"

Jane nodded, a well of emotion caught in her throat. "Every morning...and every night." Jane lifted her satchel and stood up. Charlotte handed the photo back to Jane. "It's yours." Jane hugged the child and whispered in her ear. "Make them proud, Charlotte."

Jane hoped the drive back to Denver would ease the numbness within her heart. But by the time she arrived at her doorstep in the early morning hours of January 11, her thirty-sixth birthday, the unnatural emptiness still persisted.

Jane turned on the living room light and set down her bags. Mike had dutifully stacked her mail on the kitchen table next to a pile of *Denver Post* newspapers. Jane scooped up the mail and shuffled through them. A bright yellow envelope caught her attention. There was no return address, but the January 5 postmark was from Oakhurst, California. Next to the stamp was an ink imprint that read, HOWDY! FROM THE BONANZA CABINS! The handwritten address looked familiar. She opened the envelope and removed a greeting card. There was a drawing of a red-tailed hawk on the cover of the card. Its wings swept upward as, beneath it, a snake slithered against a rock. A vibrant blue lotus flower emerged between them. Jane felt a catch in her throat as she read the quote at the bottom; the same quote by T.S. Eliot that Kit had left on her computer.

And the end of all our exploring will be to arrive where we started and know the place for the first time.

Jane opened the card. The two missing sobriety chips fell to the floor. Jane collected them. They still had bits of embedded sand from where they'd fallen in Cousin Carl's front yard. A long handwritten letter filled the inside of the card.

Dear Jane P.,

I imagine you've never received a birthday card from the newly departed. So let me be the first dead soul to wish you a happy birthday.

First, let's get some business out of the way. Contact Barbara and tell her to look behind the bookshelves in her living room. She'll find my life insurance policy there and the information she needs to collect the $500,000.

Now, for you. I'm writing you this card because you've been a true friend to me and you deserve to know the truth. I never intended to return to Boulder. I left with a clear intention and a plan to carry out that pure purpose. It might be hard for you to understand now, but as one nears their demise, the need to complete and come full circle is obvious. I don't fear death. I welcome it. Take away the fear of death and one's courage soars. One is able to do the thing that could kill them. If my intuition is correct, then my plan will have succeeded. So don't grieve a day for me.

As I feel the light of God coming closer, I have a sense of calm and inner knowing. It's not by chance that you and I met, Jane. Our souls chose it. We choose everything, Jane—every heartache and each breath of joy. My choice was obvious, perhaps only to me. But I knew that before I died, I had to do what I could to stop the wheel of destruction. I had to forgive him and, hopefully, allow that seed of compassion and love to grow in his soul. My hope is that during his dark night, he remembers that moment and purges his pain forever. One's touch on another is not always evident, but years later, God willing, that connection is remembered by the heart and the pattern of hatred can stop.

It's all right to forgive, Jane. Holding on to hate

is futile and will only destroy you in the end.

Be courageous and find out who you really are. Self-analysis is not for the weak, but it's infinitely more satisfying than running blindly into the night.

And please don't give up on finding love, Jane. To deny yourself that pleasure is to choke the breath from your heart. Risk it all and be vulnerable. Lead with your heart, my dear, and you'll never go wrong.

Seek contentment rather than happiness. Contentment holds water. Happiness leaks.

In Spirit,

Kit

The clear, winter sky in Denver stretched a swath of pink across the horizon. Jane drove around the bend of the cemetery where the two trees converged. That was the only way she remembered the location, since her previous visit had been so brief. She got out of the Mustang, crushing the butt of her cigarette against the pavement. Walking across the matted, brown grass, she checked one headstone after another before finding the one she wanted. Jane stared at the simple engraving of the name on the stone: DALE PERRY. Minutes passed before she spoke with choked emotion.

"Wherever you are, I hope you find peace. I hope your pain stops." She pulled the snakestone totem from her pocket and tucked it under a mat of grass in front of the stone. "This will help you." Jane wrapped her hand around the top of the stone. "I forgive you," she whispered.

That was her first step.

CPSIA information can be obtained at www.ICGtesting.com
Printed in the USA
LVOW091824181011

251060LV00001B/13/P